The Glassblower's Daughter

Frances Clarke

Wordclay
1663 Liberty Drive, Suite 200
Bloomington, IN 47403
www.wordclay.com

First published by Wordclay on 4/1/2011.
ISBN: 978-1-6048-1874-1 (sc)

Printed in the United States of America.

This book is printed on acid-free paper.

Also by Frances Clarke
UNUSUAL SALAMI AND OTHER STORIES

The Glassblower's Daughter

By

Frances Clarke

Part 1   Garden of Paradise – 1955

Part 2   That Explains the Accent – 1968

Part 3   A Dark Wood – 1971

Part 4   Trick Errand – 1975

Part 5   The Mother-shaped Portion of Space – 1979

Part 1. Garden Of Paradise – 1955

The Woman In The Bottle

It caught her eye the minute they went through the swing door into the workshop and she pounced on it; a pretty, shining thing like a snapped off twig made of glass. Between the big machines the floor was strewn with oddments of balsa wood, flitches of dust and other, less perfect glass shapes. "Can I have this?"

"Naw, hen, yon's sherp…….." but she clutched it up against her chest, "a'richt, let's see if yer daddy can smooth it for ye." He rasped the broken edge of the glass twig with a file then rubbed it with emery paper.

"I won't be bored today," she said, as he tested it on his thumb then handed it back to her. When he smiled she said, "what is that smell?"

And he said: "propinol." Still smiling he put on his lab coat.

So she said: "Where have Mummy and Deborah gone?"

"A've telt ee they're awa tae the hospital, the special hospital. Keek in, a'll mak ee yer very ane glass bubble."

Greta watched her father as he blew. His cheeks reddened. His lips pressed the tube. The tube dangled in a long loop from his mouth. Black hair stood out over the strap of his goggles and his whiskers caught the light. She thought of him standing at the washbasin in his vest, shaving; raking off cream. He was handsome. The mask hid his eyes. Her bubble grew. When it was the size of a tomato he put his flame back in the holder and got the bubble on the end of a metal stick. "Yer very ane," he passed it to her. On the end of the rod the bubble swayed.

"I'm going to look after it and take it home." She went to her father's bench and sat down on her box.

"Weel, if ye dinnae mind stayin' as still as a wee mouse the hale day." He began to whistle as he fixed a big glass tube to his machine.

"You can hold it for me if I want to move," she said.

Her father gave a shout of laughter. "Dinnae you be touching ma condenser, mind now," he darted his finger at her with such an abrupt shift of his arm that she looked over her shoulder thinking the condenser might have crawled forward to peer over the edge of the bench.

"Listen!" Harold's voice. His bicycle clips missed his pocket and clattered to the floor and he shook a green and cream thermos flask at her, making a slushy tinkle of noise. She kept her eyes on her bubble. Harold had teeth that tilted forward, hanging out of his mouth. He smelt of something horrible but she didn't know what the smell was.

"Fall in, quick march, where do you think you've been?" called Wilfred, appearing from the grinding room. "You're late."

"Listen," persisted Harold and shook the flask again.

Wilfred winked at Greta.

Greta liked being at her father's work. Good-natured Wilfred and Harold with their Leicester accents were a change from the familiar Scottish of her father. Mrs Primrose up in the office spoke so posh the men called her 'the duchess'.

"I dropped my bike on the ramp and it rolled out of my bloody saddlebag," complained Harold.

"Mind your language," Wilfred winked at her again, "a little mouse is sitting over there." Greta liked Wilfred. He called her 'the faculty mouse' and though she didn't know what 'faculty' was; the name sounded nice. Wilfred's face was young, but oldness had caught up with him in patches. The top of his head was bald but hair grew in clumps above his ears. She had wanted to watch the wings go spinning round so he had worked the glass turbine for her.

Her bubble reflected everything. Wilfred got the bench burners roaring and the bubble showed a sea of lavender flame tipped with golden waves. The pale flames that stood up out of the hand burners were like feathers curved in the rounded surface. She could see parts of her face reflected and the sky behind her through

7

the window. She wanted to feel the bubble. Without breathing, she touched it with her fingertips.

And then it was floating down. It landed on her knee, reflecting the navy pleats of her pinafore dress. The metal stick fell out of her hand. Sudden silence descended as her father threw the switch that stopped his rod rotating. Greta curved her fingers to slide them under the bubble, to coax it into her hand. Wilfred came to fetch a clamp from the cupboard, his head crimson from the heat. The bubble sat on her palm. "Look Wilfred."

"That's a regular crystal ball," said Wilfred, "You can see the future in there."

"Rubbish," scoffed Harold. His rounded shoulders drooped over his lathe and his neck poked forward out of his overall collar like the neck of a tortoise. Wilfred was different. Greta liked his big, gentle eyes and his shiny head. The things Wilfred said were like stories. Maybe Wilfred could tell her when her mother and Deborah were coming home.

Her father was whistling a song off the wireless. *Step we gaily, on we go, heel for heel and toe for toe; step we gaily…*The jaunty words danced in her head. Wilfred clashed clamps in the cupboard. The bubble stirred on her palm. It was so light that all she could feel was its warmth. They never lost their heat. "Wilfred."

"Yes, Pet."

"Heat is their skin," she said. Her father's lathe hissed and the rod began to rotate.

Wilfred closed the cupboard. "Go and watch your Dad putting on the side-arm."

The glass on her father's rod was glowing deep orange. He directed the violet points of his burners at the glass and turned them up to roar out in golden flames. The glass was like syrup. Any minute it would begin to pour. There was a hiss and a thud as the rotation stopped and then the row of burners went back to violet points and he lifted the hand jet. In his other hand was a black cone on a stick and he poked it into the red mound, holding it there while he blew. He was making a hole. The glass he was getting rid of swelled into a bubble. He took the tube out of his mouth and pointed at the bubble. "Noo where does this yin gan?"

"In the flash," said Greta.

"Aye," he knocked it off and she watched the pieces float down to join the sparkling layer on the floor. He picked up the side arm and heated the mouth of it. When its rim was red, he heated the rim of the hole in his big tube. When they both glowed red, like two open mouths, he pressed them together. Together they sagged into the softened wall of glass. He pressed them and pulled them and shone the flame on them until he was sure they were joined and then he slammed on the rotating rod and round it all went, the red gone, the gold fading to transparent and the new side arm sticking out like a little waving limb.

Her bubble lifted and she put her hand over it, pressing its wobbliness until it cracked open and became warm, curved pieces to scatter in the flash.

At lunchtime her father lifted her up and she ruffled his hair with both hands to get rid of the indentation where his goggle strap had pressed. "There you are, Daddy," she said.

"Haud the snap," he passed her the tin. Inside was her jam sandwich, wrapped in greaseproof paper. Her father had cheese and piccalilli. "Ere ye gonnae gies a hawnd making ra tea the nicht," he said as he shouldered through the swing doors with her. His lab coat smelled of machine oil. He had bought a gas cooker, "*Fer yer Mammy gin she comes hame,*" and every day they were trying out recipes from the little cookery book that had come with it.

As they went down the steps into the darkness she hid her eyes against his neck. Above their heads was an overhead pipe lagged with sacking. Once, he had shone a torch to show her. The humps of sacking frightened her. She felt his hand over her head. The humming of the basement engines was all around them now. Her father turned the corner. "It's a braw sunny day oot here onyway." He kicked the door open, spring sunshine flaring round them as he put her down.

"Ask me questions." It was her favourite game. She had tried with Wilfred and Harold but not any more because they asked what have I got in my sandwiches? How much is a tin of elbow grease?

"De've ee ken the kind o glass yer Daddy uses?"

"Bora-silicate," she said.

"Boro," he corrected her. "Ony mair?"

"Soda glass."

"Aye. And fer whit would ah use soda gless?" He stopped in his tracks to light a cigarette, cupping his hands around the match as he carried it to his mouth.

"Windows."

"Super! Aye. Yer a canny wee lassie."

"Can I blow that out?"

"Aye." He held the match down for her. She blew. They crossed the road to the cemetery. Gravestones tilted over as if the ground had heaved up and flung them sideways. Greta sat by her father on a bench and they ate their sandwiches.

"Is it a long way to the special hospital?" She gripped his face with her hands. He didn't look pleased. She knew it wasn't the same hospital as the one near their house. "Can we go and see them?" His face twisted away from her hands. Birds sang in the graveyard trees. "Can we?"

"Naw we cannae dae that."

"But why?"

The pages of his newspaper snapped as he opened it up.

"Why can't we go?"

He lit a cigarette but didn't let her blow out the match. She leaned her head against him then slid down to pick the daisies and celandines that grew in the uncut grass around the old graves. When she heard him folding up his newspaper she ran back with her flowers and he lifted her so she could put her cheek next to his face. He scraped her with his whiskers to make her laugh. "That's ma bonny wee lassie," he said, "Pit doon yer wee bunch o' flowers, ye cannae bring they in ma lab." He hugged her and she let the flowers fall, breathing in the lovely warm smell of him; aftershave, tobacco and some other part that was just him.

During the endless afternoon she sidled into the grinding room up to Wilfred's elbow: "what's that, Wilfred?"

Wilfred jumped. The grinding wheel went round.

"What is it?"

"Carborundum powder: two hundred grit."

"Wilfred…"

"Yes?"

"Do you know where Mummy and Deborah have gone?" Wilfred's goggles pointed down. The grinding wheel went round.

Greta went back into the glassworking room sniffing in the smell of propinol. With her colouring book on her knee, she sat on the floor by the annealing oven and coloured in a fairy's dress with a pink wax crayon. Bored with that she put on a Perspex mask and a pair of the big asbestos gloves the men used. On tiptoe at her father's bench Greta stared at the condenser. It was like a bottle, and inside it was a shape that looked like a lady made of glass. Greta stared hard. It was a glass lady who was trapped inside a bottle; and out of her head… "What's that curly tube?" asked Greta, but Harold passed by and didn't answer. The glass tube curled up from the lady's head, coiling round and round, until it reached the top of the bottle. But there was no opening at the top. The giant gloves fell off her hands and Greta reached out for the condenser.

"Whit are ye daein?" Her father was back.

"Nothing," she said.

"Jist ye dae yer colourin'." He picked up the condenser and hurried out. The telephone rang.

"Answer it Harold," Wilfred's voice was loud above the roar of his lathe, "don't stand gawping, you daft ha'porth."

The phone stopped before Harold got to it. He looked at Greta. "See this?" Harold proffered a round white biscuit. She drew back from his tortoise face and tried not to breathe in his awful smell or look at his teeth. *Tell me where Deborah is. Tell me when she is coming home again. Tell me why Mummy took Deborah and not me as well.* As she reached out for the biscuit, he snatched it backwards. "No; tell me what it is first;" he said.

"A biscuit?"

"'Tisn't a biscuit! It's glass."

"No it isn't," she said.

"Yes it is."

"No it isn't."

"Yes it is. It's sintered glass."

"I don't care."

"How old are you?" Harold asked.

"I'm five."

"And you don't know about sintered glass," he teased.

"Deborah's gone to the special hospital."

"So you said."

"Do you know what she's got?"

11

"She comes home in a few weeks. Here…" he gave her the sintered glass.

"How long is a few weeks?"

"Too long, if you ask me. Why don't you go and help Mrs Primrose up in the office?"

"Harold – Get over here," shouted Wilfred and Greta ran to her colouring book as if he had shouted at her.

Fairy Tales

Weeks and months went by. Summer became autumn and autumn merged into winter. There was frost on the window panes every morning by the time they came home. Deborah had a new hairstyle, short; puffing around her face like a dark chrysanthemum. Maybe that was why her father was angry but Greta liked it very much. Her mother's hair was the same but she smelled as if she had been keeping her clothes next to the Vim under the sink. She lifted Greta up and held her so tightly that Greta squeaked. "Do you like the new cooker?" she clamoured, desperate to have them eat their tea; another recipe from the little cookery book.

"What's this?" her mother tilted the plate.

"Shamrock Savoury." Greta glowed with pride. Her father had made fried bread and she had spread the pieces with fish paste and helped arrange three slices of hardboiled egg on each to form a shamrock. Her father had added a dab of chutney in the center of each slice of egg.

"Dad cooked and I helped," said Greta turning to Deborah.

And Deborah lifted Greta and said: "sit on my knee to eat yours. Pass her plate to me so she can reach. I'm not letting go of her."

Everything went back to normal except that now there were the arguments: Deborah and their mother; Deborah spraying lacquer. "What's the sense of doing that to your hair," their mother demanding, "after that expensive perm?"

Deborah snapping: "It's my head Mother; I can do what I like with my hair."

And instead of answering, her mother made a noise as if she had accidentally cut herself with the bread knife.

For Christmas, Greta had a walkie-talkie doll with chestnut plaits whose eyelashes were jutting fringes of real hair. Inside her open mouth a red tongue was about to touch two baby teeth at the top. "*Mama*," she said, in a cat's voice, when Greta laid her down.

The voice came from the small of her back where she was drilled with a pattern of holes like the telephone receiver at the glassblowing lab. Greta called her Pearl, which was Deborah's middle name.

"Look, this is the Devil, Pearl," Greta held out the picture at the front of the Edgar Allen Poe book, "he's sitting on the laird's coffin. What's a laird, Mummy?"

"That's a desperate book." Her mother, knitting Greta's new jumper in some tan-coloured wool Brother Isidore had brought round, tutted sharply; "put it away."

"Edgar Allen Poe," chanted Greta from behind the sofa, as amused as ever because 'Poe' meant 'potty' as well. She lay on her tummy next to the bookcase. It was her favourite place. As well as Edgar Allen Poe there was an incomplete pack of playing cards, her game of Snap, copies of the *Readers' Digest* that Wilfred passed on to her father and a book, from a jumble sale, her mother said, which Greta loved. The pages of the book were fibrous and soft and had black and white pictures; among them a sad postman, an awkward bridge and the one Greta looked at most which was a big lady lying down with no clothes on. Why was she bare like that? Her flesh looked so pocked and goosepimpled that several times Greta had dug her nails into it, convinced the lady could feel it. The nail marks were retained in the thick padding of the paper. Deborah had read the title of the book to her: The Artist Van Goff.

Pearl fell forward onto the picture of the Devil. Greta sat her up again. "Are you scared, Pearl? I'll read what it says at the bottom: Twas the foul fiend in his ane shape, sitting on the laird's coffin..." Greta couldn't really read it but Deborah had told her the words.

In March, for her birthday, they gave Greta her own book: *Hans Andersen's Fairy Tales* and at bedtime, Deborah, with sensational dramatic expression, read her the stories. By June they had reached *The Garden of Paradise* with the four winds telling tales of polar ice and walruses, of dromedaries and sandstorms. In order to find his heart's desire, the man had to cross a high white bridge. "Read me that bit again," Greta said, gripping Deborah's moving finger as it traced the words.

"Lions and tigers, perfectly tame, sprang like cats over green hedges," repeated Deborah.

"Can we go there?"

But Deborah went on reading.

Soon Greta clamoured once more: "Read that again!"

"You will come, said the Fairy, to where the tree of the knowledge of good and evil stands. I shall sleep among its branches. You will bend over me. But if…" here Deborah paused, "… you touch me," her voice dropped low, "Paradise…" she hissed, "will sink beneath the earth…" she waited, then; much louder: "…and be LOST…"

"He won't do it will he?" Greta asked. Deborah's voice had gained a terrifying, menacing volume.

"…The sharp wind of the desert will blow," thundered Deborah implacably, "the cold rain will drip from your hair and sorrow and care will be your lot."

"He won't do it will he?" Greta was weeping, undone by the conjuring of such dreadful loss.

"Greta, it's a story, don't cry;" Deborah said, and her doom-laden tone had vanished and her arm went round Greta, her face laughed down and she used the edge of her skirt to dab the tears. "We'll stop now. See – nothing." The book snapped shut. "Sweet dreams," and Deborah kissed her and was gone.

Hot as a boiled potato, Greta kicked her covers off. The summer evening light was rose-pink through her red curtains and she pictured the high white bridge and the tame tigers. If only she could go there. All summer Greta made Deborah read and re-read the mysterious story to her.

It was September by the time they began on *The Wild Swans* and Greta became acquainted with Princess Elise and her brothers. "Don't call me Greta," she said, "I'm Elise".

"Why?" Her mother was impatient and uncomprehending which made Greta shy so she shrugged as she had seen Deborah do. She had begun to read the book to herself; slowly deciphering the words. One bit said: *Elise was too good for magic to have any power over her*. Greta dug her fingernail into the paper so that a crescent marked the place.

"Can we go to the sea?"

"No, it's too far."

"Elise goes to the sea and finds the swans. Elise gets carried by swans."

"Swans?"

"The swans are her brothers; she's looking for them; they're by the sea."

"Nonsense." Knives and forks jangled into the drawer. The cat flitted out from under the table, tangling in her mother's feet. "Damn you, cat," she cried, suddenly furious, "I'm fed up with Deborah reading you that book. It's giving you ideas."

"I want brothers," stormed Greta. In the doorway stood Deborah, silently pulling hideous faces at their mother's back.

"Tell her we're reading *Bunty*," she said that night, while she was showing Greta how to play Patience. Her hands layered the cards into place. "She'll be at work. She won't know." Deborah had left school and started a shorthand and typing course. A smell of cigarettes clung to her.

To save her brothers, Elise took a vow of silence and wove shirts out of nettles. Greta cried. Behind the garden shed were plenty of nettles and she let them sting her hands to see if she could bear it. She couldn't. By November they were nearing the climax. Elise was to be burned as a witch. Her nettle shirts were taken with her to the stake. "Greta!" came a shout, "what are you up to?"

Greta gave a guilty start, caught in the act of trying to bind herself to a garden fork that she had thrust into the centre of her father's bonfire pile. One minute her mother was rapping on the kitchen window, the next minute she appeared by Greta at the bottom of the garden. "Get off that. What have you done to your poor doll?" Pearl stood with her legs rammed into a pile of soil to keep her from falling over.

"She's the wicked archbishop, Mummy. Leave her."

"Is this game something to do with that book?" Her mother straightened up sharply, gripping Pearl. Greta's hand sneaked into the pocket of her gabardine mackintosh. Folded in there was the nettle shirt she was going to throw over her princely brothers. It was a leaf she had picked from the last marrow plant; its dark palm as rough as the cat's tongue. It was the same colour as nettles. "What are you playing?" Her mother persisted.

"Guy Fawkes," said Greta.

16

"Well don't. You'll wreck your Daddy's bonfire. Pearl's getting filthy, look at her legs."

"She's my doll, Mother; I can do what I like with her legs."

The secret game continued. Greta sat at her mother's dressing table and stared into the mirror as she brushed her hair. Pearl; now the king; spoke in a deep voice: "is it true Elise? Have you been gathering nettles among the witches?" To ensure silence Greta pressed her lips together so tightly that they went into her face, leaving a line like the scar on Deborah's stomach and she burst out laughing

Questions tormented Greta before she fell asleep at night. To weave nettles was agonising enough, but to have to keep silent and not explain why, even though helpful people surrounded her, was terrible. And God; where was he? Elise prayed to God but he never helped her, only made things worse. Why did he let the wicked queen turn the brothers into swans? And couldn't he have led the hounds away from Elise until she finished the shirts?

A Tale of Hidden Treasure

Deborah went out more and more. "Don't get in my way," she warned Greta, who had come into the bedroom with her drawing book.

Greta sat on Deborah's bed. "I made up a poem," she said, holding out the page.

Deborah,who stood brushing her hair; angled her body away from the mirror to read it out.

"Humpty Dumpty lived in a shed
Humpty Dumpty fell off the bed
Humpty Dumpty had a sore *hed*
Humpty Dumpty was *ded*,"

she intoned and both of them burst out laughing. "What a lovely poem, Twig."

"I'll make it longer," said Greta, sucking her pencil. From the radio in the kitchen The Archers music floated up. "What rhymes with dead?"

Deborah pointed at the pictures sellotaped onto her wall which were all of ladies wearing bridal gowns that Deborah had cut out of the papers "Wed?" She rested one foot on the chair as she eased a stocking over her toes and unrolled it up her leg. "Tread?" she suggested, "Fat-head?"

Greta laughed. The net flounces of Deborah's petticoat were frothing round her wrists as she fastened her suspenders. "Can I do one?" asked Greta.

"No, I'm in a hurry." Deborah dropped her skirt down over her head; a lasso of sky-blue gingham, her elbows like porcelain jug handles behind her as she fastened the zip. She dabbed White Fire scent on her wrists. It was Friday so the rest of the house was full of the smell of grilled herrings. "Pass the nail file," Deborah said; and after a while, "Reach me that compact."

Greta gave up on the poem. "Are you going dancing?"

"No;" Deborah drew lipstick along her stretched lips and Greta's moved in a copy of the shape Deborah's were making; "the flicks." Deborah compressed her lips, printing coral bows together.

"Sing me the fountain song," said Greta.

"*Three coins in the fountain…*" the lipstick twisted back into its golden case. "*Each one seeking happiness…*" into the pointed shoes went Deborah's toes. "*Thrown by three hopeful lovers…*" stiletto heels raised clear of the rug. "*Which one will the fountain bless…*" as Deborah's husky voice finished the song she twirled and Greta watched the flaring circle of skirt and the gorgeous peony of petticoat.

"Do it again," she said. Her pencil fell to the floor and her laughing sister spun. "Can I come with you to the kennels tomorrow?" Deborah had a Saturday job and Greta longed to work there too. "Can I come, Deborah?"

"Maybe," Deborah buttoned her cardigan; "out you go, you know the rule," Greta knew the rule. She skipped out onto the landing and leaned over the banister looking down. Deborah followed, closing the door and began to descend the stairs. *You are NOT to go in my room when I'm not there!* Deborah had made her say *I promise.* Halfway down the stairs Deborah looked back up at her. "Bye, Twig," she called.

Greta sat on the stairs and peered between the banister rails to watch her sister swish into the kitchen. Only Deborah called her Twig. She heard the two voices, Deborah and her father. Bumpety-bump she progressed, on her bottom, a stair at a time, all the way down and waited. Deborah, gloves on, came out of the kitchen shrugging on her coat and when she opened the front door, Greta stepped forward to hold it.

"Damn," said Deborah, "it's raining." She grabbed her umbrella from the hallstand and raised it as she stepped out onto the pavement and set off. A gust caught the umbrella and Deborah shrieked and ran a few steps.

"You're flying," Greta called and the thought of her sister lifted into the air made her laugh as she slammed the door. The letter box made a friendly clang.

In the sitting room, the chair by the window was Greta's vantage point for watching the street. She put her head under the lace curtain, pressing her forehead against the glass. At the bus stop Deborah furled her umbrella. The bus came. As it drove past the window towards Wexford Street, Greta saw Deborah inside, reaching up to the silver rail and walking towards the back as if she was trying to come home even though the bus was taking her away.

The glass was cold against Greta's forehead. Deborah had gone; her mother was at her part-time cleaning job at the off-license, her father was listening to the radio then he would do the crossword in his Reader's Digest. She could smell the smoke from his cigarette. Greta crept upstairs into Deborah's room. Her heart was beating harder and harder making her open her mouth to breathe. It was frightening but she longed to see Deborah's treasure. The floorboards dug into her knees as she knelt in front of the dressing table. The bottom drawer slid open and she removed the angora sweater and saw the tissue paper. Without making it rustle Greta lifted it out and revealed the bed of cotton wool with shiny cloth on it.

And there they were. The glass animals. Against the purple satin they gleamed as if polished with light. Greta loved them. There was a roe deer, its crystal antlers as tiny as the horns on a snail. Her favourite was the galloping horse. She held it up, marvelling at its radiance. Her fingers traced the outflung mane. The tail was a feather of glass; each hoof a shining nib. She replaced the horse and lifted the peacock, holding it to the light to see the scrolled sequins of its plumage. The spread fan was as delicate as the skin of ice on a puddle when frost first catches it. Greta's heart thumped. If she pressed with her thumbnail, would the peacock's tail flake into crystals like salt? Curiosity gave her an urge to do it.

Once she had borrowed Deborah's shantung ribbon for Pearl. Deborah had discovered her. "You've been in my room – damn you to hell, you're a thief. You'll rot in hell!" Her dark-brown eyes had looked black. She had snatched up Pearl, torn off the ribbon and dropped the doll back into Greta's lap. Cheeks red with anger, lashing at Greta with the ribbon she said: "don't you ever go in my room unless I say so."

Now, covering the animals up, Greta closed the drawer and looked for the ribbon. Deborah had taken it off a chocolate box at Mrs Griffin's and ironed it. If you held it one way it was deep rose red. If you tilted it, the colour changed to violet.

Next day, at Mrs Griffin's kennels, Greta stared at Terry as he opened the big five-barred gate for her and Deborah. "Hello Terry," said Deborah and reached up and gave him a pat on the head as if he were a horse. Greta, twisting to watch him over her shoulder as they crunched across the gravel, saw him rub his cloud of straw-soft hair and smile after them. He collected things from Deborah and kept them in the pocket of his dungarees. He had shown them to Greta: a toffee wrapper, two cigarette cards, a bus ticket: he called them his 'business'.

They went to get Captain, Mrs Griffin's golden retriever. "Morning Debbie," called Mrs Griffin.

"Morning Mrs Griffin." Deborah strode on, leaving Greta squatting on the kitchen floor patting the sleepy old dog.

"Come to help us today, Greta? Have a biscuit," Mrs Griffin offered the tin.

"Thank you," Greta took one, hands cold inside her woollen mittens. The dog sat up and Greta fed him her biscuit.

"Lucky boy, Captain," said Mrs Griffin.

Mrs Griffin was fat and dipped custard creams into her tea, sitting at the kitchen table adding up lines of numbers. She had a gramophone and listened to Edmundo Ross and Pat Boone and sighed when she got up to change the records as if moving was hard. Terry was her son. Deborah said he was backward. The howling and yipping of the foxhounds broke out. They had heard Deborah coming with their food. Chow time: that's what Deborah called it.

Greta clipped on Captain's lead and set off around the paddock, another biscuit in hand, the heavy dog floundering alongside. Ice creaked and snapped on the puddles and muddy water oozed over her Wellingtons. Captain was old and took a long time to get all the way round. When they got back to the kitchen door Greta sat on the step to remove the lead.

"Dry his feet," Mrs Griffin passed an old towel. Greta watched Deborah talking to a tall man wearing a trilby hat like a film star. Greta knew how big and sparkling her sister's eyes would be. "That's Oliver Robinson talking to your sister. He's the hunt master. He's taken with your Debbie," said Mrs Griffin as if she could see what Greta was thinking.

Deborah beckoned, and Terry came into view. Deborah passed him the bucket she was holding then moved off slowly, her hands in the pockets of her tightly belted overalls, laughing up at

Oliver Robinson. Greta hugged Captain and the panting dog turned to lick her face.

When boyfriends came and collected Deborah, Greta thought that maybe they were not very nice because it made her father angry. It annoyed her too, because it meant she couldn't have her story. "Can your heart really break because it is so full of gladness?" she asked after *The Red Shoes*.

"No," said Deborah.

"Have you ever seen a night-raven?"

"There's no such thing."

"Deborah, let's be the birds in *The Galoshes of Fortune* – you be the parrot and I'll be the canary," and off she went: "Once I flew about among green palms and flowering almond trees..."

Deborah, angling a look at the page whilst painting her nails, stuck to the book. "You have genius but no... prudence..." she said, pausing to dip her brush in the nail varnish.

Greta improvised. "Shut your beak, parrot – I'm going to squeeze through these bars and fly to Africa, Goodbye!" And she jumped off the bed in her pyjamas and ran about the room waving her arms. "I escape. But you must chase me, Puss, chase me! I'm flying..."

And the cat blinked.

That year Santa Claus brought Greta a picture book of jungle animals, a new pack of cards and a compendium of games. As Christmas Day grew dark she and Deborah played pontoon for matches by the sitting room fire, cards balanced on their mother's sewing box and Greta's legs mottled from the heat of the coals. Later on, she, Deborah, and their mother and father too; sat around the table in the kitchen eating iced Christmas cake and playing Snakes and Ladders and Ludo until the counters were sticky and Greta had hiccups from laughing.

The next day Deborah announced she was leaving college, she hated shorthand, and she was going to work full time at Mrs Griffin's kennels instead. Both her mother and father were furious and no one ever wanted to play Snakes and Ladders again.

"What's it to be, a fried egg?"

"Yes," beamed Greta, plumping into her chair next to Deborah's. Her mother obligingly pulled a funny face and imitated the spitty noise of an egg frying which always made Greta laugh herself silly. But the humour didn't last long.

"Put that paper down, Deborah and finish up your toast."

"I have finished," said Deborah, who was cutting out a picture, the part-eaten slice ignored on the plate in front of her.

"Why can't you be more like Celia Furedi?" Their mother would not get over Deborah giving up her shorthand course. "You're as bright as her," she fumed; ripping the top off a packet of tea.

"Oh is that what you think now? When she first went you said: *oh, so Leicester's not good enough for her*," sneered Deborah.

"Leave off your insolence, Deborah."

"Well don't go *on*. Just because she's gone away to college! Celia wants to be a teacher. I don't. The Kennels pay well enough. I give you my keep." Deborah frowned with concentration as she turned the scissors to go around the top edge of the picture. It was another bride.

"Keep? Hah! Keep she says. Just listen to her."

Deborah wobbled her head, mouthing the words: "Keep? Hah! Keep, she says."

"I've dripped egg on my sleeve," said Greta, trying not to laugh.

"Don't interrupt," said her mother, staring at Deborah with hot cheeks. "I suppose I'll be glad you're not in one of the garment factories. Now that is a skivvy's life." Into the caddy went the tea.

"Celia's right about one thing," said Deborah, "she thinks Leicester's a dump and I agree with her." The scissors made two snappy bites and the picture was sheared free.

Greta jumped as her mother slammed the tea caddy down yelling: "why would you say that?" Deborah just waved the picture backwards and forwards and Greta craned to see it. "Amn't I doing enough for you, Deborah?" What their Father called her Irish side always came out when she was angry.

Deborah thrust the picture at Greta. "Hold it for me, Twig. I'm going to stick it on my wall later." Greta reached out with her free hand as the other conveyed a forkful of egg to her mouth. Her eyes were on the picture and at that moment Deborah gave her a well aimed nudge in the shoulder and the fork went upwards giving Greta an eggy moustache. Both girls screamed with laughter but their mother's anger increased.

"Why are you so bold? Stop laughing…" Deborah was off. "Come back here Deborah."

"I'm going to work," her head came back around the edge of the door, "see ya later Twig." The front door banged. Clang went the flap of the letterbox.

Grace Kelly's lifted arm, in its white sleeve, was painted with light. She looked to her left out of the photo as if she was waving goodbye to Deborah. Greta tried to count the pearl buttons on the long cuff. Grace Kelly had been made into a princess, Greta could tell by the half-bonnet of a headdress that held yards and yards of gauzy veil.

Apple Blossom

The arguments got worse.

Shouting ricocheted up and down the staircase. At the top was Deborah, buttoning her new red and white print dress. It was a shirtwaist with three quarter length sleeves and a full skirt. "She's seven Mother, not three," Deborah was buckling the matching belt; pulling it tight to make her waist as tiny as possible. "She's old enough to know what to do – it's only Mass for God's sake and I've told you already; I'm going to Bruciano's to meet Greg."

"I'm warning you, Deborah…"

"Well I'm telling you."

"You can't defy me and besides it's barely half an hour and you know I rely on you for this. For the love of God couldn't you have met him later?"

"Greg said six." Deborah's hands gripped the white collar of her dress and stood it up. "I'm going. She's not a baby, Mother; we've done it a thousand times. You shouldn't take me for granted. I'm not your slave." Deborah sank into a ballerina curtsey to pick up her clutch bag. The stiff petticoat billowed under her skirt.

"Greg! What kind of a stoaty name is that? And a cardigan isn't enough, it's not even the end of May; you'll be skinned once the sun goes down, the wind is biting. Wear your duster coat." Deborah slung her white cardigan around her shoulders. "You defy me my girl and …"

"And what? Don't worry. I'm getting out of here for good. You won't see me for dust." Their mother retreated from the white winklepickers, stair by stair. Deborah swept past and opened the front door. Evening sunlight poured into their narrow hallway. "Bye Twig," she called, "take your animal book. You'll be right as rain. See ya later alligator…" She was gone and the door banged shut, letterbox echoing, the hall dark again.

Muttering under her breath, their mother put on her camelhair coat and went to the kitchen dresser to rummage in the drawer for her headscarf. Greta darted to her side. "Jesus Mary Joseph you made me jump. Not that one." Greta's hands were offering the silky one with the huntsmen in red coats against a turquoise sky. "I want the purple one with the chevrons on it and the paisley border – that's the one – grand, Love," her mother was not smiling as she took off her beret and put the scarf over her head and tied it under her chin.

They hurried up the street, crossed Museum Square under the chestnut trees and went down the avenue to the church. "I'm last, oh Jesus Mary Joseph no one's as late as me," said her mother as they entered and crossed the wide nave. "Sit there while I'm gone and don't move." Her mother hurried towards the heavy oak door that led into the Lady Chapel.

"Look Mummy, Twig's waving," Greta held up her glass fragment. Amid the faint odour of candle wax she saw her mother's pale face glance round; heard the groan of the hinge and the thud of the closing latch. Sunlight filled the church. The windows were huge. *I'm not your slave.* What did Deborah mean? Greta began looking through her picture book. *I'm getting out of here for good.* The African elephant. *You won't see me for dust.* The giraffe. *It's only mass for God's sake.* The sloth. Greta dug her nail into the ugly sloth then spat on her finger and began rubbing at its offensive shape, until it wore away into a hole. The okapi over the page had Victorian bather's thighs with alternating stripes of cream and black. Its white socks were girlish. The silken hide of it looked so velvety that Greta imagined her hand imprinting a palm shape in the bronzy shine. It extended ears like a butterfly bow above its devoted kangaroo face. Greta tenderly turned the book sideways to adore the way it nuzzled its okapi calf. To her horror the baby had disappeared. There was a hole. The mother okapi now peered into a ragged mess.

Angels, high up by the ceiling, stood on stone platforms just big enough for their feet. Their outspread golden wings were edged in scarlet. The hateful sloth had spoilt her book. If only an angel would fly down to her. "Come and see where I stand," it would say and would carry her up. She would hear the air in its wings, like Elise being carried by swans. Her wounded mother would not know where she had gone.

"I'm here," she would shout and people would look up. The angel would bring her down and her mother would talk to it. She would stand with Greta the way Greta liked; when they both faced the person her mother was talking to, her arms round Greta from behind, her gloved hands clasped a little way below Greta's chin like the collar the milkman's horse wore. Greta would stand on her mother's shoes and be held there while her mother and the angel talked.

From beyond the door Greta heard Brother Isidore and then the sound of people's voices all rumbling together. She heard Brother Isidore again then once more the responses. She began counting. *One, two, three, four, five, six*: six angels. The words of Brother Isidore were fast now and urgent. They went up high and loud. Then silence. *One, two, three, four*; four candles burning in the stand. The magenta cloth on the altar was beautiful. *I'm getting out of here for good.* The ceiling looked like an upside-down boat; narrow planks and every now and then, curved strips of wood, like sprung bows, to brace them. *One, two, three*: three statues draped in purple with only their feet showing. Greta felt hollow. *I'm not your slave!* She wanted to go home; wanted to read about being lost in a dark wood. She was in the middle of *The Snow Queen*. It was even more exciting than all the other stories. Little Gerda was lost in a dark wood, searching for Kai. The robber maiden wore a scarlet hat and with her long dagger she tickled the reindeer's throat so the poor animal struggled and kicked. Greta wished for a friend with a dagger just like the robber maiden. She wanted to ask Deborah why did all the people in the story undress Gerda?

"Because she's pretty, like a little doll," Deborah replied, a few nights later. Greta slipped her bare feet into Deborah's white high-heeled shoes and clopped around the room, one hand on her hip. "Oh Twig, you sweet little thing," cried Deborah, and lifted her up in a tight hug.

Time drifted by.

"Stand still." It was March the eighteenth, the day after Greta's birthday. Greta bobbed and twisted, trying to see the scarlet wool, to gauge the effect of the white daisy buttons. It was her birthday present, a shop-bought cardigan, the knitting smooth and soft. "Let's get the tangles out of your hair. Keep still."

Deborah swept into the sitting room. "Hold out your hands Twig," she said and shook talcum powder onto Greta's palms. "Rub them together," she said, "now pat your face," Greta obeyed, breathing in the ravishing scent. Her head was yanked sideways as her mother did her parting and gathered up a bunch of her hair. "I'll put the ribbons in, Mother," Deborah seized the brush. The red satin ribbons were her birthday present to Greta.

"Beautiful," said their mother. "Do up your cardigan so your old blouse doesn't show." For the first time ever, Greta was going next door to play with Bridget Furedi.

"Lift me up to see in the mirror," Greta stood with her arms raised. Deborah lifted her then pretended she was too heavy and they giggled.

"Mind your p's and q's next door," said her mother but Greta was not attending.

Her father slammed his paper down. "Carmel dinnae fash yersel…" he told Greta's mother, "…Bridget's ma jist wants her wee lass to hae a pal."

"I," said Deborah, putting Greta down, "am going," and she swished out as their mother began buttoning Greta's cardigan.

"Greta," her father struck a match, "throw yon auld thing awa;" he nodded towards the mantelpiece as he lit his cigarette. "Ye're no a wee lassie ony mair." He shook out the match and took her glass twig off the mantelpiece. Greta watched. He flicked the match into the coal-scuttle then tossed and caught her glass twig.

"Daddy…" She held out her hand for it, stretching round her kneeling mother, who was reaching up under Greta's skirt now, and with hefty tugs, pulling the bottom edge of her blouse down tight.

"See now ah could melt it doon and mak summit o' it," said her father.

Greta tore loose and snatched the glass twig off him. Her heart pounded with indignation as she tucked it into the pocket of her skirt.

"Don't tease, Walter. Go on Greta. They're bound to let you play again but don't get above yourself."

"Michty me wumman calm yersel," she heard, as she let herself out of the front door.

Next door, Mrs Furedi answered her knock. Behind her was Bridget with her fingers in her mouth. "What a smart cardigan." said Mrs Furedi.

"I'm eight now," said Greta.

"Would you like a pineapple cube? Bridget loves them." Mrs Furedi gave Greta a paper bag. "Go on, have one."

The yellow cube was too big for her mouth; the acid taste awful.

Mrs Furedi sat them in the front room. "Don't touch the dog if he comes in, he bites," she said and left them to a Snakes and Ladders board set out on the table. Sedately the girls began to play. Bridget didn't notice when Greta took the dreadful sweet out of her mouth and put it in her pocket alongside her glass twig.

"What's that of?" asked Greta when Bridget finally won. She pointed at a picture in a silver frame.

"Wedding photo," Bridget took her fingers out of her mouth at last.

"The dress is nice," Greta went to examine the picture.

"Wedding dress." Bridget came to stand by her.

"Who is it?"

"My Ma."

"It doesn't look like her," said Greta.

"Yes it does," said Bridget and pinched Greta's arm so hard it was like being burnt. Greta tried to snatch her arm away. Bridget wouldn't let go.

"It looks like a princess," said Greta, staring at the picture so Bridget wouldn't notice that she was nearly crying. "Why don't you have a sweet?"

Bridget let go of her arm. "Ma said they were for you."

"Have one," Greta held out the bag.

"Thank you," said Bridget primly taking one, "do you want to come upstairs and play on my rocking horse?"

"Will your dog bite me?"

"Kick him if he does."

"I don't want the sweets; you can have them."

Bridget smiled. "You can have the wedding photo if you like it," she said.

But later, when Greta was going home with the photo under one arm, Mrs Furedi said she couldn't have it at all and she smacked Bridget. Bridget cried very loudly.

"Where is your wedding photo?" asked Greta. Her mother swung round from the sink and stared at her.

"Why ask me that?" she shouted. Greta was too surprised by the shouting to feel upset. She tried to correct her mother's peculiar mistake.

"It should be on the sideboard in the front room. It is at the Furedi's. Have you lost yours?"

Her mother turned back to the sink and finished washing the gravy boat she was holding. She put it upside down on the draining board. "I don't remember. It was just after the war. Things get lost. I don't know where it is."

"Did you have a long dress?"

"No. It was just after the war," she repeated. "Go upstairs and wash your hands and face ready for bed."

A noise of pounding. The shed was ringing with it. Maybe her father was making her a rocking horse. Greta had always said she wanted one. He must have come home from work early. Her satchel bumped on her back as she ran towards the shed. Inside, raising the bolster hammer and pounding it down over and over, her mother stood at the workbench.

"Mummy," said Greta.

Her mother leapt; face white and eyes like snowman eyes; two orbs of blurred coal. Her open mouth dragged breath into her. In silence she put the hammer down and walked past Greta out of the shed. Greta stood on her crate. The purple cloth made the workbench look like a messy altar. On the cloth were broken legs and snapped off tails; animals lying smashed, a horrible slurry of powdered glass. The jaws of the vice held the glass horse. The shank of the vice-clamp yielded to her push; gave way, loosening the bite. The iron ball on the end of the shank clanged on the socket-rim as it fell through its hole in the metal. Her hand followed its fall and grasped it from below. Her right hand held the horse and her left hand eased the shank to part the lips of the vice. She laid him on the pile with his broken legs beside him.

By reaching over and gathering the corners of the purple cloth, Greta could lift the whole destroyed collection in an inverted parachute. Tears threatened to overwhelm her. The thought of Deborah finding them made her feel out of breath. Greta's heart began punching her ribs. The treasure was ruined. Why had her mother been smashing them? She stepped awkwardly down with the heavy parcel dangling from both hands. The oblong of the shed doorway framed a picture of where she lived. There were more bees than usual flying among the Sweet Williams; she saw the lettuces, the beetroot leaves veined with red and the house beyond. The dustbin, its lid crooked, stood level with the scullery door. Just next to it the little window of the outside lavatory was open, glass flashing as the sun slid from behind a cloud. No sign of her mother at the kitchen window. Birds were singing, Furedi's dog barked. What if Deborah was coming along the street? There was a clang from somewhere further down the terrace. Furedi's dog again; *bark, bark, bark*; surely trying to tell everyone about the destruction of the glass animals.

She hurried towards the dustbin, the purple bundle hammering her knees, setting it down while she got the sun-warmed lid off. She heaved the bundle up then into the dustbin it went. Braving the stink she leaned over and rearranged the rubbish so that the treasure disappeared under cinders, tea leaves, orange peel, a Camp coffee bottle, cigarette ends from her father's ashtray and something slimy that was soaking through the newspaper it was wrapped in.

"Weel. That's richt 'e ken." said a voice as she wiped her hands on her skirt. Her father bent down and picked up the dustbin lid. Without looking at her, he crunched it into place, twisting it slowly, first one way, then the other, as if screwing it tight. He kept his eyes down. "We'll nae speak aboot it. Ah thoucht ye'd be roon at Bridget's." There was complete silence. "Weel?" Now he glanced at her. To nod seemed the best thing. "So?"

"I had to come home. Bridget's got a violin lesson."

He crouched down and put his arm round her. "It's a'richt. Yer mammy had a wee bit fight wi yer sister ye ken."

"Deborah's at work."

"She isnae. Yer mammy foun' Deborah in the hoose wan she brocht hame the shopping frae the market." He was in his vest but smelled like chicken soup. Greta squirmed from his arm and shed her satchel. He stood up.

On the step of the lavatory her skipping rope lay twined around its wooden handles. "I'm going to skip," she announced.

"A'richt then." He took out a cigarette and patted his trouser pockets for matches.

Rushing away through the house helped. Greta held the snake of her rope and let the handles fly. She swung the rope and the wooden handles banged against the stair rails as she ran past. It helped a lot. So did the noise of her shoes on the wooden floor and the slam of the front door as she pulled it shut much too hard. Chanting calmed her as she skipped on the pavement at the front:
"Salt… mustard… vinegar… pepper,
Salt – mustard – vinegar – pepper,
Saltmustardvinegarpepper…" Faster and faster she skipped.

Soon the man in the black suit who gave Bridget her violin lessons came out. Greta dropped the rope and was about to knock on Furedi's door when it opened and Celia Furedi; Bridget's big sister; dashed out, followed by her mother. "I didn't expect you to come home looking like a beatnik that's a fact," yelled Mrs Furedi. Celia didn't look round, walking away fast, her circular skirt flaring. It was made of scarlet felt. Her tightly belted cardigan was on backwards. It was black. The light winked off the buttons between her shoulder blades. She wore flat black pumps and a red scarf with white polka dots knotted at her neck in a triangle. Greta liked the scarf. "Black! Black! Who wears black unless it's a funeral?" screamed Mrs Furedi. Celia was Deborah's age but had passed her eleven-plus and gone to the grammar school. Now she was at teacher training college. "Tell Bridget Greta's here," called Mrs Furedi, leaning backwards into her house. "If only Celia dressed like your Deborah. You wouldn't catch Deborah Buchanan biting her nails… She doesn't bite her nails!"

Parts of this were screamed after Celia, parts addressed to Greta and Greta couldn't think of anything to say. But the drama of the scene blotted out the image of her mother in the shed, so she sat on Furedi's wall and drank in the swirl of Celia's red skirt, the tap and clatter of Mrs Furedi's high-heeled shoes as she stormed in tight circles on the pavement and the music of the charm bracelet zithering on her enraged wrist.

An old woman appeared, holding Bridget by the shoulders. "So is this Bridget's little friend, Greta?" She demanded. Bridget nodded. "Greta Garbo," said the old woman and laughed until she doubled over coughing. She had iron-grey hair under a brown hairnet and no teeth. Greta stared at the repellent mauve cavity in her face.

Bridget ran away down the street, fair pigtails flying. "Come on," she shrieked.

Greta took off, chasing her down towards the prison, heading for the park where there were swings and a slide. "Who's that old woman?" She asked.

"Nanny Furedi," said Bridget, "my grandma. She's staying with us for a fortnight. Celia's boyfriend has a beard. " This made them laugh. "She's got a black boat-neck jumper with batwing sleeves," continued Bridget: "she smokes now as well."

"Deborah's been smoking ages," said Greta. The slide smelled of metal, inches from her nose. She liked its worn gold. She was lying on her front on the flat part at the bottom. Bridget hung upside down on the climbing frame; her knees hooked over one of the bars.

"Celia won't have milk in her tea. She says tea's common and she wants black coffee," said Bridget. "Me Mum's gone mad."

"Where does Celia live?" Greta couldn't imagine what the teacher training college was like. *Me Mum's gone mad.* Maybe her mother had gone mad too and that's why she had smashed the animals.

"There's halls at the college where they all live. Celia shares a room with a girl called Penny."

"Why has she got her cardigan on back to front?" said Greta.

Bridget started laughing so much that she had to come down. "Let's do it to ours," she said. They buttoned each other's cardigans down the back, giggling. "I want to show my Mum," said Bridget and they ran back up the street.

"I've got to go in now," said Greta as they arrived. Greta didn't want another confrontation with the toothless old woman. She wanted her mother. She burst into her own house, slamming the front door. In the kitchen her mother was cutting bread. The only odd thing now was that her pinafore wasn't fastened. Greta crossed over to her. "Shall I do up your pinny?" No reply, just the steady sawing of the bread knife as another slice peeled off the loaf. Greta took up the two long strings and began to do the bow. She tied it carefully, making the loops even. "There, Mummy. All done."

Silence.

"Have I got any Grandmas?" The quiet rasp of the knife began again, through the bread. "Because if I have, I don't want them to have no teeth."

Her mother suddenly did things very fast. She slammed down the bread knife, grabbed Greta in her arms and began to laugh. "Your Daddy came from a children's home in Scotland so there's no Grandmas or Granddads for you there and the ones you might have had from me..." her voice sounded as if it was sobbing now. Greta couldn't hear clearly because her mother's arms were pressing her ears tightly to her head. "...There's no telling where they might be. The nuns reared me and I burned my boats when I left Ireland. I'm cut off now from all that went before. Never ask. Never ask."

Greta was making up rhymes again. Loudly. Because it seemed to her that she was the only one of them now who ever said anything. A scent of steamed cotton drifted in from the kitchen where their mother was ironing. Greta and Deborah were in the sitting room; Greta laughing herself silly. "What about this – listen Deborah," she clamoured to her sister's profile: "Deborah-Pearl and Greta-Marie went down to the river to bathe..."

"Enough," screamed their mother, shockingly, "get to bed, Greta before I take a strap to you." Silence engulfed them. Deborah left the room. A wedge of light appeared in the hall and Greta saw dust motes. The front door closed and the light vanished.

The days were long and hot. Greta; cotton frock tucked into her knickers, had to be dragged away from the paddling pool in the park each bedtime. The sun-warmed leather smell of her new satchel beguiled her – that and the taste of Raspberry Splits bought from the corner shop and eaten as she and Bridget walked home from school showing each other the pink of their tongues getting darker and darker.

"Miss Warren said I could bring this home," she called as she burst into the house with her picture. Even as she spoke, she could tell that something was different. There was a strong whiff of cleaning in the air. The orange wax in her mother's tin of polish was worn away in the middle and Greta saw the golden metal of the tin shining through.

Her mother knelt on the stairs, rubbing at the banister rails with her rag. "Close the door," she said, finally turning her head. Greta slammed it then approached, picture on display. "The deep blue sea," said her mother.

"That's Daddy, that's you and that's Deborah and me stroking the swans," said Greta.

"Swans as big as carthorses." A tired tone in her mother's voice. The nose-tickling odour of Mansion Guardshine muffled the hallway.

"Why does it smell so polish-ey?" asked Greta. There was silence.

Her mother stood up and came down the last stair folding her cloth. "I've given Deborah's room a good clean," she said. "Deborah's left home now and gone away, like Celia Furedi."

"Gone?" Greta asked.

"Yes. She's gone."

"Where to?" demanded Greta, too astonished to think.

"Australia," said her mother. There was an instant of blankness where only the smell of polish and the silence in the house were present in Greta's mind. Then her mother took the picture from her. "You can put this up on the wall. Would you like to have Deborah's room now she doesn't want it any more?"

"Can I?"

"Yes," said her mother, "you can."

Greta ran upstairs into Deborah's room and the first thing she did was look in the bottom drawer. Of course there was nothing there. The drawer was just a bare wooden box.

As the days went by, Greta's pleasure in the room began to fade. "When is Deborah coming home?"

"Jesus you made me jump. Where've you been, Greta?" Her mother was beating eggs. The fork tines clacked on the china. Over and over the glinting metal looped through the froth in the bowl. "I said, where've you been?"

"In the bathroom." Without Deborah's Silvikrin lotion and Camay soap, the corners of the bath were naked. Sadness wracked Greta. Deborah had taken everything with her, even the tube of Valderma; but sometimes in the bathroom Greta thought she could smell Deborah if she shut her eyes and breathed carefully. "When is Deborah coming home?"

"She isn't coming home; it's too far to come."

"If it's too far to come, how will she get home for Christmas?"

"She won't have time for that."

Greta felt as if she was forcing her mother to give these answers. How could she possibly want to hear them? So why did she ask? Her tongue had begun to feel strange. Maybe asking a question that you didn't want answered made your tongue stiff. "But why won't she come home?" In silence her mother added milk and continued beating. Greta stared miserably at the triangles of buttered bread lying ready in the pudding dish. "Mummy?"

"You make my head ache with all your questions," said her mother, "fetch the sultanas. I've had enough."

There had to be a way to make everything come right. "Dad, where is Deborah?"

"How de've e think yon meat got in w'ur meat pie? We've eaten her up."

"It was rabbit pie."

"Naw. Yer mammy telt ee 'twas rabbit fer to mak e eat it."

"Stop it, Dad, I saw the rabbit hanging up in the shed. Mum put the guts in the dustbin."

"How de've ee ken twas rabbit's guts? See now – that's you telt! Aye and wur stew yisturday – yon wus yer sister an' all. Weel whit a face on ee. Aye that's you telt. Dinnae ask if ee dinnae want to ken whit's true." He darted a glance at her face then scowled. "And dinnae tak the pet," he said, all joking gone, "that'll nae bring yer sister hame. Jist leave it alane."

And the weeks went by.

Greta was sure Deborah couldn't be dead. "Mum shall we go and see if Deborah still works at the kennels?"

"She doesn't."

"But how do you know?"

"Greta you ask too many questions, drop it."

"Where is she?"

"I don't know."

"Has she come back from Australia?"

"She isn't in Australia."

"You said she was."

"How should I know where she is?"

"Please let's go to the kennels. Maybe she wrote to Terry."

"Greta, shut up. I've got a blinding headache. You'd try the patience of a saint. I'm going to confession in five minutes and I haven't combed my hair."

Winter had come.

"What will Santa bring?" A smell of warm rubber as her mother pushed the hot-water bottle down the bed towards Greta's feet.

"Can I have a tinderbox?"

"Ask for something sensible."

"You haven't heard me say my prayers," Greta struggled out of the tight blankets.

"The lino's too cold…. Stay under the blankets – oh you scallywag," Greta was kneeling on the floor. "You're a good girl. No wonder Brother Isidore gives you Scripture prizes." Greta smiled as she thought of what Brother Isidore would say if he ever heard the mocking scriptures she recited to amuse Bridget; 'Now Moses kept the flock of Jethro his father in law, the priest of Midian: and he led the flock to the *backside* of the desert….' At bedtime however she often insisted on singing *Jesus Bids Us Shine* as well as saying prayers. It was because she hoped God would bring Deborah back. Greta hadn't asked him yet but she was banking up goodness so that when she did he would listen.

Prayers done, her mother tucked her back in and stroked her hair. "So what do you want for Christmas?"

"I want to be a princess, so can I have a small crown?"

"Have you been reading that book again?"

"No. Can I have a rocking horse?"

"How would Father Christmas carry that down the chimney? Catch yourself on, Greta."

"A parrot?"

"Greta!"

Greta chose a globe.

When Christmas came, another of Greta's presents was talcum powder and on the pretty tin it said, *Apple Blossom by Helena Rubinstein*. The scent was divine. It was just like Deborah's. But as the weeks went by, Greta couldn't use it because whenever she smelled its perfume she thought of Deborah and felt sick with sorrow.

She read and re-read the Hans Andersen stories and borrowed book after book from the library; *Ballet Shoes, The Lion The Witch and The Wardrobe, Lamb's Tales from Shakespeare, The Water Babies* – she didn't understand it all but devoured everything. On her ninth birthday she was given *Alice in Wonderland* and came to realise that her mother; invariably late for Mass, was just like the White Rabbit.

In May, she picked lilac. "Take it out, Greta," called her mother, hands flapping, "you can't bring that in here; it's bad luck. Put it in the shed if you must."

"There's a dead rabbit in the shed."

"That was months ago, don't be daft."

Greta left it on the path. The setting sun shone. Her father had just finished raking the lawn-mowings. He pushed the heap of grass to the end of the garden in his wheelbarrow. "We'll have our picnic here," said Greta to Pearl.

"I'll spread the cloth," came the squeaky voice of Pearl. For a cloth, Greta had borrowed the embroidered linen mat from her mother's dressing table.

"This is your plate, Pearl. Sit up straight." On the cloth in front of her doll, she put a red tulip petal. "Here are some cakes with white icing." She put some daisy heads on Pearl's petal. "Now I have to fetch the bread and butter. Twig will look after you." Greta put her glass twig down on the cloth next to Pearl, then took another tulip petal and went up the path looking for buttercups. Dismantling the shiny flowers without tearing them was difficult so she sat on the wooden step of her father's shed. There was no dead rabbit. An evening breeze threatened to blow the petals away before she could arrange them. She moved inside the shed.

Dragging her crate into position by the workbench she stood on it and began again. Wood shavings lay below the vice. She brushed them aside and set each yellow buttercup petal overlapping its neighbour, just like her mother did when she made a plate of bread and butter. The sound of her father's Wellingtons came towards her from the direction of the compost heap. He passed the doorway without saying anything. She watched. He went towards the doll, who sat alone, a small figure next to the white patch of cloth, her hands held out in front of her. "*Daddy, mind Pearl*," Greta wanted to call. The low sun stretched her father's shadow long on the mown grass. The shadow passed over the doll as he fetched his hoe from where it leaned against the fence. Greta got down off her box. The petal plate had to be carried slowly or the buttercup bread lifted and blew off. "Before you can have a cake you must have some bread and butter, Pearl."

"Thank you," squeaked the doll.

Greta pinched up a buttercup petal and laid it on the star of the doll's hand. There was a moist quality to the air. Greta could smell mown grass. A robin was singing but apart from that and the chinking sound, as her father hoed his seedbed, it was quiet. The sun was flattening behind Mr Furedi's pear trees and gilding the galvanised corrugations of the shed roof. Greta went to offer her father some of Pearl's bread and butter. He put a petal up to his mouth and made a noise like someone eating. Greta held out the plate again and pinched up a second petal for him. He bent down by her and put out his tongue for the offering. She put the petal on his tongue and he closed his mouth, smiling at her. Her knuckles rested against the supple folds of his cheek in the indent of his smile. The shiny stretches of skin around her nails, the hangnail at the side of her index finger, the nails themselves and the never-touched ovals of flesh beneath them; all felt his warm bristles and the soft edge of his lip.

"Say goodnight to Daddy." It was her mother, at the back door, calling Greta in. Up in the bathroom she washed Greta's face with the flannel, wiping off the soap with cold water. She sploshed the flannel around the back of Greta's neck then rubbed her dry with the towel. "Sandals," she commanded and sank into a kneeling position. Greta pointed first one foot, then the other while her mother undid the silver buckles and took off her sandals and socks. "Would you stop that now you little terror..." Greta was twiddling the tuft on top of her mother's brown beret. The socks were transformed into a soft ball by her mother's swiftly turning hands. Then Greta stiffened, wailed and burst into tears. "Dear Jesus what's the matter?"

"I've left Twig on the lawn..." shrieked Greta.

"Come back here Miss..." Her mother had caught her by the arm.

"Let go, I have to fetch Twig..." Greta bucked and twisted, sobbing wildly.

"I'll fetch Twig. Stop it Greta or you'll get a smack!" Her mother raised one finger and Greta squeezed her eyes shut and held her breath. "Brush your teeth. I suppose Pearl is out there as well." Her mother left the bathroom. Greta scrubbed her toothbrush in the pink cake of toothpaste. The brushing and spitting calmed her down. She couldn't put the lid back on the tin so she left it lopsided and pattered back along the landing to her room.

"Say your prayers," sighed her mother, back again, putting the glass twig into Greta's outstretched hand and sitting Pearl on the bed. "Or shall you sing *Jesus bids us shine?*"

Greta cast herself onto her knees and put her hands together. "Gentle Jesus meekandmild, look-a pon-a little child..." Prayer done, she wriggled under her covers. Her mother kissed her goodnight; then, still close enough to touch Greta with her lips, looked down into her eyes. Greta smiled and stroked her mother's face with Twig. Her mother went downstairs and Greta got out from under the covers, kneeling on her bed to look out of the window. There was her father, hoeing.

It was still light but all the colours in the garden were richer now. Her father came to where the beanpoles made a row of tall wigwams. Then he glanced up. Gnats danced in a patch of air to one side of him. The evening sun slanted towards him through the pear trees. Her father smiled at her. Then he was lighting a cigarette, his face bent into his cupped hands and as he shook the match and flicked it into the border he was already turning and walking towards the shed. She wanted to run outside to him. She wanted to be lifted as high as the top of the bean sticks.

She laughed at first. There was a tickle to his touch and his smile curved his cheeks into bumps that she could hold. But then he was breathing too loudly and he said nothing and her voice, when she tried to speak, had gone small. She meant to ask him if her mother was home yet but her voice refused to ask because it didn't want to hear the answer. "You're pulling my hair," said the new, little voice.

"Ah'm sorry ma wee pet," murmured her father, adjusting his position, as if that was all right now.

"Thank you," said the little voice. Greta heard it as if she was a long way off. Then she became preoccupied with finding a way to bear the unbearable reek of the spit with which he was coating her mouth. She imagined herself screaming, "*Deborah, Deborah, save me.*" But she couldn't imagine past the two repetitions of her sister's name.

"Hold this for me…" he said, guiding her hand. "Ah'll gie ye a wee present the morn."

When he'd gone, only the silence was left. She curled round in a ring under her covers and an echo roared in her ears and she knew she could get no smaller.

The next day, after tea when her mother had gone to her cleaning job at the off-license; her father gave her a tissue-wrapped package. Inside it was a glass gazelle. Its tapered horns were spiralled with lines and its head was lifted and turned as if at any minute it might have to run. "Pit this somewhere safe," he said, "an' dinnae tell a soul." He smiled at her. She kept her eyes down. The glass gazelle lay shining in her palm. "De've ee like it?" Instead of reacting to him, Greta imagined the heat of a real gazelle, the rasp of its hide, the explosive clatter of terrified hooves, the mess and danger from its frantic plunging as it tried to escape from among their tables and chairs.

41

Time went by, taking Deborah further and further away. Greta had a brainwave. "Can I write to Deborah? Mum? We've got to have penfriends at school. Can I have Deborah for mine? There's Malaya or Australia for penfriends – can I? Mum?" Her mother was washing the dishes. Greta sat at the table, kicking the bar under her chair. "Mum?"

"I heard you."

"Well can I?"

"No you can't."

Greta saw her mother tightening up. Her mother was like a string on Bridget's violin; a string that someone has tightened and tightened, turning the peg until the wire doesn't give its true note any more. And they keep turning the peg. They turn the peg until the wood creaks as all parts of the instrument start to buckle. Greta stood up. She had to have an answer. "Why can't I?"

"Deborah's gone!" screamed her mother, her body shaking. The visceral cry sliced the air so Greta felt a long way apart, seeing her mother begin to fold the tea towel smaller and smaller. The kitchen clenched itself.

Her father hadn't moved. Greta opened her mouth to speak. He narrowed his eyes. But before she could bring even one word onto her tongue, he thumped the table. "Leave it alane, Greta," he shouted. Her mother smoothed her wad of tea towel and her father sat upright at the table, his arms held rigid either side of the space in front of him as if he expected a plate of food. "When ere ee ever gonnae learn?" He snarled. He lunged forward and his words got louder…"Dinnae speak aboot Deborah. Dinnae say her name ever again!" Greta shrank back. Her ribs banged into the back of her chair. She ran for the stairs. … "Dinnae speak aboot Deborah …" the words followed her; Greta was inside her room; "Ere ee listening tae me?" She slammed her door… "Ere ee?" She got into bed and pulled the covers over her head… "Dinnae you speak yin mair word aboot bloody Deborah."

Every night in bed she prayed for Deborah to come home. One day after school she went to church. The stone was cool as she knelt on the dais, close to the altar. *I know you didn't go to Australia really Deborah. I know what you meant now when you said you won't see me for dust. How am I ever going to find you? God takes no notice of me either like he didn't to Elise.* This wasn't the way to pray. Greta began again, whispering now. "Dear Father God, is Deborah still in Leicester? What shall I do?" The beautiful stone of the church was silent. The idea occurred to her that she should write it in the ledger. She got off her knees and went over to the lectern. Unable to reach or even see the book, she dragged a chair into place from the end of the nearest row and climbed up. A pencil rested in the groove between the pages.

Suddenly Brother Isidore was beside her, lifting her down; a sensation like flying, mixed with the blanket whirl of his robe against her legs and the smell of tobacco and sweat. "What are you doing Greta? I heard the chair scrape-scraping."

"I'm writing my question for God to answer," she said, mortified at being lifted down.

"That isn't what the book is for," he said,

"I've prayed but he doesn't answer," Greta's cheeks were hot.

Brother Isidore patted her shoulder then put the chair back. "Sit here," he said, "and maybe God's word will come to you and answer your questions." His eyebrows and his forehead made little movements of encouragement for her to sit. He was smiling at her. Brother Isidore's face was wise.

Greta believed him. "What will his word be like?"

"I don't know," he said, walking away, "but you will know, when it comes."

She sat and waited for a long time. The altar cloth in the sunlight; the shadows on the stone, the candles in their stands; all was calm emptiness and waiting space. Greta waited. When the church clock chimed the hour Greta counted. Seven o'clock. She could walk to meet her mother from the off-license.

On a day not long after, Greta fell down the stairs. Blows hammered into her tumbling body as she crashed from the top to the bottom. It all ceased as her head slammed into the floor.

"Keep the compress on until the swelling goes down," The doctor loomed above her and tucked the thermometer back into his top pocket. He shone a torch in her eyes.

"Is witch hazel good, Doctor?" came her mother's voice.

"…mild concussion…" she heard. They were going. The doctor giving her mother instructions as their combined footsteps descended.

The flannel on her forehead dripped cold water into her ear. "There's water in my ear," croaked Greta.

Her mother's footsteps came flying back up the stairs. "Dear God. Dear God." Her mother put the flannel in the basin. Greta heard the musical notes of water falling into the enamel whiteness.

"Wring it out," Greta begged as the soaking cloth covered her eyes once more. Tears were trickling into her ears, hot droplets along with the cold.

Greta was kept off school. Her mother, who was a dinner lady as well as a cleaner, took Greta to her canteen. Silver: the whole noisy shebang; everything made of metal. Greta crouched on the cushion she had been given and tried not to let her knees slip off it onto the knobbly sisal PE mat. She felt like Alice in Wonderland. The big legs of the women went to and fro. They wore green overalls and squashy green cloth hats.

"That's a terrible bump you've got," bawled a huge woman towering above Greta with a stack of baking tins. Greta didn't know what to say. The kitchen smelled of custard and jam tart; beef stew and onions. "She's very like you, Carmel," the woman bellowed. A machine began a furious clattering.

Her father brought home a present for her – a Barbie doll. Greta heard him telling her mother that Professor Nightingale had brought it back from a research trip in America but Mrs Nightingale wouldn't give it house room let alone allow their daughter to have it. Gripping the doll's elongated legs together as if they were pliers; Greta stared at the ethereal prettiness of its tiny face and then undid its elaborate coiffeur and spread out the shiny hanks of hair.

By the end of the week Greta had abandoned her mat in the corner and become the canteen pet. Her bruises turned purple and yellow and green and the ladies each gave her jobs to do. She stirred the cornflakes into the syrup for Marjorie and helped smooth the mixture over the pastry with a palette knife. Esther let her shell peas and Vera let her slice the beetroot. She counted out the cruets onto the tray and put tea-towels into Brobat suds to soak. They called her: "Good Girl," and "My Darling," and praised her dexterity and quietness. In the aftermath of dinnertime, when the big sterilizers filled the air with steam, Greta polished the cutlery dry and sorted it into compartments.

"Why do I keep finding Barbie on the hall floor?" demanded her Mother, once Greta was back at school, "what game is it this time?"

"No game," said Greta.

"Shall I knit her a dress? What have you done with the clothes she came in?" her Mother persisted. Greta just raised her book higher in front of her face and didn't reply.

You Won't See Me For Dust

The year after, Greta started at Four Pools Secondary Modern. Her father grunted at the sound of the name because he was disgusted. "Ye should o' passed," he said, when they heard she had failed her 11-plus. "Ye've aye ways bin a clever wee lassie – far too clever so says them at ma work, whit wi all yon questions all the time."

Disgusted. Not looking at them when he spoke and her mother sighing and patting her as if there was something on her that had begun to crumble away. But she loved the school. The boys and even some of the girls used terrible, foul language and she was Deborah Buchanan's sister.

"How is your sister?" the teachers all singled her out.

"She's in Australia, Miss."

"Goodness, how wonderful." And she was famous.

Boys, as big as men, stopped her in the ruckus of the playground and asked her to say something to Deborah. "Tell your Deborah I've finished with Heather," said one.

Another day it was: "Say that I'll see her in the Casa Bolero." The boy; hair like Billy Fury, looked her in the eyes.

And she looked straight back. "I can't. She's in Australia," she said, "haven't you heard?" At her side Bridget gasped and giggled, clutching Greta's arm, suggestive, nervous and to Greta's mind, silly.

"OK," said the boy, "you'll have to come instead then won't you."

Greta found that when she stared back into their eyes the boys smiled at her more and really looked at her; up and down. She began to backcomb her hair and chew gum. With her Saturday pocket money she bought pearlised pink nail varnish and Miners foundation. But homework was her favourite thing. Greta had not stopped being clever after all and her books were full of red ticks and exclamations: Excellent work. 10/10. Well done.

"Off ee gang noo, tae yer bed," there stood her father, at the bottom of the stairs.

"I need to learn this, we've got a geography test tomorrow," Greta, curled on the sofa in the sitting room, made her voice urgent.

"Dinnae bother yersel wi yon. Here wi ye. See whit a've made ye – anither yin." He was holding out a small package.

"I don't want it. I have to learn this by tomorrow, Dad."

"Weel hurry up then. Gie't tae me, ah'll test ye," and he came into the room and took her book impatiently. "Whit's the capital o' Venezuela?"

"Caracas."

"Whit's the capital o' Bolivia?"

"Um…Quito?" (oh, she knew the correct answer) .

"Naw hen, La Paz." By the time they got to Paramaribo, her mother's key was rattling in the door and there she was, shaking the rain off her headscarf; smiling at them and breaking into song … *Catch a falling star and put it in your pocket, save it for a rainy day…*

At school she got into trouble every day. "Greta Buchanan stop talking at once. Stand up. Address yourself to me. What were you saying?"

"The water buffalo, Miss, ploughing the rice field."

"What about them?"

"Doesn't the plough rip all the roots out and stir them up in the water?"

"Malaya is weeks ahead Greta. You are meant to be labelling Newfoundland."

"I finished, Miss."

"Sit down and don't ask irrelevant questions. You may read about Malaya but do not talk." But Greta could never not talk and was often put in detention to write out: 'I must learn to stop talking in class' one hundred, two hundred sometimes five hundred times.

"Here's a bonny thing noo." Her father held out a tiny swan as she followed him into her bedroom. Greta took it. The glass wings were raised as if the swan was about to take to the air.

"De've ee no like it?" he asked.

"Put it with the others," said Greta tonelessly, handing it back. She heard him open the wardrobe, then scuffles and clinks as he put the swan in the old sock where she kept the rest of her animals.

"See noo, ee could pit them all happed up in cotton wool?" he was closing the wardrobe door.

"Don't make me any more," she said, "I don't want them." She saw the sag of his shoulders. It felt as if she had hurt him. The bedsprings creaked as he sat with his back to her and lit a cigarette.

She took a step away; then another. No movement from him, no sound. Blue smoke from the cigarette rose in helical curves. Another step returned her to the room's threshold and she stood there, poised. And then, when he still didn't speak she said: "I'm going to meet Mum from the off-license," and left the room.

Greta's connection with religion broke when she was confirmed. Other girls at school excitedly planned white dresses, sheer veils, tiaras. Was an ivory half-crown with sequins better than a petal wreath with embroidered trim?

"I'm having a bun crown in organza and a beaded double veil," said Anita Fulford.

"Oh a *bum* crown, how perfect," said Greta, and she and Bridget snorted with laughter.

Her mother was scornful when Greta asked if she could have a tiara. "You don't need ornaments." She shook the tea towel and it made a snapping noise.

"Can I have long lace gloves? Bridget is having gloves." Her mother took the iron off the stove and spat on it to test the heat. The spit bounced off with a crack.

Right up to the day of her Confirmation, Greta hoped her mother was making her a dress in secret; imagining the scene. Her mother would come in with a big box. She would remove the lid and layers of tissue paper like they do sometimes in films, and then, the dress. She would lift it by the shoulders. It would unfold like swans' wings from the diaphanous paper.

But on the day of her confirmation Greta wore one of her mother's white blouses and had a lace-edged tablecloth over her head. Her mother smiled. "There." She stood back from Greta, holding her by the shoulders, "a proper little bride of Christ." Greta went to the mirror and the dome of the cloth over her head reminded her of the houses in her picture bible; white houses with rounded roofs on the hillside in Bethlehem. Tears welled up and spilled onto her cheeks. Her mother said: "What's the matter with you Greta?"

"Don't make me go," Greta started sobbing. "I look like a whited sepulchre."

Christmas came and went and then another Christmas; the question always the same. "What do you want Santa to bring, Greta?" Her mother asked it teasingly, these days.

"A diary." And through her morose bleakness, Greta felt triumph at the baffled expression this answer produced. It was practically a duty to annoy her mother. "Shit a brick..." she would exclaim as she broke a nail heaving the coal scuttle.

"Greta!"

How satisfying to observe her mother's pained horror. Disappointment, and her attempts not to care about it, began to appear to Greta like a permanent state of things. In a rage one morning because her hair refused to flick out, she tore the comb through it, standing at the mirror and yanking at the backcombed knots until her scalp was seared with pain. "Whoa, Neddie." Her mother had come up behind her. But Greta twisted her shoulders out from under the friendly arm and left the room without speaking.

As she mooched along their narrow street one day she saw a laughing Bridget Furedi sitting on a low garden wall further ahead. Kneeling before her, a handsome prince held her gracefully extended foot. The sun shone. Beyond them rose the battlements of Leicester prison. Bridget's long hair was blowing, golden, about her face. Bridget must have been to her dancing class. Her lips and cheeks were flushed to a bright colour that magnified detail in her face. The man's hands clasped Bridget's foot. He laughed up at her and she radiated beauty. It was only Mr Furedi and he was just rubbing Bridget's foot better for some reason, as if she was a little girl again. Maybe she had twisted her ankle. It was not serious because he was laughing and she was radiating beauty. He rose to his feet and Bridget stood up and he put his arm round her shoulders and they walked towards Greta. A thudding sensation began in Greta's chest. *I'm going to run away*, she thought; *they won't see me for dust.*

"Hello Greta."

"Hiya Bridge."

"Are you coming round to watch *Z Cars* tonight?" Bridget said sweetly.

"Yeah." There was no television in Greta's house, nor a fridge; not even a telephone. Her father called everything *modern rubbish*. Later, at home, she threw Pearl in the dustbin and covered her with tea leaves and the bones from yesterday's lamb chops. Her mother didn't see what she had done. "Can I have dancing lessons like Bridget?" She asked, slouching in the kitchen doorway.

The movements of the rolling pin speeded up. "No you can't, there isn't the money. Your father's buying the house on a mortgage." The furrow between her mother's eyebrows twitched and she put down the rolling pin and pressed her forehead with the back of one of her floury hands. Greta had no idea what her mother meant. "Get me a couple of Phensic, Greta, would you? My head's bursting."

"What good will it do taking that modern rubbish?" asked Greta spitefully.

Greta never came down for breakfast now until her father had left for work. On her birthday there was a tiny package lying between her knife and fork. "Oh well, don't laugh then," said her mother when the spitty sound she made with her mouth, to imitate a frying egg didn't even raise a smile. "Your face is as long as a fiddle. Open your present."

Greta removed the tissue paper and there was exactly what she wanted – a poodle charm bracelet. The gilt links felt cool and supple. The adorable poodle stood on her palm daintily cast in pearly blue plastic.

"Do you like it?"

"Of course I like it."

"Happy Birthday, Love, there's a card as well." A shadow slanted down the wall by Greta as her mother reached into the cupboard. Greta watched the salt cellar appear, her mother's hand withdraw.

She opened the card and stood it up in front of her. "I feel sick," she said, slumped in her chair, satchel on her knee.

"You're hungry. Sit and eat your breakfast."

"I don't want any vile breakfast. I've got stomach ache." Greta found it hard to speak to her mother. Her tongue felt stiff and her lips paralysed, as if they couldn't bear to form speech. Here at home her voice worked best if the words she spoke were nasty and unkind.

"Vile? How can you say vile?" Then her mother changed tack, moving over to her, resting a hand on her shoulder. "Buck up, love."

"Leave me alone," Greta shouted.

Her mother slammed the plate of bacon and egg down on the table. "What's the matter?" She demanded, "I don't get you at all. I'm fed up with your rudeness. As far as I'm concerned I've cooked your breakfast, so eat it now." She wiped her hands over and over again down the front of her pinafore.

"I will then." Of course the bacon was delicious, the egg blended perfectly with its saltiness but Greta gobbled it down in seconds and ran upstairs to the bathroom, the poodle bracelet in her hand. "I'm going to be sick," she shouted and slammed the door and pretended to vomit. Her mother rattled the handle and banged on the door; calling shrill angry words. Greta ran taps and flushed the toilet, coughing and spitting. "Can't hear you…" she yelled. Her mother retreated. Greta looped the bracelet round her wrist, twisting herself over and using her knee to keep the chain level while she snapped the tiny clasp shut. Then she wetted the two bits of hair either side of her face and plastered them into kiss curls before going down.

Her mother, face mottled with fury, seized her by the shoulders and pushed her out through the front door. Greta imagined screaming: "*We're having sex education today and I don't want to go!*" She leaned back against the pushing hands. "*I'm afraid to go to school Mum – help me.*" As they struggled Greta heard her shoes scraping along the pavement and the gasps of her breathless mother. The hands she was leaning against were all that supported her, her entire weight cast back against them. They supported her and yet they were pushing her away. The lack of words was unbearable; their silent scuffling not dignified by anything. Greta wrenched herself upright. "You bitch…" she screamed at her mother's flinching face, "…you might as well be unconscious."

"Unconscious?" There was no volume in her mother's voice.

"You don't understand anything, I can't even remember what Deborah was wearing the last time I saw her and you're too thick to care." Her mother looked as if she had been punched. And Greta walked away up the street.

At school, among pupils heading for their classrooms, Greta still felt like screaming. Bridget held her hand, admiring her bracelet. Danny Scott's ginger hair and freckles bobbed alongside. "Hiya Greta," he said, "Rumboldt says he'll wait down the field at break." Baby-faced Danny; a first former, was often the messenger for senior boys like Jimmy Rumboldt who invited Greta to meet them behind the groundsman's shed. Greta ignored Danny but he didn't take the hint. He carried on jumping in front of her, calling out her name, just his usual grinning self but she couldn't stand it.

Wrenching her hand from Bridget, she hooked her arm round his neck. "Got any chewing gum Danny?" she said, yanking him backwards. She put her other hand into the pocket of his trousers. His hipbone jerked away from her. His pocket was empty. He writhed. She jabbed her hand into his blazer pocket.

"Greta's killing Danny," laughed Bridget and others clustered round. Danny stamped and kicked. His hands gripped her forearm, trying to lessen the pressure on his windpipe. His round face was dark red. Under her nose was the smell of his scalp. As they fought, clumps of his red hair, flopping and shifting, gave off a sad, breakfasty egg and fried bread smell. Her hand found a stick of toffee in his pocket and the onlookers cheered.

But Greta turned him loose. "Here," she muttered, tossing the stick of toffee.

"Fuck off, you spaz," he croaked, letting it fall to the ground. His expression was about to explode into crying under the seething marigold of his hair. He pushed his way out of the group, his too-big blazer making a shaky rhomboid of his fleeing shape.

"We'll be late, Mrs Dean'll kill us," clamoured Bridget, dragging her arm, offering her a box of Toffets, towing her down the corridor. While the film was on Greta ate Toffets. She wrote a note and gave it to Bridget to pass on. It was addressed to Anita Fulford and asked for a lend of her manicure set. The note went from hand to hand until it reached Anita. Anita lifted the lid of her desk a few inches and slid her hand inside. The triangle of pink vinyl was passed back. It fastened with a pink stud and when this was unpopped, the case opened out like a book and the silver implements inside were displayed, fanned out in clear plastic pockets. The nail file was tiny, the tip sharp. Greta began to file her nails. She put her feet up on the desk

"Remove your feet, Greta," ordered Mrs. Dean.

"Can't Miss, they're attached." She crashed them to the floor. One nail after another was filed into an oval that narrowed to a point. *The male organ of reproduction is the penis...* She held her fingers out at an angle, ostentatiously examining them, trying to shut out the film's voiceover...*the means by which the sperm, carried in the semen, are introduced into the female reproductive organ...* And in the end, only using the nail file to carve a letter G, into the desk lid, gave her any way to keep a grip on herself. The desks were new. *Once conception has taken place the baby can grow in complete safety...* The varnish furrowed into powdery lines. The metal dug into the wood and the plummy voice on the soundtrack of the film crackled with volume...*the neck of the womb is called the cervix...* Greta whispered sneering remarks to her friends. Sweat soaked the armpits of her school dress. Leaflets were handed out. They explained periods and pregnancy and condoms. There were diagrams and instructions on how to put tampons in. It had a section on masturbation. Greta put it in her pocket. She yawned loudly. Mrs Dean was talking about babies. Greta gave a grotesquely exaggerated sigh. She was sent to the Head. *You are an obstreperous troublemaker Greta Buchanan.*

She read the leaflet over and over again. Her periods had started not long before. She made a plan. The time came. Hearing the customary scrape of his chair on the kitchen floor as her father rose from the table and turned off the radio; Greta jumped up from the sofa, her heart thumping and was standing waiting as he appeared in the doorway of the front room. Waving the leaflet, she confronted him. "I've started, Dad. It says in here I'll get pregnant." How breathless it made her, to say that. There was a feeling like empty space where she imagined her heart to be and below that a regular spasm like a clock's tick, amplified.

"Dinnae worry yersel hen," he just nodded his head towards the stairs, "we'll get around it."

"Condoms, you mean?" She turned the leaflet over and held it up, aware of a trembling in her arms that she fought to control. He looked shocked and although he opened his mouth to speak, he closed it again then scowled. At that moment there came a loud knock on the front door and Greta pushed past him out into the hall and ran to open it.

"Hiya Greta. Are you coming to watch *Bonanza*?" It was the innocent Bridget, bang on cue.

"Yes," said Greta, "I am." Glancing back as she stepped over the threshold she saw the expression on her father's face. Now that she had carried out this manoeuvre his helplessness astounded her. She slammed the door.

Come in the front and staun' by the office to wait fer me he had said. The vestibule of the university chemistry department had various exits and Greta was imagining it as a stage. Vending machines twinkled as part of the set. The students were the cast of the play and the action was laced with laughter, cigarette smoke and the smell of coffee. Typewriters clacked from inside the office and Greta heard occasional lines of dialogue. "These can go in Professor Nightingale's pigeonhole; his secretary will collect them this afternoon." Greta yawned. "Take the agenda down to Mrs Primrose." The office door squeaked open and a young woman clicked away up the corridor on black court shoes, carrying a sheaf of large white envelopes.

"*I'll see you in the workshop,*" she had said to her father. "*Naw ye will nae Greta.*" Crash, went his teacup into the saucer and he wiped tea from his Clark Gable moustache. His temper was awful these days and her mother would look from one to the other of them sighing with anxiety "*Dinnae you mak it herd for a body. Jist you come in the front and staun' at the office.*" Greta considered going down to the workshop anyway. What could he do about it? *Enter Greta stage left. The glassblower drops the condenser he is holding*…Were her crayons still there? Would Harold still smell awful? Slap slap went her chisel-toe shoes on the parquet as she slouched along to the lavatories. This was where Mrs Primrose used to bring her when she needed to pee. She would make Greta wash her hands, letting her stand on the chair to reach the roller towel.

Then she would lead her back to her father in the lab. The old roller towel was gone; in its place, a machine released blue cotton cloth in ratcheted half-yard loops. Clank, clank. The inside of her duffel bag smelled of ink … *please wait at the gates of Heaven for me…* Singing to herself, Greta took out her steel tailcomb and hair lacquer. She backcombed hanks of hair, spraying them, smoothing them into a dome, flicking the ends up, rolling them round one finger. Blazer sleeves looked better pushed up to three-quarter length, yes, and she loosened the knot of her tie, opened her top two shirt buttons, turned up her collar then smoothed foundation on her face and applied her white lipstick.

By the office, leaning against the wall, duffel bag hoisted aggressively on her shoulder, she saw Mrs Primrose coming down the corridor. Mrs Primrose flicked a look at her, a look that needed confirmation from Greta, an answering smile that would seal their mutual recognition. "*How you've grown,*" she would say. But Greta stared through her blankly. Greta had turned the waistband of her school skirt over so many times that the skirt flared, inches above her foal's knees. She wore diamond-patterned stockings and smelled of Body Mist deodorant and chewing gum. Mrs Primrose was almost sure. "Aren't you the glassblower's daughter?"

"No." Greta held Mrs Primrose's gaze for a fraction of a second and then turned her head languidly, as if to see who else might be coming by.

"Sorry," said Mrs Primrose and carried on into the office. The door closed. Greta felt a triumphant fluttering in her stomach. *Fooled you*!

A man and woman approached followed by a teenage boy in the Grammar School uniform. They don't know me, Greta thought. I could be a princess or *anybody*. The man and woman disappeared into the lift and the boy sat on one of the benches. Greta stared. He knew she was looking; she could tell, but he wouldn't return her look. She kept staring. Black-framed spectacles weighed his face down. His neck was strong but Greta despised the swotty short hair. And then he surprised her by walking over. "Boring isn't it," he said.

"What is?"

"Being interviewed." He put his hands in his trouser pockets. "Are you doing single honours or joint?"

"What, in Chemistry?"

The boy smiled and shrugged. "This is the chemistry department."

"I'm waiting for my Dad," she said, "he works here."

"Are you doing A-levels?"

"No, O-levels... I'm fifteen."

"You look older."

"I'm at Four Pools Secondary Modern."

"A boy from Four Pools came to our school to do A-levels last year," he said. "Ian Hirst. Do you know him?"

"He was a right swot." The boy turned away and she modified the scorn in her voice, preferring to keep him talking, pleased that he thought she was his age. "Was that your Mum and Dad?" She nodded towards the lift.

"No. Lecturers. Interviewing me". He was not planning on coming here though, even if they begged him on bended knee. He was leaving Leicester. He wanted to go to London; to get away from his family and live in a Hall of Residence. His parents made him have short hair and wear grotty clothes.

"See ya," she said, breaking away. Her father was walking towards them, frowning. He summoned her with a jerk of his head. A red line marked where the rim of his goggles had pressed on his forehead. His hair was indented from the elastic strap. Greta felt an urge to reach up like she used to and ruffle his hair until the indentation had gone. *There, Daddy.*

"Whit kind o face is that, ye wee tart? It's the dentist yer gaun tae no a party," said her father in an enraged undertone. "Ye canny gaun wi me looking like yon." His eyes challenged her to answer. He gave her arm a shake. "Gan tae the ladies and clean the make-up aff yersel."

Today I found out how you get out of this dump... Yes. She could see herself writing it in her diary. She smiled at her reflection as she wiped off the lipstick. *...Please wait at the gates of heaven for me... Te-e-erry ...* She unrolled her waistband until her skirt went back down to just below her knees.

"So you're a swot now Greta or what?" said Bridget Furedi, the first time Greta appeared at the bus stop wearing the brown and gold of the Grammar School uniform. Bridget was at the Tech doing shorthand and typing.

"Yes. But at least I don't go to church any more," retorted Greta; a nonchalant reply, that masked profound uneasiness. Her mother's despair over her refusal to go to church was terrible and although Greta felt her mother deserved it she couldn't work out why she thought that and she didn't feel any triumph at having caused it. They had not spoken to each other for days.

One morning Greta came down to breakfast to find a packet of Cornflakes on the table and she knew it was a peace offering. Cornflakes were unheard of in their house. *Modern rubbish*. Greta shook Cornflakes into her dish and poured on milk. But for some reason it made her want to cry. The tears were hard to force back as she ate. When she had finished she put her spoon down silently in the empty dish. In equal silence her mother came over from the sink and put a cautious hand on Greta's head. Greta turned towards her and leaned her forehead on her mother's apron and her mother hugged her like that, warily at first and then tightly, before letting go, so that Greta could stand up and leave the room without crying. They were both under a spell of silence.

That Christmas Greta asked for a suitcase. As an experiment she packed it to see how much it would hold. All her clothes fitted in with room to spare, even her shoes; one pair of white stilettos, one pair of tan suede Chelsea boots and her slippers. She didn't count her clumpy school shoes. She wouldn't be taking them. She began saving her pocket money so as to buy a weekend case to match. If she had not been so occupied with homework and revision, she might have taken a Saturday job; but she was afraid to give up the hours she spent studying in the town library, in case her plan didn't work. Although they were drifting apart, Bridget was still officially Greta's best friend. They went to see *Mary Poppins* and afterwards in the rain, arm in arm under Bridget's umbrella they danced up the avenue together; raucously trying to fly. Greta loved the film and went again. Mary Poppins had the same dark hair and porcelain complexion as Deborah. It was like watching her sister floating towards her through the air.

On Saturday nights, she and Bridget went to the De Montfort Hall, standing at the front pressed against the stage, screaming and reaching up to their idols: The Kinks, The Small Faces, Geno Washington and the Ram Jam Band, The Zombies, Traffic. Exhilaration, and the rum and black she drank, transformed Greta into a thinly-clad siren, dancing in stockinged feet up against any boy she fancied and losing herself in the sweaty heat and thunder of the dark hall. It was a contrast to the devotion she showed towards her studies. Greta loved the Grammar School. She loved the cryptic teachers in sacerdotal clothes whose elusive smiles betrayed their passion for their subjects; calculus and probability, Einstein and relativity, fission and Fourier, Russian poetry, French literature – and she loved the reading: *Candide, The Idiot, Passage To India, Riders To The Sea*. She haunted the school library. In her diary she wrote: *I have discovered Rabelais*.

The library was empty but for herself. "*There is no shadow like that of flying colours, no smoke like that of horses, no clattering like that of armour…*" read Greta. The book was *Gargantua and Pantagruel*. Pantagruel itched to get back to battle, but: "*…there is no shadow like that of the kitchen, no smoke like that of women's breasts and no clattering like that of ballocks…*" rejoined his companion, rather to Greta's mystification. She whispered the words as she read them and they wove a pattern. The words were not instructive but they intoxicated her and drew her in. The world of this book was like a place she felt something in common with and she walked in it wearing her incomplete understanding like a blindfold. She felt sure she was the first person to discover that this book was in the library. It was a really old book but looked brand new. She knew that no-one had ever read it before because when she had first found it, the pages had been uncut. She had used the edge of her set-square to slit them open. She was fascinated by it. It referred blithely to copulation, to shit and piss and it contained elegant illustrations that were jaw-droppingly crude and explicit.

The swing doors at the far end made their gulping noise and she raised her head to see who had come in. Christ! It was the headmaster, Mr Grogan; Grog, as he was known. Furtively she lowered *Gargantua and Pantagruel* into her lap. As Grog's oblong head swung the other way she dragged her cardigan swiftly off the back of her chair and laid it across the book. Grog approached and leaned over her. His hands moved the layers of books and sheets of foolscap on the table in front of her. An odour of tobacco clung to his hairy suit. "Homework?" His breath whistled in his nose.

"Yes, Sir."

"Calculus eh?" he remarked, tapping her slide-rule, "How are you finding it?"

"All right, Sir."

"And what is this? Can you read me a little? Translate it for me?"

"Lermontov, Sir; it's a poem," she read a line in Russian, translated it. *"A single sail appears, white in the blue sea mist…"*

"Remarkable. Remarkable." His voice contained an un-coughed cough. His nose emitted its whistle. Eyes down, Greta kept her hands on the warm wool of her cardigan and the hidden pages beneath. There on her lap, the giant, Pantagruel, was farting. A pen and ink drawing showed his lanky propped legs, the rude tilt of his naked buttocks, his arsehole and a race of small people curling and tumbling in the cone of gas he emitted. *"Go, go,"* she willed. Grog was going. Chalk dust floated in the beams of sunlight he traversed on his way to the swing doors. Greta watched his tweed elbows, the black gown brushing his heels. *Phew*. The windowpanes projected a hopscotch of sunlight onto the parquet. The whole library was hers. The books were beautiful. If only she lived in a house with a library where all you could hear was the tick of the clock and birds singing outside. In the distance she heard a creak and squeal of hinges and then the clank as a metal bucket was put down. Handy, the caretaker, was getting closer. On his left hand he had only a thumb and one finger. He never smiled. My bookworm, he called her, since she had started helping him. She scattered the sand on the library floor and swept it up again for him. In return he ignored her being there and only came to kick her out when he had finished. *"Here you are Bookworm,"* he'd say, scooping a shovelful of pungent sand into a conical pile on the floor. Then he would lean a broom against the wall for her. The sand was impregnated with Jeyes fluid.

Grammar School was not like Four Pools Secondary Modern. It was better than church. It was geared towards launching people out into universities and that was Greta's plan. She was letting it launch her. Nottingham University, her first choice, had accepted her as long as she got a grade A and two grade Bs for her A-levels.

You won't see me for dust.

Part 2. **That Explains The Accent – 1968**

Barbie

"Urgh. What's that?" said a girl in the communal kitchen.

"It's milk," Greta carried on rinsing tea out of her mug.

"But it's *sterilised* milk." The girl's clothes; white lace tights and a navy vinyl mini dress with white dots and puff sleeves; were very unlike her own. "There is a fridge here you know…" Condescension and disapproval in the voice.

"We have it at home," said Greta, and took the sterilised milk back to her room. She stepped into her white stilettos, smoothed her red tartan mini skirt and pushed her cardigan sleeves up to three-quarter length. No one else would know she had the wrong milk. Sod them.

The lunch queue in the refectory was loud. The girls in front of her stood heads together, like a swarm of bees. Jesus. How come there were no barefoot hippies smoking Gauloises and arguing about Hegel? What was that in the sandwiches? It looked like conkers mixed with marmalade. What were the dark balls covered in dead leaves?

"Do you know what's in the sandwiches?" said a conservatively dressed girl in beige swivelling round: "I'm Viv, by the way," an eager, cultured voice. She had a pale, round face like a peeled chestnut.

"These are chimp and pickle," said Greta, "or there are assorted balls if you'd rather."

Viv looked confused, calling: "sandwich, Pippa?" A girl barged in from behind; hair like Sandie Shaw, black patent T-bar shoes and a sensible shift dress. The two ignored Greta.

"I thought you were funny," said a voice.

Greta turned her head; saw a slender girl with long brown hair. "I like your dress," said Greta. It was short, empire line, high neck and flared sleeves; bright pink with paisley swirls in orange and green.

"Thanks. My name's Clare Candy, what's yours?" Clare's lips were well defined, the lower one full and her top teeth stuck out a little bit.

"Greta Buchanan." They moved along the counter loading their trays.

"Have you got a middle name?"

"Marie."

"Me too," said Clare raising black eyebrows like Deborah's.

A babble of voices around the table: "...this is the best place for Social Administration....and I was head girl ..."

"Guildford...A-levels in Domestic Science, Geography and French... reading Social Administration..."

"...hockey for Surrey...lots of favourite hobbies..."

"Riding?"

"Oh Riding!"

"...and philately...and I'm doing Social Administration too."

"...your turn..."

Squeals of recognition, murmurs of admiration.

And then: "You don't say much..." They were all looking at her.

"My name's Greta Buchanan." Her heart beat rapidly. The air, as she shaped the words, was drying her mouth out. "I'm from Leicester..."

"That explains the accent," chirped a wag.

"I went to Four Pools Secondary Modern... "

"Hence the tart's make-up," hissed another.

"What A-levels did you get, Greta?" asked Clare, sweetly.

"...pure maths, physics, English, French and Russian. All grade A. I'm doing Russian and Philosophy."

"A communist tart!" oh the wittiest joke ever. Some shushed, some giggled, and some called out: "hobbies – what hobbies?"

OK you snobby bitches, thought Greta. "I like poetry," she said, "especially Verlaine, but my favourite activity is having sex."

There was a stupefied silence.

She left the table, carrying her tray to the clearing bay.

"Greta?" Clare drew alongside on the stairs. "Take no notice. Some people are disgusting." Her face was solemn. "I like poetry, especially the Romantics." Her hair hung almost to her waist. Around her neck on a velvet ribbon, she wore a cameo. "I'll write you down my room number…" she said. Clare looked like Elise as pictured in Greta's Hans Andersen book – Elise, sitting in a tree weaving nettles. The sleeves of Clare's dress flared into tapering points like the ones on the gown in the picture. All she needed was a circlet of flowers on her head. Her shoulder bag had an appliquéd suede flower on it. They reached Greta's corridor. Clare was writing in a tiny notebook, still talking. "Ferlingetti is my favourite – we poetry lovers must stick together. Here, take this." She tore off the page and gave it to Greta. It said: *Clare Candy (likes poetry too) room 313.*

As they parted on the landing, she gave Greta a sweet Mona Lisa smile that hid her teeth.

Lectures began. Greta settled down, soothed by reading lists, the parquet floor of the Philosophy corridor, note-taking and forays into Sisson and Parkers, the bookshop in the Union building, where she bought a paperback *Gargantua and Pantagruel*, devouring the biography of Rabelais in the introduction.

The University buildings were white marble. Portland's baronial sweep of steps filled her with delight as did the polished ballroom floors inside and the beautiful views over the lake with its boats and willow trees. It pleased her to take the curving underground tunnel, emerging to the monastic solemnity of the Trent Building with its clock tower and archways. She loved the campus; the paths winding beneath pines and chestnut trees and even if she didn't fit in with the other girls she loved brand-new Cavendish, her Hall of Residence with its carpet tiles, convected air heating and the smell of bacon in the morning. At night, feeling hidden and secure, she slept well but during the day loneliness plagued her. She looked out for Clare at every meal but never saw her. One evening after sitting alone at dinner among the noisy throng, she plucked up courage and went and knocked at the door of room 313. There was no answer. No-one wanted to be friends with her. No-one liked her clothes.

"Is your rumbler broken?" she asked, the next evening, as a canteen lady served her with boiled potatoes and carrots.

"How can you tell?" said the woman.

"You've hand peeled these spuds and you'd only do that if the rumbler was broken."

The woman told everyone in the kitchen and in the next few days they singled her out, a question here and there, until they knew all about her time helping her Mum in the school canteen. "Hello Greta," they called, whenever she appeared.

One Sunday morning, when Greta came down almost too late for breakfast, there was Clare at last, eating boiled egg and soldiers. "Hi there Greta," Clare's face brightened. "How are you getting on?" And, "you've braved a fried egg I see. You must be the only one."

"I think I am," agreed Greta, well aware that fried eggs were derided as revolting and slimy (some girls brought packets of Ryvita down to breakfast). "Fried eggs remind me of my Mum," she added and when Clare laughed, she said: "my Mum can make a noise like an egg frying: listen…" And she imitated her mother's trick.

Clare laughed and Greta saw that there was a gap between her front teeth as well as the slight sticking out; it was like a child's mouth. "Who's your tutor Greta?" Clare patted her lips as if coaxing the laughter to stop, "someone nice I hope."

"No. He wears brown carpet slippers. His pipe stinks and he cleans out the dottle when I'm talking."

"That's foul. Mine's Dr Braithwaite," said Clare, "Sean Braithwaite. He's a bit of a heart-throb actually – not that I fancy him," and Greta giggled at her look of alarm. "Have you got a boyfriend?" Clare added.

"No," said Greta, so emphatically that they both laughed.

"Do you know Pippa… from the first meal we had…?" Clare raised expressive eyebrows.

Greta nodded, "yes; we share a bathroom," she managed, through a mouthful of fried egg and toast.

"She told me she's here to experiment." Clare widened her eyes.

"Meaning what?"

"She says sex this year and drugs next."

"How clinical," mused Greta, "I don't know whether to be repelled or impressed."

"Me neither."

"I've come here to study," said Greta, "which makes me really boring."

"To be fair, you do a great fried egg impression," Clare joked.

"Yes and Pippa would approve of the experimenting I did before I got here," The words were out of Greta's mouth before she could stop them.

"Oh?" Clare's intrigued relish was devoid of censure. "Everyone but me seems to have had a sex life already," she said, "I feel like such a baby. Is sex nice? I'm sure it must be." She clapped both hands over her mouth and looked round, an expression of embarrassment on her face.

"To be honest," said Greta, "I've only had one-night stands." She wondered if she should be talking like this.

"Tell me more," begged Clare, "I need a crash course."

"Saturday nights were my speciality…" said Greta. Around them the canteen staff noisily cleared up; other girls finished and clattered out. "My friend and I used to go to dances at the De Montfort hall and get plastered and when they ended…" Clare's attention made Greta bolder and bolder as she told of her exploits.

Ten minutes later she was stricken with disappointment when Clare excused herself to go and get ready to meet her parents who were driving up to visit her and take her out to lunch. "I really miss them, and my sister," she told Greta, as she carried her tray away.

Nottingham Castle: a desolate pie-crust of stone atop its massive rock. Greta stood there shivering the following Saturday morning. Far to the right, rows of terraced houses merged into fog; smoke rising ragged from their chimneys. The air smelled of coal, like home. She leaned over the battlements feeling the roughness of the damp stone under her palms. There was a jerk and she couldn't straighten. She was trapped by the wrist. The links of her poodle charm bracelet were wedged between two massive stones in the wall, and she was held in a stooped position. And then, mortifyingly, a smiling girl strolled up. "Hello," the girl was vivid in a scarlet hat and matching coat, "I've seen you in Cavendish. I'm Alma Etheredge." Bushy curls fanned out over her shoulders and escaped in wisps around her face.

Greta; awkwardly braced against the stones, said: "I'm Greta."

"I used to play Robin Hood with my brother…he was always Robin Hood though," Alma's lips were narrow, "…we had a den in an old quarry…" each pointed corner of her smile revealed a canine tooth; "…we had some big rocks where we'd sit and when it was sunny, lizards used to come out… God, you're stuck!" She bent over, lifting Greta's wrist a little. "Your bracelet's wedged," she reported, "I can't see the catch either. Is it hurting? What's your name again?"

"Greta Buchanan." Greta wanted to hear more about the lizards. Her wrist was killing her.

"Maid Marion to the rescue…" Alma drew a folded knife out of her bag and clicked. A six-inch blade sprang out. "Is it OK to break it?" she glanced, eyes bright, dagger poised. "Obviously not," she said. "Alright. I can do it by… prising…" she dug the knife into the stonework, "… out…" Greta heard chinking and scraping, "…some of this…mortar…"

Alma's efforts caused painful tugging and then all at once Greta was free. "Thanks," she said, rubbing her sore wrist. "Why the knife?"

"My brother gave it to me," said Alma, retracting the blade.

You remind me of the robber maiden in the story of The Snow Queen, Greta wanted to say but a quick pain of unshed tears made her think of Deborah and she daren't speak. Alma Etheredge turned theatrically. "Oh well," she said, "see you back at Hall sometime." She sauntered off. Her red hat and coat stood out against the misty walls.

A Friday night. *Anaximander's Indefinite* wrote Greta; and underlined it. Formal dinner. Every Friday; which Greta hated. Compulsory black academic gowns. Best dresses. In the corridor girls already flapping past. On her one foray Greta was appalled, standing eyes closed *…benedictus benedicat piesum christum dominum nostrum…* enraged at the pretentiousness of it. Canteen ladies dressed as waitresses had served them, perspiring like ignored relay runners between the long tables and the hatch. "What's Miss Girly Swot doing then?" cooed Viv, poking her head through the interconnecting door. Today even her thick, diamond patterned tights were beige. A smell of medicated shampoo wafted in with her from the bathroom where Pippa had been washing her hair

"The concept of The Indefinite," said Greta.

"Greta, did you hear our plan?" Chimed Pippa, "we're going to wear nighties underneath our gowns to formal dinner one night."

"Let's do it in Rag week, Pippa!" Viv squealed, "You and your friends could do it too Greta," she added, patronisingly. Greta pretended to be amused. That week she had seen Clare twice as they passed each other on the way to lectures but apart from greetings they had not spoken. Should she knock on Clare's door again? Thinking back to that breakfast she winced. Telling Clare about being fucked standing up behind the De Montfort Hall every Saturday night had maybe been going too far. But Clare had laughed at her imitation of a frying egg.

"Are you going to dinner Greta," called Pippa.

"No. I've got work to finish." *If only they'd go.*

They went. Bolting the connecting door, Greta lay on her bed, reaching under the pillow for her diary. Pages flicked by: dancing, a boy's arms around her, the crunch of his leather jacket, its cold smoothness in the January night, the smell of beer as he kissed her with freezing lips, Nothing recent apart from: *Appointment at Health Centre to register.* She had the feeling that there was something important she should write. Her teeth dented the plastic top of her biro. The nib advanced. *Friday October 18th. I feel as if I'm waiting for something…*she wrote. The slipper fell off her left foot and she used her bare toes to push off the other one before tucking her feet under the folds of her disordered blankets. Footsteps stopped in the corridor and there was a vigorous knock on her door.

It was Clare; with a smiling Alma Etheredge. "Can we come in?" said Clare, "We've joined the poetry society and have to recruit more freshers. Alma says she met you in poetic circumstances. Would you like to join it with us?" She brandished a tubby bottle. "We're having *informal* dinner; beans on toast and Mateus Rosè. Have you got a glass? Then after that let's go to the union building and have a drink in The Buttery."

More than usual, they stared at Greta as she carried her tray over to Clare. Greta had teamed her white stilettos with black ski-pants and a sloppy Joe sweater. Her back-combed hair stood out around her face and she wore black eyeliner. She was going out. "Clare," she said, "the Poetry Society accepted the poem I sent in. It's in the magazine. Will you come with me to the meeting?"

"Whereabouts?" Clare was subdued.

"The Fox, on Parliament Street. What's up?"

"I've got a tutorial tomorrow," Clare untucked her hair from behind her ear and let it swing forward. "We were supposed to read Dryden's *Rape of The Lock* for it and I haven't even started." A tear fell onto the table.

Greta reached across the table to pat Clare's arms. "It's Pope's *Rape of The Lock,* not Dryden's," she said, "you're getting very absent-minded, what's wrong?"

Clare pressed her sleeve to her eyes. "Nothing. I'm just tired," she said, too wan to even bother drawing her top lip down over her teeth.

"But you're crying." Greta was troubled. "Clare?" A sniff from behind the hair. "Shall I help you? We could read it together."

"No," said Clare, "It's only homesickness. I'm so weedy. You go. I'll come next time." She blew her nose.

"Alright," Greta speared a chip on her fork, giving Clare a final pat on the shoulder. "I'll go with Alma," she said.

In Slab Square as they got off the bus, a group of lads swerved towards the Flying Horse, whistling at a troop of white-booted girls with gauze headscarves tied over their hairstyles. A newsvendor called. Drizzle sparkled in the streetlights. Alma and Greta reached Parliament Street. Tyres hissed on the tarmac as taxis delivered people to the Theatre Royal. In The Fox, quiet rooms with wooden floors led off a stone flagged passageway. There was a regular thud as darts hit a board. The girls turned towards the sound. A man stuck his head out of a hatch. "Oi! Not in there. Are you students? Front parlour, back along the passage, on the right."

Alma jutted her chin and marched off; wiry and small, in the direction he pointed. Blushes brightened her cheeks. "Greta," she commanded, "look out for Camilla."

Greta went to the bar. "Half a lager and lime and a Cinzano and lemonade please."

At each pedestal table were ink-black chairs with curved frames, the tapered legs like line drawings. Alma unbuttoned her scarlet coat. She pressed her palms on the tabletop. "Marble," she said. There was a tramping of boots on the dark floorboards and a crowd of students came in.

"There's Camilla," said Greta. Camilla was a lanky, beautiful girl with what Greta's mother would have called a 'cut glass accent'. She wore clothes that were straight out of a *Vogue* photo shoot yet they were grubby; stained with wine; marred by cigarette burns. Her hair was cut in a stylish wispy crop yet her scalp had on it small, bloody lesions that she scratched again every time they scabbed over. Greta sat behind her in metaphysics lectures and had observed her doing it. Her fingernails were bitten and on both her hands, the index and middle fingers were yellow with nicotine. Her voice was hoarse and throaty; in fact her style was everything that Greta had expected from university. To cap it all, Camilla didn't live in Hall like the rest of them; she shared a flat with some second year students in Nottingham's trendiest area: The Park. Camilla had failed her part-ones and was nonchalantly repeating the first year.

"Camilla," called Alma, "where's the meeting going to be?"

"Through there," Camilla pointed with a skinny arm. She was wearing a narrow purple velvet mini-dress, matching suede knee-boots and white tights. A long grey fur coat was slung around her shoulders. "Clive, darling, fetch me a gin and tonic would you?" She passed a pound note to one of the young men clustering around her then came over.

"Where did you get that fabulous fur coat?" asked Alma.

"In The Meadows; there's a shop down Arkwright Street sells them second-hand. They've got hundreds – a bit moth-eaten but ever so cheap. This was only two quid." Camilla offered them her Gauloises saying: "got a match? My fucking lighter's gone awol."

Greta struck a match. "Who's that bloke you sit next to in metaphysics, Camilla?" she asked.

"Col. What a gorgeous bloke," Camilla uttered a deep groan, "Colin McLean. If I wasn't so mad about Dr Braithwaite I'd definitely go for Col. He plays the saxophone in a jazz band you know. He's got such balls. You fancy Col then?"

"No, Alma does," said Greta. Alma went red.

Camilla nodded at Alma and blew out a plume of smoke. "I don't blame you – he's definitely got a zillion balls," she said.

"Well he hasn't, not according to today's lecture; not if we're going to be empirically accurate," said Greta.

Camilla caught on immediately. "True, we'd have to say just the two," she acknowledged, "two balls. Good old Two-Balls McLean."

"Actually no, if I understood that lecture right you couldn't even say that," said Alma, looking amused, "not unless you'd taken off his pants and checked."

"Are you going to the Students' Union dance on Saturday, Camilla?" asked Greta when they'd finished giggling at Alma's remark.

"No. I'm not a Spooky Tooth fan. I'm going to London. My friend's coming over from Morocco with some stuff."

"You live in London?"

"My flat is there. Mother lives in Oxford, Father's in Barcelona. Divorced."

"How do you afford the rent in London?" said Alma, "I wish I had a flat."

"I have an allowance," said Camilla, "come and stay – any time you want. And you," she said, smiling at Greta. "Here's the editor, let's go."

"Which one?" Alma craned to look.

"Dark curly hair and big overcoat," said Camilla, "David Hayden-Fox."

"Dishy," said Alma, "he's put a poem of Greta's in the magazine."

"Well done, Greta," said Camilla. "David's the English department's postgrad superstar. He's doing a thesis on something to do with plants and poetry and apparently he's already had an offer from a publisher."

"Blimey," Greta was awed.

"Yeah, he started by editing *Gongster*," said Camilla, "He reviewed poetry books and was spotted by someone at Macmillan. His uncle works there, I believe. I love older men." She exhaled smoke, angling it away from their faces.

"How old is he?" Greta asked.

"About twenty four. But alas he's too short for me." And with that, Camilla, all six foot of her, gracefully followed the other students through to the adjoining room.

Greta looked at David Hayden-Fox. "Not too short for me," she murmured to Alma, as they stubbed out their cigarettes.

"We're the only freshers." Alma hissed as they joined the others, "are you nervous?" Greta shook her head. But she had butterflies in her stomach and couldn't breathe properly.

David Hayden-Fox called the meeting to order. "Sean's coming later," he said.

"I'm saving him a seat," Camilla patted the chair next to her. Her crush on Dr Sean Braithwaite was legendary.

"OK, let's start with Zoot." Zoot; patterned neckerchief bobbing beneath his Adam's apple, declaimed his poem. A respectful silence ensued. David asked who his influences were.

"God! Why does it always come down to influence?" Zoot flicked strands of tobacco off his red velvet trousers. These had sewn-in psychedelic inserts at the bottom of each trouser-leg. His roll-up had gone out.

"We all have influences," David smiled obliquely.

"Sure…" a pause, Zoot snapping his lighter, sucking the roll-up, "…sure…" firing the word through nostril-jets of smoke.

"Own up then," said the one with the heavy moustache who had fetched Camilla's gin and tonic and whose Afghan coat stank to high heaven.

"Shut up Clive, he's hardly got a word in edgeways," protested Camilla.

"Sorry."

"It's a protest – you know – futility of war," said Zoot.

"Can you be influenced without knowing?" said Alma.

"Nice try Alma," said Camilla, "course you can. But the question has not been answered. Zoot, stop squirming."

"I wrote the bloody poem and David printed it and he says it's good," Zoot flicked ash, his heavy-lidded eyes half closed.

Greta didn't like Zoot's put-on air of indifference. "It may be a coincidence," she said, "but...*the son is killed, he no longer carries on*: ...your first line; is an exact translation of a line in *Familiale* by Jaques Prévert."

"Told you," said Clive, "French was one of his A-levels."

"Sean!" pealed Camilla. It was Dr Braithwaite, saturnine and distinguished in his black polo neck and leather jacket. He apologised, took his seat, and David Hayden-Fox moved the discussion on to consideration of Camilla's poem; *Brain Fuck*. Several poems later it was Greta's turn. She gulped air and began to read.

"Barbie."

How loud it sounded. She felt a muffled pop inside her skull and now she had an echo in her head as her voice went round a feedback loop in her inner ear:

Look at that; see down there
Lying polite at the foot of the stair
Toes straight up and perfect hair
Barbie, smooth and pink and bare.

What has happened? No-one knows,
Glinting hair and slender toes
Trusting eyes are open wide
No-one knows how Barbie died.

Somebody removed her clothes
Took the ribbon from her hair,
Someone didn't like her; killed her,
Left her by herself down there.

Why was nothing ever said?
Barbie; Barbie; Barbie's dead."

As Greta finished there was hush for a moment. Then Camilla said: "Shit, Greta that's a seriously groovy poem." And Alma patted her on the back. Zoot's chair scraped ferociously on the floorboards as he shifted his position and Clive sniffed meaningfully. Greta smiled in gratitude, aware of Dr Braithwaite nodding approval. Beyond him, she saw a reflection of them all in a mirror decorated with a Pernod advert. Reading out her poem had not been the amusing diversion she thought it would be. Her heart raced and her hands were cold and sweaty.

Clive took a gulp from his pint of Mild then wiped his frothy moustache. Greta had a glimpse of his teeth as he said: "Are you coming from a women's lib viewpoint?"

"Not really," she answered, "but I think maybe it um…. could be, subconsciously. I don't know."

At that point, to Greta's relief, Camilla broke into applause shrieking: "Shut up Clive. She deserves a gin and tonic. Be a sweetheart and go to the bar for me will you? Get the girl a drink."

"Let's break there," said David. Everyone stood up and people crowded in from beyond as if they had been waiting for the poetry to finish.

"Greta." David Hayden-Fox spoke into her ear softly, and she felt his breath like a tiny impact. The bar was so crowded that his technique for holding a conversation was as good as standing a few inches away and bellowing but Greta felt as though he was being intimate nonetheless. His eyes were dark. She looked away. "That poem is very resonant," he said, "Have you written any more?"

"I did when I was little," she focused her gaze on Alma who was in the corner of the room, pressing buttons on the jukebox.

"You should write more," he said. "What exactly is that accent of yours?"

"Leicester." She had to look at him now.

"Simon de Montfort, John of Gaunt – it's a great place."

"Is it?"

"Robert Dudley, Earl of Leicester!" he said. "He even had his own theatre company. If you were free on Saturday would you like to come to Southwell Minster with me? They're doing the *Missa Solemnis* and the BBC is broadcasting it I believe." He had an Elizabethan look; standing very upright, as if the black velvet jacket he wore was really a doublet, slashed with satin. An invisible ruff made him hold his chin high. With his cloud of dark, courtly hair and his Botticelli eyelids, the effect was one of authoritative contemplation.

"Was the Earl of Leicester a contemporary of Rabelais?" Greta babbled.

"Lord knows," he gave her a smile of amusement; "There's the Quorn of course. Do you ride?"

"My sister used to look after a pack of foxhounds."

"Actually in Leicester?" Elegant eyebrows queried the fact.

"A village; just outside. She used to take me sometimes, on the bus."

"On the bus! You're fabulous Greta… if your hair was black you'd look like Juliette Greco." The jukebox was blasting Sergeant Pepper and at that moment the whole bar erupted into the chorus and he sang a version of the line too, "*…I'd like to take you home with me I'd like to take you home…*" looking straight at her.

"Where do you live?" It was all she could think of to say.

"On a farm in Rutland."

"So your Dad's a farmer."

"God no. The farm manager looks after the muck and middens. Dad's a high court judge." He was laughing.

"It's a pity about Saturday but I've already arranged to spend the day with someone," she lied, stung and exhilarated at the same time. Her mind revelled in astonishment that she should ever have met such a person let alone be exchanging banter in a pub with him and having him breathe into her ear. "But thank you for the invitation," she added, "excuse me, I said I'd buy Alma a drink; I'll go and find her," and she slid away from him into the crowd. She wanted to seize Alma by the arm and scream with excitement.

"I think David likes you Greta. Here, have another drink – was he kissing your ear?" It was Camilla, thrusting gin at her; pouring tonic into both their glasses. "Are you looking forward to Christmas?" she yelled.

"No." The sudden mention of Christmas unsettled Greta. It seemed impossibly far away. Surely they were caught now, in an eternal present? "Are you?"

"Yes. It'll be a hoot. Ohhh – do you have to spend it with your parents? See that's where I'm so lucky. I can please myself. I went to Father's last year but I think this year I'll stay in London. Come to London. Do your folks do anything at Christmas?"

"No, not even drink." Greta laughed although she didn't think she was saying anything funny. And Camilla smiled back in a way that made Greta feel that they were both gripped by sadness.

"Parents," Camilla said, "I leave mine well alone. Here's to us." She prodded Greta's glass with her own. "To me and little Greta. Cheers," and without taking her eyes off Greta's face, Camilla tossed back her entire drink. Greta followed suit, unsure if Camilla fascinated or scared her.

In fact to be separated from this bright, gregarious life was a prospect that had begun to make Greta feel anxious. Why had they all been woven together into this great rug of raucous conviviality and intellectual effort, if all that happened, at the end of twelve weeks, was that the rug was shaken in the air? There went the crumb that was herself, flying into the void and where was she supposed to land if they did that to her new life?

Clare grew sadder. The night the three friends went to the Pictures to see *Camelot* at the Lenton Essoldo she cried so much that when the film finished they couldn't get her to stand up. The auditorium emptied. Clare sobbed. One either side, Alma and Greta practically carried her out. Lenton Boulevard was deserted and they sat on the wall by the bus stop while Clare told them all about Ray Meo; the architecture student she had known since they were children. Ray was in his third year. He had said he would see her when she came up to Nottingham. She had expected to be with him from the start, had written to tell him which hall she would be in. But that was in July. He hadn't written since. Not knowing what to say, she hadn't written either. She'd been waiting for him to turn up. And he hadn't.

"So what's the plan?" said Greta later, hauling her quilted nylon dressing gown off the floor to retrieve half a packet of digestives from the pocket. They sat squashed together on Clare's bed in their baby doll pyjamas drinking cocoa. "Did you say Ray was in Wortley?" Posters all over campus declared the next social occasion at Wortley Hall to be a Firework-Night Fancy Dress Party. "Don't worry," said Greta, "we'll sort him out."

No mail ever came for Greta but the other girls were always checking their pigeonholes; Clare exchanged letters as often as three times a week with her sister. Thus Greta learned that Clare planned to go home for the weekend. Despondency struck her. But she hid it. Their Friday morning was free so she suggested seeing Clare off at the station. Clare was warmly wrapped up in a navy blue reefer jacket. She proudly wore her green and yellow university scarf against the bright chill. Greta thought she looked cute although she considered university scarves an unnecessary expense. Drifts of autumn leaves covered the campus roads and they kicked their way through them, talking excitedly. Winter hardened the morning air, condensing in clouds as their laughter surged ahead of their striding feet. The sun shone, despite the cold and Greta tried to cheer up. Nearing the station they stopped by Redmayne and Todd's, the big toyshop on the corner, gazing in the window, exclaiming over the dolls in their velvet hats and coats. Clare pointed at a bride doll, exquisite in white satin and sparkling net veil. "I had one like that," she said. Greta thought of Deborah cutting out pictures of brides. She stared at some Barbie dolls. Despite their sweet smiles the Barbies looked nude and vulnerable with their small dresses and elongated legs.

At the station the metallic slamming of train doors set the girls running. ....*Loughborough, Leicester, Market Harborough, Kettering, Wellingborough, Luton and London St Pancras...* The tannoy incantation of names accompanied them as they crossed the bridge. A whistle blew and as they clattered down the steps an express was gliding by. At platform three Clare's train stood waiting and she hopped on and leaned from the window, ready to wave. What did she see? The train began to move. Greta tried to imagine what Clare could see: herself and Alma, growing small on the long curve of the platform; Alma a traditional doll, curly brown hair and a red hat and coat; herself a Barbie; shivering in spike-heeled shoes; pale legs seeming too uncovered, too revealed by her scrap of a skirt and her short suede jacket.

Later, after her three o'clock lecture, Greta went to browse in Sisson and Parker's. She bought *The Queen of Spades* by Pushkin. But as she left the shop, instead of looking forward to reading the book she was engulfed by a painful feeling that there was something else that she should have been doing .She felt like crying. Was it because Clare had gone home for the weekend? The low sun tinted mouse-coloured clouds with bronze as she walked up past the staff club to cross the quiet campus. Among cedars on the side of a hill Greta paused. Slabs of rock broke through the lumpy carpet of pine needles and she sat down on one, thinking of Alma and her brother as children waiting for lizards in the old quarry. The memory of waiting for the word of God came back to her. What would Deborah be doing now? The sun sank lower and the tawny light faded until it was too cold to sit there and she went back to the warmth of her room and the comforting smell of biscuits, unwashed bed linen and Kiku talcum powder.

Next day Alma hustled her to the refectory at teatime to meet her parents who had driven all the way up from Barnstaple to visit. Over cod and chips it transpired that Alma's father knew Leicester. "I was there during the war," he said. He had a cleft chin and merry blue eyes.

"Dad, don't start on the war."

"Did you consider Leicester University Greta? Right on your doorstep."

"My Dad works there."

"Aha," he joked, "Anything to escape from Dad!"

"That's right," Greta, laughed with him, blushing.

"What does he do?"

"He's a glassblower."

"Interesting," he encouraged her.

"Yes."

"Scientific apparatus I suppose – test tubes and so on?" he queried and at Greta's nod: "You normally think of glass blowing as being to do with goblets and crystal decanters."

"Well when he was young he was an apprentice at Edinburgh Crystal," Greta blurted. There came a great clanging of metal trays from the kitchens.

"So you didn't want to blow glass yourself?" teased Mr Etheredge. The anodised handle of the jug slipped in Greta's hand as she poured. Water missed the beaker and splashed onto the table. "Whoops," he reached forwards.

"I used to go to my Dad's work sometimes when I was little, when my Mum took my sister to the hospital when she had something wrong with her."

"Is she OK now?" Alma cheerfully slathered butter on her roll.

"She emigrated to Australia when I was young." Greta felt hot. Sweat trickled under her arms.

"So you put on a little white coat and helped your Dad did you?" said Mr Etheredge.

"He used to keep my crayons in one of his drawers and I'd draw pictures."

"A midget student," said Alma.

"They all knew me," said Greta, "they used to point me out – that's the Glassblower's Daughter."

Alma's Mum made the cooing sound that Greta's own mother made at pictures of puppies and kittens. "The Glassblower's Daughter," she echoed, "like something out of a fairy story."

"Greta!" Came a fluting call, "come here love," Delphine; a big black kitchen assistant who scowled at all the students except Greta, leaned over the steel counter beckoning.

Greta came back from the hatch with a small tray of sponge pudding and a pitcher of hot syrup, "Delphine says keep quiet," she announced, "or everyone'll want some and there's only this bit left."

"They love Greta," explained Alma, reaching for her slice. "Her Mum is a school dinner lady and Greta knows the names of all their machines."

Alma poured a stream of golden syrup. Greta heard the roar of flames on molten glass.

It was Sunday night and Clare was back. "Is this your rosary, Greta?" The rosary hung from her fingers. A snort of laughter formed in Greta's midriff at Clare's reverence. The delicacy of the way she was handling the rosary was touching. Greta felt the laugh dissolve. She put her bookmark in place and closed the book on her knee. "Were you lonely?" Clare turned a sympathetic face towards her.

"No," said Greta, "I went to a disco in Cripps." Cripps, the largest of the Men's Halls, was famous for its parties.

"By yourself?" Clare put the rosary back in Greta's open drawer.

"Zoot was there and Colin McLean."

"Look at the handcream my Mum bought me," Clare said, seizing her bag. She produced a pretty flowered tube and unscrewed the top, smoothing cream onto the back of her hand. "Sniff…"

Greta bent her head and sniffed. *Apple Blossom*. Like Deborah's talcum powder. Sorrow loosened her self-control and halted her indrawn breath. An aching in her jaw made her open her mouth. Tears ran down her face.

"What's wrong?" Clare knelt by her.

"The handcream," she sobbed, "it's… my… sister…had…"

"I didn't know you had a sister. What's her name?"

"Deborah."

"You miss her. Poor Greta," Clare proffered a handkerchief. "Is she older?"

"Yes," Greta wiped her eyes. "She emigrated to Australia ages ago. She didn't get on with Mum and Dad…" she stopped, head bent.

"Oh dear," Clare patted her knee. "Don't cry, you're making me cry now. Look." There actually were tears in Clare's eyes.

"I've stopped now," sobbed Greta and pressed the handkerchief to her face. The book she had been reading slid off her knee.

"Whoops…" Clare made a grab, "here you are – oh – what's this?" She picked up Greta's glass twig, which had fallen out of it.

"My bookmark," said Greta, reaching for it.

"How sweet. It's like a one-sided wishbone made of glass," said Clare.

Things Have Gone So Wrong

To snare Ray, they wore witch costumes made using their academic gowns, black fishnet tights and a lot of eyeliner. A few ciders in The Buttery made them confident. Their walk across the frosty campus made them uproarious. A group of male students leapt out at them from the dark pine trees and they ran, screaming and laughing towards Wortley. In the distance fireworks exploded.

Ray Meo was tall and meaty like a rugby player, with handsome features and tidy dark hair and eyebrows. He was dressed as a devil and danced in the red light, surrounded by friends. Clare turned tail. "Hey," shouted Greta above the noise of the band. She seized Clare's arm, "turn round. Come on, stop struggling!" *...and it's Hi Ho silver lining...* The whole room erupted into the chorus and they dragged Clare to the bar and made her drink more cider, and then they lit up a pretty cocktail Sobranie each; mauve, turquoise and pink; so as to smoke glamorously. The walls were hung with black and purple crepe paper. Cardboard Halloween bats dangled on long strings from the ceiling.

Greta could see Ray coming towards the bar. He recognised Clare and did a double take and his smile was replaced by a look of stunned bashfulness. He said: "Clare?" Clare turned round in such agitation that she didn't notice that her gown was in contact with Alma's cigarette. There was a flurry of batting hands as both Alma and Ray noticed the singeing.

"We're going to dance now and leave you two to talk to each other," said Greta. She pulled Alma's arm and they sashayed off, chortling over their matchmaking success.

Freezing blizzards swept the city and then the clouds cleared. Snow covered everything, spliced onto every branch and twig. Light expanded the world and made the air echo. "Here comes a vision for you Alma. It's Two Balls wearing shorts," said Greta on the Sunday morning. It was bitterly cold and coming towards them was Colin McLean. Alma slipped and grabbed Greta to steady herself and Greta felt her feet sliding on the snow. They clung together shrieking as Colin approached. Greta was bent double in her attempts to prevent falling and laughing too much to do anything useful.

Colin drew level with them, walking easily. He was wearing sports kit revealing legs like the Belvedere Apollo. He passed them; gave a brief smile. "Hello," he said in his aloof way.

"Hello Col," they chorused.

"Tell us next time your jazz band's on," called Alma as their sliding pulled them nearer to the edge of the slope that fell away to Wortley Hall below. Colin McLean, laden with sports equipment, walked comfortably by in his spiked boots while Greta toppled into the pristine palm of the snow's hand, dragging Alma with her. If Col had looked back, he would have seen only that they had vanished. They were rolling down the hill by then. The snow was so prickly and cold that to Greta it felt like heat searing her cheeks. They couldn't stop laughing. Everything was hilarious; the fact that Col played rugby in the snow, the fact that Alma had seen his legs; the fact that he could walk with grace and they couldn't; the fact that they were in danger of wetting themselves because it was so insanely cold: it was all achingly hilarious. The hill ruckled up into toppled piles of linen napkins in their wake.

Later, in The Albert on Derby Road, the four of them sat in one of the ornate mahogany booths with engraved glass partitions. Etched windows glittered and winter sun bounced off the chandeliers. Amid the aroma of Ray's cheese and onion sandwiches, Alma recounted their sighting of Colin McLean "…and guess what Clare, he plays football."

"Rugby you mean," corrected Greta.

"He was carrying two footballs," insisted Alma. The landlord's pet toucan uttered a squawk.

"Yes," interrupted Ray, "but let's just say he plays a ball game and he was carrying the requisite balls: and?"

"He's got the most epic legs," said Alma.

"If you fancy Col so much Al, why don't you get off with him?" said Greta, aware of their reflections in the enormous mirrors.

"Hey – he could audition for the part of my gentleman caller." Alma sat forward holding up her hands to halt the conversation in its tracks. Alma had joined Dramsoc. "We're doing *The Glass Menagerie*," she said, beaming.

A churning sensation filled Greta's insides and the angle of the sun through the window made her feel as if the glass all around them was splintering into fragments. "I hate that play," she burst out. "We had a school trip to see it when I was in the sixth form. I couldn't sit still. I kept having the urge to shout obscene things at the actors. It was awful – I started muttering to the boy next to me …"

"Why?" interrupted Alma, "it's a fantastic play, I'm going to be Laura…"

"Oh no, not bloody Laura," ranted Greta.

"What's wrong with Laura?" Clare wanted to know. An offended Alma stared. Clare turned to Ray, eyebrows raised. He shrugged. "I don't know the play at all," Clare persisted, turning back to Greta, "why don't you like it?"

"It's about a crippled girl who has a collection of glass animals," said Greta. "Her Mum tries to get her off with a bloke but she's too scared…. *Oh Ma, I can't, I simply can't* she'd go and oh fuck your stupid animals I'd go to this boy."

"Greta!" Clare sounded scandalised.

Greta felt cold wetness under her arms as sweat soaked her blouse. But now Alma was laughing and Ray, grinning, was checking to see if anyone had overheard

Colin McLean did not audition for *The Glass Menagerie* and Alma began going out with Zoot instead. "It's because he's a poet," she said, when Greta expressed reservations about how stoned he was all the time. There was a Christmas tree in the Common Room, a party and then term was over and everyone went home.

"Ent yer goin' 'ome duck?" said the hall porter as Greta returned from a trip to the library. He leaned from the hatch of his lodge, a half-completed crossword in front of him.

"I wish this was my home," she said, blowing on her frozen fingers. It was four thirty and dark outside. Cavendish Hall was ghostly. Greta went and stood in the dimness of the unlit Common Room to look at the decorations. There was a scent of pine needles. Her father had never allowed a Christmas tree. Light from the vestibule gleamed on silent foil garlands. It was eerily deserted but the building hummed with warmth. Late the next day, Greta packed her smaller case and reluctantly caught the train home. In Leicester the brick archways were wreathed in fog as she came out of the station and headed off through the smoky darkness. By the museum, on impulse, instead of turning off towards their house she carried on along the avenue towards the church. Mass would nearly be over. Her mother would be there. It would be a surprise. By a wrought iron lamp post, Greta paused. A woman passed, haloed in lamplit breath, footsteps echoing under the bare trees. Greta listened. Her fingers, despite woollen gloves, were glacial. She approached the church door and went in.

Everything was the same: the sweep of the parquet floor, the faint smell of candle wax. Greta sat at the back and hugged her little suitcase to keep warm. The angels watched from above. Then the door of the Lady Chapel opened. People streamed through. And there was her mother, but what was this? She was going over to the wooden lectern with the great ledger open on it, where Greta had climbed up all those years ago, the ledger where you wrote down the thing you wanted others to pray for on your behalf. Her mother was picking up the pencil. Several minutes went by as she stood hunched over, slowly writing. The church was empty now but for the two of them. She could call out. *Mother…* She stared at the absurd liripipe of her mother's headscarf against the camelhair coat. *Mum…* Now. Call out. But she sat, paralysed. Without looking left or right her mother hurried out.

Light a candle. Greta walked stiffly over to the candles. Slanting the wick into the choir of flames, lifting her flame up, setting it next to those that quivered at her proximity; these actions calmed her. Candle heat warmed her face. To stay facing this hot light would be good. *You can't just stand here. Put some money in the box.* Was it twopence for a candle? Greta put in five two shilling pieces, clank clank: one after the other. Then she went to read what her mother had written. In one way, she didn't believe that there would be anything. But there on the page was her mother's careful, shaky handwriting in a small menu-shaped prayer.

Pray for me
please
things have
gone so wrong now

As Greta hurried back up the avenue she heard the metallic sound of a long train easing over the points. She stood, just beyond the museum. To her right lay the way home, to her left was the way to the station. Frost quenched the evening into silence. Her fingers, holding the strap of her suitcase, felt raw. She changed hands and blew through the wool of her gloves, staring at the pointed toes of her shoes. The cold laid icy hands around her insteps. The soles of her feet were numb and she felt pain where her heels rested in the high cradles of her stilettos. *I can't go home.* Maybe if her mother had looked round, that would have been different. *People run away to London. Maybe Deborah is there.* Greta's feet began to walk again; towards the sound of the train wheels. She speeded up along the path and each knee in turn felt the rush and bite of the terrible cold as her stride quickened and her certainty grew. She caught a train to London and phoned Camilla's flat.

Next morning the girls went shopping to Fortnum and Mason where Camilla ordered hampers. "And I need to buy a bottle of champagne to drink now," she said. Her fur coat flowed behind her as she strode along, manhandling a staring Greta through the panelled rooms. Christmas as glittering as a fairytale was piled around them; pillars of sugared almonds packaged in ribbon-wrapped cellophane and turrets of bottled peaches and candied cherries. Golden tables were stacked with glazed fruit cakes. Greta smelled good coffee, women's perfume and the sharp tang of ripe cheese from a delicatessen counter somewhere out of sight.

Camilla bought champagne from a softly spoken man whose grand suit and polished shoes made Greta think he was the managing director rather than a shop assistant. "A beautiful wine," he said, "yellow tint, notes of iris." With priestly white fingers he began to roll the bottle in tissue paper. "Hints of citrus peel," he continued, ringing up the purchase on his harmonium of a till, "and a finish of honey. You'll enjoy it I'm sure."

"Let's do the Kings Road," Camilla croaked, once they were back on the pavement. "You must buy some new clothes, Greta. I'm determined to get you out of those winklepickers. And I've got to convert you to tights. Suspenders and stockings are out," and she rolled her eyes and hailed a taxi. "Buckingham Palace," she said. The cab pulled away from the kerb, swung around and roared off. Camilla popped the champagne cork. "I can't show you the sights without a drink," she declared, "and it's my belief you'll let me choose clothes for you if you're sloshed."

They swigged champagne straight from the bottle.

Greta loved Camilla's flat. Black walls were hung with Indian cotton bedspreads in shades of saffron, cobalt and lavender. More, in crimson, emerald and gold, draped the sofas. There were mattresses on the floor and psychedelic cushions. Camilla lit the fire. Logs, piled in the recesses of the massive stone fireplace, made Greta think of being lost in a dark wood. She curled up on the sofa with a plate of fresh dates, smoked salmon, celery, Stilton and cold chicken and sipped champagne from the stockpile of bottles in Camilla's enormous fridge. The heat from the fire stroked her face and the champagne chilled her throat. *Dear Mum and Dad, I won't come home for Christmas, I've got too much studying. We've got exams in January. I'll come and see you after that I expect. I don't want a present, I'd rather have the money instead if you wanted to get me one – Have a nice Christmas. Love, Greta.* Counting on her fingers Greta thought the card would get there on Christmas Eve at the latest. She thought of going out to post it there and then. Instead she nibbled a date and basked in the firelight. It would do in the morning.

January came and went but Greta didn't go home. A letter arrived. *My Dear Greta, I hope you are well. Dad will send a cheque. He says to leave you be. You will come home if you want and not to worry but I would like to see you. Your mother.* And Greta, who had taken to saying: "We don't get on," in answer to any questions about her parents, realised that she was on her own and drifting away like a little boat carried on the current. It was hard to imagine what might cause her to go back. It was hard to see what would provide the motive force against the strength of such a current. So she had escaped. But now what? She screwed up the letter and threw it in the bin, re-focusing on her task. *In this essay*, she wrote, *I shall show that in their article: 'In Defence of a Dogma', Grice and Strawson fail to make a case against the argument Quine expresses in: 'Two Dogmas of Empiricism'.* But she felt a new uncertainty creeping over her, as if her hold on what things meant was slipping and soon she would fall into a state of ignorance.

Ten minutes after; Alma, back from a lecture, breezed in putting her hands over Greta's eyes from behind and yelling, "Guess who?" Her woollen mittens smelled of throat sweets and perfume.

Greta leaned back against her friend and said, "let's get drunk."

Greta In Love

At dinner one evening in May, a girl leaving the refectory paused by their table. "My friend's in the room next to Alma and says she's in there crying," she said. They found Alma distraught because Zoot had dropped out and gone back home to Tunbridge Wells.

"I'll never see him again," she sobbed, as Clare hugged her.

"Good riddance," said Greta and was about to say more.

But Clare was shaking her head. "No," she mouthed, her sweet, bunny teeth uncharacteristically stern.

The last time Greta had seen him; Zoot had been throwing up in Alma's washbasin while Alma held his hair back. "Oh well," she said, "I'll see you both later." And she set off to stroll across the campus in the evening sunshine amid the scent of hawthorn and mown grass. There was always Camilla

Camilla, to whom exams were such a tedious inconvenience, pounced one day. "Greta, come out with us tonight." Even when Camilla whispered she sounded like a fourteen-year-old boy whose voice was breaking. In the library, heads lifted then sagged down again, deep in intense revision. The sun blazed outside. "Come on, we're going to the Trip."

Greta was tempted. In parts, The Trip To Jerusalem was a series of caves hollowed out of the great rock that Nottingham Castle stood on. "I've got my Pushkin exam on Monday," she breathed, "I need to revise" The smell of the wooden table was resinous in the heat. The floor of the mezzanine creaked as footsteps prowled the shelf stacks.

"Come on, just for a little while, David's coming, and Dr Braithwaite."

Greta looked at Camilla's bony sun-tanned shoulders. "You're peeling."

"Bring Alma," wheedled Camilla, turning her head to squint at her shoulder. She rubbed at the flaking skin.

"She's rehearsing." Alma was in *A Winter's Tale*, which was going up to the Edinburgh Festival Fringe. She was playing Perdita and had taken to wandering barefoot on the slopes of the campus, gathering cow parsley and strands of ivy.

"So you'll come then," Camilla mouthed, "we'll meet you there at seven."

"OK." Greta smiled. Irrepressible Camilla. There was a sense that Camilla rescued her. Camilla; always there at crucial moments. So later, in The Trip To Jerusalem Greta bought herself a drink and found a table. Leaning against the bulging stone of the cave wall, she began to read Pushkin and didn't notice the others until they came to sit down. "Where is everyone?" she said.

"This is a select group," said David.

"I'm just going to the machine to get some fags," said Camilla, gaunt and leggy in her hot-pants and Roman sandals. She rummaged in her Biba bag and counted change.

"Smoking's bad for women," David set his pint of beer on the table and sat next to Greta. "I like your skirt," he said, with an appraising glance at her turquoise leather mini and sleeveless white polo-neck. "You smoke too much," he added, to Camilla.

"Well, there's no smoke like... Like something," Camilla laughed, "it's a proverb... what am I talking about?"

"*There's no smoke like the smoke of horses,*" quoted Greta.

"God knows, won't be a minute." That was the last they saw of Camilla that evening.

"Who said: *There's no smoke like the smoke of horses?*" David enquired.

"Rabelais."

"You're incredible," he said, "is it from *Gargantua?*"

"*Pantagruel* actually," she said. "I used to stay behind after school and do homework all by myself in the library. One day I found an old book which still had uncut pages. I used the edge of my set-square to slice them. You should have seen the illustrations! God knows what the headmaster would have said. It was my favourite book."

She was surprised by David's earnest response. "But Rabelais is so crude," he said, "scatology and sex – you were so young – what … sixteen?"

"Well he wanted people to know the value of education. He knew that sex sells books," she joked. David smiled sceptically. "The stories are funny," she insisted, "there's one where a woman gets chased by dogs. All the dogs are pissing on her dress because a man sprinkles her with essence of 'bitch on heat' because she won't have sex with him…" David's eyebrows were drawn together but he was still smiling, "…In the picture she looks as if she's growing out of a mound of dogs – it's a volcano of dogs and she's erupting out of the top with outstretched arms…" And Greta quoted, stretching out her own arms to demonstrate: "…*These villainous dogs did compiss all her habiliments*…"

David laughed. "And pages of farting and shitting?"

"Well yes, but it's beautiful."

"Really?" up went his elegant, black eyebrows.

"Beautiful images."

"Such as?"

"There's a rosary of lemon wood with every tenth bead made of gold, isn't that beautiful?"

"Very beautiful," he said. His eyes were dark blue; the pupils enlarged and shining. "But why did you like it so much?"

Greta took a slow drink, and then stared into her glass. *It was such a relief.* But she couldn't say that. *Rabelais talked about bodily functions as if they were admissible rather than taboo.* Yes. But it was more than that anyway. She had had the sense that, long-dead though he was, Rabelais would have let her tell him about what her Dad had done to her – what she had therefore done too – and he wouldn't have been shocked. *That happens* he would have said. *Lots of things happen and some of them are revolting.* Maybe he would have said*: it wasn't your fault.* Greta shrugged her shoulders and smiled at David. "I don't know," she said, "tell me about your thesis, has it got a title?" He was looking at her too much. The question pushed him away.

"It's called 'Physicke and Aplomb: Plant Imagery and Nature in Poetry 1500 to 1700'."

"Which poets?"

"Marvell, at the moment." He widened his eyes, half smiling, at her flare of recognition.

"I did him for A-level." The ice in her glass clinked as she swirled the remains of her drink. "I prefer poets like Verlaine or Keats," she said, "I mean if you found out that Harold Macmillan had written poetry it wouldn't stop you thinking of him as a boring MP would it?"

"Is that it? You want to dismiss Marvell because he was a Member of Parliament? Christ, Greta, it was our *first* parliament." There was anguish in his voice.

"Oh so he's more of a Che Guevera then, do you mean?"

"If it helps you to like him, yes. Let me get you another." He took her glass and went through the archway to the bar. Greta smiled at him as he returned with her drink. His knee brushed her thigh as he sat down again. The grit from the rock wall was sticking to her damp shoulder. "So you hate my favourite poet," he said laconically.

"I remember a lot of fruit," said Greta, "and puns. Some of the poems were like reading crossword clues. But I can see they would be relevant to your thesis – flowers and herbs, and mentions of gardens. Do you visit gardens?" She meant it facetiously.

He raised his eyelids and stared at her with calculation. "If I did would you come with me?"

"Yes." Would she? Why not? "*The fairest flowers of the season,*" she quoted, "*are our carnations and streaked gillvors, which some call nature's bastards.*"

"What's that from?" David leaned back his eyes intent on her face.

"*The Winter's Tale.*"

"Is it? Who's talking?"

"Perdita."

"I don't remember that bit." He took a small notebook out of his pocket and extracted a propelling pencil from a compartment on the spine. "Do you mind if I note it down?"

"I'm flattered," she said.

"Why are you laughing then?"

"It's your propelling pencil, it's really sweet!"

"And all in that kinky Leicester accent. How come you know the dialogue?" David wrote, swiftly.

"Alma's playing Perdita this year. I help her learn her lines. I'm in Dramsoc too, I'm a stagehand."

"You're bewitching." David said. "For all I know it's normal in Leicester for girls to quote Rabelais but I've never met anyone who could comment on him the way you did just now. You reckon he's funny do you?" David put away his notebook and lit two cigarettes and passed one to her. Their fingers touched.

"Yes." Greta smiled. "I reckon," she said, "that Rabelais would have invented a cartoon if he'd been alive today. He would have had a TV series like *Tom and Jerry*. He would have been in *Monty Python*."

"That's very good." He was laughing again. "Rabelais the comedian."

"He liked recurring jokes," she uncrossed her legs and felt the give as his thigh moved under the adjustment; "there are three pilgrims," she went on, "who keep getting in the way – harmless innocent people, but they get caught up in the giants' turmoil and always come a cropper. They hide on Pantagruel's plate under a lettuce leaf but he doesn't see them and eats one of them; that kind of thing." In a denim shirt with the cuffs turned back, David's forearms looked more muscular and tanned than she had expected. "You're muscly for a poetry editor," she said, facetious again.

He pressed his lips together. He might have been concealing a smile. One of his hands clenched into a slow fist then spread out again into a star. "So what else did Rabelais do?" he said.

"He fought against hypocrisy."

"You like that?"

"Yes I do."

At the end of the evening he asked Greta back to his flat in The Park. By the time they started walking there, a breeze was filtering the heat out of the night air. It swished among the leaves of the municipal chestnuts and sycamores. David took her hand. They walked past palatial houses and overgrown, mysterious gardens. "Greta," he said. He put his arm round her waist and when she turned towards him they stopped. "Can't you look at me?" He murmured into her hair, the words warm against the side of her head.

No she couldn't. Beneath her palms his biceps were hard through the denim. She raised her head but let her eyelids remain lowered. She saw the V of smooth skin at the open neck of his shirt. Her cheek came to rest against his jaw. He didn't move. She let her closed mouth drift against his, corner to corner as if she was testing for something. He waited. Her breathing took in the faint soap scent of his skin, a tang of cigarettes, a hint of laundered fabric. There was nothing to fear; no stink, no slobber, no shuddering. He sighed. She felt his lips part slightly.

"I think I'm in love with you," he whispered.

She kissed him.

David had a brass bedstead covered in white bedding. After he fell asleep Greta watched the sheets billow up around them from time to time in the gusts of air that blew in through the open French windows. David slept with one leg drawn up. As she looked across the warm curve of his ribcage, she saw his reflection in the black glass and her own possessive hand encircling his raised knee.

Next day, he hired a car and took her with him on a research trip to Sudeley Castle. "It's closed," she said as they passed a board at the entrance.

"Not to us though." He led her through a door in an ivy-covered wall where a sign said: *Private.* "I've come to see the beehives."

"With bees?"

"You needn't go near the bees if you don't want. Nick! How are you?" A man crossed the gravel towards them, smiling. "Nicholas Henton; this is Greta Buchanan."

"Pleased to meet you, Greta," the man's bony, featherweight hand was dry and warm. "Do you like bees?"

"No."

"That's all right, you can have a pass. Go where you like. Allow me." Nicholas Henton was not much taller than she was. He produced a badge on a string and, as he reached up to loop it over her head, she smelled lemons and found herself smiling.

"I expect you can smell the melissa," he said. "It's what David's come to watch. I rub the hives with it;" He pulled a handful of leafy stems out of the pocket of his leather apron, crushed them briefly and held them out to her, "the bees love it."

She sniffed; "sherbet lemons," she exclaimed.

"That's good isn't it?" he nodding his furrowed forehead at her, "you do this," he rubbed the herb on the back and arms of a wooden seat. "Sit there and you'll find you can concentrate better." He smiled, showing uneven teeth. Greta sat down. "It's in Shakespeare according to David." Nicholas Henton tapped David with the fronds of greenery. "Quote away, David, how does it go?"

Greta enjoyed the spectacle of an embarrassed David, forced, by Henton's good nature, to quote Shakespeare. "It's mentioned in *The Merry Wives of Windsor*," he said, and cleared his throat. "*...the* *several chairs of order look you scour with juice of balm and every precious flower...*" He blushed as he quoted the lines, adding: "It's lemon balm."

Greta sat dreamily waiting while the two men went into the building. When they returned in beekeepers' veils, she accompanied them as far as the hives then turned off towards the lake in front of the castle. Through a walled garden she went and a cedar grove, past a chapel, then found herself in a topiary garden where yew had been clipped into a squadron of shapes. Alone on a grassy walk, she turned towards a flight of stone steps. At the top, she found she had come to the edge. The estate was surrounded by a stone wall and beyond it, from a source hidden in the woods, smoke drifted, lupin blue, across the sloping fields. Greta leaned over the coping and watched cows grazing. Am I going to be David's girlfriend? She glanced over her shoulder as if the shapes of clipped yew might have moved when she wasn't looking and squatted down again when they saw her turn. Meringues, goblets, breasts, pillars, navels and bells: she was alone in the garden, staring at the shapes. From between two black hedges, the figures of David Hayden-Fox and Nicholas Henton appeared in the distance, walking away.

The question of whether she was officially going out with him was not resolved although a month later, when he left to spend eight weeks in America, David gave Greta the keys to his flat. She had got herself a job for the summer and she paid him two months rent.

Dear Mum, I have got a summer holiday job here at Boots. I have rented a flat. I would rather stay here than come home. This way I am near the library so I can do all my vacation essays. I got good marks in my exams. I shall go back into hall come October... she bit her pen, what else could she write? *...you witch; you won't put me in a pie like you did with Deborah.* Greta pushed the writing pad away and reached for her notebook, turning to the poem that took up pages and pages – scribbles and crossings out; half written lines that went no-where. *Can't you guess what he's done?* She wrote.

She was back in her old room in Cavendish Hall when Clare and Alma returned in October for the start of their second year. "So you lived with him?"

"No. He only got back last week. I don't go out with him. Alright?"

Clare and Alma had to be satisfied with that.

At late night cocoa sessions they now drank wine instead of cocoa, and rejected the fluorescent overhead strip in favour of candlelight. The odour of unwashed linen and talcum powder was overlaid with the smell of joss sticks.

But Greta's essay marks went from seventies to fifties. She read T S Eliot and gave her Kant to Colin Mclean. She read the *Gormenghast* trilogy and D.H. Lawrence instead of her course work, which bored her. She read *Vogue*. She dropped Russian to do single honours philosophy.

"Your Dad is an architect, Clare," said Alma, one night, "and you want to marry Ray – who you're perfect for – and he's an architect."

"So what," countered Clare, "your Dad's an auctioneer and you want to marry…"

"Two-Balls McLean," interrupted Greta, "who's a… jazz fan."

"You're not taking me seriously," Alma protested, "Greta – OK she doesn't want to marry him perhaps – but she sometimes goes out with David Hayden-Fox, and he's an academic, and Greta's Dad works at a university. There!" she finished, in triumph.

"But my Dad's a moron," Greta, scrambled to her feet, "and David isn't. Oh… sorry; here, have mine." She had knocked over Alma's wine.

"Greta …"

"I want to change the record." Greta stepped over Alma into the dark corner where Alma's record player was and lifted the needle off John Mayall.

"I'm sure…" Alma was resuming, "…glassblowers aren't morons. He can't be an actual moron."

"He can," said Greta, but she botched the groove and the stylus made a vile sound and the others held their ears. Down went the needle again, then the opening to *Nineteenth Nervous Breakdown* rang out and she stepped back into the light, dancing.

That summer, Dramsoc's Edinburgh Fringe production was *The Seagull* with Alma starring as Nina. And this time Greta went too; as the wardrobe mistress. Clare and Ray were also there. Clare's sister, by now a student at Edinburgh University, sublet her flat to them. In the days leading up to their departure Greta was jittery; haunted by the idea that behind her father's back she was returning to a place he'd once come from. Never having been there before she could not logically be returning. But 'going back' was the way she thought of it. Unable to mention this to anyone she bottled it up and it fizzed inside her.

And when they got there Greta was astonished by the great stone city. "Wait until you see the Old Town," Alma said, ushering them along George Street. They had to drag an enthralled Ray past each statue and monumental column. Halfway across North Bridge, Alma held out her arms like a figurehead; the wind blew her hair and her long hippie dress backwards and flapped her handfuls of publicity leaflets.

"*This is fantastic!*" she shrieked, above the bluster of the wind. "*The men, the lions, the eagles, the partridges, the antlered deer…*"

"Alma," pleaded Clare, "people are staring."

"*The geese, the spiders, in short every living thing… Has been SNUFFED OUT!*"

"Shut up," Clare begged, clutching her poncho round her as amused tourists crowded past while Alma thrust playbills into their hands.

The bridge held them all high up in the bright air – for a moment less dwarfed by the spires, turrets, cupolas and domes of their gothic surroundings. Below them ran railway tracks and a street lined by massive buildings. "Is that Calton Hill?" Ray asked, consulting his map. "Look at that." He was pointing at a Greek temple on a hillside above Waverley Station. The wind blew Greta's hair into her mouth. Beyond Arthur's Seat, in the distance, gleamed the ocean, blue as a budgerigar. They continued over the bridge and turned right up the Royal Mile. Dodging among throngs of people, Greta seized Alma's arm as they walked and squeezed it in rapture. Around her the Old Town leapt and reared. The tenements and cobbled courts of its architecture merged with the volcanic rocks and crags of its geography, like a landscape of legend. Alma's excited litany of landmarks echoed as they went down onto Cowgate through a chasm between towering stone walls, past flights of steps suspended over yawning basements. The ensorcellating geometry of the flying staircases filled Greta with fascination. In the darkness under a bridge (…"This is George IV Bridge, everybody…") they stepped over rank pools of water that had collected in the pitted cobbles and emerged finally into the Grassmarket.

"That place looks good," cried Greta, pointing to a building on the corner that was painted orange and bedecked with posters. "Can you eat there?" An aroma of garlic and herbs emanated from its wide-open doors.

"That's The Traverse," said Alma, "look," she added in a squeal. The market was in full swing. They dragged Greta from her contemplation of the Traverse Theatre and ran across the cobbles to the nearest stall, which glittered with velvet caftans, sewn with tiny mirrors.

"Hayden-Fox is here Greta; did Alma tell you?" Ray spoke through a mouthful of chips. The night's performance was over. …*oh the sisters of mercy they are not departed or gone…*It was a cosy lamp lit suppertime; Leonard Cohen on the record player.

"That's right," Alma paraded in a white cheesecloth blouse, "I saw him about five o'clock in front of me going along Cowgate towards our venue." She stroked the fabric of her blouse. "Do you like it? I got it off the market after the rehearsal."

"Very sexy," Greta said. "I'd better hide backstage then or I might bump into him."

"Did you know he was coming Greta?" said Ray.

"No."

"You like him don't you?"

Greta shrugged. Ray looked baffled. "I do like him," she said.

"How can you like him?" said Alma, "you're horrible to him even though he's mad about you. Pass the salt please." She sat down and began unwrapping her chips.

"He's gorgeous, Greta, and so eligible," said Clare, "I still don't understand why you won't go out with him properly. Why don't you like him?"

"I've got a chip on my shoulder," Greta replied balancing one of her chips on her left shoulder, "and anyway he looks too much like Berlioz." She put the chip in her mouth.

"So is there another composer that it would be more permissible to look like?" Ray asked, peering round Clare, who had left the table and moved forward until her shins touched the sofa between his outstretched legs. He held his arms up to her and she sank down, coiling herself round him like a treble clef, her long hair curtaining his face as Leonard Cohen sang on… *so I hope you run into them, you, who've been waiting so long…*

"I do like him," said Greta, "I spend lots of time with him."

"And pigs fly," said Ray, the words muffled by Clare's kissing.

A few days later, David had been in the audience at every performance of *The Seagull* and the others were pleading with her to relent. "He could have easily followed us back to our digs to find you, but he doesn't. He's being really restrained; he's unhappy Greta. Why are you being so cruel?" said Clare.

They were walking in Cramond because Greta had never been to the sea. Ahead of them on the path Alma was arguing with Ray about high-rise blocks. Among the boats in the harbour behind them, wind chimed insistent rigging against metal masts. The repeated lamenting of gulls accentuated Clare's question. Was it cruel?

"I don't know." Greta said. "What's that island?"

"Ray," shouted Clare, "what's that island?"

"Cramond Island," Ray turned and came towards them, "Alma wants to go and live on it with Beardy Bob."

"I only said Bob wants to live on an island!" exploded Alma. Ray dodged the seaweed that she threw at him. Beardy Bob was their name for Alma's latest boyfriend, a philosophy postgraduate who never wore socks and wanted Alma to himself all the time and wouldn't come with her when she did things with her friends.

"Hi Beardy," yelled Ray, waving at the island, "what's that? You want Alma to come over there for a dish of sprouts?" Beardy Bob ate only raw vegetables.

"You pig," yelled Alma, leaping onto Ray's back, "stop being so mean," But she was laughing. "He's a philosopher," she bellowed, "philosophers are bound to be different from ordinary people."

Greta half listened to an argument about whether to walk out to the island. A causeway of wet concrete, revealed by the falling tide, joined it to the shore. Greta stared at the depleted stretch of water. The beach was covered with black drifts of seaweed. A plastic carrier bag caught in the wrack made a sizzling noise in the wind. Birds in the distance prodded their beaks into the exposed mudflats. "Aren't there any swans?" She called, shivering.

"You funny little townie!" said Ray, "oyster catchers, yes, or curlews. Why swans?"

"Greta," exclaimed Alma, slipping an arm round her, "you look cold. Let's walk back. What's the matter?"

"The sea is grey," said Greta. Ray dropped his donkey jacket round her shoulders and she shrank into its warmth, gripping it round herself. "I feel too small."

David wasn't at the performance that night. At the end, Alma, her face looking transparent and sore where she had rubbed off the stage make-up with baby-lotion, came out to where Greta was folding costumes into the basket. "So no David," she said.

"He's given up," said Greta. Alma handed over her long white Nina dress. The cast of the next show, (*Hamlet*), were congregating backstage doing voice warm-ups. Greta put away the dress and strapped up the basket. "Let's go," she said. Along the passageway they squeezed past a mass of bamboo canes leaning against the wall. Hamlet and one of his stagehands cheerfully reversed a coffin back out onto the dark pavement so the girls could get by.

"Greta!" came a shout. A Dramsoc girl flattened herself against the wall to let the coffin through; sidling towards them. "David said to give you this."

"Thanks." Greta ripped open the envelope then took a deep breath. The malt-scented breeze was welcome after the heat of the makeshift theatre. She passed Alma the note. "Read it."

"*I am staying at The George Hotel*," read Alma, "*Come now. Ask for me at reception D.*"

The two girls looked at each other then simultaneously began running along Cowgate towards the steps. Laughter was spurting out of them in shrieks of jagged breath as their feet drummed on the pavement.

"What does your father do, Greta?"

David's bathroom was awash from their lovemaking in the bath. By the window a sodden towel marked the spot where the ice bucket had fallen over. The empty champagne bottle had rolled under the armchair and the sun was rising. Greta noticed these things as she raised her head, surprised by David's sudden question. "He's a glassblower." With her cheek against the soft black hair that grew down the centre of his ribcage she inhaled, kissing his skin.

David uttered a murmur and then, as though to speak was an effort, said: "Good job he didn't make you out of glass."

Greta moved her lips up his body to his mouth to feel him speaking. "Why?" She held her lips to his.

"It's a liquid, you'd melt." Her lips felt the shapes of his words as they entered her.

"Glass is a solid," she said.

"No, it's a super-cooled liquid."

"Really? A liquid?" She drew back to look at him. He stroked her hair back from the side of her face, his fingers warm; tracing the shape of her ear.

"Yes," he said, "The base edges of panes in very old church windows are thicker than their top edges. The glass is flowing downwards."

"Is it the same for blown glass?"

"What does he make?"

"Scientific stuff – condensers." Greta thought of the condenser, the glass woman trapped in her bottle with her hair coiling up in an unexplained vortex.

"Yep. Put the condenser in a pot and wait a million years and the pot will be full of glass."

"Melted," she said, and laid her head back down. His hand traced the bones in her spine and a sensation like goosebumps contracted the skin all over her; scalp, wrists, ankles, nape; every one of her pores crisping and stiffening. Heat flared up from inside her to meet it. He lifted her onto him. The sun turned the room pink and golden.

In her final year at university Greta spent more and more time at David's flat in The Park and less and less in her room at Cavendish Hall. He had hundreds of books and was constantly giving her new things to taste. He loved food himself and often went shopping for exotic treats. His favourite shop was Burtons, the big delicatessen in the arcade under the dome of the Town Hall. "Here's your tea," he said, one afternoon, squatting down and placing the mug next to her, "try this," and he put a bone china plate next to her book. The plate held wafer thin slices of a dense-looking fruit cake.

Greta, wearing only pants and one of David's blue denim shirts, lay reading at the foot of a bookcase, her elbows resting on a velvet cushion. She took a small bite of the delicacy, "Mmmm…"

"It's panforte," he said, "Italian."

"What's that flavour – cloves?"

"Probably, and cardamom and pistachio and… " she held her mouth open, "have more," he fed her the other slice and they laughed as she pretended to bite his finger. He kissed her. "I'm off to my seminar now." He was gone and she returned to the big art book, sipping tea, absorbed in Surrealist painting and revelling in the blissful quietness. As she read, she could hear birds singing outside and in the distance, a lawnmower.

Some time later, something struck her as odd. She raised her head. Her forgotten tea had gone cold. The peace and quiet had gained an odd intensity. It wasn't that the birds had stopped, although the lawnmower had. She had the sensation that the room was holding its breath. Her heart gave an extra bump. Concentrating, she listened. Was someone creeping towards her in the empty flat? Unnerved she stood up and edged barefoot towards the doorway. The black and white tiles of the floor beyond came into view. David's hallway was wide and spacious. She took another step.

There was the old church pew and the iron umbrella stand. There was the coat rack and the grandfather clock.

The clock had stopped!

Flooded with relief and a silly happiness she ran across like a child, and took the special key down from the hook on the wall. It required several minutes of careful winding to raise the weights back up to the top of their lines. She set the pendulum going, as David had shown her, and closed the door in the body of the clock. And then, for no apparent reason, she went straight into the bedroom, seized a pad of foolscap and began writing:

Once upon a time there were two beautiful sisters called Deborah and Greta. Their father, whom they loved, was a glassblower. He made exquisite flagons of sparkling crystal and the whole world marvelled at his skill. The glass birds he made were so realistic that unless you kept them in a cage they flew away, singing. "How do you do it?" the people asked. But he would not tell them. In truth he was a wizard. He had magical powers and sometimes he turned animals into glass and gave them to his daughters. These were their toys. One day when Greta woke up, she found that her sister had vanished. When she asked where Deborah was, her parents said that she had gone to a far-off country and would never come back. In secret the glassblower made Greta help him with his magic spells. "Never tell your mother," he said, "or you will be turned to stone. If you even think of telling her I will strike you dumb and your mother also." So the glassblower's daughter helped him with his magic every night. But she couldn't stop thinking about telling her mother and it came to pass that he struck both of them dumb. One day he died and the child was about to tell her mother everything when on the instant she was turned to stone. The drink in her hand grew cold. The world moved on around her but the glassblower's daughter was frozen in time and even the clock stopped ticking…

At that moment Greta heard the sound of David's key in the lock. She jumped as if she had been shot. The cheerful slam of the front door was followed by the sound of his footsteps heading into the kitchen. Greta ripped her story in half, screwed it up and stuffed it into the bottom of the wastepaper basket.

"I got some fresh garlic in the shop on Derby Road," called David, "I'll make a lasagne. What are you up to?" This last spoken, as she appeared, carrying the wastepaper basket.

"Tidying up," she said, pushing her hair off her face, and she went past him in the garlic-scented kitchen and out into the yard with its pots of herbs. She emptied the wastepaper basket into the dustbin then came back inside. He smiled at her and she kissed him until he dropped the garlic-press.

Revising for her finals was happy; all done in a haze of passion; the sun beating down. "Test me on this Wittgenstein," she held the book out to Clare.

"My hands are covered in sun oil," warned Clare.

"Never mind. If I ever open this book again it will remind me of summer," said Greta. They lay on the terrace below the Trent Building, grit from the flagstones sticking to their oiled legs. From the lake came the knocking of oars in the rowlocks of the boats. There was the cluck of water against wood, the voices of the people in the boats coming and going. Greta was content. What could possibly go wrong? She had moved in with David, she was in love. So after graduation, when everyone finally said goodbye, she wasn't sad at all.

Part 3. **Dark Wood – 1971**

The Folly

"What is that?" Greta pointed to bright washes of mauve on the hillside below the pines.

"Rosebay willow herb," replied David. "Mother hates it. The seeds get everywhere – look." White filaments drifted in the breeze.

"I like them," Greta put out her fingers to catch one; unexpectedly thinking of Deborah, carried through the air towards her like Mary Poppins under an umbrella.

"Over here we have the folly." David took hold of her head to align her gaze with a tower. Terracotta tiles on its roof glowed in the sun. Greta leaned against him, enjoying the touch of his warm hands either side of her skull. He was holding Deborah inside her head. She twisted round and pressed herself against his body. He tilted her face towards him and they kissed.

From the distant terrace that stretched along the back of the house a voice called and they could see David's mother waving at them. "Tea on the lawn. You're honoured," said David as a white cloth fluttered. They began walking back. "Ah. Dad's there now." A second figure had appeared on the terrace; Judge Hayden-Fox presiding. Greta saw no sign of scarlet robes or a curled white wig.

David's mother was fierce, like the Red Queen in Alice in Wonderland and as they approached the garden here she was, coming to meet them. "Did you get as far as the folly?" she called.

"Yes," said Greta.

"Get David to serve you cocktails on the balcony as the sun goes down," said his mother brusquely, "you'll have plenty of time before dinner. Eight o'clock sharp," she added, to David.

"The garden is fabulous," offered Greta, as they crossed the lawn past a glory of dahlias, goldenrod and michelmas daisies.

"It's taken me years," said his mother.

"You do all this yourself?" Greta was amazed.

"I have someone to dig and mow, and do the topiary. But I plant and design. It keeps me busy." She sounded dismissive.

"This is beautiful, what is it?" Greta spread admiring fingers among the dancing motes of a delicate airy plant with flowers like white knots.

"Huh! Baby's breath," sniffed David's mother, "comes up everywhere like a weed."

"Il faut cultiver notre jardin," gabbled Greta.

"*Candide*," responded his mother as if it had been a test.

"Dad, meet Greta," said David, as they reached the terrace.

"I'm very pleased to meet you, Greta, welcome to Wychwood," said David's father. A neat moustache half hid his allusive smile. His eyes were bright and he shook her hand warmly which mitigated the severity of his lined face. "So you're a croupier," he said, "how are you finding that?"

"It's only temporary – until she gets a proper job," interjected David, before Greta could reply.

"It's interesting learning all the different odds," said Greta, "because…"

"Freddie, will you fetch me my sunhat?" called his mother, "milk and sugar, Greta?"

Greta hastened over and sat at the table. "She's applying for lecturing in the FE sector," she heard David say. These days David was always arguing the case for teaching in further education. He joined her at the table, smiling.

"Are you two coming to drinks at the Lipkin's after dinner?" asked David's mother, as her returning husband planted the straw hat tenderly on her head.

"No," said David, "I'm showing Greta around the house. I've promised a game of billiards and she's interested in the library."

"The library?" David's mother looked in astonishment at Greta. Greta's mouth was full; she having just taken a bite of her

104

unfamiliar slice of rather dry, marbled sponge cake. It clung stickily to her gums, so she just widened her eyes. Her cheeks felt red. Pigeons cooed in a tree at the edge of the lawn.

David's cup gave a bone-china echo against the saucer. "Rabelais," he said.

"What, the medieval monk?" His mother looked incredulous.

Greta's a scholar," he said, "she's eager to see if we have anything by Rabelais in our collection – we probably do, if my memory…"

"Look I got you lebkuchen…" interrupted his mother, proffering a plate of little rattling cakes.

And he leaned forward and took one as he said: "…and, by the way, sod the Lipkins Mother, I can't stand the Lipkins. They won't miss us. If I do take Greta into Uppingham tonight I'm taking her to the pub in any case."

Greta swallowed her cake, saying, "maybe tomorrow…?"

"Tomorrow's Friday," said his mother, "David won't stay for that – he hates Friday nights." David shrugged, stuffing another of the lebkuchen into his mouth. A wasp landed on Greta's plate and she gave a partially suppressed squeal of alarm. With a deft stroke of his knife, Judge Hayden-Fox swatted the wasp and then, with a gallant flourish and a smile at Greta, flicked its body into the petunias.

Greta roared with laughter. "You're like a conjuror," she said.

"More tea, Greta?" David's mother was already pouring it so Greta obediently drank.

"Only the female stings," declared the judge and Greta listened as he launched into a disquisition on the life cycle of *vespa vulgaris*.

Soon his wife interrupted, saying to David, "can't you have a look at the library now, with Greta?"

"Come on Greta, the Lipkins won't get you," laughed David, rising. He bashed crumbs off his jeans and leaned sideways to kiss his mother. "We're going to the stables now," he said to her, "and then we're having a swim and then I'm giving Greta champagne on the balcony just like you said." He eased Greta out of her chair, "see you later, Dad," he touched his fist to his father's shoulder in passing, then with his arm around Greta's waist he swept her away with him.

And when Greta said: "David, do you think maybe we should do what your mother wants?" He seized her, laughing again, and lifted her right up into his arms, running away with her across the grass and round the corner of the house while she shrieked, overcome with involuntary giggles.

"What did your Mum mean about you hating Friday nights?" asked Greta later as they sat on the balcony of the folly.

"It's the Jewish Sabbath," said David, "you knew I was Jewish didn't you?"

"Vaguely," Greta said, "It's not as if you're religious though."

He leaned over to pour more Champagne into her glass. "Would you ever consider converting to another religion?" he asked.

"Christ no!" she laughed, "It's taken me until now to stop thinking I'll be struck dead for not going to Mass any more." At her feet lay sloping meadows and wooded hills. She pointed at the sunset, "look at the golden clouds," she said.

The casino provided svelte high-necked gowns and Greta was instructed to buy silver evening shoes. The other trainee, Rosalind, had the elongated bulky elegance of a giraffe and shiny, platinum-dyed hair. "Can we smoke in the casino?" Rosalind demanded, when the manager, fearsome Miss Norma, asked if they had any questions.

"No," was the curt reply. "Leave your cigarettes in the rest room."

"She does though," said Rosalind, grimly, as they followed Miss Norma down the stairs.

A beautician taught them how to apply elaborate make-up. She smiled at them in the rest-room mirror as they sat meekly on their plush stools. Miss Norma stood and frowned. "This lady knows how I want you to look," she said, "so do as she tells you." A green shantung dress set off her pale skin. With her full lips and large eyes she was like the wicked queen in Snow White. "She needs it most," Miss Norma jabbed her cigarette towards Greta, making a vortex of smoke. Her eyes locked on Greta's in the mirror. "You should dye your hair," she said.

"What's wrong with it?" Greta was taken aback.

"It's no colour," said Norma, "it reminds me of… I don't know – digestive biscuits. Put it up." She swept out.

"Let's get that racoon eyeliner off you," said the beautician to Greta, in a soothing voice, shaking cleanser onto cotton wool. "You've got a lovely long neck; your hair will suit you, up."

"Norma's a bitch," snapped Rosalind, lighting a cigarette and inhaling a decisive lungful of smoke.

The shifts were nine at night to four in the morning. Make-up hid the effect when she was at work but during the day, unable to adjust to working nights, Greta looked haggard. "Give it up," urged David, "I don't care about you paying half the rent, wait until you get some proper work."

"No," said Greta.

"Apply to Central College for part time lecturing, then; it's right on the doorstep after all." David had continued to circle further education lectureships in *The Guardian* so in the end she decided to apply. It was a step down from being an academic; which Greta would have preferred. But she had not achieved a good enough degree to do postgraduate work. All the urgency went out of her studying in her second year. She had coasted to a 2:2 and sold all her books. The only book she had ever wanted to own, she realised, was that copy of *Gargantua and Pantagruel* that she found in the school library. Sometimes she thought about going back there and stealing it. She didn't feel as if she had got anywhere. Sometimes she wondered if David would ask her to marry him. Meanwhile she carried on as a croupier.

The Gamble

Greta took a deep breath. *Pull the wheel one way and send the ball the other.* Two experienced croupiers were there to help her. The brass crown in the centre of the wheel was easy to catch. *Catch it by one of its tines – send it in the opposite direction to the previous spin and then apply the ball to the underside of the rim.* "Place your bets," she called. Her only customers were two dowagers in evening dress. The one with the fox fur wrap put a chip on red. The one with elbow-length black gloves put one on the centre column and dotted others across the board. The wheel went so fast that all the numbers merged. Greta poised the ball. Pressure and a flick should propel it in a centrifugal rush, round and round. She pressed. She flicked. The ball managed a few lazy circuits then lost its momentum and clattered into one of the numbers. She bent towards it. "Zero," she announced. To her relief all she had to do was collect the chips. She swept them off to her left. The girl at her side sorted them deftly, her plump arm brushing Greta's thin one. The dowagers were expressionless. "Place your bets," said Greta, and tried to pick the ball out of its little brass pocket. She failed and the heavy wheel whizzed round. She waited, fingers hovering. Here it came. She tweaked at it but it fell back into the wheel, landing in number two and the wheel span it away again.

"No spin," called the chief sharply.

Oh God.

The chief leaned forward on her high stool and picked the ball from the blurred race of the wheel. There was the faintest of clicks as her long red nails brushed the flying metal. Without any apparent strain on her graceful wrist she slowed the wheel down then sent it one way, the ball, the other. The dowagers made their cautious bets as before. The ball buzzed round and round. The chief smiled at Greta and relaxed back again. The ball went on and on. *What if I can't get it out of the wheel – what if I mess up the next spin?* Sometimes, in training games, Greta had flung the ball right out of the wheel. The ball slowed. "No more bets," said Greta,

"Five, red," she added as it dropped. She cleared the losing chips and went to spin again.

"Pay red, croupier. Winning bet on red," warned the chief. An embarrassed Greta matched the winning chip. "Two to one, croupier," the chief snapped. Greta, more flustered than ever, added the missing chip to the glaring dowager's pile. "Spin the ball now please Greta," said the chief, adding, "place your bets." She gave Greta a smile of encouragement. Greta spun. The ball managed two feeble loops. "Short spin!" rapped the chief, "No more bets!" But Greta had yanked the wheel too hard again and it was racing so fast that once more the numbers had vanished in a blur. The ball clattered into the brass cups, bouncing in and out of several numbers before settling and she couldn't see which number it was in. "Zero," called the chief. Greta's mouth had seized up. Heart hammering, she slid the chips off the baize with sweaty fingers and her skin rasped on the surface, leaving a painful sensation, like carpet burn, down the sides of her hands.

"She's spinning zero a lot," observed Black Gloves, sliding a chip onto zero with an unsmiling look at Greta. Fox-Fur put a chip on number thirty.

Greta spun, but again she had yanked the wheel too hard. The dropping ball ricocheted wildly off the brass and out it flew, into the room. Both dowagers claimed it had landed in their number just before leaping out. "God Almighty Greta, what am I going to do with you? You're useless." Miss Norma arrived in a hiss of silk. "Go upstairs and have a break." Greta made for the mahogany door marked *staff only*. Norma's tuneless voice rose behind her. "Good evening ladies, sorry about that. I'll take over here."

Beyond the door, odours of pounded garlic and frying steak filled the air. Ahead was the kitchen. The waiters liked playing tricks. Greta hoped they wouldn't notice her go by. The swing-doors burst open and a commis chef dashed towards the cold-room along the corridor. Greta hurried upstairs. In the rest room her reflection goggled back at her. Damn. One of her false eyelashes was peeling off. Would she ever get a proper job? She had not anticipated it being this hard. But maybe because it was, she now definitely wanted to be a lecturer in a college of further education. She had sent off several application forms, but so far no-one had asked her for an interview. Why was it so difficult? Alma, Clare and Ray had begun good jobs. Camilla and Col had moved into planned careers. David was finishing his PhD. Tears welled up in her eyes. Rosalind came in. "Norma's such a cow," she said, after a glance at Greta, "everyone's pissed off with her. Have a fag." And she offered Benson and Hedges.

"I don't know what's the matter with me," Greta took a cigarette; "She's only doing her job. I'm being stupid."

"She's jealous because you've been to university," said Rosalind, "*So much for having a degree – she said – when am I going to see some brains...* She's a bitch."

"I shouldn't cry," Greta pressed a piece of loo roll under one eye.

"No," said Rosalind, "Your eyelashes will fall off. The bitch told me to tell you to have a coffee, and then come down. She's going to train you on Blackjack."

"It can't be any worse than roulette," Greta inhaled deeply. The cigarette was calming her down.

Rosalind put the kettle on and spooned Maxwell House into a mug for Greta. "I'd better go," she swished back out, flashing a beautiful smile. She had angular cheekbones and a haughty expression that reminded Greta of Cossacks. It was the first time Greta had seen her smile.

Going back past the kitchen Greta stepped as lightly as possible. In her sharp heels it was difficult to walk quietly on the hard stairs. Two commis chefs carrying live lobsters were coming from the cold-room. As soon as they saw her they cornered her, brandishing the lobsters and shouting in Italian. She screamed, trying to dodge the slow lashing of the tentacles and the waving claws. The commis laughed and shouted all the more. One of them bent and put a lobster on the stair by her foot and she screamed again, gathering her long skirt in a tight bunch around her legs. There was no other sensible response. This was the world of Gargantua and Pantagruel and she was the screaming one who has to run, be caught, scream and run again: like the pilgrim who hides in the salad and gets eaten along with the lettuce.

Right at the end of September Greta was interviewed at Central College by the suave head of the Liberal Studies Department who offered her five hours a week of part time teaching. He took her to the staff room. "Tim, here, will show you around and give you some induction notes," he said, and left her in the care of a likeable young lecturer about her own age with a friendly smile and nicotine stained fingers. Greta took to him immediately.

At the end of an intense tour *…these are the art rooms*, and receiving page after page of notes from various filing cabinets… *this is the resources room*, and an hour of earnest discussion in the drama studio… *I'll teach you how to use the lighting board*, Greta was shown out clutching an armful of folders. "Oh, and this is Gordon," said her guide, as a lecturer in a tweed jacket came by, "he'll be one of your colleagues too. I have to go; I've got a meeting."

"Thank you," called Greta as Tim loped off. "Hello," she said to the newcomer over her pile of folders.

"Has Tim shown you everything?" asked the bespectacled young man, genially, "I hope he made you welcome."

"Yes thanks," said Greta, "we're going to meet up for a pint later so he can show me some student projects to give me an idea of the level. I'm starting next Thursday. Sorry; what was your name?"

"Gordon," said the young man. "So – a pint, eh? Can anyone come? I'd better not tell his girlfriend," and with a roguish smile, he pushed his heavy spectacles back on his nose as if they were slipping off.

Back at the flat David was delighted, and cooked steak Béarnaise; opening a vintage bottle of claret to celebrate. "You'll be able to give up that bloody casino now," he said.

But she didn't. Things were looking up. And Greta showed a positive talent for Blackjack.

"Greta," snapped Miss Norma, "practise your shuffle. The restaurant's packed, it's going to get really busy."

Greta was glad. The first two hours had been boring and the piped music drove her mad.
Sha la la la la lala la
Sha la la la la lala la

Sha la la la la lala la
And sweet Marie who waits for me…

She pulled back the block and took the released cards out of the shoe. There were four packs and she began practising a waterfall shuffle. What if Deborah walked in now? Greta's dreamy gaze rested on the French roulette table in the centre of the room. *Come on, Twig, let's play Pontoon…* The ball fizzed like a wasp around the glittering rim of the wheel. "No more bets," called the croupier. The ball clattered to rest. "Thirty-one, black."

There wasn't long to dream. Greta's table filled up and soon she was flying. The hours slid past. "Eighteen: twenty: stay madam?" The woman nodded, setting her golden Bambi earrings dancing. "And you Sir – fourteen?

"I'll twist." His crew cut bristled at her.

"Twenty four," said Greta, dealing a picture and scooping away the losing hand. Crew Cut thumped his fist on the padded edge of the table in a fury.

"Stick," said the last customer.

Greta had a queen. She pulled her new card from the shoe and flipped it over. An ace. "Blackjack," she announced and her spry fingers plucked their chips from the baize in front of them. Then, with an arcing hand she swiped away their losing cards.

"Fluke!" said the one with the Bambi earrings, laughing as Greta swished out the new cards. "Can I play two hands?"

"Certainly Madam," Greta paused to let the woman put another chip on the table. Her new cards were a ten and an ace and Bambi clapped her hands.

A rustle of taffeta was followed by a tap on Greta's bare shoulder. Norma, in a beautiful black halterneck gown, had come to give her a break. The table was tense. Norma waited silently. Crew Cut had bought a card on both his tens and had scored twenty on each hand. Bambi had blackjack on one hand and twenty on the other and the rest of the table had strong hands too. They all stared at Greta's Jack of diamonds.

"She's got to bust this time," said the friendly man in the white tuxedo.

"Blackjack," she said as she drew the ace of spades. The players gasped and laughed. Crew Cut swore. Her right hand began clearing the losing bets. "Ègalitè," she said, and passed over

112

Bambi's blackjack without taking the chips. She scooped up Crew Cut's and cleared the cards then clapped her hands together and opened them out like a book, as she got down off the stool.

"Good riddance," said Crew Cut, lighting a cigarette.

Upstairs Greta made coffee and took out Alma's letter. Alma, who had taken a first in philosophy, was about to complete a three-month contract with a community theatre company in Bristol. *October 15th 1971. Dear Greta, remember when we did 'The Seagull' in Edinburgh? – Well I'm going out with a musician who saw me in it. He's with Floodgate Theatre Company. His name is Mick and his guitar playing makes me swoon. I am planning to audition for Floodgate so we can tour together. I hope I get in. I saw Clare last month. She's doing social work in the department that sorts out foster homes. She was telling me awful things about why children have to be taken into care. I don't know how she can do it. It upsets me just to hear about it.*

Greta pictured their delicate happy Clare finding out about neglect and cruelty and children taken into care. What would have happened to her if someone had found out about what went on while her mother was out cleaning? But they didn't find out. So she had received a normal upbringing. And now no-one would ever know. And she was normal. *I'm impressed that you've got the lecturing but how's the casino? I can imagine you in that sort of place; it sounds glamorous no matter what you say. I want you to meet Mick. Write to me and tell me when you get some time off. Love Alma.* Greta put the letter away and lit a cigarette. She and Alma were twenty-one. Here at the casino Rosalind was only nineteen and yet she was married and had a baby son. Her husband had no qualifications or job and was teaching himself to play the saxophone. At nineteen, Rosalind was a mother and the breadwinner. A glance at the clock showed it was midnight. Four hours to go.

Rosalind came in carrying a plate of dried up steak and rattling chips. The tough bits of meat and chips – some said they were customers' uneaten chips – fed to the croupiers at midnight were awful. "How's your lecturing Greta?" Rosalind settled herself down.

"My Thursday one is OK but on Tuesdays it's at nine o'clock," said Greta, "it's hardly worth going to bed by the time I get home and have a wash – I feel shattered."

"I bet your students are bigger than you aren't they?" laughed Rosalind, "all those hulking apprentices!"

David, now a teaching fellow, went to New York for six weeks on a research visit. It was December. He was disappointed that she wouldn't come with him. "I don't believe you," he said, when she told him it was because of work, "It's something else," and his eyes were hooded with anger.

I get triple time for Christmas at the casino," she wrote in a Christmas card to her parents, *and I really need to think up lesson plans*. But David was right. Those weren't the reasons. *I like lecturing but it's hard work*, prattled her card. Greta was almost afraid at the way David sensed she was hiding something. She knew what her reason was but she couldn't tell him. *Merry Christmas Mum and Dad. And by the way – just to let you know, my new address is: c/o Hayden-Fox, Flat 2, 31 Newcastle Terrace, The Park, Nottingham*. The card showed a wooden angel praying and Greta prayed for inspiration as she tried to devise entertaining ways to present current affairs to her unruly mobs of apprentices. Term was underway again by the time David came back and she still refused to give up the casino. He protested. He would be waking up just as she was coming home to bed. On her nights off she would be too exhausted to go out.

She got to grips with teaching; dressing differently for a start; midi length brown pinafore dress over a skinny polo-neck and black boots of wet-look leather with clumpy heels. The lads noticed. "where's your mini skirt, Miss? You wore it when we first had you," they bantered. Day-release mechanics, sheet metal-workers, plumbers and carpenters, like the boys at her school, they identified with her accent and said she was more like they were than the other lecturers. When Floodgate Theatre Company came to the College in June, Greta tried to persuade her apprentices to attend, explaining the plot of *Romeo and Juliet* to them.

"Guess who," hot fingers covered her eyes.

"Alma… You were wonderful," the pre-Raphaelite clouds of Alma's hair tickled Greta's face as she hugged her friend, breathing in the familiar after-show fragrance of baby lotion.

"Thank you. Are these your students?" Darting figures around them stacked chairs and swept the floor.

"No. These are all O and A-level. None of mine came."

"This is Mick," said Alma and the lanky young man behind her, the production's lute-playing Mercutio, smiled; big teeth white in a strong face.

"You were fantastic," said Greta, "especially the music, and the sword fight."

"What about me?" demanded Alma, who had played Lady Capulet, and still looked like her in the ankle-length Indian cotton dress she wore. "Where's David?" she added, as Mick draped a purple crocheted shawl round her.

"Meeting us in the pub," said Greta, still annoyed that David had gone to an English department seminar instead of attending the play. "And you were brilliant. It was effective – the way you underlined the fact that Juliet was so young by playing her mother young too."

Mick hugged Alma, nodding in approval at Greta's words and then turned and hollered: "we're going to the pub." Other actors emerged from the wings and followed him as he strode towards the door. Not many men could carry off jeans tucked into unzipped biker boots but with his long black hair flowing down over his Che Guevara tee shirt Greta was amused to see that Mick turned the head of every girl in the hall.

What's That Plant?

"Those are my words." Greta's incredulous voice came out higher than she had expected, "my ideas. You thief!" she broke off coughing. David became stiffly controlled. He would not look at her. Remained sitting; biting his left thumbnail. "Look at me," she said, "deny it…"

He said nothing. On the floor at his feet, where she had thrown it, lay the transcript of *Tom and Jerry meet Rabelais: The Rhetoric of Comedy as a Didactic Tool*, an article he had just published in *Renaissance Overview*. He took a breath, which sounded too loud to be natural, then started to speak in a monotone. "The conversation we had was after I'd done most of the research and…"

"Liar!" She took a step closer. "That whole piece is based on what I said. You've just hi-jacked…"

"What are you accusing me of exactly? Stealing words?" He shot a glance at her.

"…you never even told…"

"Stealing words?"

"Fuck off! They're all my ideas."

"Oh is that so?" He glared at her. Beethoven's Kreutzer Sonata was playing on the record player, its poise and harmony highlighting their lack of it.

"…I didn't say topöi… or… anarchy is the edge of paranoia and all that alienation bollocks …"

"Bollocks is it? So they're not all your ideas then…"

"Shut up! Yes you've put in bollocks but the ideas are mine. At least admit that you…"

"Stop being so melodramatic."

"Melodramatic?" She stepped another pace forward.

"Take your hands off your hips, Greta, you look…"

"Shut up! Shut up with how I look. You look. You look me in the eye. Come on!" He turned his head away as she came and crouched next to him, staring at his averted profile. "Look at me David: you took my ideas didn't you." He shifted his head a fraction

116

more to the right, another degree away from her. In a fury she balanced one knee on the edge of the couch and reached over and gripped his hair in two fistfuls either side of his head, trying to force him to face her. He grabbed her wrists but his hair was long and curly: her fingers were buried in its black, soft mass, twisting the roots tight against his scalp. "At least look me in the eye," she said, "you betrayed me."

"Betrayed?" he said, trying to speak quietly, "you can't help using this sort of word can you. Get off me for God's sake; you're making a fool of yourself." He was flushed scarlet.

She let go and hunched into the opposite corner of the couch, staring at the layer of dust on the coffee table. Neither of them ever did any housework. She began again. "Who's been keen on Rabelais since they were sixteen? Me. Who said that if he were alive today he would have invented a satirical cartoon? Me." David said nothing. "Who did a third year essay on the visual and plastic qualities in Rabelais' work for the aesthetics course? Me." She looked sideways at him. He didn't move. "They were my ideas David."

"But you weren't going to use them for Christ Sake!"

"It doesn't matter – it's my brain and I can do what I like with my ideas."

He didn't move. The sweetness in the music was now a painful counterpoint to the bile in the atmosphere. "Well," he said, slowly at last, "you weren't going to use them for anything were you." Greta stared at her lap. "Were you?" The quietness of his voice deflated her. No; she had not been going to use them. It wasn't fair, but somehow she was in the wrong and she had no answer. "You've got a problem," he said, "you're only half engaged with the world; you don't analyse your position in it do you? You don't formulate goals." His fluency suggested that he had been thinking about this for some time.

"Shut up. What do you know?" she said scornfully.

"What, indeed," he said and he faced her; dark eyes sombre. She scrunched herself further down into her corner. There was a pause. "Why do you aim so low?" he said, "you got fabulous A-level results and in the first year you were on target for a first. Then you stopped trying." Silence. He stared at her. "You could have been a brilliant academic. You could have developed those ideas but you're more interested in earning money, so why blame me for doing it now?" She made a futile snuffling noise that was meant to express contempt. He hadn't finished. "I'm a writer and an academic. I want ideas to be published. Everyone should be able to share good ideas. You have to take responsibility for it, not snarl at me when I do it."

"I write poetry – I might be a writer too." she flung at him.

"Yeah? Well. Choose to be a poet. Not a… croupier," he spat the word. "It's *all* about choices. Choose to come with me to California instead of going to Clare's wedding."

"Shut up," she said, violently. The wedding made her think of Deborah, of pictures of brides cut out of magazines. Weddings were supposed to be a good thing but she remembered Mrs Furedi's wedding photo and Bridget pinching her, her mother shouting when she had asked *where is your wedding photo*? Clare's wedding made her feel nervous. But it had been her second excuse for not going to California with David. Her first – that she had no passport – was, although true, a poor excuse and he hadn't accepted it. "*It's something else*," he had said, "*your usual murky secret*." She stormed to her feet. "I'm going out." She kicked a fallen cushion out of her way and slammed the door as she left the room.

Outside, mist cloaked the horse chestnut trees, which were heavy with white cones of blossom. The day was cool. Persistent drizzle soaked the silent crescents as she walked along under the trees listening to the rain pattering on the leafy canopy. Water seeped onto her flip-flops making her feet slip awkwardly on the wet rubber. David was trying to uproot her. This wasn't the first time he had tried to make her go to America with him. His prescience was beginning to frighten her. It was impossible to go away – to go all the way to America. She felt a tightening sensation in her chest. *I won't go anywhere Deborah, I'm here. I'll still be here if you come back*. The thought filled her with sadness. And David wasn't going to ask her to marry him. The clue had been there in an exchange whose significance she had completely missed at the time. *Greta*, he had said, *would you ever consider converting to a different religion*? And what had she said? *Christ no!* All she had noticed was the heavenly view from the tower. How shallow she was.

The aimlessness of her walking saddened her and she turned back towards the flat in frustration. Hugging her thin shirt round her in the moist air she felt as if she wanted to cry. But her eyes were dry. Only the tight feeling remained, like something binding her ribcage, preventing her from breathing properly.

A gift from David reconciled them; black and yellow, an Ossie Clarke dress in clingy bias-cut crepe to wear to Clare's wedding. It appeared demure, finished with a large floppy bow tied at the throat, but this decorum was subverted by the sensationally low-cut neckline. The loops of the bow concealed her cleavage but only as long as she didn't move. Shortly before he left they went shopping again and chose a scarlet soda siphon for Clare's wedding present. And then David went to the States.

August arrived.

The wedding was in Elmley Castle; a village near Evesham. There was no direct train from Nottingham. To reach Evesham, Greta had to change trains at Birmingham and again at Worcester Shrub Hill. She grew impatient as the morning wore on. David would have hired a car, planned a route, and no doubt they would have taken in a garden full of medicinal herbs on the way.

A memory occurred to her as her train drew in to Evesham station: Sudeley Castle. In her memory; the Greta-figure trailed behind the David-figure while he walked between the black shapes of clipped yew, deep in conversation with a bee-keeper. Their figures were as small as chess pieces. The veils they wore, and the smoke drifting from the canister in the bee-keeper's hand, gave it the air of a film memory rather than a real one, as if it had been nothing to do with her; Nicholas Henton and the lemon scented herbs he offered.

An old taxi chugged her to Elmley Castle. By now it was almost two o'clock and Greta had a vision of the wedding starting without her as bells rang. She arrived to see Clare and her father walking towards the little church and Greta dashed to overtake them; running between lopsided gravestones alongside the path, her high heels catching in the churchyard grass. The uneven ground seemed to bounce beneath her so that she felt as if she was about to fall. Clare proceeded up the path with her father like a seraphic bridal doll. In the sunlit church doorway stood a group of bridesmaids; little girls in primrose taffeta. Greta heard them giggle at her haste as she burst through them and scrambled into a pew at the back. She steadied her breathing, trying to spot Alma. The church was full of families, of couples, of sets of people. Greta felt disconnected. Even though her relationship with David troubled her she would have fitted in better if he had been with her. The organ pealed; the congregation rose and, as Greta turned to look, Clare swept by and smiled radiantly, straight at her.

Later; an express whammed through Evesham station as she waited alone on the platform. The wind of its passing cuffed her hair; raising it in tails about her head. A sudden despair pierced her. The wedding guests, her friends; even those who knew her well; were unaware of the efforts she made to keep certain things hidden. The question was not: when would she begin to be like everyone else – the answer to that was never: the question was, could she keep up the pretence that she was as normal as they were for the rest of her life? The slow train to Worcester Shrub Hill drew in. It was just a matter of getting aboard; keeping going. Maybe it would get easier. She went home, August gave way to September. David returned from California, life went on. The months passed.

If only she hadn't gone to the meeting. No. If only David hadn't come to it. Or if only she had known he was there. The crowd was thick that evening. Nottingham Poetry Society had many members and the turnout, for the Annual Competition-Winners' Night, was impressive. Greta had told the people she worked with at College and had even invited her first year carpenters and joiners who she was persuading to write poetry using Bob Dylan as an inspiration. None of them turned up but Tim, the lecturer was there and so was Gordon. The swing doors blabbed open and shut time after time as more and more people came in off Shakespeare Street, each bringing with them a draught of smoky November air. Greta had come third. Prize-winners were invited to read their competition poems plus one other they were working on. It was that *one other*. If only she hadn't written the penis poem. If only she hadn't read it out.

Spotlights dazzled her as she stood on the dais and she was aware of black shadows criss-crossing as people fetched drinks from the hatch. The audience applauded her prize-winning poem. "And this is my other one... recently finished," she said. Sporadic coughs faded to silence. "It's called: What's That Plant?...

That's the withered penis-plant
That is, old man's beard.
That is a disgusting plant
Next to a disgusting plant
Surrounded by ground cover plants
Ground that's needing cover plants
Ashamed and needing cover ground
Ground with an embarrassed plant
A dreadful withered penis plant
An over Love-Lies-Bleeding plant:
It was a Love-Lies-Bleeding plant.
Let's hurry past the bleeding plant
The sorry plant
The cover plant
And talk of plants like you instead
Or him or her or me."

Silence. Broken, as someone went through the swing door so forcefully that it crashed against the wall. Then a detonation of laughter and applause. Greta laughed too, feeling as if she had created something both vicious and amusing. She bowed.

It was the end. People crowded round, congratulating her. The lecturers from her college came up, smiling. And here was Clive looming out of the crowds, with a beard now as well as a moustache. "Well done," he enthused. Clive taught English at the girls' grammar school in Clifton, on the outskirts of Nottingham. He still wore the smelly Afghan coat.

"This is Tim…" Greta said, "…and Gordon," introducing them, "some of my fellow lecturers at Central College."

"Hi," Clive, like a big brown bear paid them no attention; turning the coat's grimy back on them. "Greta, you should get published. You're really good."

But when she got home, she found that she was not good at all. David stood in the hall by the grandfather clock, his hair standing out round his temples as if electrically charged. Fury drew his black brows together and his eyes looked black too. "Is that how you see me?"

"What?"

"I decided to come to that meeting and I was just in time to hear you read." He grabbed her arm as she tried to pass. "Did you know I was coming?"

"No."

"Would you have read that poem if you knew I was there?

"Yes – no!" He was twisting her arm. "It isn't about you David."

"It's full of anger and hatred."

"It isn't about you!" She couldn't deny that the poem expressed anger but even with her arm twisted behind her back she insisted it wasn't about him. She could smell the grandfather clock, a faint odour of linseed and polished elm. She could hear it through the wooden panel by her ear: precise metal hammers with long handles: two faraway men; each with a hammer; and they struck alternately against a finely-wrought metal surface so that each stroke had its own tone, its own weight and resonance: far, far in the distance. "Let go of my arm," she said.

"I don't think you've ever loved me at all have you," he said, as a statement not a question. He let her go and she went into their bedroom. "Yes!" he shouted, as she dragged her suitcase down off the top of the wardrobe, "I think it's time you went home. Get off home, to your… your… backstreet in Nowheresville and the… plebeian obscurity you take such care to avoid mentioning."

She could have retaliated; told him that he was a pretentious academic, a stuffed shirt, with his incongruous rider's thighs and his neurasthenic obsession with Elizabethan Physicke. But she didn't. She felt like comforting him, although that wasn't going to be possible. "You don't know anything about me," she said through dry lips, and a dizzy feeling assailed her as if everything she had run from was threatening to materialize. But he just made a scoffing noise and she layered one garment after another clumsily into the case in thickening silence.

"When I think of what I was offering you…" he said. A glance at his face showed it white with a dark red patch on each cheekbone. "All you've ever done is fuck me. It's all you're good for." At intervals he spoke again, leaning in the doorway, as she packed her things. "Prick-tease," he said; emitting the words as if he was aiming darts at her. "Flashing your cunt at me," he said. When she had filled her case, she tried to pass him. He blocked the doorway and seized her wrist. He had never been rough. His words and actions were always precise, delicate even. But now his fingers tightened painfully. "I thought your unselfconsciousness was natural," he said, "I thought the sight of you naked; painting your toe-nails; drying your hair – never caring if you were covered or uncovered – I thought you were a true innocent. But now you sicken me."

"David I'm going to the spare room. You're hurting my wrist."

He let go.

With the door closed she mechanically began to get ready for bed. Her heart was pounding and she pulled off her skirt and jumper, dropping them on the floor. She took off her petticoat and rolled down her tights. His words echoed in her head. He had made her sound like some sort of animal *…never caring if you were covered or uncovered…* She sat on the bed and bent forward to take her left foot out of the tights. *Flashing your cunt…* The coke oven of her cunt with its hot, mineral reek didn't scare her but it didn't explain itself to her either. There was a volcanic edge to the smell she caught sometimes. It was how she imagined melting rock would smell but she kept clear of the thought. The next step along that path was to think of hell.

Her heart thudded as soon as she woke the next day after finally falling asleep at dawn. Her mouth was dry and she couldn't breathe properly for the churning sensation in her stomach. A year ago she would have caught a train to London and phoned Camilla. Camilla would no doubt have plied her with tequila. But now she had the casino. And she had students.

For hours, Greta sat nervously in the spare room, even after she heard David leave. Then she packed her smaller suitcase, gathering her diary notebooks, the folder with her tax papers, her foolscap pad, the typed out poems, her lesson plans and her spongebag. She hesitated over her portable typewriter; a gift from David, but finally packed that too.

She lugged her cases into town and sat drinking coffee in the Kardomah until it was time to go to work and then she struggled to the casino. She wasn't due to teach again until the following week and when she asked Rosalind if she could stay a few nights with her,

Rosalind's blue eyes filled with concern and she insisted that Greta could stay as long as she wanted.

It was a long bus ride into town from the tiny terraced house in Basford that Rosalind shared with her husband and baby son. After a week Greta felt unbelievably tired trying to cope with both her jobs on top of all the extra travelling. She was full of admiration for Rosalind. How did she stand it? The arguments were constant because the husband had never done any of the chores while Rosalind slept. He bought the paper every day and took it to the pub to read: the baby parked outside in a pushchair. He was meant to be finding a job. When he'd finished with them, Greta used the same papers during her breaks at the casino to try to find a bedsit. Within three weeks she found one in Carlton. It was still a bus ride but the bliss of being able to sleep without hearing a crying child was immense.

Fly Posting

The poem she was trying to write was no further forward. Over a contented Christmas dinner of Spam and spaghetti hoops in front of the gas fire in her new bedsit she tried again …
She cannot come home, she cannot come home
No matter how badly you've missed her
The damage is done and her mind is made up
And she's going to look for her sister

Greta crossed out '*going*' and put '*trying*'.

In the New Year she applied for a full time post that came up at her College, and got it. Full of elation she wrote to Clare: *Dear Clare, I've packed in the casino and finally got a proper job – full time Liberal Studies lecturer at Central College of Further Education which is not far from The Trip to Jerusalem, if you remember. I like it. Some of my students are rough but I'm fond of them and now I'm full-time I get O-level and A-level students as well. And I've got nice fellow lecturers – all blokes…* She stopped writing. Clare would smile maybe, or would she sigh? And why had she written that anyway? *All blokes.* What about other aspects of her new job, and the yoga; what about that? Greta had started doing a yoga evening class. Telling Clare she had become interested in physical movement was the last thing that occurred to her. Yet she loved yoga and was looking forward to a residential course she had booked, come the summer break. The nib placed itself on the paper. *Maybe I wouldn't have mentioned the blokes, but I fancy one of them. His name is Tim Duprès. He's about my height, very thin with long blond hair. Unfortunately he's got a girlfriend. I might join the Labour Party. (Tim is very left wing; he's in The SWP.) David and I broke up. He got a lectureship at Berkeley so is in California now. I have my own bedsit, in Carlton. I feel guilty because I haven't been down to see you. I hope you and Ray are well. Have you seen Camilla lately?*

125

Biting her pen, unable to visualise Clare reading the letter, Greta wondered what else to say.

The sleeve of her sweater smelled of Players Number Six. Tim Duprès, the young lecturer with nicotine stained fingers who had shown her round on her first day at the college, smoked them constantly. If she inhaled, she could envisage him; conjure the look of his bony frame, the hang of his jacket, the quick lope of his walk.

By the time summer came she was certain he liked her too. In the echoing staff canteen one morning Greta looked up to find Tim gazing at her from an adjoining table. He lifted his cup of coffee, narrowing his eyes through the steam. "Going somewhere nice this summer?" he asked.

"No, just staying here as usual," she said.

"What? I imagined you as a traveller. You're not off to Greece?"

"No. Are you?" she asked.

"Yes. I'm going to Crete as soon as we break up."

"With your girlfriend?"

"Nicki? No. She's going somewhere with her parents," he said. "Nicki's not like me," and then, "I can't wait," he added. It felt as if he was entrusting her with his profoundest heart's desire.

And this grew even more intense in September, once the new academic year started. Sometimes in staff meetings Tim would sit opposite her. He would look at her and hold her gaze. From across the table his eyes were aquamarine. The black pupils gleamed. Was this how he looked at Nicki? As autumn progressed, the colours of the trees looked more beautiful than she could ever remember as she rode the bus to work, gazing out of the window. As the days shortened and the darkness fell earlier and earlier a tense happiness inside her grew and grew.

One overcast winter's day, when the weak midday light was already draining into thick fog, Greta and Tim met; quite by chance; on Bridlesmith Gate and they strolled along together, talking. Like a married couple they went into the bank on Middle Pavement and she drew out some cash. Then they walked in the slushy snow towards college and he asked her if she'd do some team-teaching with him.

It seemed natural to plan projects with Tim Duprès. They started a college magazine, publishing student paeans to the Bay City Rollers; statistics about motorbikes, commentaries on Giant Haystacks and analysis of Nottingham Forest matches. Greta was purple to the wrists from the cyclo-styling machine. They produced and directed a student play which Tim encouraged her to write. The title was *Penelope*, and it was a swiftly created version of the Odysseus myth in which Penelope went on the voyage too and gave Odysseus all his best ideas. Their teenage Penelope had bright blue eye-shadow and auburn curls that glowed against the black tabs of the drama studio. Greta directed. "Smashing," she called as Penelope vanquished Circe for the umpteenth time, "but if you don't know those lines by Tuesday we're in trouble."

"You're good," said Tim. He had a way of tilting his head and peering at her through his long blond hair. His eyes were perpetually narrowed against his chain-smoking. "Is it still snowing?"

Greta pressed her face to the window. "No."

"Sir are you and Miss coming to The Trip with us?" came the imperious shout of Cameron Valentine; their slender Odysseus.

"Yes," called Tim, winding a woollen scarf round his neck, "See you down there."

"We're not going there with them, are we?" said Greta, as they walked to the car park, "they're underage."

"Christ, Greta, it's the seventies. I bet you went in pubs when you were a kid."

"That's different." She held her long skirt clear of the slush as she waited for him to unlock the passenger door of his old blue van.

"Hypocrite," he said.

"We're in loco parentis," she protested, getting in.

He laughed: tried the engine. "My Dad always bought me a drink if he met me round the pubs when I was out with my mates."

Greta shut up. When it came to knowing how parents were supposed to behave she always shut up. The engine started at the third attempt.

Something about her expression must have changed Tim's mind. "OK," he conceded, "we'll go to the Berni Inn. I fancy a steak. And there's something I want to ask you. How about we take this lot up and do the show as a Fringe Production in Edinburgh next summer?"

Her heart leapt.

They drove the short distance to King Street, wiping frost off the inside of the windscreen, their hands bumping together as they did so, making them laugh for no real reason. Inside the pub the juke box was playing *Tiger Feet* full blast. Greta ordered the house speciality, a schooner of draught sherry, and sipped greedily. "Let's dance," she said.

"No!" He recoiled, aghast, "I don't dance. Sorry." While they waited for their steaks to arrive, Tim drank lager, dropping cigarette ash over the Fringe Programme registration forms he had brought to show her. "I got these last year but never did anything about it. But with you I could. The students could chip in for accommodation, they can sleep on the floor," he said, "I bet the Principal would fund it – it would be good for the trendy image of the college."

"I've been to Edinburgh," said Greta, "I was a stagehand at University."

"So you know all about it then. It's settled."

She loved Tim's eagerness, the way he assumed she would go ahead with him; loved his ambitious dreams for their students. His hands were bony, the knuckles prominent, his wrists thin. She would do it. He only had to say. What would he say if she told him that she had fallen in love with him? She suspected that the reason they got on so well was precisely because she never said such things. And what about his girlfriend? Would she come to Edinburgh? However, when they asked, the Principal wouldn't give them college funding for their Edinburgh plan after all.

Greta began writing another play. The weather was bitterly cold and she drew her red curtains and ate toasted crumpets in front of her gas fire, wrapped in her quilted dressing gown. She wrote and wrote – whenever she wasn't working she was writing. It took her mind off Tim.

The months passed.

"Greta," Gordon asked, "are you coming to The Playhouse bar tomorrow night?" Then he added, "Tim isn't," and indicated the lounging Tim Duprès at his side. The refectory chairs were moulded plastic but Tim managed to make his look as comfortable as a sofa. "He's spun a fucking pathetic excuse about going to a christening," Gordon said, frowning; wiping coffee froth from the thick hair of his moustache, using a downward motion of his closed fingers.

Tim addressed himself to her, leaning back in his chair, his hands in his pockets and saying in his drawling voice: "Oh dear. Comrades aren't supposed to go to christenings."

"What's on at The Playhouse bar?" Greta changed the subject because she could tell that Gordon was angry. And she was on Tim's side. Tim's foot tapped against her ankle. One light tap and then another. He smiled complicitly.

"There's a blues band on…" Gordon said, and then, as if jolted out of anger, "…cripes; look at those sexy boots." A leggy girl walked by outside the window. Gordon leaned on the table, his bulky forearms either side of his coffee cup and levered himself upright. "I've got to go," he sighed. He squeezed round Tim's reclining figure, "I've got Mechs 3 and it's over in X-block."

Tim ignored Gordon's receding back. Greta looked out of the window. Spring had come. The wind shook blossom off the trees and three girls laughed and raised their hands among the floating petals. "I suppose," Tim recalled her attention, "there's a good chance we won't be all that late back from the christening. Gordon's organised this Playhouse bar thing that's why he's being shitty. It's a miners' welfare benefit."

"I'll probably go to it," said Greta.

In her long, tiered cotton print gypsy skirt and tight vest top; her platform espadrilles held on by sexy ankle ties, Greta paraded from friend to friend at The Playhouse bar. It reminded her of her wild nights at the De Montfort Hall, herself and Bridget Furedi. She stood near the band, joining in applause for a harmonica solo, knocking back vodka-and-lime. After a while, to her delight, Tim Duprès came in, stylish in a brown suit with flared trousers, matching shirt and wide striped tie. He went straight to the bar, disappearing through the crowd. Without hesitation she followed, leaving the band like a carousel behind her. The lights changed colour. Tim glanced round and saw her. Perfect timing. "What's that you're drinking?" he said.

"Vodka-and-lime."

"The hard stuff. Yeah. Why not? I got pissed at the christening." He lit a cigarette leaving it smouldering in his mouth as he waited for the barman to get his drink. She took in the sight of him as he lounged there, as he pocketed the change without checking, as he took the cigarette out of his mouth, squinting at her through coils of smoke. She was with Tim. They stood by the bar looking into each other's eyes.

"Where's your girlfriend?" She asked.

I'm gonna wait 'til the midnight hour.... "She went home." He yanked at his tie, "fucking christening..." the tie came loose and he stuffed it in his pocket. Noise; wonderful brassy noise. Noise and drinking. Noise had always made Greta feel bold. Nothing awful happened in a noisy crowd. All the trouble happened when it was quiet. "Do you like this music?" He asked, undoing his shirt collar.

"Yes."

"Me too.

The lights changed again, the band announced a break. "Gordon and some others are at a table over by the wall," she told him, "Gordon's with a dark-haired girl."

"That's Trish; his girlfriend. He lives with her," said Tim and then he reversed his cigarette and held it to her lips. She took a tiny puff of it, made breathless by a flutter of excitement. Tim, leaning his elbow on the hammered copper of the bar, lazily scanned the room. She cradled her glass. "Greta..." he said, waiting until she met his gaze, "we're going to do something about this." He touched her hand and then peeled it away from her glass and stroked it. He stroked her forearm. Then; "we've been spotted," he murmured, glancing beyond her then back into her eyes, "Gordon's heading over." Their hands parted unobtrusively.

Next day she went to see Rosalind on her cane stall in the Victoria Centre Market. This, in addition to her shifts at the casino, was Rosalind's Saturday job. Rosalind's mum, pushing Rosalind's baby boy in a pushchair, was emerging from among the baskets, wicker chairs, cane mats and plant holders. "Say hello to Greta," cooed Rosalind. All three gazed down at the child who arched back against his pushchair and smiled, tilting his head on one side. He was much bigger than when Greta had seen him last and even more like Rosalind with his silky hair and light blue eyes.

"Wave bye-bye to Mummy," said his Grandma and he obediently raised his hand.

Over bacon sandwiches fetched from the adjacent café, Greta told Rosalind all about Tim and the Playhouse Bar. "And what about his girlfriend?" Rosalind narrowed her eyes and blew cigarette smoke upwards, a knowing look on her face, "what's her name?"

"Nicki," said Greta unwillingly.

On Sunday at four o'clock Tim Duprès arrived at her door almost as if it had been arranged that he should. Greta was dressed in jeans and an old velour tee shirt. Her feet were bare. "Oh. Hi." She was astounded. "I was just going to have a bath."

"Carry on." He stepped in, hands in the pockets of his bomber jacket, shoulders hunched as if it were cold. "Can I crash out?" He lowered himself into a languid sprawl on her floor, dragging a cushion off her couch. "You can run me one after," he said, "I've been playing five-a-side football." He closed one eye and squinted up at her as if she was bright sunlight.

Greta went and had a bath and washed her hair and when she came out he was asleep. She ran a bath for him and put some bath foam in it. He slept on. The scent of roses filled the room and she was tempted to just sit and watch him. His blonde hair was long. His fingers were thin; the nails bitten. But watching made him childlike so she woke him and he staggered into the bathroom. He looked lost and sleepy and she wanted to take him in her arms but she just smiled instead and showed him where the shampoo was.

He didn't bother closing the door. "Greta," he called, after a few minutes, "come in."

"We haven't got any lessons to plan," she said, leaning on the doorframe, inhaling the steam. His face was pink, his hair darkened by water.

"Nicki went to her parents for the weekend," he said, holding out his hand to her, "come on." She took his outstretched hand. "Join me," he said.

He didn't stay all night, and they didn't talk about where they would go from there but: "I guess we should keep this quiet," he said, as he left her, "or it'll be all over college and I don't want Nicki to find out until I work out what I'm going to do."

"Miss…"

"Yes, Parminder?"

"Are you going out with Sir?" Parminder swigged from his can of Vimto and glanced round. The rest of them were draped over chairs or on the floor in attitudes of heat and fatigue. The double doors at the end of the drama studio were open wide and a scent of mown grass came in on the warm air.

"No, he has a steady girlfriend. They've been together for years." Greta looked at her group and they all laughed because everyone had stopped talking to hear her answer.

"You two get on so well," continued Parminder, "we kind of thought you ought to be together…" much giggling accompanied this. Some of the cast looked at her, a little alarmed while others indicated, with nods and knowing looks that they were in agreement.

"Don't be cheeky," Cameron Valentine, gave Parminder a push. "Miss has a private life you know," he grinned at her. "Take no notice of us," he said, "we just all think you make a good couple." Again the wave of sympathetic laughing and Greta felt warmed by their acuteness rather than embarrassed.

"Come on – break over," she said. "It's your line Parminder: start from the beginning of that last speech."

Although she hadn't joined the Socialist Workers' Party Greta started going to their meetings that Autumn to just be with Tim. Meetings were held in pubs in districts like Gedling, Sneinton or Basford and never the same pub two meetings in a row. Greta had no interest in politics; her knowledge and understanding of it hadn't progressed beyond what they had been when she was twelve. Discussions at the meetings were intensely theoretical or involved different people reporting on union meetings they had attended. Greta tried to listen, *blah blah social contract* but lapsed into daydreams about herself and Tim, hoping her duplicity wouldn't be exposed. Gordon, chairing the meetings, *blah blah TUC boycott* took pains to include her, checking to make sure she was following the discussion *blah blah referendum.* A nod would satisfy him and her lascivious thoughts of Tim were barely interrupted. After meetings the group split up and a few of them would go into town for a drink at The Bell. It was Greta's favourite pub. The main bar at the end of the stone-flagged passageway reminded her of *The Peasant Wedding* by Breughel with its beams, wood-panelled walls and heavy oak tables and benches and it held happy memories of when she and Alma used to come to Jazz Night in an effort to bump into Two-Balls Mclean.

Sandwiched between the hairy sleeve of Gordon's jacket and the denim-clad warmth of Tim, Greta drank beer. Gordon would sometimes take a book out of his pocket and present it to her. *Culture and Society* had been one. His finger pushed his spectacles higher up on his chubby nose as he earnestly explained the merits of each writer he recommended. Gordon was her age and it amused her to see him taking on roles like chairman and mentor. Sociology was his main subject but in his good-humoured manner he constantly took on the task of widening everyone's political awareness at Central College. "Here Greta," he said, angling his body forwards to get something out of his jacket pocket in the squeeze of the seating. "I nearly forgot." The book he laid on the table was *Marx and Engels; Basic Writings on Politics and Philosophy.* "Got to go," he said, "Trish is expecting me. Cor blimey – look at her." A girl in a tight sweater went by.

"That's subtle, Gordon," said Tim. "Greta's impressed." They laughed.

Greta volunteered to go fly posting with Tim. When the pubs closed they waited, locked together in the back of Tim's van while the roads emptied. Their bower was a duffel coat, a tarpaulin, his fishing cagoule, sweaters. "See what I do for you," he murmured. Greta watched the shape his hand made as he straightened her skirt. He smoothed the fabric tenderly, as if she were a doll and he was dressing her. Torch-light shone rose and gold on the trapezium of skin between his thumb and cantilevered finger bones. His fingers moved from the hem of her skirt to her thigh, stroking. Greta heard herself breathing; pressed herself against the corrugations of the metal floor to arch nearer to him. His long hair dipped against her face, hiding the torch light. Coldness and heat mixed themselves up, as instead of dressing, they began making love again. His stomach, chilled by a few minutes of withdrawal, slid against her warm one. Her legs were cold; his were warm through his jeans, which he didn't remove.

The back of the van had a volatile scent, part mineral and part creature, the odour of their bodies, engine oil from the jack and wrench; nicotine from the endless cigarettes. "I look after you," he said, pouring her coffee from his thermos as she dragged overalls on ready for fly posting. His look was quizzical. His looks were signs that she loved to see. He looked at her hopefully. He looked at her enquiringly. He looked at her sardonically.

Fly posting was exciting. "We're breaking the law so be quick. The police hate us," Tim warned. The wind was freezing but she found gloves a nuisance. Tim drew up by a road sign and she got out with the paste and slapped some on. The gel blew back into her face in gummy strings and her hair, escaping from under her black woolly hat, became clumped and sticky. Tim would pass her a poster to unroll against the pasted sign. *Rock Against Racism!* Even in a high wind she could do it. Riskier but more satisfying was getting a couple of A1 sized posters up onto the big motorway signs. *The National Front is a Nazi Front!* Tim kept the engine running and as soon as she had slung the stepladder in and dived in after it he pulled away, while she slammed the door, laughing. It was like being Bonnie and Clyde.

Greta got a letter from her mother. *Dear Greta. Dad not well at the moment. It might be lumbago. He has a pain in his back. Why don't you come and see us?* Greta stared angrily at the sheet of paper. "Well why don't you tell me where Deborah went?" But she sent her Dad a get-well card. Tim had gone south to visit his parents. Nicki had gone with him. Greta tried to carry on writing her new play but it was a struggle. It was based on *Pantagruel and Gargantua* by Rabelais and was about the daughter she imagined Pantagruel having. The daughter's name was Pantagruelle and Pantagruelle had a daughter called Gargantina. Another verse of her poem appeared in the margin…

You told me my sister had gone round the world
or was dead and you said hold your tongue
But why did she go, tell me that, are you blind?
Don't you know? Can't you guess what he's done?

The students said they didn't like Greta's new play so she gave up
writing it and they did *The Threepenny Opera*. Of more concern to
Greta was the fact that Tim Duprès did not seem to realise he had
outgrown his relationship with Nicki. In an effort to dress more
enticingly *(then he'll leave her,)* Greta took to reading *Vogue* again
and studying the fashions. But Tim made no effort to break out of
his deception of Nicki. Far from feeling free to discuss it with him
Greta suspected that if she began to question him he would blame
her for the impasse. In *Vogue* the following Spring, there was a
lustral ivory tulip of a wedding dress. Its veil shone like a sunlit
cloud. Greta cut it out.

By July she had others.

You Don't Have To Be One

The summer vacation dragged. Greta lay on her bed, listlessly writing her diary. *14/8/75. When I was five, Dad used to hold his watch to my ear so I could hear it ticking. I could never hear it at first and I wouldn't let go of his wrist until I did. It was so faint and far away…* Her hand flopped on the page.

At least there was yoga. Greta, folded into the 'Plough' position, could smell varnish as she stared at the pink lycra folds of leotard across her abdomen. The floor's colloidal gloss tackily sucked at her bare shoulders. The voice of the teacher filtered into her consciousness *…and breathe out….* As sometimes happened in yoga class, Greta's thoughts flowed in lucid sequences. And she decided to visit her parents. Drifting this far from them in time, she felt as if they were museum exhibits, not real people. *…Clasp your ankles…* A door slammed elsewhere in the building and a car engine fired up right outside the open window. *…Roll onto your tummies…* The shellac odour ascended. She would go and see them. It would be fine. Tim had disappeared to Greece so there was nothing to keep her in Nottingham. Yes. She would visit her parents.
    But the next day she was busy doing all her washing and the day after that she and Rosalind took Rosalind's little boy to the park. Greta held his hand in the paddling pool, laughing. Next day as she queued in the supermarket with her small basket of groceries it entered Greta's head that Tim might come back from Greece early. She ought to go to the off-license and get some Dubonnet to put in the fridge. The wire of her basket was cold against her thigh. Because it would be awful if he were to come round to see her and she wasn't there. "Do you want your Green Shield stamps?" asked the girl at the till.

September arrived and soon term began again.

Greta's father died.

An autumn sun shone over Leicester. A terrible pain in her back struck Greta as she emerged from the station. It rooted her to the spot. Gasping for breath with the agony of it she inched towards the taxi rank. The taxi stank of cigarette smoke. Her back was rigid. She sat bolt upright swaying with the movement of the car, tensely maintaining her position and unable to lean back in the seat. Her legs felt as if they were coming unhinged from her hips. *Greta your Dad is died.* (The '*is*' had been crossed out). *I didn't expect it. The funeral is on October 2nd at 2.30 pm at the Crematorium. Please come to the house before to go in the car with me.* The letter was signed: *Your Mother, with love.*

Theo Bernstein, her Head of Department, granted her time off to attend the funeral. Compassionate leave. She felt like a sham. The taxi drew up and Greta paid and inched her way out. A funeral car stood waiting. Two little Indian girls in green satin trousers and matching tunics hopped on and off what had once been Furedi's doorstep. In her mother's house a beautifully dressed man who was sitting at the kitchen table, rose to his feet as Greta came into the room. He wore a white shirt, black suit and tie and a black overcoat. His pale skin and black hair made Greta think of Dracula. He was clean-shaven but under the smooth jowls she could see bristles waiting. He shook her hand ceremonially, his fingers warm and soft. "Mr Jensen," he murmured, "my condolences for your loss."

"This is my daughter, Greta," her mother said, as though Greta had just popped out for a breath of air a moment before. "We can go now."

"I sent flowers," said Greta, as they were driven along. Molten pain flowed from her right hip to her ankle. "Have the Furedis moved?"

"Years ago," said her mother. "And the other side is empty." She was staring out of the window. Greta looked at the back of the driver's Brylcreemed head. She didn't know what to say. Silence filled the car. Where was her father? She didn't want to ask. He was in a coffin. It was taken care of. It must be or her mother wouldn't be so calm. "The hearse is bringing the coffin from the funeral parlour," said her mother. There it was, that way that grown-ups knew the thing you wanted answering.

"Right."

"The funeral people bring all the flowers as well. Did you send yours to the funeral parlour?"

"Yes."

"Did you remember a card, Greta?"

"Yes." Greta found her voice coming out as a peculiar whisper.

"They're very good with cards at the funeral parlour. I didn't know what to put and they were a help. I left it to them."

"So did I," said Greta, trying to inject a more normal volume into her voice.

Her mother was wearing a maroon felt hat with a dotted veil of black net. Greta remembered it from a parents' evening at the grammar school. On that occasion the veil had been pushed up into a ludicrous cockade but today it was pulled down and hid her mother's eyes. The crowd waiting for them at the crematorium took Greta's breath away. Her mother could hardly get out of the car. Mr Jensen stepped up to take her arm. Greta saw how her mother's face was collapsing. She had been all right a minute before. Massed sympathy emanated from the crowd. Mr Jensen curved his arm round her mother's bent shoulders. Greta didn't want him to. Her mother was stricken: it was terrible the way her handbag had come out of her hand and landed on the gravel at her feet; unbearable. Ignoring the pain in her back, Greta stepped forward and picked up the bag and said: "I've got your bag Mum, I'll look after it," and she took her mother's other arm. At that her mother let go of Mr Jensen and grabbed onto Greta with both hands. Greta felt a rush of tears. They clung together.

But Jensen had not let go of her mother. He was holding her in a professional grip. It both separated him from them and held them up. Greta blessed him as she concentrated on steering her mother up the path. Without him she wouldn't have known where they were going. The solemn people gave her compassionate looks. Mr Jensen briefed her softly: "These are all his colleagues and friends from the University." She saw reddening eyes. Many held handkerchiefs. The people were falling in behind them. She and her mother led a dignified procession and all these people were silently and clumsily making it happen. Greta and her mother and their supportive minder arrived at the door. And Greta saw the coffin. As she and her mother drew level, the coffin was raised onto the shoulders of the bearers and among them she saw men she knew; Wilfred and Harold; grown old.

Mr Jensen, when he had escorted them to their seats at the front, gave them each a printed sheet with the order of service on it then courteously melted to one side. Greta could not look round. All the people filed in and took their places. She and her mother were right by her father in his beechwood coffin: they were the little heap of flotsam that was his relict and his daughter. And where was Deborah? Her mother was crying. The maroon hat and its black spotted veil gave her a gravitas and a mystery that had not been apparent at the parents' evening all that time ago. Greta kept her mind fixed on giant lathes, the smell of machine oil, propinol, acetic acid: on burners and gas bottles, on the grinder, the apron, the asbestos gloves: on lathes turning, on protective eyewear, on the annealing oven, on glass tubes. Her teeth were clamped shut and only that prevented her from shivering with intense cold. And yet she felt hot.

When they stood for the first hymn her mother's body shook and she clung with both hands to Greta's arm, her hymn sheet crushed. An organ sounded and the congregation sang. *Lead kindly light amid the encircling gloom, Lead thou me on…* Greta drew in the breath to continue. *The night is dark and I am far from home…* Her voice failed her and she drew a ragged breath which sighed out again in scalding tears and each breath she took did the same. She bent her head and alongside her mother wept throughout the hymn.

Back in her flat that night, Greta, a stony feeling in her throat, tried to write in her diary. *Once I asked my dad about the children's home and he said to leave the past alone. He could have been left on a doorstep when he was a baby, or just given away because his family couldn't afford to feed him any more. Maybe he had brothers. Maybe he had sisters…* The pen remained poised above her page. Her thoughts had receded into some strange internal distance where they clustered just out of reach and because of this she had not been able to think clearly ever since boarding the train home. An image of the kind face of the chemistry professor who had taken her to the station was followed by the thought of her mother saying: "*It's a good send-off. Walter would approve,*" to the same professor.

Once she got to the Welford Arms for the wake, as she called it, Greta's mother became regal and efficient. "Take a tray, Greta," she had said. Two stout grey-haired women appeared, handing round sandwiches and sliced pork pie. "You remember Marjorie and Vera don't you?" Greta helped them with trays of bridge rolls and fruitcake and an enormous pot of tea. The lounge bar with its new vinyl seating had been filled with a respectful hum of conversation and the mixed aromas of beer, cigarettes, scotch eggs and ham.

"Is there no-one from church here?" asked Greta, at one point, looking around.

"I stopped going," said her mother. "Brother Isidore died. It wasn't the same." At the thought of all the years that had gone by without her knowing that her mother was no longer the White Rabbit, Greta felt even bleaker. Her back settled into a fiery throbbing. A dreadful headache made her feel sick. Although her hands were icy, she sweated; cold patches soaked the underarms of her jumper. The old idea came into her mind that Deborah was dead, lying buried, alone all these years. Greta had pleaded an early start and a lot of marking still to do and had left.

Now she closed her notebook and clicked off her bedside light. Her mother would be alone too. For hours Greta lay in the darkness, thinking. Her headache dilated nauseously. Inside her cranium she imagined there was an arrangement of wire hooks and rubber bands to hold the moving parts together like in her doll, Pearl. And it was fraying. It was only a matter of time before something gave way and then, the inside of her head would be a mess of hooks and broken bands. And just as Pearl's eyes had opened with an audible click, so hers would tumble backwards into her skull, clattering.

Morning might dispel the sense of defeat that was torturing her. She would never see Deborah again. She had failed. She longed to cry but couldn't. If only morning would come.

A version of normal life resumed. Greta yearned for her relationship with Tim to be out in the open. The secrecy pained her. Sometimes she would hear Tim and Gordon laughing together; planning social engagements in which she wasn't included. Tim and Nicki would be invited round to dinner with Gordon and Trish, or vice versa.

Photogenic Trish, Gordon's girlfriend, with her long black hair and PhD, had an administrative job working for ASLEF. Then Tim took Greta to see *One Flew over The Cuckoo's Nest* and she thought it was a breakthrough until she found out that Nicki had gone home that weekend for her Mum's birthday.

The clocks went back. Mornings were frosty but Greta's mood wasn't lifted by it as she remembered from student days. The splashes of de-icing salt looked like vomit on the tarmac as she trudged between the college buildings clutching a thick cardigan round her. Walking in the snow with Alma flashed into her mind. Alma and Clare no longer wrote. Her habit of not answering was to blame, she knew. By now there were seven wedding dresses sellotaped to her wall.

"**A**re you coming to the battered wives disco? Come on," said Gordon, one day. "You don't have to *be* one!" He smiled, pleased with his joke.

"Give me some posters to put up but I won't go," she said.

"Why?"

"I don't know anyone else going; I'd feel stupid by myself."

"Tim and Nicki are going, myself and Trish; you know us."

Then Tim told her that Nicki wasn't going because Friday was parents' evening at her school. Greta began to plan what to wear. If Nicki wasn't there the chances were good to very good that Tim would come back to her place after. On the night she took special care, blending blusher below her cheekbones and applying mascara. A squirt of *Charlie* and she was ready. The disco was at the Unitarian Chapel Hall down Alfreton Road. The first thing Greta saw was Tim – with Nicki. Greta went to the freezing ladies loo, balanced her bag on the washbasin and took out her cosmetic face wipes. Staring into a flecked mirror, she ritually removed the ignominious make-up with a Quickie. The striplight magnified her bitterness. *Why don't I say something*? The cologne scent and coolness of the circle of moist fabric mocked her. *He'll go on doing this to me because I act as if I'm happy with the way it is. Can't he see I'm pretending*? She peeled off another one. *A Quickie.* That's what she had been hoping to have with Tim. And it rhymed with Nicki. Greta took a deep breath.

Trish, it transpired, had not been able to come after all, so Gordon asked Greta to dance. The hall remained chilly and the air became a sour fug of cigarette smoke and beer fumes. Their dances were constantly interrupted by people who engaged Gordon in procedural discussions about SWP tactics on various issues. Standing by Gordon while he talked politics was unbearably boring. In the background Tim smooched with Nicki, as though asleep on his feet.

"Eleven-thirty, I'd better go," she said, as the lights came up.

"Me too," said Gordon, "thanks for coming." She looked at him. He rubbed his eyes, reaching under his spectacles, which wobbled awry. He gave them a shove into place on his nose. His hair was brown and curled thickly.

"You're tired," she said. Poor hard-working Gordon. The oatmeal polo-neck sweater he wore accentuated the pallor of his face in the fluorescent lighting.

"I'm shattered," he answered, and then smiled, "fancy a coffee? I could do with a comfy armchair. Come back to our place, it isn't far."

"Trish will be cheesed off."

"She won't," assured Gordon, "would that worry you?"

"Yes, I hate the thought of keeping someone up."

"No danger of keeping Trish up," he said, "when Trish is ready for bed she goes to bed. Come on, I won't talk about politics!"

As they stepped into the freezing night, Greta glanced back, hoping to give Tim a wave goodbye. Tim stood alone, outlined in the artificial brightness, staring after them. He didn't return her wave but called: "See you Gordon," and Gordon gave him a friendly thumbs up. In Gordon's yellow 2CV, they headed back to Canning Circus, then into town and up Mansfield Road. After zigzagging through narrow streets they arrived in Colville Mount. Few houses in this dilapidated Victorian terrace were inhabited. *For Sale* signs stuck out of tiny, rubbish-filled front gardens and there were two skips in the road. A tarpaulin, covering a roof, flapped in the wind. "This was all rented at one time," said Gordon, "most of it is derelict. You should buy one – they're dirt cheap and the area's just had a preservation order put on it so they'll be worth a lot soon."

"Can a Marxist say that?" she said, shivering as they went in.

"Come through," he countered.

It was warm inside. Greta removed her scarf. He led her to the kitchen, then filled the kettle and put it on the gas. "Take your jacket off, I'll just nip up and see what Trish is doing; probably reading." He ran upstairs. The floor was stripped wood. The table was painted blue and the chairs orange. Floor to ceiling bookshelves filled an alcove. Greta examined them. As the kettle whistled Gordon came back into the pretty kitchen. "She's falling asleep," he said, "and says please excuse her. She was at a conference in Loughborough all day, didn't get home until eleven. Coffee or tea?" He turned, kettle poised.

"Coffee please."

He ushered her into the front room where the gas-fire cast a glow over chic furnishings. "She left the fire on for me that's why it's so cosy in here." He turned on a table lamp. More books lined the walls.

"What a lot of books."

"More upstairs," said Gordon. They sat in beige, corduroy armchairs. "It's all Trish's doing," he waved at the décor. "I just put up shelves and obey orders."

"It's lovely." Greta relaxed in the soft chair, gratefully sipping the hot coffee. Relief spread through her. They talked about shopping in Habitat, about novels they were reading, about college. For the first time in weeks Greta felt at ease.

"You worked at that casino before you got the job at college, didn't you?" he said. She began telling him about being a croupier. Blackjack intrigued him. The coffee was finished. He fetched a bottle of Bells and two glasses and they sipped whisky as they chatted. "Impossible," said Gordon, "if the bank has to draw on sixteen and the customer doesn't, the probability is in the customer's favour."

"I know," said Greta, "but if I'm the bank, I'll still win."

He got a pack of cards. "Prove it," he challenged.

"But I'll win," she laughed.

"No way," he said, "no-one's that lucky," and handed her the cards.

Kneeling, she dealt them on the floor. "Don't play with real money," she said, "you'd be skint. Use matches."

He fetched matches. Their hilarity increased as the game proceeded and Greta won and won. After losing four boxes of matches, Gordon had to concede that weird though it might be, she was right. "It's witchcraft," he said and then leaned over the cards and seized her by the shoulders. He spun her round and laid her flat on her back on the floor and kissed her. "If you only knew how long I've been wanting to do that," he sighed, propping himself on his elbows above her. He removed his glasses, smiling tenderly.

She laughed. But she wanted to wipe her mouth. *Oh my God,* she thought, *poor Gordon.* She was prepared to forgive it; especially in the light of the whisky, the sleeping girlfriend upstairs and the fact that they were friends. She had to say something to get them past this unexpected faux pas. She took a breath to go on speaking and began to get up. But she couldn't. Her breath whooshed back out again. Gordon was holding her down. She put her hands against his shoulders to push him off. "Get off Gordon," she said. "You can't do this."

"I can do it," he said, "I am doing it." Again he kissed her, forcing his tongue into her mouth, his moustache like animal hair against her face. Desperately squirming she wrenched her head to one side. The moustache went into her neck and she heard him say: "Don't struggle Greta, you must know I think you're gorgeous, you do now anyway."

"Get off!" she was frantic with embarrassment, afraid to speak louder in case Trish caught them. "Gordon; I mean it; I don't fancy you. Get off me, now. You're drunk."

There was a pause and he raised his head. His weight pressed down. Her hands were painfully flexed at the wrist as she pushed against his chest. "I might be a bit drunk," he said, "but you needn't worry, it won't affect me. Don't worry about Trish either. She isn't here. I made that up."

Next day he eventually gave her back her clothes and unlocked the door and let her go. Greta walked to Mansfield Road and caught a bus into the town centre. By then it was late and the Saturday crowds were thinning. She headed for Jessops, the big John Lewis department store.

A girl walking ahead of her wearing tight black trousers caught Greta's attention and she felt forlornly akin to her. It was cold, yet the girl had no coat on and there was evident anxiety in the

144

way her fingertips delicately checked her left buttock. It was as if she was feeling the extent of an injury. On the other buttock a patch glistened. Greta thought of a horse with blood soaking its flank. The girl was bleeding through her clothes. The jet-black fabric of her trousers had a racehorse sheen to it and she was bleeding. Her scared fingertips patted, trying to feel the extent of the damage and then she veered off towards the public toilets in an agitated clatter of high heels.

Greta was aware of an unpleasant odour rising from the skin of her face; the smell of Gordon's constant attempts to kiss her. Gordon's voice was somehow between her and the normal sounds of the street. "Trish is on the pill," was the only thing he'd said when she told him she had no contraception with her. She was trying not to think but thoughts fogged in her head as if her recent experiences were trying to cling to her: Gordon's heavy limbs; the wiry hairs on the pastry-hued skin of his thighs. She could still feel the sensation of friction burns. On her retina an image was branded: the ghost of the pine wardrobe she had stared at to avoid looking at his body.

Although it was only a memory, the grunt of his pushing was still in her ears. Her mind oscillated with repulsive impressions; his knees damp with sweat, the stubble of his chin scraping her skin, a cold fried egg on a plate that met her eye as he dragged her broadside across the bed, turning her onto her stomach to face the floor. (How incongruous, his jolly morning promise of a cooked breakfast. How bizarre, the concern in his voice as he presented her with that plate of food… *you must eat*….) There was a cruel ache in her neck from hours of twisting her head away from him.

What would Camilla do if she was me? Skinny Camilla, with her stash of Moroccan Black and her croaky voice, using men she liked the look of for sex and then discarding them and never, apart from her eternal crush on the lecturer Dr Braithewaite, attaching herself to anybody. This thought gave Greta a shiver of comfort as she entered Jessops, passing the warm jewellery counters. Her sore-looking lips were a shock but as she studied herself in a mirror: denim jacket, cord skirt flaring to mid-calf, boots and long scarf, her reflection was weirdly normal. She bought foaming bath oil scented with carnation. She bought baby powder, baby soap and baby shampoo and imagined herself immersed in hot water; soaking and washing and rinsing.

Back home in Carlton, crossing the road from the bus stop, she saw a startling thing. The low sun, almost setting lit the object obliquely with an intense glare. It was a piece of split sugar-cane, exotically green and vivid. It lay on the tarmac. How strange. She paused to look a little closer. Then she realised it was not sugar cane. It was a cucumber. A cucumber had been run over lengthways and squashed flat. Its dark rind striated its luminous, lime-green flesh. She had just been shopping in Jessops. It was a parallel. Someone might look at her in the same way and say:

"Look at that, a girl in Jessops."

Then say, after a closer look:

"Not a girl, a whore."

On Monday, Gordon took her to one side in the college refectory and said he needed her to confirm that they were going to be a couple before he finished with Trish. She said she had no intention of ever letting him near her again. She refused to look at him. "I'm sorry if I was a bit… passionate the other night," he said. It hurt her to walk. She said nothing. "I need to know if I'm going to finish with Trish," he said. Poor Gordon.

A few days later he forced his way into her flat but she ran out immediately and began to walk up the street. "Go away Gordon or I'll phone the police," she warned him. For days he was back at her door, begging her to re-consider. And finally, through the crack, his mouth bisected by her safety chain, he tried to get her to promise never to tell Trish.

Greta went to see Doctor Staite, who she'd had since student days. "You look well, what can I do for you?" he said. He had a catarrhal snuffle that always accompanied his speech.

"I need an abortion."

"Have you checked that you're pregnant?"

"I am pregnant. I haven't checked. But I must be." She told him the circumstances. Of course he tested her. He came back into the room to tell her what she already instinctively knew, that the test was positive. He glanced at her notes.

"You're Catholic."

"No. I was brought up by a Catholic mother. I'm not Catholic. Have you got a diagram? I want to know what the foetus looks like."

He went and got a booklet, showed her some diagrams. "It looks like this at the moment."

"She," Greta corrected him. Dr Staite made the snuffle and appeared to stifle something he had been about to say.

The fallopian tubes in the diagram were like the horns of a meekly yoked water-buffalo. It was a picture from the past; from school geography, days when all she had to do was learn. It dawned on Greta that she had believed herself to be practising liberation all her adult life and yet she was a slave. Her liberated behaviour had been of benefit to others not herself and those others were men. The enormity of the trick she had been played stunned her. She stared at the tiny bean in the diagram. Here was another slave: one who, if this had not been nineteen seventy five, would have followed her mother's path in a pre-destined, patient walk like a yoked buffalo. "How soon can I have the abortion?" she asked.

"I can book you in tomorrow but I won't," he said, "because I think I'd be acting irresponsibly. I want you to mull it over. I realise that the circumstances of the... er…. are regrettable, very adverse, but I want you to be certain – and the father has a right to know. What does he think?"

"I haven't told him."

"Think about it for a week then come back. If you still want to go ahead, I'll make the arrangements." He looked at her from under his bristling eyebrows.

"I want the week off work then," she said. He wrote out a note for her.

For a week she never left her flat. Winter sunlight shone and the light turned rose-pink through her red curtains. She revelled in the fullness and tenderness of her breasts. The only food she wanted to eat was porridge and toast. All she wanted to drink was hot milk diluted with water. When she collected her pint off the frosty doorstep in the morning she smiled at the day outside, at the pavement, at the lorries parked in the haulage yard opposite. Her locality. She felt full of possessiveness: it was the home of her baby.

Until now she had paid it no attention. She had eaten chips from the chip shop, caught buses from the bus stop, washed clothes at the launderette. She had given schoolboys pennies for their Guys and walked through the cemetery on the hill: but all without thinking. Now she loved it.

In her flat she swooned into a delicate nausea that ebbed and flared, emanating from a place in her body she couldn't pinpoint. Feeling more alive than she had ever imagined you could be, she didn't want to bathe, or wash her hair. Keeping the musk odour of her own, new body was paramount. It grew more familiar and comforting as the week progressed. She felt like a mother with a baby. Her daughter. She was certain. She knew it was a girl.

On the Friday morning, Greta woke to see rain falling in a heavy shower on the bedroom skylight. It looked as if the pane of glass was melting. The water rippled down in syrupy layers. She imagined the glass reverting to its liquid state; slipping away; a delicate avalanche of transparency. Greta cradled her baby in the curve of her womb while time ticked towards the moment when they would be separated.

She went back to Dr Staite and confirmed her decision. He handed her an appointment slip for the hospital abortion clinic at two o'clock the following Monday. She took it as if it was a holy wafer. Silently she blessed her doctor, his sausage fingers, his warthog eyebrows, his reddened face. She blessed his prescience in making her the appointment; he had granted her a week with her daughter. He was helping to free her from enslavement. He was freeing her daughter also. He was not on Gordon's side. He was on her side. Then she went away to spend her final weekend with her baby.

Monday was December the seventh. Greta went by taxi to the hospital. She stood alone in the windy car park on the hilltop. She looked around her seeing no people just winter grass alongside the grey tarmac and a line of naked almond trees with a few yellow leaves scattered beneath them.

As she lay on a high couch in the dark green tank of the anteroom she curled over on her side and began to savour the feeling of being there to its fullest extent. *Just for now, we are both here, you and*

148

me, she thought, for now, which might as well be all the time there is, we are together; like we were in our bedsit, like we were just now in the car park. Her wrists loosened, her fingers uncurled and her breathing became deep and refreshing. She felt warmth spreading into her cold feet and her whole body sank against the hard green vinyl. The cellular, cotton blanket felt deliciously comforting. She thought about the nurses. She was using a detached outer segment of her brain, which allowed her, simultaneously, to follow a line of thought and to continue doing the yoga breathing. The red-haired nurse had given her water; the older one had taken some blood. She began to half-doze, but she was alert to noises and movements, and when the nurse came back to look at her she opened her eyes and smiled.

"Are you doing yoga?" the nurse whispered.

"Yes," she allowed the word to feather out along with the air she was exhaling.

"Good girl, carry on. We're just waiting for the doctor to arrive." The nurse lifted her wrist, took her pulse.

They came to fetch her into the next room. Like the last one it was tall and tiled. Lamps cast pools of light. They helped her onto the central bed, which was draped in white. The nurse rested a cool palm on her forehead and said: "Try to carry on with your breathing." Greta tried, feeling a raggedness breaking in. "Doctor is just going to inject a local anaesthetic into the neck of the womb – it may hurt a little but it will stop in a second as the anaesthetic takes effect. You won't feel a thing after that."

But there came a moment, during the procedure which followed, when Greta felt a groan begin from deep inside her and the nurse at her head said: "do you want me to hold your hand?"

"Yes." It was a sob. She held out her hand. The nurse clasped it strongly.

And the quiet doctor, perched on the stool at his end, said: "Nearly done, nearly done," in a low voice.

Tears poured into her ears.

Afterwards, as arranged, the nurse phoned Rosalind who came striding in through the swing doors, listening as the nurse explained something. Greta was in a wheelchair, a blanket over her legs, letting everything wash over her. Rosalind had not long passed her driving test and as they drove towards Basford in an old Morris Minor Greta smiled and nodded her head in slow motion every time Rosalind asked if she was OK.

A derelict factory with leafless buddleia sprouting from its walls towered next to the side street where Rosalind lived. Once helped out, Greta stood by the side of the car and couldn't move. She leaned on the bonnet and said, "I'll get going in a minute," to reassure Rosalind. Her bones felt marrowless. Rosalind darted inside and fetched her husband. Greta mustn't get cold. Should he carry her? "No," insisted Greta, "I'd like to stare at the factory for a while."

An inch at a time she set off across the pavement to the front door. She leaned there for five minutes before the strength arrived to lift her feet up the step. Once inside with the door closed, she sat on the floor in the hall. Rosalind and her husband were talking in the kitchen, their voices urgent and muffled. Mark, Rosalind's little boy, appeared, staring at her expectantly. He brought her a puzzle and did it for her, fitting vehicle-shaped pieces into matching recesses; a fire engine, an ambulance, a bulldozer and a motor bike. "Do vis," he said, belting up the narrow hall on all fours.

So she crawled into the living room and dragged herself into the armchair by the fire. Rosalind came in, smiling, and asked if she was ready for a cup of tea. Greta nodded and stared at the fluctuating heat of the coals. The tea, with sugar in it, tasted like nectar. She knew she was smiling too much but she couldn't help it. Rosalind smiled back but tears ran down her face. "It's OK," said Greta, in weird, slow motion speech.

"I know. I'm making you egg and chips but don't have it if you don't want it. I've sent Patrick down to the corner shop for some vinegar."

The egg and chips were like the ambrosia of the gods. Greta had more tea. She felt as if this was the first meal of her life; as if she had been condemned then reprieved and granted freedom. A kitten appeared from time to time pouncing like a shadow from around the backs of the chair legs. "I like your kitten," said Greta to the child. He picked up the kitten and put it on Greta's lap. Its paws; when she took one between finger and thumb, were so delicate, that she could almost flatten them. It was as if any bone or sinew inside the fur was liquid, running in gossamer capillaries which fluidly separated and rejoined, according to where she pressed her fingers. The kitten gazed at her, its eyes wide open.

Mr Bernstein steepled his fingers. His brown eyes in the smooth tan of his face, regarded her with a look that was impartial. It was like the grip of the nurse's hand in the abortion clinic. "I will speak to the Principal on your behalf and I will do my best for you but I have to warn you that he may not like it," he said.

"OK." The clock on the wall said ten-thirty. Outside it was lashing with rain.

"You understand me, Greta, I'm warning you of the consequences in relation to future employment opportunities. You need to have all these facts clear so you can be sure you're making the right decision." The rain teemed against the huge windows. The office was like a third-floor aquarium.

"I know," she said.

In profile he looked like Rudolph Nureyev. Greta had always liked Theo Bernstein. He was the perfect boss. He had supported all the teaching projects she had wanted to pursue, he had backed her and Tim when they proposed merging some of their groups and team-teaching them. He had fostered creativity. He was the only person that she had told about Gordon. He was the only person apart from Rosalind that she had told about the abortion. He had let her do everything her way. "The Principal is entitled to refuse you a reference if you don't work out a notice period."

"OK," she said. The clock moved on to ten thirty-one. Ten minutes before, she had come into his office and said: *I'm sorry Theo but I resign. I want to leave right now.* And ten minutes before that she had been happy. It was the last day of term. The Christmas tree glittered in the refectory. Tim met her for coffee. She had decided to tell him everything; certain that once he knew, he would stand by her at last. Her mouth shook. It could hardly form words. It tried to twist into a smile. The words *Gordon raped me*, when she finally said them produced a reaction she could never have imagined. Tim was jolted. His head made a movement like a recoil. It was as if he was a handgun that had just been fired. His fair hair gleamed about his bony face. His eyes glittered at her, ocean blue.

But then he said what he said. "Are you sure?" And smiled. He had put his head on one side. He had made a quizzical look. *Are you sure?* She had endured one whole night and most of a day being repeatedly raped and he was asking her if she was sure. And then it began to dawn on her. Tim *already knew*. An image flashed before her: Tim outlined in white light and Gordon's thumbs-up sign. It was so obvious: Gordon and Tim, Tim and Gordon: the two comrades.

And now Theo Bernstein rested his steepled fingers against his pursed lips as if demonstrating a kiss. "What about your work here – your career?" he said. Even as he spoke, her work ceased to count. It mattered; it mattered a lot to her. She loved her students. It just didn't count.

"I'm sure," she said. The wind fired volley after volley of rain against the windows.

"Do you want me to explain the full circumstances to the Principal?"

"If you think it best." Their voices had to be raised over the noise of the storm outside and the drumming of the torrent on the glass.

He picked up the phone and dialled. His Tartar eyelids lowered until they half hid his eyes. He was speaking to the Principal; an exchange that took seconds. Theo Bernstein rose. "Lucky," he said, "the Principal is free now. Would you like to sit here and wait for me?"

"Yes please." *Strike off my chains.* The cataract against the aquarium walls was a tempest of heartbeats that stunned her into muteness. As she waited, the thought came to her that she had never really been a lecturer. She had been a mouse; a Rabelaisian cartoon mouse and it was for that quality she had been selected at her interview. And they were cats. Big cats. And she had been put into the post so that they, in the end, would have something to play with. The dark wood lay all around; her friends were far behind. Now she must set out again; alone.

When he came back, Theo was smiling and she was free. "What do you want me to tell your colleagues?" he asked her.

"Tell them I was offered a job in London."

"You'll need an umbrella," he said, cocking an eye at the deluge.

"I hate umbrellas," said Greta. The flash of her fury showed in his startled face, and he wished her luck.

Part 4. Trick Errand – 1975

She Thought I was Her Sister

Camilla. That's where she went; straight to Camilla, saying only
that she had chucked in her job because she needed a change.
Camilla looked different, long hair like one of Charlie's Angels;
done in layered waves. A lean white shirt; top three buttons undone;
revealed a gold medallion. "You look awful, Greta," she said. Greta
put down her cases, took in the long pointed collar, the frilled cuffs;
the olive-green princess line tunic and matching flared trousers.

"I like your outfit," she replied, intensely grateful to have
arrived.

"You could go back to being a croupier," suggested Camilla once
Greta was installed and their food had been delivered. "It's a
transferable skill," she said, "and there are loads of casinos." Greta
agreed and speared a water chestnut on her fork, conscious of
Camilla's shrewd eyes on her uneaten takeaway. She put the morsel
in her mouth. Camilla pushed off her shoes and curled her long legs
under her. There was only a leather couch to relax on these days.
Costly hardbacks were piled on a glass and chrome coffee table.
Beyond the furthest window a black ash dining table with six chairs
stood isolated on the shining floorboards as if on a stage. Greta,
cross-legged on a sheepskin rug in front of the fire missed the
scruffy Indian cushions and squashy sofas she remembered from
before and was glad of the cinders and ash that messed the hearth up.
Slivers of bark made a homely litter around the log basket. "I get the
impression," said Camilla, "that just now you don't want anything

154

with too much responsibility." She stared hard at Greta through her cigarette smoke. "You're like a little refugee with your two suitcases," she sighed, "that's everything isn't it?" she nodded towards the cases by the wall, "that's your worldly goods, I bet."

"Yes."

"You look as if you need a rest actually," Camilla said. "Perhaps you should take a couple of months off – give yourself a chance to see things in perspective."

And Greta almost blurted: "*It's because I was raped. I've had an abortion.*" Tears heated the rims of her eyes. "Yes, I think I will," she managed to say, then: "my Dad died in September – cancer of the pancreas." Oh to explain the agonized paralysis in her throat; *lacrimae Jesu. Lacrimae sanctus.* But she let no tears fall.

"Shit, that's rough," Camilla uncoiled and pushed the Marlboros towards her. "I'll make you a coffee." On her way past, she patted Greta on the shoulder; three awkward impacts. "Don't worry," she said gruffly.

Camilla's whole flat was different; the spare room now an office; filing cabinets and two desks facing each other. There were Habitat table lamps, an electric typewriter, two telephones and a telephone answering machine. Camilla taught Greta how to re-route calls to the States. "What do you actually do Camilla?"

"I work for a casting company," she replied. "You know, organising auditions and try-outs. Films mostly but sometimes for stage productions too. We have an office in Soho but headquarters is in Manhattan. I'll be going there in January – for maybe a year or two." Indeed, Camilla was so busy these days that her only concession to Christmas was to take Greta to an intensely fashionable party at a Hampstead restaurant where all the surfaces were brown or gold and the festive decorations consisted of oranges and bay leaves. After two glasses of an admittedly delicious mulled wine Greta felt ill and had to get a taxi back to the flat.

A fortnight into the new year, when Camilla went to the States; she offered Greta the role of custodian of the flat in lieu of rent. "Just field any stray phone calls, pay the bills whenever they arrive and forward the mail," she said.

So much space and nothing to do intimidated Greta after Camilla's departure. In its new incarnation, the lounge, with floor to ceiling black velvet curtains and bare floorboards reminded her of a theatre. In the echoing silence she did her yoga exercises and yearned to see Clare and Alma. "*How are you!*" they would chorus. And she wouldn't be able to say. Imaginary conversations with them unscrolled in her head. *You look sad Greta, and pale. What's wrong? I was raped and it made me pregnant and I aborted the baby. Oh my God Greta, that's terrible. How awful. Did they catch the man who did it? He was a good friend of mine from work. My God – why did he do such a thing?*

Exactly. Why did he? And the image of herself in that strappy vest and peasant print skirt strutting towards the bar in sexy shoes accused her. Yes, she had been swaying her hips. Yes, she had been drinking vodka. And on many occasions wearing tight jeans and drinking beer in the pub with them; laughing and joking. Knowingly seductive. But for Tim; not Gordon.

She had made Gordon mad about her.

Everything was her fault.

Deep-breathing, she concentrated fierce efforts onto the yoga and forced herself into difficult positions, straining her body to its limits to banish the thought of Clare and Alma's dismay as they saw at last what she was actually like.

Her half-written play, *Gargantina and Pantagruelle* turned up among the papers in her tax folder when she unpacked her second suitcase. Unexpectedly comforted, she started working on it again. But being alone in the flat was dismal and she went to a Soho casino; only an interview, she reasoned; she didn't have to take the job. She pushed through the revolving door and came face to face with Deborah. That settled it. She no longer took pride in her luck with the cards. It was just a job; the attraction was the dark-haired girl who looked like Deborah. The girl; her name was Julie; liked recalling Greta's utter shock. "She thought I was her sister," she'd laugh, little white teeth flashing then hidden as she painted her rosebud lips with Chanel lip gloss: "she had her mouth open…" more lip gloss, and then: "…like this:" and a cute demonstration. Deborah, born in nineteen forty-one, would be thirty-five. Julie, in her wide-leg trousers and big platform shoes, was nineteen. It was like looking at a Deborah who couldn't possibly exist. Greta didn't know how to position herself between these images but found Julie's resemblance to Deborah comforting now that she was used to it. One night she dreamed she saw Deborah and their mother walking away in the windswept car park of the abortion hospital. Deborah's full skirt billowed as if at any minute she might be lifted into the air.

Pantagruelle. Pantagruelle. The casino rest room mirror was surrounded by light bulbs. Greta's eyelids glittered with amethyst eye shadow. The question was, what would Pantagruelle say when her daughter Gargantina, returning from an assignation with her boyfriend, announced that she was leaving? Greta retrieved the notebook from her locker and settled down with a mug of coffee to do twenty minutes writing.

Living rent-free allowed her to save money. She worked out a budget. In February she sent for accommodation brochures and a venue list from the Edinburgh Fringe Office then booked a one and a half hour performance slot at Old St Pauls, a church hall opposite the back entrance to Waverley Station.

    The Fringe registration forms were spread out on the desk. The radio played softly. The sound of it usually soothed her but filling in the forms made her sick with excitement. Afraid to put pen to paper but also certain that she was going to do it anyway she poured herself wine. Camilla's wineglasses were huge. The wine freed her from her anxiety as she began to fill in the boxes. She would create a world that would fit on a stage where all was calm emptiness and waiting space. Maybe if she paid them her former students would come and be in her play. *Name of Company*: she drank wine and considered. To call a space *the stage*, to call the way you arranged it *designing the set*, to light it, to create the action: this, Greta thought, felt safe. Big swallow of chilled white. *Name of Company*: leave that box. *Name of Contact*: Greta Buchanan. *Title of Show*: 'Gargantina and Pantagruelle'.

A card from her mother arrived; bronze chrysanthemums; gilt edging. *I bought a niche in the Garden of Remembrance,* it said, *for the urn with Dad's ashes. Somewhere to take flowers even if not a grave but he said cremation. I hope London suits you. Please keep in touch. Much love, Mum.* The subdued mourning sentiment hinted at by the chrysanthemums was soon covered up by a newspaper; by a packet of Kleenex; by mugs of tea; by her paperback copy of *Gargantua and Pantagruel*; by junk mail, a Fry's Peppermimt Cream, her copy of the Edinburgh Fringe programme, a props list, a telephone directory and by the re-written drafts of her script which she spent all her spare time on.

Come June she was wound up tight with excitement and fear.

The letter was typed on college headed notepaper. She unfolded and re-read it for the umpteenth time. *June 14th 1976. Dear Miss Buchanan, Thank you so much for this opportunity. I will be down for the auditions next Monday as required. I expect some of the others will come. I have told those as I've seen. Thanks for thinking of us, it will make a change from this dead-end job. Yours sincerely, Cameron Valentine.*

Oh God. Breath faltered in her windpipe and she was sweating with nerves. What if they turned her down? Don't think about it. Camilla's office was impressive and businesslike. The script was ready, there were spare copies (*I expect some of the others will come*): Christ it was nearly time.

The lounge furniture, couch excepted, was piled into her bedroom and she sidled by to fetch her cigarettes. Heading back into the office she heard the buzzer and swerving to the door she spoke into the grill, her gullet compressing. "Yes?"

"It's Cameron Valentine, I've got an audition with Miss Buchanan."

Biting off the impulse to shriek a welcome and rush to meet him; she pressed the door catch without saying anything. So many minutes went by that she began to think he had chickened out. Then the doorbell rang. "Cameron – And Parminder as well! It's great to see you. Come to the office."

Their gazes took in the Aubrey Beardsley posters on the walls. They followed her like lambs: no hint of their college bravado. Their Nottingham punk personas were abashed. They sat side by side in their chairs and their heads swivelled and their eyes rolled. "This is posh, Miss," said Parminder. He wore a tartan scarf tied round one wrist; trouser bottoms folded to reveal big Doc Martens.

"It's nice isn't it," she agreed, smiling. They listened as she outlined the project. Like good pupils, they nodded and sniffed and hunched themselves up and accepted the coffee she gave them. They made use of the little pre-packs of milk she had nicked from work and tore open sachet after sachet of sugar.

"Is this a stirrer Miss?" Asked Parminder humbly; picking up her glass twig off the desk.

"No Parminder, it's a keepsake. Have a teaspoon. Any questions?"

"Yes Miss, can we live here when it's time for rehearsals?"

"Certainly."

"Cameron only got your letter because he works at the college now," Parminder said.

"Really Cameron? What doing?"

"Reprographics office," he said, "it's dead boring. Parminder's unemployed."

"No I'm not! I'm a free-lance DJ," countered Parminder, huffily. Then: "What will you pay us, Miss?" He changed his position noisily.

Cameron shoved him in the ribs and looked annoyed.

"Parminder don't call me Miss any more," she said, "I'm not a lecturer now."

"Shall we call you, 'Miss Buchanan'?" he asked.

"No. Call me Greta." She stood up. "Let's do the audition. Cameron first." He bounced to his feet.

The couch stood against one wall of the lounge. "This is our rehearsal room," she said. Light washed through the windows, chequering the floor.

"Wow," said Cameron. He was heartbreakingly ill at ease. Her proud Nottingham rooster had transplanted himself because she had offered him a chance at what he thought was stardom. She could hardly bear to see how shaky he had become.

"Relax; shake yourself out. Do you still play the recorder?"

"Yes."

"We could work that in – come on, let's limber up." She went through stretches and deep breathing with him. "See? It's just the same as college."

He was loosening up. He walked the floor, thin and leggy. This was better. He walked faster, round and round. Then he spun towards her. His Rasta curls created electric dusk in a shaft of sun as he launched into Lucky's long rant from *Waiting For Godot*, word perfect and full of rhythm.

Parminder, beautiful as ever with his chocolate skin and blue-black hair, did his Polyphemus speech from their college production. It was just as dire now as it had been then. But Parminder, as he had been then, was just as serenely convinced that it was fine.

"You'll be great, I'll see you next month for rehearsals," she said cheerfully, showing them out. The wages she had promised were below the Equity minimum and they didn't mind but she felt like the wicked stepmother who sends Hansel and Gretel into the dark wood on a trick errand.

"Greta!" Cameron leapt back up the stairs, "What's the company called?"

"Trick Errand Theatre Company," she said.

The casino were philosophical when she explained what she was doing and said she could come back to work again when the show was over. She had glossy leaflets done. Cameron and Parminder turned up in July. Britain sweltered. They rehearsed barefoot in the heatwave, Cameron and Parminder without shirts, Greta in a bikini top and shorts. The boys slept on the rehearsal room floor. All the windows and doors stood open to catch any breath of air. "I am the director of Trick Errand Theatre Company," she told herself as she walked up Great Titchfield Street with their suppers of fish and chips, "I am the producer of the play *Gargantina and Pantagruelle*."

The Scotsman, August 12 1976.
RABELAIS COMES TO TOWN
'Gargantina and Pantagruelle' at Old St Pauls.
Though this Rabelaisian love tale resembles a cross between traditional storytelling and a circus, it taps into universal emotions

160

*exploring mother/daughter relationships. As in Rabelais's original
text, the characters are giants. Here, two black actors play all the
parts, helped by a cast of hand puppets. These are made before our
eyes, breaking into speech as soon as they are assembled so that you
have the impression that socks and potatoes are erupting into life. A
mop has a starring role as the troubadour who seduces Gargantina
and in one erotically charged moment Cameron Valentine
(Gargantina) and the mop, perform a sensational tango.*

*Parminder Singh plays Gargantina's mother, Pantagruelle,
as a housewife of few words. Singh is monumental and his impassive
countenance contrasts with Valentine's frenetic outbursts. He is so
deadpan that a blink of the eyes is a major facial expression and his
occasional lines have great appeal. "Fark what?" he says on being
told that Gargantina's troubadour is proposing to travel to "Far
Cathay."But this is more than a transvestite caper. Someone has
done their homework; hats off to both writer and director. The
Rabelaisian themes are coherent and there are moments of startling
power. Glycerine tears roll down Pantagruelle's face as she realises
that her daughter has left home forever. As the lights fade, she
begins to sweep the floor. From far away we hear the recorder
playing. It fades into the distance. Blackout. Knockout.*

"Greta there's a man looking for the producer, I said talk to you but
I didn't let on you were in here." Cameron put three glasses of rum
and Coke down on the table.

Greta lowered the newspaper. "Very wise." They were in the
Traverse bar.

"Well we've got to protect you," he was pleased.

The routine was: sleep late, fetch rolls from the bakery (they
took it in turns), make breakfast, go leafleting in the Royal Mile,
have lunch, do the show, go and have food at the flat, get ready, hit
the town. They had taken to ending up at the Traverse, partly
because it was the place to be and partly because it was near their
flat. "Which one is he?" She asked. Cameron indicated a tall bulky
man, leaning against the wall at the far end of the bar. His greying
brown hair was tied in a ponytail and he was talking to a well-
dressed woman and her companion. "He looks interesting," said
Greta, "I'll go and see what he wants."

161

"He's too old for you Miss," Parminder was laughing. She had given up correcting him; to Parminder, she would always be "Miss".

"Excuse me." Up close the man's pony-tail was immaculate and a gold stud gleamed in his left earlobe. He gave no sign he had heard her. She felt snubbed. "Excuse me," she said again and this time tapped him on the arm. He recoiled with a startled look. "I'm sorry," Greta said, "I didn't mean to interrupt but did you want to speak to the producer of *Gargantina and Pantagruelle?*"

"Yes I did. Forgive me, I'm deaf in that ear, I didn't hear you. And you are?" He had the kind of melodious voice you hear on the radio, reading poetry.

"I'm Greta Buchanan, the director."

"Would you excuse us," he said to his companions, "Darling," this to the woman, "I'll see you at the art gallery tomorrow – this is someone I have to meet," and he kissed the woman, shook hands with the man, took Greta's arm and led her to a table. "Could you give us a moment," he said to a young man with red hair and an enormous bunch of keys on his belt. The youth and a girl with him rose from the table obligingly. "It's all right; they're in one of my companies. Let me introduce myself. Matthew Tarry." He held out his hand and she shook it. "Sit down," he urged. "I'm a producer, Greta, and I concentrate on small scale touring productions. I love your show. Did you find that your review in *The Scotsman* helped?"

Greta had seven copies of the review clipped from discarded papers she'd picked up that day. "Oh yes," she blurted. She wanted to leap up and scream in triumph; to stamp her feet and clap her hands; to open her mouth and keep it open so the elation could gush out. She had no idea what to do with such feelings and drank the rest of her rum and Coke.

"Let me get you another." He was up and getting served straightaway. How glad she was that she had painted her nails. How lucky that she had washed her hair and put on the new dress. Greta had heard of Matthew Tarry. He had a sell-out show at The Assembly Rooms and another at The Traverse, which had won a Fringe First. The Guardian had interviewed him the week before. Her prized review in *The Scotsman* had indeed boosted their ticket sales but this was much, much better. He was back like a magician with her drink. "I hope you wanted ice and lemon."

"Thank you."

"So you are the director." He studied her in a shrewd yet kindly way. "Who wrote it?"

"I did. And actually I'm the producer as well."

"Good Lord. Forgive the impertinence but are you a student?"

"No. I'm a croupier. I'm twenty-six."

"You should be very proud. Is this your first?" It felt as if they were talking about a child. She was weak with gratitude and felt a surge of love; for Edinburgh, for the sweet, garlic-flavoured, smoky air of the bar, for Parminder and Cameron and for this big, seal-shaped man with his grey velvet jacket and long hair. She wanted to cast herself into his arms and say *let me stop now, just let me rest here.*

Permanent Darkness

For *Gargantina and Pantagruelle* Matthew Tarry undertook to produce a tour of British Arts Centres followed by a year of appearances at festivals in Singapore, Toronto, Lyons, Milan and Frankfurt. From the profits, should there be any, Greta was to have a percentage as the writer, a percentage as the original director and a percentage as the original producer. Cameron and Parminder got their Equity cards and two years' guaranteed work. For Matthew, Greta undertook to write a one-man show for the following year's Fringe which he would direct and which they would produce jointly. "Who is the character going to be?" she asked.

"Rabelais," said Matthew, "the man himself. But Greta," he warned, "don't give up the day job."

That Christmas; curled up in a nest of blankets on the sofa, she wore fingerless woollen gloves and all her sweaters to write her cards. A letter to Camilla, asking how to order logs for the fire had received no reply. The news about her deal with Matthew Tarry was so good she sent Christmas cards to Clare and Alma, along with a copy of her *Scotsman* review. She put a copy of the review in her mother's card also. What would her mother make of it?

Clare sent a card by return of post along with a photo of herself, toddler astride her hip and Ray beside her, his hands resting on the shoulders of a dark haired little girl. The family smiled out. A card from Alma arrived three weeks after Christmas. It was a budget card from a very cheap box. Greta was surprised. There was no photo but Alma said she had a two-year-old son called Ben. *I'd love to see your play about Rabelais but we can't get up to Edinburgh. Let me know if it tours this way. Have a happy 1977! Stay in touch, love Alma.*

The year went quickly. *Rabelais The Rabble Rouser* was fun to write. Matthew cast an actor friend of his as Rabelais and all Greta had to do was pay half the production costs. In August it went up to the Fringe and her success repeated itself. Matthew wanted another play. Greta began to think. He sent her postcard reproductions of Renaissance art from the various European cities he happened to be in. *Any news on the new play?*

But no subject presented itself.

Nights at the casino took a toll. She felt as if she could no longer stand daylight. Her skin craved the wrap of sheets and blankets. Slipping into the sunless canyon of Great Titchfield Street by taxi at five in the morning in her make-up and sequinned dresses, a butterfly going back into its cocoon, she emerged from the bathroom like a pale grub and flopped into bed.

"We are the knights who say Ni…" So Steve; the resident mimic and Monty Python fan; would say in his laconic Liverpudlian accent; leading the shift into the casino, and "Ni more bets…" solemnly, to make his chief crack up. Greta liked him. Steve. He swaggered in through the revolving door, his gaucho moustache jaunty above the pointed lapels of his jacket. A lilac grandad tee shirt hugged his narrow ribcage and he had a Ford Capri. Greta liked his belted trousers, tight over his matador's backside. Attracted by his humour, his Torremolinos tan and lop-sided smile she shared breaks with him; intrigued to find he was a politics graduate from UEA, impressed that on his breaks he read Zola and Dostoevsky, and amused by the fact that even though he was the casino Space Invaders champion – hunched over the machine in the foyer after every shift – he approved of *The Female Eunuch*. In the space of a month on various days off, they went to Regents Park Zoo, to Madame Tussauds, to The Tate Gallery, and on a boat ride up the Thames.

After a meal on their fifth date he put his arm round her as they left the restaurant and stroked her hair as he opened the car door for her. Reclining the passenger seat to its fullest extent she lay compliant and content listening to his Billy Joel albums on the 8-track stereo that was his pride and joy. But in his flat, when he kissed her, it felt something like two slugs connecting softly with her mouth and then, to her horror, a thing like a piece of raw liver gliding between her lips. In an agony of embarrassment she hid her revulsion and they progressed to the bedroom. He was considerate and courteous but her dryness disconcerted him so much that he suggested that he call her a taxi. "Perhaps we should just be mates," he said with a comradely smile, patting her on the back as she left. That feeling of slugs haunted her. His good looks and sweet character did not deserve her revulsion.

Something had happened to her.

And then the new play crept forward to be written.

Her new play was not fun. The subject of it repelled her.

The phone woke her one winter afternoon, and she rolled to the other side of Camilla's massive bed to answer it. "Hello?"

"Have I woken you, Sweetie? It's Matthew."

"Matthew – I should have been awake…" a glance at the clock, "… an hour ago. Hang on a second." She padded along the hallway and clicked on the central heating. This year, when the frosts came, a gas-man, summoned in desperation, had explained it all to her. "Sorry, Matthew," she said, scuttling back to the warmth of the bedcovers and seizing the receiver again.

"Are you free on Thursday evenings Greta?"

"No, why?" There was a clunking as the boiler started up.

"There's a project at The Royal Court to encourage young playwrights. My friend there wants to know if I can nominate anyone. I'd like to suggest you." The clunking gave way to loud gurgling in the pipes. "Greta?"

"I'm thinking," said Greta.

"Might you like it?" Matthew's voice was persuasive. An image of his warm velvet jacket and wise forehead formed in her mind. "There'll be wonderful writers giving workshops. Wouldn't you be interested?"

"Oh… I probably would…"

"But?"

"I'll mull it over… see if I could swap my night off. Thank you for thinking of me, Matthew."

Weeks went by. Matthew reminded her about the workshops on a postcard from Germany. *And P.S.* it said, *I've found you in the Renaissance. Look at the central figure. That's you, with your pensive little face.* Greta was huddled at the table in Camilla's uncurtained kitchen with the radio for company. She turned the card over. *Sistine Madonna*, by Rafael. The Madonna carried a huge baby and he too had a pensive expression. Greta stared at the baby. Snow drifted down outside the window. Only its mothy movements were visible through the black surface in which her reflection waited for her to act. Her cornflakes had gone soggy. She dwelt in a permanent darkness eating breakfast at five as the winter night fell. What might the workshops be like? But she couldn't go. No-one at the casino wanted to swap Thursday night off anyway.

1978 dawned and at the end of January Camilla wrote saying she would be home soon.

"You all right?" Julie; still the image of Deborah; gazed fondly at Greta. Sleety rain lashed the window and slicked the road. Afternoon darkness pasted the sky shut like an eyelid. Greta took out a tissue and blew her nose. That winter she had suffered cold after cold. To pass time before work she and Julie were drinking hot chocolate in a Soho café, their steam clouding the plate glass beside them.

"I'm failing to write a play," she said, balling up the tissue and stuffing it in her pocket.

"What's it about?"

"Female sexuality."

"You're too serious Greta, come out with Zoë and me one night." Zoë; an ex air-hostess; was Julie's best friend and the fastest croupier in the casino.

"Oh yeah! Put her back up." Zoë was jealous of Greta and called her, 'Professor'.

"She likes you, Greta," said Julie.

"Oh I know, I was just joking."

Julie; Estée Lauder perfume wafting like thurified incense from her poppy sleeves of gathered silk, spooned froth off her chocolate.

In March, coinciding with Greta's birthday, a royalty cheque arrived from Matthew. Greta, in Camilla's office opening letters in her dressing gown, put it on the desk by the card from her mother. Two pigeons on the window ledge outside made murmuring sounds. Greta switched on the radio and picked up the cheque again.

Matthew. He would incline his good ear towards her; she could visualise his bulk and his benign eyes. *How's it going, Greta?* She missed his harmonious baritone. The workshops at The Royal Court were probably over by now. Was he disappointed in her? The mournfulness of the song on the radio and the cooing of the pigeons suggested that yes, he was. In a fluster she rang his office. No answer. On the radio the klaxon outburst of the saxophone solo wrung her heart and she imagined Deborah trudging along a street by herself. *…it's just coming up to five o clock and that was Gerry Rafferty with Baker Street taking us up to the News headlines…*

At work, glueing her false eyelashes, Greta told Julie it was her birthday.

"Great!" said Julie, "come for a drink after work."

"Not too posh to get tanked-up with us are you, Professor?" Zoë arched round at the mirror to get a rear view. Her backside shone like a satin Comice pear in the tight dress.

"No." Greta slashed the zip of her cosmetics bag shut as if Zoë was caught in its teeth.

"Come to our place, Greta," Julie coaxed.

"OK. Thanks."

"Bingo," exclaimed Zoë, adjusting the drape of her satin jacket.

It was a mistake. Greta felt it as soon as they arrived at the small terraced house that Julie and Zoë shared. Plagued by the knowing looks they cast at her from time to time she ravenously ate the bacon they cooked. Julie poured Cinzano and Zoë laughed as ice-cubes spurted from the tongs and landed on the carpet. The other two moved on to Tequila Sunrise, but Greta stuck with Cinzano, watering their cheeseplant with it to fool them she was drinking. Night gave way to sombre morning; rain against the windows. No-one opened the curtains. Julie, too drunk to change the music on the cassette recorder, switched on the radio as their talk wrangled its way closer to Greta's personal life.

"Sexuality?" said Zoë, "Why write a play about that?" She dragged on her cigarette, cheeks hollowed and eyes like greeny-blue marbles, opened wide.

"Shut up Zoë," Julie, back from the phone in the hallway, fumbled to tune the radio to another station.

"Yeah," said Zoë, "but why? Women's lib?"

"I just said I thought I should try."

"But why would you want to? Sex is sex." Zoë slurred the words.

"I don't think it's that simple," said Greta.

"Sex is sex," Zoë laughed scornfully, "you get turned on – wham! Bloody simple," she said.

"Not to me," Greta insisted.

"There must be something you're not telling us then," slurred Zoë, ominously.

"You're good at writing Greta, that's what matters." Julie poked stockinged feet at her silver shoes. "Let's show her our clothes while we wait for the Chinkie to come…"

How Greta wished she had not agreed to the Chinese takeaway. But the order had been phoned in; she was trapped.

"… bring the drink, Zoë."

Greta stood up, glass in hand. Zoë snatched the Dubonnet out of the ice bucket then passed the bucket to Greta, her agate eyes challenging. The tongs clanked among the melting ice-cubes. Greta registered the sound of the radio simultaneously as if her ears had popped. … *coming up to the Midday News… first, The Stranglers…*

"Come on," Zoë thrust big belligerent lips close to Greta then swooped after Julie. They climbed the narrow stairs. The bacon odour gave way to perfume.

"What's that perfume?" said Greta, crowding onto the landing.

"Cabochard," Julie took a purple glass atomiser off the windowsill.

"I've got Arpège in the bathroom," said Zoë; unexpectedly affable, "in here, come on, I'll squirt you, it's gorgeous." She capsized into the bathroom. "We decant our perfume," she announced, tilting at a mirrored cabinet and rebounding with a crimson atomizer. Greta remembered Deborah's tiny bottle of White Fire, crowned with a stopper like a long white evening glove.

Zoë and Julie, blinking and lurching in the confined space, reminded her of puppets. Yet they were guilty of nothing, other than blundering about. She, on the other hand, had committed an error. How had she allowed it? The make-believe that she was searching for Deborah was a hoax and she herself had spun the yarn;

conferring a spurious significance on Julie by making her into a facsimile Deborah. Self-disgust overcame Greta. She was deceiving the oblivious girl. "Don't squirt me, Zoë," Julie squealed.

Greta, encumbered with ice-bucket and drink, had to present her neck. She raised her chin, angling her head. Her hair fell back and Zoë squirted. The projectile mist of scent tingled against Greta's warm skin, like a freezing scatter of pinpricks. Why should she stay here? Adrenaline flowed in a sudden spurt. She had to get out.

Ding-dong.

"The chinkie…" screamed Zoë.

Pale sun gleamed between clouds. Greta walked twenty minutes in her high hccls before a cab appeared. "Great Titchfield Street please." She stumbled in, wrenching the door closed. The chilly wind had sobered her but she was cold and exhausted, her toes agony where the sparkly straps of her shoes dug in. She imagined Camilla in a yellow New York taxi. The problem of finding a flat reared up. Camilla was due home. The taxi took a corner so fast she had to grip the loop in the ceiling to avoid being thrown across to the other side. It went hard into the Chiswick roundabout and Greta slid the other way and was pressed against the door. The wide sleeve of her jacket exposed her arm to the elbow reminding her of biology lessons: radius and ulna. Her skin was bone-white against the old-gold satin. Already it was late afternoon. Another shift began at nine. In a flash Greta knew that she was never going back to the casino. They roared towards Hammersmith flyover. She'd had enough. The flyover was a surrealist bracelet, and the vehicles, enamel charms. The taxi charm would come off. The Thames glittered. In her imagination, the taxi crashed through the barriers and fell towards Hammersmith below. An idea seized her and she knocked on the partition, shouting: "Riverside Studios; stop at Riverside Studios!"

The driver slid his window back, repeated, "Riverside Studios," in a calm voice and changed gear. Before the window closed she heard Beethoven's Kreutzer Sonata.

In the Riverside Studios café, ordering a cup of tea, she noticed a sign: *Staff Wanted.* The air smelled of pizza cooking.

"Do you need staff?" she asked.

"I get Rhonda." A Japanese girl with a French accent. "Please fill this form."

Frowning to stay awake, Greta took her tea and sat down yawning while she completed the form.

"Hello;" a buxom young woman with a mass of curly black hair joined her. "I'm Rhonda Perrine. Where are you working at present?"

"Nowhere." Greta; conscious of Rhonda taking in her sequined outfit and kohl-rimmed eyes, hoped she didn't smell of drink and took a big mouthful of tea.

"Hmm," Rhonda scanned the form. "You can start tomorrow. We're desperate – she's supposed to be in the box office." Rhonda indicated the Japanese girl at the till.

Greta could hardly believe it. "Thanks," she spluttered.

"You've got a degree," Rhonda looked up from the form, staring at Greta as if how come Greta thought she could get away with a bombshell like that?

"I write plays," said Greta.

"What have you written?"

"*Gargantina and Pantagruelle* …"

"We had that here a while back," Rhonda smiled.

"*Rabelais The Rabble Rouser*, and now I'm trying to write another one."

"Well, you can begin tomorrow – ten in the morning. I see it was your birthday yesterday. Happy birthday," said Rhonda and: "are you going far?" And Great Titchfield Street was far, she decided and she lent Greta some plimsolls and an anorak. "Not glamorous," she laughed as Greta covered up her evening clothes, "but you can walk and be warm at least."

On the way towards Hammersmith tube Greta studied the small ads in all the shop windows and collected four telephone numbers advertising flats. Back in Great Titchfield Street she began phoning.

The Glassblower Is Dead

It wasn't far from Hammersmith tube to Greta's new flat. The street was wide which made the dustbins appear further apart; the piled black bin bags less obvious. Greta liked it better than Camilla's cloistered neighbourhood. On her walk to work she passed under the awning of a florists, cheered by ranks of furled gladioli, bright as toucans' beaks, in their rows of tin buckets. Chrysanthemums crowded the doorway, astringent petals releasing a medicinal tang. The takeaways and shops were handy here; there was a library, which Greta immediately joined, and opposite that, a park with swings, a slide and scuffed tongues of earth where the children's feet braked. A tarmac path circled a brown lake with willow trees at one end. Moorhens sailed in and out of the dangling fronds. Parents hovered over toddlers who squatted at the water's edge throwing bread to the ducks. On sunny days Greta lingered in this park after work; picking at a doner kebab or bag of chips – feeding most of it to the pigeons. One day the thought came to her that maybe nineteen seventy-eight was turning into a good year. The false eyelashes were binned. She bought comfortable clothes; a peach wrap-over cardigan, some black cord jeans and a pair of Scholl's clogs. Her appetite improved and she found herself wanting to write again even though she dreaded starting. Imagining his ponytail shining against the velvet nap of his jacket, she wrote to Matthew saying she was confused and stuck. Matthew; pleased to hear of her new job; invited her to lunch.

On the way to meet him, TV screens in a shop window multiplied images of the white-clad Israeli singers who had won the Eurovisian song contest the night before. Greta paused, staring at their routine. But how to write her play about sexuality? The froth of their ballerina skirts gave the girls a child-like quality. But female sexuality was hateful. Did she mean the injustice of it? In princely white doublets the three boys turned and swayed. Silver lamé glittered on their erect collars. Her subject was repulsive. The girls had demure sweet bodices, the boys had their shirts open to mid chest. Greta hurried over the zebra crossing. Her subject was disgusting but it filled her thoughts and no other presented itself.

The restaurant was busy and fragrant; basil, garlic and tomatoes cohering. "A broken sloth?" boomed Matthew, laughing, "How do you feel like that?"

"Kind of… unable to move," she began. The noise of conversations all around them comforted Greta and allowed her to say anything that came into her head. Being in Matthew's company also had that effect; he was so large and absorbent with his ample torso and good quality clothes. Nothing shocked him and while she had no intention of putting that to the test it reassured her.

Matthew tilted the wine and she inclined her glass for more. "Why do you feel like a broken sloth," he teased.

In her mind she saw a drooping creature like a bag of pepper-coloured fur. "I hate female sexuality," she said, "I hate calling it that."

Matthew mopped juice from his plate of moules marinière with a chunk of freshly baked bread. He ate seriously, napkin tucked into collar. "What happens when you try to write about it?" he asked.

"It's like there's nothing there," she said, "just a mess." Matthew offered the basket and she took bread, put some in her mouth and had an instant vision of herself in the church, rubbing at the hated sloth with her wet finger. It came with such force that she wondered how she had ever forgotten it. "I'm a rubbed-out sloth," she said with a laugh. The way David Hayden-Fox had sensed that she was hiding something came into the back of her mind. The bread was delicious. The wine warmed her. "Maybe I have to climb a tree."

"No," said Matthew and to her alarm he reached commandingly across the table for her hand. His white cuff and gold watch were perfect, his fingers tanned from weeks in LA. What had he guessed? "Look," he said, turning over her nervous palm, "look at this hand of yours. This isn't a sloth's paw." He let go and dabbed essence of moules from his gleaming lips with the linen napkin. "Let your hand write. Leave your brain out of it. What might surface?" He smiled. "You might not see yourself this way," he said, "but I see a successful playwright. You're stuck at the moment but don't be hard on yourself. You're only twenty-eight and already you've got two fabulous plays to your credit. Finish your mushrooms. Let's move on to our osso bucco."

His words never ceased to surprise her.

She took his advice and sat in the park writing about the people she saw: the children on swings, old men on the benches reading their papers, babies in pushchairs, young women smoking as they watched their kids, Hassidic Jews with black coats and hats. She spent hours trying to write down exactly how things looked; the peeling bark and albino patches on the trunks of the plane trees; the pigeons' ruby feet.

I am the glassblower's daughter, she wrote one day. *The glassblower is dead.* She sat writing until it grew too dark to see properly. In the next week or so she wrote and wrote. She bought wine at the Cypriot off-license and some nights got drunk as she wrote. She typed bits out on her portable typewriter. She sent some to Matthew.

In the Garden of Remembrance she found him at last. Walter Buchanan. Her father. Dead. At the end he had been Walter Buchanan. Not her Father, not her Daddy or her Dad. He was much respected; the funeral chapel packed. She remembered how packed. The whole Department, even some students, had come. The funeral of her Dad, Walter Buchanan. Dead. He was much respected but he died unloved.

She thought of what he had done; a man breathing life into glass capillaries for threads of liquid to run; threads so fine, that the liquid in them amounted to less than a human hair in diameter; a man making tubes within tubes, precision-mapped hermetically sealed wonders that chemistry could not do without; a man creating mercury diffusion, condensers like women trapped in bottles, spiralled wishes emanating from the tops of their heads. She remembered the transparent turbine, glass wings spinning on the spindle so that gases could circulate like breath, in the body of the apparatus.

She stood and stared at the urn in the niche. It was held in place by bolts; its lid bound. So he must be in there. Her gaze took in the empty Garden of Remembrance. Cypresses formed underworld torches; tormented blue Van Gogh trees. The wind wove between raw brick arches. Walter Buchanan, in your niche. Unvisited. And Greta was suddenly racked by a strange retching. It was not nausea but reminded her of it. The spasm stretched into the furthest cavity of her body and she felt like a glove that was trying to turn itself inside-out. Her face contorted into a mask, eyes like slits, mouth downturned. Molten tears were mounting. The mask was rigid. To fall, the tears needed her eyes to relax and they couldn't because every muscle in her body had locked. The dreadful wrenching of it gripped her. Here she must stand before this niche, racked; here, by this small area of nothing that was all her father had come to from the place in Scotland where he had existed as a child. His entire past, which he had never spoken of, was, because of that unspoken-ness, obliterated. There was nothing in this niche. There was no Walter Buchanan.

Her breath came back, like it does in small children winded by their howl of anguish when they are hurt. It siphoned into her lungs bringing with it a piercing sensation. Then it went out in a long, terrible sound. *Keening*. The breath shivered agonisingly back in and as it went keening out again made the sound of words. "*My…*" lasted seconds; then the next word, barely audible, relentlessly enunciated … "*Dad*." Those were the words. Saliva and tears gushed through them as her breath was dragged back in. Her mouth stayed open, running with drool. Her hands hung by her sides until some conscious part of her prompted them to action and they brought the sweatshirt tied round her middle, up to her face. She sank to her knees on the concrete path, weeping into the sweatshirt. She sagged against the wall by the niche of Walter Buchanan. Walter Buchanan with his unspoken, unspeakable history, his deceptive success and the respect and affection of colleagues who couldn't tell what a shipwreck he clung to.

Eventually, she dragged herself to her feet. Tear-blinded, she fumbled in her bag and; made clumsy by unstoppable sobbing she began to arrange, at the base of the urn, the things she had brought with her. The glass animals. Her glass animals.

For a while afterwards a twitchy Greta brooded about how she had gone to Leicester to visit her dead father but hadn't made any effort to see her mother. Taking refuge in her job she was able to leave this thought behind. Because Greta loved Riverside Studios. She had begun a course of their weekly adult dance classes. The teacher was a supremely graceful dancer with perfectly chiselled features and silky dark hair. Her name was Sue and Greta loved her too. Sue had a robust sense of humour and no pretensions at all. "Avoid this area for a while," she called in the studio one day, "I've just farted. Sorry!" Reflected in the mirrors, a frieze of balancing women collapsed with laughter.

When in May an invitation from Matthew arrived, Greta rushed to work and arrived at the café yelling: "Rhonda, look!"

"*Dear Greta,*" read Rhonda, "*You are invited to dinner to celebrate the inauguration of The Scotsman's Playwriting Award, August 8th at The George Hotel Edinburgh. RSVP, Matthew Tarry.* Get writing," commanded Rhonda, "then you can have the dinner *and* win the prize," and they had a toast to Greta in hot chocolate.

Rhonda with her mass of black hair and solid, curvy body was a comfort to Greta. The café used ready-made pizzas and all they had to do was put them in the ovens, but whenever it was quiet, Rhonda baked. Rhonda loved baking. Gingerbread, shortbread, lava bread (she was Welsh), cinnamon buns, saffron buns, coconut pyramids, coffee kisses, date and walnut slice, and Greta's favourite, jam tarts. Rhonda collected biscuit cutters. She ground her own nutmeg and cardamom and kept vanilla pods in a big jar of sugar. "It's a shame you live all on your own, Greta," she said, rolling out pastry one quiet afternoon. Several pink petals dropped onto her pastry board from the blossom Greta had brought in from the park. Greta moved the flowers. She was busy cutting out circles and putting them in the baking tins. Rhonda spooned jam. "You must have had some friends once," she added.

"They're married – got kids," said Greta.

"What are their names? Don't you ever see them?"

"Alma," Greta said, "Clare... I send Christmas cards."

"Alma's a cute name," Rhonda, clanked a tray of tarts into the oven. "What's she like?"

"I remember her telling me that when she was little, she and her brother used to play in a disused quarry," said Greta. "They had a place in the centre with big rocks and if they waited quietly, lizards came out and basked in the sun."

Rhonda listened, arrested. "That's lovely," she exclaimed.

"That's what I'd like to do: wait for the lizards," said Greta, dreamily, and was comforted by a sudden idea of Deborah, baking, just like Rhonda.

"You should go and see your friends," said Rhonda. "Why don't you?"

Which is why in July, Greta went to see Clare, who had the same address she'd had since her wedding. "Six years," Clare lowered the abacus of her fingers and smiled across the table at Greta, allowing a pause as the waiter took her order. They had come to an Okehampton restaurant while Ray babysat. Greta admired the glint of wine in her glass. There was something seductive about big wineglasses. She watched Clare quizzing the waiter. Yet if you were a wineglass, it would be safer to be as short and compact as possible. A memory came into her mind – herself aged nine, curling up very small, a ringworm of silence under her covers – and her throat constricted, making her swallow instinctively as she said: "I'll have a medium steak too," the image like a stone going down inside her.

"I can't get over you writing plays. How do you do it?" asked Clare.

"It's hard. Actually I haven't written anything for ages," observed Greta, "I work in a café though – that's my real job."

"But at the Riverside Studios. Even I've heard of Riverside. And it makes a lot of sense for a playwright to work in a theatre; and you have a producer? Matthew is it?" Clare was beaming.

"Yes, Matthew Tarry. He's asked me to a dinner at the Edinburgh Festival next month and David Hayden-Fox is going to be there." Greta had received a list of invited guests a few days previously and had been pleased at first to see David's name. With each day that passed however, she worried about it more.

"Really? So is this the dinner to celebrate your first night?"

"I haven't written a new play for ages," Greta reminded her.

"Sorry, yes you said. I'm hopeless at the moment – I'm expecting and it's making me absent-minded."

"Clare! Congratulations. I couldn't tell." The waiter offered a basket of rolls. Greta waved them away.

Clare took one. "This hides everything," she said, tweaking the sprigged cotton of her Laura Ashley smock, "It's due in January. Tell me about your new play."

"I'm trying to write a new play," said Greta, "but the dinner's to inaugurate a new award. Lots of theatre people are invited and press and so on,"

"Can I have the script to read?" said Clare, "as a work in progress of course."

"There isn't one! I'm stuck," Greta said, "that's the thing, I can't get started on it."

Clare laughed. "But here's to you. Well done." Their glasses clinked. "What are you writing about that you're so stuck with?" Clare's brown hair still almost reached to her waist.

"It's... to do with sex."

Clare gave a small yelp, "really?" A look appeared on her face.

Greta was afraid to go on. She tried to rally her confidence as the waiter served them bowls of coleslaw. Be like you are with Matthew, she told herself, Clare used to work with disturbed children, can't you trust her to be capable of hearing what you want to say? Clare: always the down to earth one. But her fear that Clare might be affronted or disgusted won. "Like I said – I'm stuck."

"Booze'll help." laughed Clare.

"Yes." Their steaks arrived.

Later the taxi dropped them at Clare's house deep in the Devon countryside. Greta looked up at the sky. The stars were like grains of sugar; each held apart from its neighbour by an atomic thrip of space, each with its own microscopic sparkle. With every jot of starlight, they created between them impossible fabrics; astral gossamer and gauze; attenuated clouds unrolling and billowing, layer upon layer in the pulsating of the busy void. Greta gazed. "Look at that," she said, "you never see them in London; the whole universe is hidden."

"Greta, you're crying," sweet concern in Clare's voice.

"There was a sad story I had in a book when I was little," said Greta. "A man travels the earth to find a beautiful fairy who lives in the Garden of Paradise. Every night she sleeps under the

Tree of Knowledge and she tells him he can get as close as he likes but whenever she's asleep under that tree he mustn't touch her. And that's the only rule in Paradise. He does though. He touches her and the Garden of Paradise vanishes and he's left alone on the bare ground … *he opened his eyes and saw a star in the distance, a star which sparkled,*" Greta swallowed, "… *like his lost Paradise.*" She flattened a swell of tears with her fingers because Clare's concern was evident. Greta, bitterly recognising that it was harder to go looking for someone in real life than in a story; was trying to smile.

"And you're still quoting. You haven't lost your touch," Clare said and she hugged her; "Oh Greta," she exclaimed, "you seem so desolate. Perhaps that's enough of looking at the stars."

"No, I want to keep looking." Greta was thinking of her lost father and more tears blinked out. "It's the most fantastic sight I've ever seen," she sobbed, "I'm so glad I came down. Oh god – I'm drunk," and then she was laughing.

"Me too," Clare said. "I'm glad you're writing plays, it suits you. You always were passionate. You were disgusted when none of the girls in hall smoked Gauloises or discussed Rimbaud when we were Freshers. Remember?"

"Yes." Their feet made small crunching sounds in the gravel as they crossed the drive. "A walled garden and a starlit dovecote," Greta said, "your house is spectacular."

"It's fantastic that you write plays," Clare said, "what with Alma being an actress…it's nice that you both ended up in theatre. Not that she does any acting now, with the children so young…"

"She's only got the one hasn't she?" interrupted Greta, closing the big five barred gate.

"Two. She had another boy last September. You should go and see her."

"Christ," said Greta, "I could go next weekend." The wood of Clare's gate, holding her up, was warm and rough.

"She'd love it. She said she saw you once when she was on tour."

"That's right. Our college used to have touring productions. We had our own studio theatre."

There was a long peaceful silence, which Clare broke, saying: "I thought you were enjoying being an FE lecturer. Why did you give that up?"

Greta stared up at the stars. "I … just… felt like something different," she said eventually; then: "do you remember Col? Camilla told me he went to Cardiff on the journalism MA after graduation. Oh dear, I must lie down." Her neck ached from tilting her head back. "What's that lovely smell?"

"Night scented stock," said Clare. Skirting the spacehopper that Greta had brought as a present for the children, they went across the grass to the sun loungers. Lying back on the cool fabric they spoke quietly in the silent garden as they watched the firmament. "Col!" Clare gave a sudden giggle. "Why did we call him 'Two Balls'? Did you know he's had a novel published?"

"Really?" said Greta, "I'm impressed. Have you got a copy?"

"No I haven't. I think it's called *The Right Angles*, something like that."

"How do you know about it?" asked Greta.

"Camilla told me."

"You still see her?" Greta was startled. She had assumed Camilla was only part of her world; a glancing visitor to it maybe but nevertheless someone belonging only in her universe.

"*Human Trigonometry*," Clare yawned, "that was it."

A shooting star flared across the cambered sky. They both saw it; both gasped. It was gone. "Make a wish," said Clare.

They went to bed in the quiet house. The children's bedroom doors were open and Greta saw Clare pause, first at Francesca's and then Luke's before going into her and Ray's room. Greta looked at herself in the dressing table mirror, leaning her face close to the glass and angling her chin. There was the faintest trace of frown lines between her eyebrows. Her body was the same shape and size as when she was eighteen. She could still do the splits. *A five-foot four size eight but with a cleavage! It's so unfair*, As Clare once said. Greta had a vision of them all in The Buttery, the tiles underfoot sticky with beer and Camilla, next to her in the rough box bench, hugging her with a sudden snaky arm and saying *ribcage like a rabbit and double-jointed hips. Ooh, sexy little Greta.* Clare's shape was different now, heavier, and although her wrists and forearms were still delicate, above the elbow her arms had developed a peasant wideness. At eighteen, Ray and Clare were Romeo and Juliet, totally enamoured, so sweet and ardent. It must be having children. That was it. Clare looked motherly. The thought of her own mother occurred to her. Would she have found the glass animals? And Greta was back to thinking of her father. She opened the casement wide and leaned out, looking up at the stars.

After That Dinner

Greta's bus crossed the river out of Southampton over a high white bridge. Further along, rounding a bend alongside a towering wall they emerged parallel to a shore. Greta was astonished at the shining blue water. A shingle beach curved into trees ahead. And then; swans! Her breath caught. The swans glided at the edge of the calm lagoon. *One… two… three…* Greta pressed her forehead to the vibrating glass; *four… five…* The bus plunged between trees and a slope hid the sight. They emerged into the sprawling village where Alma and Mick lived and, manoeuvring the paddling pool she had bought, Greta descended into a quiet sun-baked Saturday afternoon and walked past a row of shabby little closed shops, grateful for the shade of a canopy held up by wrought iron columns. A warm breeze blew. Further down, the word *bakery* was painted on a board. The pavement was dusty and overhead a metal sign saying *barber* squeaked on an iron rod. A man riding bareback on a grey horse nodded as he passed. On the other side of the road, a dirt track led down to the sea past big neglected houses.

Alma's house was in a shabby terrace of Victorian cottages. The front path was made of blue bricks. Grass grew yellow in the cracks. Red paint flaked in stiff curls from the bay window-frame. A lace curtain sagged off a wire stretcher. Greta knocked, the paddling pool suspended from her head like a giant sombrero.

The door opened. "Is that your paddling pool?" said Alma's little boy.

"No, it's for you and baby Andrew. You must be Ben. I've brought it for you and Andrew as a present," she said, taking the pool off her head.

"Greta, you haven't changed a bit," said Alma, who had put on weight, "let me take your bag."

Greta presented the bottle of champagne she held in her other hand. "You live by the sea," she said, "I saw swans on the shore!"

"Southampton Water is a work-a-day sort of seaside," beamed Alma hugging her.

Ben said: "come on," dashing into the house.

The front door opened into a cramped sitting room where ten-month-old Andrew lay asleep on the grimy sofa. Greta heard a Spanish guitar.

They followed Ben past a dark staircase, Alma calling: "Mick! Come down. You can play the guitar later." A pram almost filled another little room then it was up a step and into the tiny kitchen.

Alma put the champagne in the fridge while Greta eased the pool through the back door and stood in the concrete yard. The sound of guitar playing had stopped and Mick loomed in the kitchen entrance. There was no door there, just a lopsided gap. A small face pushed past his knee and baby Andrew squeezed by, holding onto his father's leg.

"Your baby walks," exclaimed Greta, reverently. Andrew made for Alma, who proudly lifted him up. He sank against her.

"They both walked at nine months," Alma cuddled him, her face in his hair, swaying him gently.

"Greta," Mick's handshake was warm.

"Daddy, look at this paddling pool, come and put water in," Ben, zoomed in, then out, like a dragonfly.

By the time they had eaten plates of pasta and the children had been put to bed Greta had found out that she was sleeping on the sofa and that, upstairs, you had to go through the children's bedroom to get to the bathroom.

"What's it like living in London?" asked Alma, "Mick went on that big anti-Nazi rally didn't you, Mick."

"Yeah," Mick nodded; embarrassed. Alma's relentlessly expectant look made him clear his throat. "We marched," he elaborated, " you know, from – oh, miles it seemed, um, down Bethnal Green Road and into… um… Victoria Park…"

"To the concert," prompted Alma.

"Yes," he agreed, glancing at Greta.

"*Rock Against Racism*," declared Alma, "I expect all those lefties you worked with at college were there, Greta, weren't they?"

Momentarily chilled by this reminder of Gordon and Tim, Greta said: "was there any violence, Mick?"

"Surely you saw it?" interrupted Alma, amazed.

"No," said Greta, "it was miles away."

Mick blushed. "Outside one pub we passed there were some skinheads and some of them shouted fascist stuff – but there was a hundred and fifty thousand of us marching past and a line of policemen guarding the way. So there was no sense of violence really; no."

"Are you going up to the Edinburgh Festival?" asked Alma, sipping her champagne.

"Only to attend a dinner," replied Greta, "are you?"

"I wish we could."

"Why can't you?" Greta only expected one reason – they were doing something else. But it was not that. Alma went canoeing down a torrent of explanations. Here came the obstacles; baby, finances, Mick having to sign on and back to baby again. Greta felt sorry for her.

"…otherwise we would," Alma concluded.

"Do you play mainly classical music Mick?" Greta asked. He was sitting there so quiet, eating peanuts. They talked about the Bach Lute Suites. He recommended Barrios and Sor and the *Concierto De Aranjuez*. Alma had fallen asleep on the sofa. Then came a baby's cry and Alma began to get up; her eyes closed. "Alma, stay there," Greta rose, surprised that Mick hadn't already sloped off. "You obviously need the sleep, let me go."

"It's no good, he'll only start crying in earnest," said Alma.

"What about Mick? Let him go, you rest…" The other two exchanged glances. "You can do it Mick, can't you?" Greta asked.

"I can give it a go," said Mick. He lobbed a peanut into the air and caught it in his mouth then rose and went out.

Greta was scandalised. "You're so tired; you poor thing. How do you cope?"

"I'm OK. I bounce back after a good sleep. Was I asleep long?"

"About ten minutes. You've got two wet patches Alma – is that normal?"

Alma looked down at herself. Two patches darkened the tight cheesecloth over her nipples. "Shit, I should have put some breast pads in – I forgot. Ah well; never mind, no-one can see me."

"What causes that?" said Greta.

"The sound of Andrew crying – even the thought of Andrew if I haven't seen him for a while." Alma was beaming. "He doesn't always wake up so soon; I expect it's the excitement. He goes back down again if I feed him."

The crying came closer. Mick's tall figure appeared carrying the baby. Andrew sat upright, his head turning like an owl's, trying to locate Alma. She took him in her arms and the crying stopped. "Excuse my orthopaedic bra," she opened her blouse, "nursing bras are hell." She unhooked a flap and offered her left nipple. It was dark; like conkers. Greta imagined the fierce grip of gums, the press of the baby's tongue as he squeezed out the milk against his palate. Andrew bopped his head a few times against the great bulge of the breast above him then his mouth fastened on and he fed for about five minutes before popping off the nipple, fast asleep, his cheeks flushed. Mick's hand caressed Alma's hair. Alma took no notice. To Greta, Mick looked lonely, as he sat on the arm of the sofa. He resembled a weary Warren Beatty. "You must phone me," murmured Alma, "and tell me… " she broke off crooning: "*there there* … all about Edinburgh…" her face hovered inches from her sleeping baby, "…after you've been to that dinner."

As the day of the dinner drew nearer, anxiety about David Hayden-Fox made Greta want to chicken out.

"I don't think I should go. I'm really worried about seeing him," she pleaded on the phone to Matthew.

"Nonsense," Matthew insisted. "I'll be there, Greta. Relax."

She set off from Kings Cross full of apprehension, but her spirits leapt in excitement when the train crossed the Tweed into Scotland. As they drew, finally, into Waverley Station; the sight of the castle above; even grander than she remembered; made her stare, awestruck. A taxi took her to Broughton Place, wheels whirring on the cobbles. The scent of Edinburgh, of the sea, of malt from the brewery – was just as she remembered.

A flight of worn stone steps that spanned a deep basement, led her up to her bed and breakfast. The entrance was imposing despite faded paintwork. The landlady showed her up. "Ah'll gie ye yer ane key so's ye can let yersell in an' oot," she puffed, "it's an awfie climb up they stairs, ah hope ye're fit." To Greta it was like hearing her father speak. The bathroom was along the hall. Greta shivered in her room after her bath. The dinner party was going to be crammed with theatre people and writers. Matthew Tarry and David Hayden-Fox were the only two she knew and her mouth went dry at the thought of how much David hated her. From her suitcase she chose her black trousers and tucked in her silky aubergine top. She put her denim jacket on. It was already half past seven and she wasn't sure where The George Hotel was, although the tenderness of that night there with David Hayden-Fox was vivid in her memory.

Her heart raced and the air was full of the tang of hot vinegar as she ran up the hill past the fish and chip shop and turned right, along Queen Street. The turrets and parapets that spiked the sky gave the buildings a fantastical appearance and she felt dwarfed as she scurried along. Pain sliced into her chest as she panted for breath. Above the basements, flights of steps arched up to grand porticos, only now for some reason, the slant and tilt of the city caught her off balance. The architecture with its escutcheons and saltires in stone – how stern it was, how dark against the luminous indigo sky. Traffic passed. A church bell was ringing. She felt intimidated; unequal her task. She hailed a cab. "The George Hotel please."

"It's jist o'er there," the cabbie laughed.

But she got in all the same. "I've got a stitch!"

The cab turned up the hill, then left, and drew up outside The George making Greta laugh too, at how near she had been.

"Hae that yin on me hen," said the driver, "enjoy yersell."

Inside, Matthew came to greet her, his bulky frame elegant in a beautiful suit. He began rapid introductions, steering her through the crowd. In the heat of the opulent bar she struggled out of her jacket between handshakes. A waiter offered her wine from a tray. She sipped; jacket and bag awkward over her arm.

"This is Greta Buchanan, my collaborator on *Rabelais*."

"Hello Greta, pleased to meet you," the woman shook Greta's hand. Oh God. There was David Hayden-Fox.

"And this is David Hayden-Fox, whom I believe you already know, and his wife Naomi, who's an actress."

David was married. Thank God. Naomi was a hugger and kisser, which made it easy to respond with reciprocal warmth. "Greta. Hi," her voice was husky and beguiling. "Remind me; did we meet at our wedding? I'm sorry, I can't remember all the friends from England but that day was wild. It's so nice to meet you."

186

"You too," as she turned to David, Greta's relief burgeoned into exhilaration. "It's amazing to see you …" David was more solid; portly in fact, a suave Mr Pickwick; benignly smiling. He was almost bald and his remaining hair tufted out over his ears. The skin on his head was tanned a California brown. "…. So are you in the theatre now, David?"

"Sort of."

"Of course you are…" exclaimed Naomi, "you must read his book on Shakespeare, Greta. He's my own personal dramaturge." Naomi, her forehead too domed for beauty, was striking, her smile accentuating high cheekbones.

"How did you two meet?" asked Greta, beginning to have an odd feeling as she listened. The wedding was sketched in, then the plays they'd worked on. David nodded occasionally. They had a four year old and a two year old. Greta's odd feeling grew stronger. And then, (…do you have kids yourself Greta?) she had the feeling pinned down. She had finished her wine. That was it. She wanted another drink. "I must get some more wine, can I get you some?" She even seized Naomi's glass.

But David took both glasses off her. "I'll get them," he said, "Back in a jiff," and disappeared towards the bar.

"…what about you?" Naomi was saying. "You're the writer I've heard them mentioning….the Rabelais plays; what are you writing at the moment?" Such a gentle question. David came back as the spectre of Greta's new piece reared up.

"I'm… trying," Greta said, "thanks David," she took a big gulp of the wine.

"Good for you. It must be so hard," Naomi had a truly sweet smile.

Greta's odd feeling had not gone away. Her wine had been replenished but the feeling was getting stronger. She finished the glass. "I should circulate," she said, "I need to find out who I'm next to at dinner." They beamed at her. When she glanced back, Naomi was kissing the corner of David's mouth.

She squeezed between two women and ducked under the arm of a tall man who was reaching out to introduce somebody to his companion. All at once she knew what the feeling was. She was feeling alien. The taxi driver had sounded like her father too; and it had comforted her. In here she didn't fit. She took more wine from a tray. There was Matthew. "Who am I sitting by?"

"I'll introduce you – it's Liam Kennedy, a friend of mine; he's an administrator at The Royal Court. He's the one who organised that series of workshops I told you about. And actually Greta, he asked if he could meet you because he likes your work. He saw *Rabelais* last year in Paris."

"If I could just welcome you all…" A voice began to make a speech, a fork chiming against a glass. "…Er…people?" The tumble of talk continued. "People!" Liam Kennedy was introduced to her in an awkward diagonal of hands, reaching across, as they were all ushered to the tables. "If I could… People. Hey…" Cutlery danced as the speechmaker thumped on the table, Bang. Bang. Bang.

Liam sat at the end of the long candle-lit table; she was on his left. "Are you Irish?" she asked.

"My Dad's parents were," he said.

"My Mum's Irish," she told him.

"Oh dear," he said, "we're cousins."

She couldn't stop laughing. "I love the Festival," she said, wiping tears from the corners of her eyes, "it's kind of outside normality."

"I know what you mean," he said, "when I'm up here I make myself pledges about what I'm going to do next."

"Pledges? How very knightly," she said.

He paused, then: "what's the best thing you've done this year?"

His look challenged her. The question evoked a flash of memories: herself crying in the Garden of Remembrance; Rhonda removing a tray of pizza from the oven; Clare on her starlit lawn. "Seeing the stars when I went to my friend's house in Devon," she said.

He nodded. "I suppose it's isolated?"

"Totally. Her address is just: Burton House, Near Torrington," said Greta.

"My Mum lives in Burton," he said, more affably, "Burton-On-Trent though."

Avocados filled with prawns and French dressing were served. There was an uproar of voices, the chime and clang of cutlery against china. The waiter replenished her wine. "All these women have children and babies," she said.

"Children *and* babies," Liam was gently mocking, "how greedy." His eyes were deep brown and specks of gold from the candle flames burned in each pupil.

"My Mum had two of us," said Greta, "but I never got the impression she was as pleased about it as they seem to be."

"Have you gone round and asked them all? They might be putting on a brave face in the public arena. It isn't like you," he said, "not to check."

"How do you know? You've only just met me."

"From your work. That's what I like about it – you have an empirical approach." He was on her side. Matthew said so. Her work had gone on ahead of her and this man liked it. His face was austere, with an arrowhead mouth and he might have looked melancholy if his hair were not so loose and long. He speared a prawn and with a wave of his fork, indicated the dinner table. "This is what it's all about…" A sequin of dressing fell onto his soft blue shirt as he transferred the morsel into his mouth. He raised his wineglass as if toasting her and then took a drink.

"Prawns?" she said.

"No – well yes – about eating prawns with people whose company you've chosen; in a geographical location that you find amenable…" He was playing along and he strung it out further, because she maintained her unconvinced look. "…under circumstances you helped to arrange," he finished.

"About being a control freak." Greta's facetious remark was verging on rudeness. Why was she doing that? And she regretted it because that look appeared on his face again. What was it, irritation? Impatience? The look came and went and the engaged warmth was replaced with a neutral blankness.

"I'm sorry," she said. "Don't take any notice of me. I get edgy sometimes; I shouldn't have mentioned my mother."

"Have a prawn," he looked friendlier. "Empty stomach. You'll get drunk."

Greta ate one.

"I've been wanting to meet you," he said.

"Am I a legend or something?" It was hilarious. Laughter mixed itself up in her mouth with the prawn. "I'm eating a sea-creature, you realize," she said and could hardly stop laughing.

"Jesus, you're pissed," he said, laughing also, "good for you."

The meal went on, roast duck, game chips, something fluffy that turned out to be creamed parsnips. Greta wondered at the fact that she had tried to be combative and he had objected. It took them past a barrier of some sort. She felt as if she had granted him the right to mention her mother. She noticed this in the time-lapsed way you do when you're drunk and just-spoken words float in the air around you. And why had she brought her mother into the conversation at all? Maybe seeing David again... she remembered the bitter vehemence in his voice long ago. What had he said? Skulk off home to the back streets and your weird working class family who you never talk about... "I never talk about my Mother," she said, "do you?"

"Not really," said Liam. "I talk *to* her a lot though; I go there as often as I can. It's not such a long way to Burton-On-Trent. Why were you so nervous about meeting Hayden-Fox?"

She was surprised. How did he know that?

"Matthew told me," said Liam.

"I was dreading it," she said, "we had an awful break up." She laughed. "But it was OK," she added and laughed again, because all around them people roared with laughter and shouted for more wine and called out to friends further along the table. Greta felt woozy. Liam's teeth captivated her; a straight white edge.

"Matthew says your new play is about female sexuality; have you got a particular angle?" He swept her calmly on. "I mean is it the politics of sex..." to hear him better, she leaned close amid the hubbub, "...or more from a social observation perspective?" A series of explosive guffaws from somewhere mid-table caused a surge in volume; "...it's one hell of a difficult subject I should think." Liam was almost shouting.

"Yes it is."

"Do you have a title?" He bent his head near to her.

"*Why Some Women Don't Enjoy Sex*," she confessed, "working title. Too grim though. Maybe it isn't a good subject for a play."

190

"Why write it then?"

The noise rolled around her like protective pillows. It muffled the secret she was about to tell. "I started writing it because I …I'm talking about… you know, libido. I lost my libido."

"Why?" Liam covered her wineglass with his hand so that a waiter missed her out then he poured a glass of water and handed it to her. Bowls of fruit were placed down the centre of the table and Liam took an orange and began to peel it. *Why*? Can you tell someone something so horrible as they peel their orange?

Liam's fingers were tanned; he had gaunt expressive hands and she noticed the shape of his wrist and felt an urge to touch it. He was eating a segment of orange and waiting for her to reply; attending to her and waiting and in the meanwhile he ate his segment of orange. "I've never met anyone as calm as you before," she said.

"Mind if I smoke?" said Liam, "Would you like one?" She took a cigarette, bending towards him so that he could light it for her.

"I had a job once," she said; "as a college lecturer." Liam's face was calm; listening. In the pause he said nothing. "I was raped by one of my colleagues," she said. Liam took a deep breath. His eyes met hers. Still he said nothing. "We were good friends," she went on, looking down at her plate. "He was a socialist and it happened after a Battered Women's disco he'd organised." There was no need to look up to see what Liam was doing. She knew. He was listening. "His name was Gordon," she said, "I was in his house. He told me his girlfriend was upstairs asleep but she wasn't. He kept me there until the next day. That was when his girlfriend was due back. He wouldn't use contraception and it made me pregnant…" her voice dropped, "… and… I had an abortion."

"Is that when you left your job?" He bent his head closer again.

"No. What made me leave was when I told…" she faltered, "the man who I thought…"

Liam was tense. His hair fell forward. He smoothed it back. "Did he work there too?"

"Yes. I'd been having an affair with him and I thought he was going to leave his girlfriend for me so I kept it secret. I told him about Gordon once the abortion was over and he didn't believe me. I said *Gordon raped me* and he said: *are you sure?* I went in to my

191

head of department and resigned on the spot." The hollow of her chest felt empty as a bell and her heart hung inside, a heavy clapper, silently tolling. With every heartbeat she felt a sensation like missing a step on a steep staircase. "You're the first person I've told," she said and gulped water.

"You're clearly very brave," said Liam. He protected her wine-glass from the waiter again. She looked at him and he said, "sorry, shall I call him back?"

"No, that's OK. I'm drunk." She saw that his face was sombre. The banquet had come to an end, un-noticed, waiters were removing plates and glasses; guests were standing and bidding farewells. Matthew came over and Liam said: "Are you ready for a lift back to the hotel, Matthew? Can I drop you off somewhere Greta?" The three of them left together, she was dropped off and Matthew and Liam drove out of Broughton Place.

In the soft salinity of the buffeting air, Greta went up the steps of her guesthouse then leaned against the iron railing, facing the street. A smell of metal conjured a sudden thought of Bridget Furedi hanging upside down on the climbing frame and herself lying on the slide with the polished golden surface inches from her nose. Affection surged through her; for Edinburgh; for the dustbin on the pavement; for the cobbled street; and the steps, each one worn in the centre, like stone cakes that sank. She folded onto the top step and watched the clouds flying across the moon and the moon sailing into pools of clear sky. "I'm in Scotland," she said.

At that moment, there in her head, isolated in clarity like the moon, another image came to her: her daughter; her baby. "All this time," she whispered, "all this time I've been ignoring you." Her baby had become a secret. She had been its mother; no matter that it was primitive and brief; she had known what loving her child felt like. And she terminated her life. And then she never spoke of her existence. "You would have been two, by now." Greta said the words aloud, and smiled, wanting to stay like that, with the moon and the blowing wind. "I told Liam Kennedy about you," she said. She rose to her feet and put her key in the lock, taking a long look round at the rapturous wild night before stepping inside and closing the door behind her. Instantly she missed the wide spaces of the air, the smell of malt, the wind's movement. Instead she felt a muffled pressure against her eardrums as her blood rushed round her system in an intoxicated wave.

Liam

Carpenters were sawing partitions in the foyer. The barking of metallic teeth in timber and the smell of sawdust lulled Greta as she stood in a patch of autumn sunshine, topping up the display stand by the box-office. And there was his name, on a leaflet: Liam Kennedy. He was chairing a panel at The Cheltenham Literature Festival discussing contemporary theatre with Serena Blay, the Canadian playwright and a director from The Royal Shakespeare Company. Greta borrowed the box office phone and without hesitation, booked herself a ticket.

Day after day, the skies were periwinkle blue with clouds blown across like milk and pigeon feathers. The euphoric weather contrasted with a feeling that was affecting Greta more and more. A hateful feeling. Glimpses of her younger self would flash onto her consciousness. At each glimpse she felt another stone being loaded inside her in a secret place she had never known about, until now. It was as though the time had come and perspective itself had triggered a mechanism that revealed this place. The flashes of memory were beyond her control. The stones inside were mounting up.

Drifts of yellow leaves hushed her feet under the sycamores as she crossed the park to work. From on high, oak and beech scattered offerings of russet and brown that fell around her like spice in the air. Such beauty kept her hopes up. She couldn't wait for her trip to Cheltenham. She was pleased to have a plan and maybe this was what you do. You don't write a play, you have a plan. Your own life is the thing; you can either write about it or do it, but not both at once. Thoughts of Liam Kennedy kept coming into her head. In the café she felt happy: "*I hope that someone gets my... message in a bottle...*"she sang, as she re-filled the squeezy ketchups and piled flapjacks onto lace doilies.

Rhonda was intrigued. "So what are you going to buy for your trip then?" The air smelt of the cucumbers she was slicing.

"Buy?" Greta stacked cups and plates in the dishwasher.

"To wear!"

Greta laughed, clanking the door of the machine shut and switching it on.

"Come on Greta, buy a nice dress, or some shoes." Rhonda held a chunk of cucumber to Greta's lips for her to bite.

Amused, Greta bought some boots and wore them to work over her black cords.

"Cowgirl boots! Let me try them." Rhonda caressed their curved tops and pointed toes. "So who is all this for then?"

Greta just smiled.

"Did you meet someone up at Edinburgh?" persisted Rhonda.

Greta put her fingers in her ears and walked off shouting: "can't hear you!"

The next week she went into Miss Selfridge and bought an amber coloured velvet dress because she liked the look of it in the window.

"Come on Greta, when are you going to tell me who it's all for?" demanded Rhonda.

The bedspread in her Cheltenham hotel room was martyrdom-red. Greta lay down and spread out her arms and legs to see if she could reach the edges. There were shapes on the liturgical crimson, lilies in gold and indigo. Liam's event wasn't until noon the next day. Greta had a lazy bath then went for a walk. The white Georgian terraces had wrought iron balconies that reminded her of black lace stocking tops. Eventually she arrived at The Everyman Theatre for the reading by Saul Bellow. It was packed.

In the friendly hubbub of the bar afterwards she bought a gin and tonic and asked a woman the time. The woman pushed back a blue cashmere sleeve then a cream linen one and exposed a tiny gold watch. "Ten to seven," she said.

"Thank you." Greta liked her smooth white hair. She looked as if at one time she had been a ballet dancer.

"Are you going to something good?" The woman asked. A very slight overbite made her look endearingly schoolgirlish, even though she was clearly old enough to be a grandmother.

"A poetry reading; Edwin Morgan at the Town Hall."

"Oh he's a lovely man; so astute." Greta wished this really were her grandmother. Greta's experience of grandmothers consisted solely of Nanny Furedi chivvying Bridget out of the house, the mauve toothlessness of her mouth like a wound. Leaving The Everyman, she was hit by the realization that her aborted baby had had a living, available grandmother and yet she, Greta, had made sure the two could never meet. She hurried towards the next venue wanting to duck her head as if insights were birds and being out in the open exposed her to their swooping attack. She ran up the steps of the Town Hall. Inside it was hot and she peeled off her denim jacket.

The Pillar Room, true to its name, had marble pillars. They were the colour of stewed rhubarb and Greta was thinking how funny it would be if it was called the Rhubarb Room instead. And then, as she got towards the middle of the front row, to her astonishment she saw that the man coming towards her from the other end was Liam Kennedy. "Hello Greta," he said, "what brings you to Cheltenham? I like your dress."

"Liam…" she gabbled, "it's fantastic to see you again." She brandished her programme, "I see you're in an event yourself tomorrow." *Oh the guile!* Surely he would see her transparent heart pounding away.

"I am. And you?" He indicated a seat then sat next to her.

"I came to see Saul Bellow," she said.

"I've just been at that. Did you like it?"

"Wow, I didn't see you there," she said, and they both laughed. "I thought he was amazing."

"Me too." His eyes were warm, his face suddenly a smiling profile as a burst of applause welcomed the poet, Edwin Morgan onto the platform.

"What now?" he said, when it ended.

"I fancy a drink," she said, "do you? Have you eaten?"

"No. I should actually."

"I passed an Italian restaurant on the way," said Greta, "we could have pizza."

"I'd rather have a massive steak," he said pulling a face, "let's have a drink first and then decide." And it was as easy as that. They had steak and chips in a dimly lit pub; drank red wine; talked plays, Edinburgh, the miners, astronomy, the Big Bang.

"Were you confirmed?" she asked.

"No, I was a Methodist; does that count?"

"Yes. So are you religious?"

"No. I think it's mumbo-jumbo and I gave it up at the first opportunity," he braced his body backwards to extract a packet of Marlborough from his jeans pocket, "holy people smell." The antique bench creaked as he rocked forwards again.

"Not all of them," she spluttered, laughing, and wiped a dribble of wine off her chin.

"Yes," he said, "mothballs and halitosis."

"You must be… a bit holy." Greta accepted the cigarette he offered; noticing the way he'd taken out two.

"Christ – have I got halitosis?"

"No, I tell you things though. I told you things when we were having dinner in Edinburgh that I still haven't told anyone else."

"Did you get your libido back?" he asked.

"Possibly, but I don't use it any more," she replied.

He uttered one syllable of laughter. Then said: "but you shouldn't joke about it because that's you you're talking about and if you want to, you can take yourself seriously; and you should. As well as joking I mean." His eyes were steady and he was smiling, so that his words, no hint of criticism; were like a magic spell.

And then, out of the blue: "I've lost my sister," she said, "not my libido." Her arms and legs went floppy. All the air had gone from her lungs and she felt as if the back and front of her ribs had closed together and made her as flat as a card.

Liam leaned forwards to retrieve her cigarette and put it in the ashtray. He said something half blotted out by the buzzing in her ears "…do you mean dead?"

Her heart thudded. Liam held her fingers, pressing her knuckles as if to soften them. "I don't know what happened to her," she said, "it's as if she doesn't exist."

He let go of her hand, poured water, held out the glass. "She does exist," he said.

Greta sipped water, her hand regained its co-ordination; she picked up her cigarette and with a deep inhalation she talked about Deborah; bedtime stories, perfume and make-up, bridal gowns cut out, full-skirted frocks, the pack of hounds. "I set out to look for her," she said.

"Didn't your parents know where she was?" asked Liam.

"They used to say she was in Australia." Greta sighed. "Maybe that's a euphemism. Sometimes…" she stopped.

Liam re-filled their wine. "Go on."

"…my Mum said things which seemed to mean that she knew something… oh I'm not sure. They told me never to ask about her. Then maybe I forgot I was looking for her."

"It's hard to do things which have been forbidden. It's frightening," he said.

"I am afraid," said Greta, "afraid of not finding her. But at the same time I'm afraid that if I search I'm getting closer and closer to her, and the nearer I get the more this feeling stirs up and if I find her I'll be having some completely unknown emotion that I've never had before."

"Do you look like her?"

"No but Julie did – a girl at the casino."

"Matthew told me about the casino."

Sipping wine, Greta realised she had run away from the casino with no explanation. From Julie's point of view, she had vanished. She began telling Liam; laughing. But he said: "That's quite an extraordinary thing to do – vanish. Quite … cynical." The word felt like a blow. And then he looked straight at her and said, "why don't you ask your mother where Deborah is?" She didn't reply and after a silence he said, "when did you last go home?" And then, "Greta; don't look so… haunted."

A feeling of great shame was making it hard for her to speak. Her glass crashed against the ashtray as she put it down. "I went a few months ago," she said, "I went to visit my Dad's grave. To put something on it," she shook her head, "it isn't a grave…" the words now helter-skelter, "…it's an urn with his ashes in a special niche in the wall in the garden at the crematorium not near our house at all…"

"Christ," he said, "it's OK!"

"What do you mean?"

"I don't want you to feel so bad about this," his smile was kind again, "you did a good thing but you're in agony. Believe me," he insisted, "trust me – you haven't done anything wrong."

"But I didn't go and see my mother even though…"

"That's OK. You're allowed to choose. And you chose."

"I left … something… there. By his urn."

"That's good."

"But…"

"No – it's good."

The shame turned to blushing discomfort and she sipped her wine. "I did… um… think…" she stopped. In a room beyond, a Spanish guitar began to play. Liam was waiting. "I wonder," she said, slowly, "what my mother thought when she saw the things I left."

"In one way," he said, "whatever you left – it was a message."

"Oh," said Greta. A deep breath made her change her position and she stood up. "I'm going to the ladies." And she was walking; gliding between tables, past laughing people; past the guitarist, until she was safely combing her hair, checking her reflection, allowing an unfocused state of mind to take over.

Liam walked her back to her hotel. "Goodnight, Miss Buchanan," he said and shook her hand with a flourish. If she had been taller she might have put her hands on his upper arms and kissed him the way Matthew always kissed her: a friendly kiss for each side of the face. No matter. She threaded her way into her hotel through the revolving door.

Next day Liam's teeth gleamed as he passionately laid into the way that government arts funding policies were starving the theatre. The RSC director droned on and on. Serena Blay leaned towards Liam and put her hand on his knee as she made a Canadian point. There was applause. Greta boiled in the stalls. It was Saturday afternoon and yet people had come to this instead of going shopping. Could there be a more boring topic? Liam wore a dark suit with a waistcoat and looked dashing, like a television presenter. It ended. He waved from the dais. She watched him jump down and approach her. "Fancy a drink later?" he asked, "I've got to go for lunch now but if you're free we could meet up in that same pub we were in last night – about six?"

Reckless with urgency she booked another night at her hotel. She washed her hair, applied an oatmeal face mask, shaved her legs, soaked in bubble bath and smoothed her body with lotion. Under her new dress she put on a lacy black bra and pants she had brought with her just in case. Again she and Liam ate dinner. Again she insisted on paying for herself. But this time they set off back to her hotel at nine, hardly speaking. This time she invited him up for coffee. He accepted. They spent the night together.

After he left the next morning she alternately dozed and lay in contemplation of bathing, of eating a big fried breakfast, of taking the train back to London, of seeing him again. He had her number. She lay there, blissfully at ease, her weekend an astounding success.

Once back from Cheltenham, Greta thought constantly about Liam. Would he ring? Yes. He had her number. November passed tiringly, the rubbish in the streets a rat-infested obstacle course. Many of the pickets holding signs outside the council offices wore heavy moustaches that reminded her of Gordon. Outside the tube the *Socialist Worker* sellers multiplied. Liam worked at The Royal Court. So should she go to The Royal Court? Pride prevented her. December began spooling past. She helped Rhonda decorate the Christmas tree in the café. During power cuts they lit candles and Greta felt as if she was in the past.

Rhonda supported the firemen's strike. Her father was a fireman in Wales. "Come on, girl, I know what'll cheer you up," she said one day. They spent a treacle scented afternoon making gingerbread and flapjacks and then bundled themselves up in scarves and mittens to deliver the goodies to the pickets at the nearest fire station. "Some of those lads are bloody gorgeous," promised Rhonda as they set out. Snow fell; isolated flakes from an iron sky. "One of them asked me out yesterday."

The snow became thicker. "It looks like it's going to settle," said Rhonda.

By the time they got back, a blanket of snow concealed the mess in the streets and London looked like a Christmas card.

A week later Greta woke up one morning sweating from a dream about a red man carved out of watermelon who painted her naked body with his fingers, groaning with love while people who were clothed and helpful looked on. Greta got out of bed. Dreams didn't have to mean anything. Her bathroom smelled of toothpaste. The bath enamel was cold under her feet. The shower curtain rattled. Under the pattering of water, she applied soap, rubbing peach scented lather into her skin with the loofah. Water dripped cleanly into her mouth from her hair. *Does Liam think I'm cynical?* "But I told Liam the truth." *Not about everything.* The shower hissed round her. "Christ, I'm talking to myself." Milky waves of lather poured down her legs leaving the skin shining. And then the phone rang, bursting the peace. Her heart contracted and she hurtled to answer it, wet feet sliding on lino, then printing shapes on carpet, her skin goosebumps, wet hair cold on her neck.

But it was Matthew, "Greta, how are things? Let's get together for a Christmas drink. Meet me in The Swan," they fixed the day, he gave directions.

Greta leaned on the bar, sipping brandy and Babycham. Outside, sleet mixed with stinging rain but inside the saloon sparkled with tinsel and red candles lit each table. Three men, as if unaccustomed to their Lord John suits, joked and snatched at each other's wide flowery ties; butting and feinting.

"Sorry I'm late." It was Matthew. His big, bulgy body interposed itself between Greta and the men. "Can I get you a re-fill?"

"Hello Matthew," Greta indicated her glass, "I'm fine thanks."

Matthew ordered a pint with his usual panache. "Shall we sit down?" he suggested, "I'm expecting Liam."

Liam? In the mirror behind the bar her face looked white among a kaleidoscopic glitter of rum and whisky optics. Framed by bottle pyramids of orange, tomato juice and bitter lemon, her hair was stringy with rain. They sat at a corner table and Matthew presented a contract for her to sign. *Rabelais* was booked for a college campus tour in the States. "How's the writing?" he asked. "Have you got a title?"

"Still only the working title," she said, with a grimace, "*Why Some Women Don't Like Having Sex*."

"Poor Greta. That's a challenging title all right. Keep going. Maybe you should book time off from your job. Go on a retreat – had you thought of that?"

Greta frowned, "I don't know…" The idea was unexpected. And appealing. She pinched at the softened wax dripping down their candle, "I'd be like a monk."

The lights went out just then and ribald cheering erupted from the be-suited men. "Bottled beer only, lads," the barmaid called over her shoulder: "until the power comes back." Arms above her head; she fumbled a switch and a powerful torch on a shelf behind the bar blazed out like a searchlight.

"Is Liam married?" Greta asked abruptly.

If Matthew was surprised by the change of subject he hid it. "No." Jumpy shadows crowded the wall behind him. "So you two bumped into each other in Cheltenham…" he said tentatively.

She nodded and smiled, "a girlfriend?" she asked.

"His last girlfriend worked in the publicity department at a publishing company."

"Recent?" The candle flame wavered. Her eyes were getting used to the tricky light.

"It's been over nine months I'd say. They were together four years or so but towards the end he wasn't happy."

"Oh?"

"Forget I said that."

"Don't worry. Safe as houses."

"I know. I'd trust you with my life," Matthew took a long swallow of his beer. "I've known Liam since before he began the relationship." Responding to Greta's eyebrows he added: "she used to work at The Royal Court too." *Oh now that he was talking let him go on.* Greta found it pleasant and simultaneously slightly painful to be listening to this whilst anticipating Liam's arrival. And then he said: "You like Liam don't you." For a moment Greta felt as if the correct thing to do was run away. "Sorry Greta; I've made you blush."

"I should be the one apologizing," Greta gulped brandy in confusion, "I'm getting you to gossip."

"Not at all. I blundered. Why do you say that?"

"I was being sneaky."

"Oh Sweetheart. There speaks a Catholic."

Liam appeared at the end of the bar. He wore a leather biker jacket, the collar turned up and Greta could see his brown hair shining with rain. He stood with his head lowered as a caution against the low beams. Her heart pounded. "There he is," she said. Matthew waved and Liam strode forward silhouetted by the torch beam.

"I'll get you a drink, Liam," Matthew made for the bar.

Greta smelled rain as Liam took off his jacket. "Greta," he held out his hand, which was very cold.

"Hello." She shook it, feeling an urge to clasp and warm it; conscious of his long legs fitting into the cramped space, the creak of the chair as it took his weight and the heavy silver watch on his wrist. "Have you got the bike to go with that jacket?" she said, while simultaneously:

"Have you made any progress?" he said so that neither speech was really comprehensible.

And in a fluster she said: "what time do you make it?"

He glanced down at his angled wrist, "Six-forty: and by progress," he added, "I meant with your play." Matthew returned with a bottle of Guinness and a glass.

"God," Greta stood up, "I'm doing an evening shift at Riverside. I'm supposed to start in twenty minutes, I have to go." She knocked against her chair, which hit the table and wobbled the drinks. Liam reached out and his hand collided with Greta's. "Ow!" Greta rubbed her hand, laughing.

"I'm so sorry."

"It's OK."

"You must come to one of our shows sometime – Matthew, why don't you bring her?" Liam rose and took Greta's jacket off the back of her chair. All three put out their hands as the movement jerked the furniture again. He held her jacket. As she struggled to get her arms into the sleeves they spoke in an overlapping babble.

"I will come to one of your shows…"

"She's not mine to bring Liam…"

"What I should do is ring you sometime perhaps…" Had Liam said that? He was speaking to her was he? Sleeves done, she turned her head, flicking hair out of her eyes. But Liam's face was towards Matthew. At that moment the lights came on and another cheer went up.

Matthew gave her a big hug. "Bye, Greta," and then she was waving, her eyes were squinting in the brightness, she was saying goodbye to them. That was it. Greta went out into the freezing rain and ran towards the tube.

Go back!

What are you doing?

No-one will mind if you phone work and say you aren't coming.

She shrieked these things in her head as she ran.

Why don't you go back and ask him why he hasn't phoned you?

But she kept on running until she had turned the corner and then, excruciated by a stitch, she leant against a wall, pressing her hand to her ribcage. The traffic had stopped, the lights red. "OK," she muttered at the carmine reflections in the gutter, "go back there. Go back." A bus, restless with passengers drew alongside and descending figures surged against her, their passing conversations dousing her with inconsequentialities. The vehicle drew away. Blowing into her cupped hands for warmth, she looked back the way she had come, one foot flat against the wall ready to propel herself forward. Snow was mixing with the rain. "I'll ring from the pub," she murmured. One push and she was launched back towards the corner. "I'll go back in, ring work, rejoin them. No: join them first, then ring work…" the corner was turned. And there coming towards her, hands jammed in his pockets; was Liam.

"Whoa! Where are you off to?" he said, "The tube's that way." He inclined his head, amused.

"I was coming back," she said.

"Good for you."

"No point though; seeing as you and Matthew have gone."

"We were only there to see you," he said.

"I'm wet."

"I like the look of you wet."

Thoughts of him naked replaced her ability to form sentences. She looked away; not sure that the neon-patched rain altered her face enough; not wanting him to see her expression. Cars hissed past, cloned wipers pushing slush. The roll-of-film darkness had to hide the way her skin blushed with sexual memories of him. They began to walk towards the tube. Greta shivered, wrapping her arms round herself, teeth chattering.

"You need a proper coat, not that skimpy jacket," he said.

"Skimpy?"

"That's what my Mum used to say to my sister." He imitated a voice: "You'll catch your death in that skimpy jacket." He grasped Greta's elbow, swinging her round to face him, "and then, she'd do this," and he briskly rubbed Greta's arms as if to warm her. She laughed. Abruptly he said: "do you want to come back to my place for a drink?" He hailed a taxi passing in the other direction. It veered into a U-turn. In the pause as the taxi waited for two cars to clear he looked down at her, *3, 2, 1...* No time to think. The taxi drew alongside. "Come with me," he said, holding the door. And in she got.

They couldn't stop kissing – in the taxi, in the lift, on the threshold of his flat, inside with the door kicked shut, in the bedroom removing garments; they were together like limpets, like ivy, like the loops of a knot, like an experiment to see how much space can be excluded from between two human bodies.

He called her another taxi at three in the morning and on the doorstep, when it arrived, kissed her again, his warm hand holding her hair in a bunch so that the arctic wind couldn't scatter it into their mouths.

Next day, amid the familiar confection of boutique windows in Covent Garden, Greta bumped into Camilla and clung to her as rain soaked their hair to glossy points like the leaves on the bay trees outside each pastel-coloured doorway. They kissed each other's icy faces, ducking into an arcade for shelter. "Fuck! I'm clutching you like a long-lost bloody sister," said Camilla, "guess what – I'm getting married. New Year's Day. I'm pregnant." Camilla's long fawn coat had shoulder pads. She wore it unbuttoned over a pinstriped shirt tucked into beige jodhpur-like trousers. A fitted mohair cardigan in a beautiful cobalt blue completed the outfit.

The bump was tiny.

Greta hugged her. "You can't be far gone."

"It's due in January – that's why the wedding is New Year."

"But you're so skinny!"

"I sometimes think it's all a hoax. It isn't; because I throw up so much." Then she said, "I'm a bitch to say this but I've only got contacts for the men we knew at university. I got Mother to send an invite to Clare – Clare never moves – but could you be a sweetie and invite Alma?"

"Clare's pregnant," said Greta, "she's due in January too." And then she blurted, "can I bring my boyfriend?"

"Of course you can and it goes without saying that Rob can come and whoever that guy is that Alma's with – kids, blokes, the whole caboodle."

"Are you still in your flat?"

"No, I'm renting that out. I'm living at Theo's in Chelsea. You'll meet him at the wedding – I can't wait to introduce you. I've got to rush; I'm going to buy a pram. Bye bye Sweetie, I'm so glad I've found you again."

Greta phoned Liam at work. A sexy female voice put her on hold and then she was connected. "What is it?" he spoke quietly as if something important was happening at his end. "That's alright," he interrupted, when she began to apologise for ringing him at work. "I'll be at my mother's at New Year," he said when she asked him to come to the wedding with her. He sounded preoccupied, "I can't think straight at the moment," he murmured, "I'll give you a ring and talk when I'm not at work."

Mouth dry and cold hands quivering she dialled Alma's number, wishing she could erase the embarrassment of what had just happened. "Please come to the wedding, it's going to be fantastic."

"Ooh, I don't know…"

"It isn't all that far from you is it?"

"An hour and a half if I drive I suppose," said Alma. The wedding was in Oxford, where Camilla's mother lived. "It would be great to see everyone again, Clare and Ray will be there will they?"

"No," said Greta, "Clare's too pregnant."

"The boys would have to stay at home. I wouldn't be able to get drunk if I had them with me. Mick would stay home I'm sure."

"Just come," said Greta, unable to see why Alma had to agonise over a simple wedding invitation.

"It's a pity Clare can't make it," Alma mourned.

"I know, but she says even without being huge she can't come because it clashes with Francesca's birthday."

"That's right. Oh no, she can't possibly come!" exclaimed Alma.

"So are you coming, or what?"

There were extra shifts to do for the Christmas shows at Riverside so apart from Christmas Day, which she spent sleeping, Greta was busy. The post was disrupted by strikes so maybe that was the reason there was no Christmas card from her mother that year. Her mother had never missed a Christmas or birthday before but Greta thought of Liam all the time and so didn't care.

On New Year's Day, it snowed and Camilla, in an empire line gown of cream brocade, arrived at the church in a carriage pulled by white horses. Instead of a veil she wore a crimson velvet cloak with a wide, fur-trimmed hood. Snowflakes fell onto clipped yew; and the golden stone of Oxford's buildings was muted into an elegant bleakness. It took Greta's breath away. The covering of snow that lay all around intensified the sense of hazard that weddings gave her. The low sky smudged over the scene, blotting out the rest of the world.

After the ceremony, as the photographer called instructions to bride and groom, Greta stood by Alma blinking as crystals of snow tapped her eyes. Guests had been given red rose petals to throw and the petals, mixing with snowflakes, caused a barrage of flashbulbs as everyone tried to capture the moment on their Nikons. A tall dark-haired guest in a long overcoat standing among the cedars opposite reminded Greta so much of Liam Kennedy that her heart leapt, and in that instant she was convinced that this was the best New Year of her life.

Limousines transferred them out into the country for the stately home reception and party.

"Unbelievable..."

"Like a fairytale..."

"Those were real candles in the chandeliers..."

At the house Greta and Alma walked forward into a golden ballroom and took champagne off proffered trays.

"Alma; there's Colin McLean," Greta widened her eyes.

"I guessed he'd be here," said Alma, "I've got his book."

"What – *Human Trigonometry?*" Greta waved vigorously at Col.

"No," Alma delved into her bag, "his new one."

"He's written another one already?" Greta took the lime green paperback. It felt silky; the title embossed in silver. Across the shining floor stood the tall figure of Col, glamorous in a beautiful suit. Alma was staring at him. "Alma, you've still got a crush," Greta exclaimed, then: "he's seen us – it's too late now." She took Alma's arm and marched her towards him. Col's characteristic aloofness turned into affection as Alma, blushing, offered him the book to sign. Greta felt winded. *It's too late now…* she'd said. And it was. Too late.

"What are you up to these days?" she heard Col say to Alma.

Too late. Like bells tolling the words rang in Greta's head. She was a fraud. No sister, no father, no Liam, no play taking shape, no past she could own up to: nothing. There stood Col, balanced and matter of fact, smiling at Alma and inscribing a special message in the new book. *How come you have no problem, Col, yet I can't write a word?* And into her head came the answer… *Because what I want to say is a tide of filth…*

"And how about you, Greta?" said Col, smiling at her, "what are you doing these days?"

"I work in the café at The Riverside Studios," she said wildly, feeling a stiffness in her tongue that she remembered from childhood.

"You're a playwright," Alma sounded scandalised. She addressed Col with great warmth, "she's had two plays touring all over the world."

"But I haven't written anything for ages," said Greta, "Christ, I'm hot. I'm going to get more champagne," and she fled.

A spinning mirrorball printed the golden room with shifting petals of light. Greta felt as if she was flying through the swirling reflections like the floating seeds of Rosebay willow herb; a child lifted into the air by an umbrella. This is me, she thought; Nothing is holding me down. There's nothing to keep me in place.

Part 5. The Mother-Shaped Portion Of Space – 1979.

The Best Stories Are About A Man

Liam didn't ring. Or was he ringing when she was at work? Greta bought an Ansaphone. On hands and knees she backed out of the corner after plugging it in behind the settee. She bumped into her coffee table. A stack of magazines and papers toppled to the floor slithering in all directions. And there were the wedding dresses she had cut out. Fanned on her carpet the images demonstrated beauty in her shabby room; the sumptuous light in each photograph like an antidote to her custodial rented interior. It would be easy to feel mocked and yet she couldn't throw them away because they were a message to her, even though it was she who had assembled them. They symbolized her mythical search for Deborah. It was just a matter of time. Time had begun to resemble a place to Greta and her own trajectory towards Deborah had a shape in her mind. It was a slingshot trajectory. Ahead in time was Deborah. Here, further towards the past in her own present stood Greta and in between was the way; curving out to the moon and back in the blackness of the universe and lit by the wedding gowns; magnolias of light with dark intervals between.

February passed, then March and Liam never rang. That was that. But she didn't believe it – couldn't believe it; was bitterly disappointed. She had Rhonda, she had the reassuring routine of work. She fought to make that a sufficient solace for her grief at the way she had been abandoned. Sue the dancer lent her books: John Updike, Flannery O'Connor, Elizabeth Bishop's poems, a biography of Jonathan Swift. April passed and then, in May, Clare invited her down to Devon for the weekend.

As well as the new baby, Greta found that the family had acquired a Welsh border collie. Clare's little boy, Luke, squatted by Greta on the stone flagged floor as they patted the dog. "She's called Jazzy," he said in his gruff little voice.

"Jazzy," said Greta and the dog cast herself down and rolled on her back.

"I've trained her myself," said Clare, "she's amazing."

"She won't come upstairs," declared Francesca, Clare's dark-haired seven-year-old, "...not even if I call her." She added, wistfully.

In Clare's manorial kitchen a birthday tea was laid on the massive oak table; ham sandwiches, a wooden salad bowl with lettuce, tomato and slices of hardboiled egg; sausages on sticks, a dish of jelly and custard and a birthday cake delectably cascading with melted chocolate. "Do you like the writing on the cake? Mummy did it," Francesca pointed.

"*Happy Birthday Greta*," read Greta, out loud.

"And she let me and Luke put the silver balls on but they sank in."

"It's gorgeous," Greta assured her, "so many candles!" She looked at Clare who was beaming at her over baby Alice's head. A teething Alice gnawed her mother's fingers. Greta was touched at the trouble Clare had gone to. Her actual birthday had passed unremarked on a cold day in March. But here and now, warm sunshine poured into the room. On the recessed window-ledge stood a jug of columbines and buttercups. A cracker lay on each plate.

Francesca picked up Greta's present and waggled it. "Don't forget to open this," she said.

They sat down to eat as Greta unwrapped the present; a pair of pink, plastic sunglasses. "Thank you," she said, putting them on. Her fingers became sticky with icing. The dog sat by her, chin on her thigh; gobbling up the bits she gave it.

"Mum, Greta's feeding the dog at the table," said Francesca.

"I know, but we can't tell her off today because it's her official birthday tea and she's a guest, so I'll tell her off tomorrow," replied Clare, grinning at Greta. They toasted her in fizzy orange.

"These crackers have girl's things in them," said Luke in disgust, holding up a miniature toy lipstick.

Later, sipping coffee, Greta sat at the table with the dog lying on the flagstones at her feet and watched Clare, who had set the dishwasher going and was now at the sink. "What a beautiful dish," Greta said.

Clare held it up; foam glistened. "Dartington Glass. We should take you; you can watch the glassblowers. It's only about twelve miles from here."

Greta got up in a qualm of agitation, "what about Mrs Thatcher," she gushed, "did you vote for her?" and she began to dry one of the matching sundae glasses.

Clare put a wet forefinger on the furrow between Greta's eyebrows. "Away with that little Greta-frown of worry. It's your birthday." She removed the tea towel from Greta's hand and sat her back down. "There. Pat Jazzy if you want something to do. And no – I didn't vote for Mrs Thatcher. Nor did Ray. Everyone in North Devon is reeling in shock from all this Jeremy Thorpe scandal so we voted Labour."

Greta wanted to tell Clare about Liam; was longing just to say his name. In one of the distant bathrooms Ray was bathing the children. From the hallway a clock chimed seven. Clare spoke. "There's something I need to tell you; now that little ears aren't listening."

"Oh?"

"Alma's left Mick and she and the boys are staying in Barnstaple with her parents."

"Oh my God. Poor Alma!"

"I know. But she's coming here tonight, to see us. She'll be here any minute."

"Why has she left him?" In her mind Greta saw again the shabby house, the contented children.

"I don't know. I only found out a few days ago."

"How come you're really energetic," said Greta, "but you've got three kids and Alma's exhausted all the time and she's only got two?"

"It's the cleaning." Clare leaned against the sink and put a dollop of handcream on.

"It didn't look clean."

"Not her house; she goes out cleaning." She rubbed the cream in briskly.

"What? But she's an actress, a philosophy graduate."

"I know."

"Why doesn't Mick do something?"

"She thought that it was a temporary state of affairs; that he'd get work again and then they'd be off benefits for good."

"She's not on benefit!"

"Bloody hell Greta, of course she is. He doesn't earn anything," said Clare, sitting down at the table with her.

"When you were a social worker, did you ever have cases of children who'd been..." Greta allowed her voice to sink lower... "subjected to incest?"

"Yes."

"You're the last person I'd think of working in that context."

"Why?"

"Well when I think of you... when I first met you... you're so delicate. Don't you remember how you cried, that time in the cinema?"

"Well I'm a toughie now," said Clare, although to Greta, she looked as gentle as ever, with her smooth flow of brown hair and arching eyebrows.

"Has she left Mick for good?" Greta touched her bare toes against Jazzy's warm furry back.

"She says she's just got out of the house for a bit. I think she may have told him a few home truths."

"I bet it's got something to do with Col," said Greta; "she disappeared with Col at Camilla's wedding. It was when we..."

"I thought you got drunk," interrupted Clare.

"I did, but I still noticed..."

"She's here," said Clare. A car engine was audible; tyres scrunched the gravel in the yard. They made for the front door and flung it open.

Alma stopped her rusty Cortina level with a stone trough dripping with aubretia and struggled out across the passenger seat, "the driver's door doesn't open," she called, holding her arms towards them. It was a shock to see how much weight she had lost since Camilla's wedding. She looked haggard.

"Boys?" said Clare.

212

"They're fine with Grandma so I'm free." Alma put an arm round each neck and looked from one to the other. "God; all three of us are together again." There were tears in her eyes and she laughed. In an instant, wild, they grabbed one of her hands each, put their other arms round her waist and carried her preposterously towards the house, laughing and squealing. Jazzy leapt and panted; fur standing out with excitement. Her yelping barks mingled with their commotion and the pigeons took off from the roof in an explosive flypast, racing away towards the woods.

Clare fetched white wine in a cooler and glasses on a tray. Jazzy wove around them as they settled themselves on sofas either side of the stone fireplace in the beamed lounge. "Where are the children?" asked Alma.

"Ray's putting them to bed," said Clare, "the baby's been asleep for an hour already. She's an angel."

"Hello Alma," Ray came in and kissed Alma's cheek, "I'll leave you girls to it. I'm off to play squash."

"See you later," said Clare. She poured wine and sat by Greta. The dog lay down on the Kashmir rug at her feet.

"You two look like an interview panel," said Alma, raising her glass in salute.

"Well we are," said Greta, "we're dying to know what happened to you at Camilla's wedding."

"How's Mick getting on?" said Clare hurriedly, as if Greta had spoken out of turn.

"He's OK."

"Your boys must miss him," said Greta, feeling awkward. From outside the pigeons cooed.

"As far as they're concerned we're just visiting Grandma," said Alma. "We phone him every day, or he phones us. Ben tells him all the things he's done each day and Andrew holds up the toy in his hand and tells Mick about it as if Mick can see it down the telephone. But talk about something sophisticated and intellectual," she cried, "and not connected at all to people whose voices are at knee level and who say bum poo willy and need help wiping their bottoms." Her hands waved. The excitable movement roused Jazzy who went over in a doggy bustle.

"OK. So did you have it off with Two Balls at Camilla's wedding?"

"Greta!" Clare remonstrated, "Poor Mick," she went on, "but he must be realising by now that he ought to be getting out and... well... I don't mean this nastily, but earning a living and keeping his family."

"Maybe it's my fault," said Alma.

"How could it be your fault?" Greta exploded.

"I could have told him to do something about it sooner," said Alma. "Maybe I've made him think that I prefer it if he's in the house all the time; or maybe..." she stopped. There was a silence. After a drink of her wine, Alma, her hand tangling and untangling itself in Jazzy's ruff, sighed. "Maybe it's got something to do with sex," she said. "I can't bear him touching me."

There was an onyx ashtray on the side table next to Greta and she wondered if they were allowed to smoke. "Do you sleep with him?" she said.

"Of course I do, I feel sorry for him some of the time and anyway we haven't got a spare room and even if we had I wouldn't move into it. I'm not trying to say he's repulsive. I've just gone off sex with him. It's not like he deserves it or anything. I... grit my teeth." The clock struck the half-hour. Alma sighed again. "He doesn't deserve that."

"No," said Clare, "but you don't deserve it either. No one does. I don't think you should feel bad about not wanting him to touch you. It isn't your fault. What about the rest of the time," she demanded, "when you don't feel sorry for him?"

"I feel furious with him, I could kill him," said Alma.

"Here's to anger," Clare held up her glass.

"So you don't love Mick any more?" Greta was dying for a cigarette.

"I don't fancy him at all."

"So you love him but you don't fancy him?"

"I don't know, sometimes I hate him. He just doesn't do anything these days. He'd have to be like he used to be, when I did fancy him – oh I don't know."

"I've been trying to write a play about sex," Greta said; after a silence. "Clare; do you remember me telling you?"

Clare shook her head.

"Last summer? We were having steak in that restaurant?" persisted Greta. Clare bent down, fussing with her skirt, sweeping her hand over her shin, grasping filaments of dog hair off the fabric. "Well anyway," continued Greta, "I didn't actually tell you the reason why I was writing about that."

"Didn't you?"

"No; but it was to do with the fact that I'd... that... I didn't have such a thing as a libido any more. And I knew that the reason was to do with things that had happened to me and not my fault and I wondered how many more people like me there were." She swallowed wine. There was a piano at one end of the room with music open on the stand. Greta imagined the children practising; Clare serenely supervising their safe existence.

"Actually I do remember," said Clare. "And I changed the subject."

"I thought it was me who changed the subject." Greta frowned.

"No, I did," said Clare, "and the reason is that the same thing has happened to me." They looked at her astounded; their embodiment of uncomplicated, youthful love, their icon of tenderness. Clare was an eternal Juliet; they had reunited her with Ray themselves all those years ago. Greta took her feet out of her shoes and curled her legs up under her on the cushions. Clare talked about having Francesca; about how it wasn't always plain sailing, that babies still get stuck; can still have the cord wrapped round their necks, that mothers can still die in labour; about how close she came. Whether it was the wine or just the sudden introduction of a surprise revelation Greta didn't know; but a disembodied giddiness was affecting her, a sense that something inside her had loosened and was spiralling up, ready to come out like steam when it reached an opening.

"Clare was in labour thirty-five hours with Francesca," said Alma.

"Thirty-eight," Clare corrected. " I felt as if I was doing a consumer test of every obstetric technique known to man; starting with natural childbirth and beanbags and progressing to crochet hooks up the fanny to break the waters and then on to foetal heartbeat monitoring, oxytocin, gas and air, vomiting and pethidine. Then it was into day two and...oh God... I had one drip for rehydration, another one for the epidural, I had catheterisation to empty my bladder, an oxygen mask, in-utero blood sampling from

Francesca's head, then a pubic shave in preparation for emergency caesarean, a high speed dash to the operating table, a massive episiotomy and a ventouse suction extraction. Then I was sewn up and had to wait ages for my legs to start working again. Having so many stitches down there means that when sensation does come back into your bottom half you wish it hadn't. But it was worth it. The people at the hospital were fantastic. I'd have been dead without them and so would Francesca; no Luke, no Alice."

Alma went over to the window and sat in the recess squinting against the setting sun. "So you still fancy Ray?" she said.

"In a theoretical way perhaps," said Clare, "but I can't feel a thing because... I don't know... something has turned my switch off. My theory is that it was the episiotomy. I can go through the motions but I can't feel anything. I'm getting resigned to it." There was a silence. "I'm not exactly bothered," she said.

Greta didn't believe her.

"Not that I think it's OK," Clare added, "what can I do? If you're not angry and you love someone, you can perform an act with them. It's consent that's necessary, not sexual arousal. It's like there are two boxes to tick: essential and desirable. Consent is essential, arousal is desirable. As long as you can tick one of them... Am I talking rubbish?"

"Well do I still love Mick if I don't fancy him?" said Alma, "I mean is that it? Are none of us going to feel sexually aroused, ever again?"

Greta thought with longing, of Liam.

From outside came the distant sound of cows lowing. Alma opened the window. A breeze lifted the curtain.

"Find a man you're not angry with. Maybe you'd fancy him," said Clare.

"Which brings us to the million dollar question..."

"Shut up Greta!"

"Shit, Clare, you are tough these days."

"It's what having children does to you," said Alma, closing the window again and, along with Clare, dissolving into laughter.

"You're both terrifying," said Greta, "I need Jazzy for protection." She appealed to the dog, bending towards her, calling her name. The dog rose and moved round Clare's knees and aligned her muzzle to fit into Greta's imploring hands.

216

"And in any case Greta, the million dollar question is what about your play?" declaimed Alma forcefully. "It seems to me, you have to write it. It's a crucial subject." She came over and knelt on the rug, fussing with Jazzy's ears as she spoke, smiling at Greta. Their hands met in the dog's fur. "Is it making progress?"

"Not exactly." Greta picked up her wine again, leaning back into the cushions, letting the other two talk. And as she did so, words came into her head as clearly as if a voice was speaking them. *The best stories are about a man. I can see him. He is fourteen and walks between the tenements down the cobbled hill carrying a suitcase. His face is without expression; pale cheeks, red child's lips. His knuckles are hidden by his coat sleeves. No one was there to say goodbye. He left the children's home. He was on his own. Say nothing. ou'll nae speak aboot it* … Greta felt the urge to write it down but she snapped her attention back to Clare and Alma.

"…perhaps it's both," Clare was saying, "you love Mick *and* you're angry with him. I think anger rules out love so that's why you can't feel the love. You probably still could fancy him. The thing is, he has to do something to stop you being angry..." She paused, frustration on her face, "is this utter crap I'm spouting?"

"No, I think that's true," said Greta, "because Alma's right to be angry, Mick's doing something that ought to make her angry, he isn't earning any money so he's letting her down."

"And the children, he's letting them down," said Clare.

"So Alma; did you have it off with Two Balls?" said Greta. This time the question provoked laughter and Clare got up and re-filled their glasses. The wine gleamed like cut pineapple.

Alma hid her face. "OK," she said, "You knew you were onto something didn't you! Well, no I didn't. But I'll admit …"

"Wait," commanded Clare, "this bottle's empty, I'm going to get another one. Don't start again until I come back." She went out, Jazzy at her heels.

Collaboration

I've got a surprise for you, Greta." Matthew's voice on the phone was vibrant as he arranged to see her. Her mood had lifted since her return from Devon but the relief and elation she felt to be seeing Matthew again raised her to a hyperactive level of anticipation. She felt a kinetic sense of energy like she did at the end of her dance classes. They met at the National Gallery.

"What's the surprise?" demanded Greta, "Are you going to show me your favourite painting or did you just want to enlighten me?"

"You'll see," Matthew said in the deep baritone that made all his pronouncements sound so wise, "this way…" Inside the gallery, as different halls merged into one another Greta felt pleasantly disorientated. They strode along. In some stretches they were the only visitors. "How is the writing going?" he asked.

"Weird," said Greta. "I've begun imagining my Dad as a boy."

"Freud would be delighted," Matthew smiled. "Whatever happens, Greta, it must be the right thing. Just let it go its own way and trust yourself."

"Watch this," said Greta on impulse and pointing her toes she held out her arms and struck a pose before launching herself in a series of balletic turns that took her diagonally away across the marble floor; spinning like a top.

"Bravo," called Matthew, "encore! I had no idea you could pirouette."

And Greta lined herself up and came spinning back towards him, getting further and further out of line until she stopped; reeling and clasping a pillar, laughing. "I'm not pirouetting," she panted, "they're called posée turns, but I can't do it from the left – I always go off-course."

"Through here," Matthew was laughing too, "pirouette in this direction," and he led her into the adjoining gallery.

"I hope that's not your favourite painting." Greta pointed, aghast.

"Greta, I don't see this side of you very often; you can be quite a mischief," Matthew said, "deconstruct it for me, then."

"Jesus has pushed those people off his tussock and these two are being obsequious in case he does it to them," she said, pleased at Matthew's amusement.

"So much for poor Girolamo and his *Transfiguration*," he said, "what scathing put-down lies in store for my surprise? There it is," he pointed ahead, "they've got it on loan from Venice," he added. It was a portrait. Greta approached, staring at the pale composed face that glanced out of the painting. Over a white cambric shirt the young man wore a black doublet. The rich silk of this garment reflected subtle gleams of light. His long brown hair was gathered back from his face. In silence together, they regarded the picture. "Can you see it?" Matthew asked eventually. Greta nodded, unaccountably timorous. The man looked just like Liam Kennedy. Behind her, Matthew stepped back and sat down on one of the benches. For such an understated picture it was extremely beautiful. The large brown eyes were looking at a point to the viewer's left. The long narrow nose and serious mouth held an expression of thoughtfulness; he seemed to be about to take a breath and speak. "It's by Lorenzo Lotto," said Matthew, "a Venetian painter. *Portrait of a Man*." Greta joined him on the bench. "It's just so like Liam," he continued, "I'm staggered." He put a friendly arm round her shoulders. "I'm going to bring him along to see it before it goes back to Venice. And speaking of Liam; he told me once that you reminded him of a Siamese cat. Isn't that sweet."

The girls were having a break on the terrace by the river one cloudless afternoon the following week. "Guess what the next production is going to be." It was Sue the dancer who spoke. With one foot resting up on the wall she bent her body until it lay flat along her extended leg.

"Surely it's too hot to contort," said Rhonda, shading her eyes from the sun.

"Tell us then," urged Greta.

"A collaboration," announced Sue, straightening and tapping the ash from her cigarette over the wall into the river.

"Is it that Polish company?" Rhonda demanded, letting her tilted chair clang back to earth. "I've heard their name bandied about lately. You weren't here then Greta but they've been before and some of them are utterly gorgeous."

"Yes," Sue confirmed, "it's going to be a collaboration between them, Riverside and The Royal Court."

"*The* Royal Court?" asked Greta.

Sue nodded and began weaving sinuously around their metal chairs, sure-footed on the grubby concrete. "This is how they move," she said, demonstrating the physical techniques the Polish dancers were famous for. "Your body has to follow the physical patterns of… a willow…say," and she jack-knifed her body, trailing her tapering arms, "… oops," Sue jerked upright, "damn…" smoothing back her shiny bob, "I should have taken the fag out of my mouth." She gave her distinctive snort of laughter. "I've burnt a bit of my fringe off."

"Sue, the pyrotechnic dancer," teased Rhonda. They were sipping iced water to keep cool. Light refracted off the river. Greta leaned back in her chair and closed her eyes. The blaze of sun on her face felt good. *The Royal Court.* She let the words sink in. It was impossible not to feel elated by the surge of hope that suffused her. *Maybe I'll see Liam again.* She counted months; her fingers moving secretly; *December, January, February, March, April, May, June*: Seven months since she'd seen him.

"You're perky," Rhonda said, as the week wore on. And: "what's got into you?" as Greta's high spirits continued, day after day. "Right. That's it!" she exploded, the morning she arrived to find Greta standing barefoot on the work-surface, whistling as she scrubbed the tops of the cupboards. "Why are you so cheerful? Are you in love?"

"It's the new production," Greta laughed, "it's going to be fantastic. I'm really looking forward to it."

"I can see that," said Rhonda, "as a matter of fact I'm looking forward to it myself. Not like you though, singing and whistling; don't think I'm not suspicious. Anyway, I've been meaning to say, I can introduce you to the writer doing the script." She turned a tap full on and for a while, water thundering into the metal sink drowned all other noise.

"Who is it?" said Greta, as Rhonda silenced the tap.

"He's a friend of mine – from the Valleys" Rhonda exaggerated her Welsh accent. "Vic Amey." Vic Amey was a well-known playwright; an ex-miner who'd begun writing after an accident down the pit forced him to retire early.

"Wow!" said Greta.

"Yes," said Rhonda with satisfaction. "Me and Sue think you should act more like a writer. You're too timid." She patted Greta's bare foot. Greta looked down; touched. Rhonda smiled; then squeezed warm suds from her sponge over Greta's foot and they both giggled.

The first week in July, when the posters came back from the printers, Greta helped Sue put them up. They laboured most of the morning, lining the walls, standing back to gauge the effect, arranging leaflets into mosaics on every available surface until Greta's fingers were sore from using the staple gun and the nails of her thumbs and forefingers were reddened from placing and extracting drawing pins.

That night she wrote to Clare, finally telling her about Liam and her excitement at the new collaboration. Clare's reply came the following week and after work Greta sat in the café with a mug of tea re-reading it.

July 14 1979: Dear Greta, Your letter was lovely. It was great to see you and Alma. I had the idea of us three going to Edinburgh like the old days. Maybe during the Festival next year? It's good that you've met someone you like. If Riverside is collaborating with The Royal Court I bet you will see Liam. But don't pin your hopes on him if he's been stupid enough to have been ignoring you. Think of all those handsome Polish dancers. I'm sure they will be very supple. Come back and see us soon. (Say yes to Edinburgh. My Mum says she'll have my three) Love, Clare.

"Ooh love letter!" called Rhonda, swooping by in a cloud of *L'Air Du Temps*.

Greta slapped the letter against her chest. "Stop making me jump; I'll have a heart attack!" she yelled as Rhonda; changed and ready to go out; disappeared round the end of the counter in a clatter of high heeled sling-backs. "And yes it is a love letter."

"What – to you?" Rhonda re-appeared, black froth of curls backlit. Under her apron she wore black leggings and a shiny blue sleeveless tunic knotted at her hip. In her hair was a matching blue headband.

"Why are you all dolled up?" asked Greta.

"Me and Sue are going to see Ian Dury and the Blockheads at the Palais." She slid into the bench opposite Greta. "Don't change the subject; it's a letter from a man isn't it?"

"*...Say yes to Edinburgh...*" read Greta, aloud, "*... Mum says she'll have my three ...) Love, CLARE.*" Greta emphasised the name, snatching the page back to her chest as Rhonda tried to grab it. To the left, doors opened and people in leotards from the advanced adult dance class trailed through fanning themselves. Just before the doors whammed shut Greta caught a glimpse of Sue, barefoot in the corridor, arms in a graceful port de bras, conducting an animated conversation with one of the theatre technicians, a Spaniard with wild curly hair. "Look, Sue's on the pull," she said.

"Don't distract me," said Rhonda, "so no mystery man?" Using her apron she wiped crumbs off the scratched planks of the pine table, lifting Greta's elbow.

"No. Do you want me to put some more lasagne in?" The early birds of the *Titus Andronicus* audience were beginning to arrive. Greta caught a tantalising whiff of French cigarettes. She inhaled. "Ooh," she said, "Gauloises. That takes me back."

"Let someone else do the lasagne," said Rhonda, "you should have gone home an hour ago. Empty the ashtrays if you like." So Greta did; then set off home.

In the Cypriot off-license the freezer gusted cold on her warm skin while she rummaged for a choc-ice. The chocolate sagged and melting ice-cream raced her attempts to eat it as she crossed the park. Along her street the leaves on the plane trees hung down in summer torpor. She licked her vanilla scented fingers, passing people grouped outside their houses in the evening sun, sitting on the walls and steps; men sipping cans of lager with their shirts unbuttoned, girls in sun frocks, lolling relaxed, smoking and laughing. Greta could smell dope and wondered if there were any tickets left for Ian Dury: she could join Rhonda and Sue. The heat produced a pleasant sensation of drugged laziness.

In her flat, she pressed the button on the answering machine; instantly alert as Matthew Tarry's cultured voice filled the room. "Greta, I've had a message from Leicester Social Services. I don't want to alarm you but your mother is seriously ill. She's in Leicester Royal Infirmary; D ward on level two. You can go whenever you like. This is the telephone number of D ward." His voice reeled off a number. "Let me know if you need any help, Sweetheart." There was a click and the red light went on blinking.

Greta pressed play again and went into the kitchenette to fill the kettle. The gush of the tap drowned out most of the message.

"*... is the number of D ward...*" She put the kettle on. Why had Social Services phoned Matthew? She stared through the opening that led into the living room. It framed an oblong of the place she lived in. She could see the window, newspapers on the lumpy settee, the telephone on the carpet, the attached answering machine. Had she forgotten to put her new address on her mother's Christmas card when she moved? She walked towards the couch and bent down, re-starting the message. What was this supposed to feel like? The kettle boiled. Unable to find a teaspoon, she shook coffee granules into a mug then poured on the boiling water. *What have I done*? No clear thoughts came to her. Nothing. She stalled; the coffee mug inert in her hand. Her eyes went out of focus. *What am I doing*? She began to imagine what it was like in that mother-shaped portion of space in Leicester. *My mother: Carmel Aurora Buchanan.* Her head was empty.The evening darkened to twilight and still she stood there. *Say your prayers now, Sweetheart, or shall you sing me Jesus bids us shine*? Greta sang the words...

Jesus bids us shine with a pure, clear light;
Like a little candle, burning in the night;
In this world is darkness, so we must shine;
You in your small corner, and I in mine...

It was an unsuspecting eight-year-old Greta who sang. Silence again. The evening faded away, its last paleness drained into violet shadows. Orange haloes expanded into slices of glare as the municipal street lamps took over from daylight. To have left the glass animals... *in the niche...* Greta stood there, frozen. The phone rang. One: two: three: four: five rings: then a click and her own voice on the answering machine. "I'm not here at the moment but leave your name and number, I'll get back to you. Thanks for calling."

A real voice broke the spell. "Greta, it's Liam." Her lungs took a gulp of air as if all this time she had been holding her breath. "There's a meteor storm tonight. I thought it would be something you'd like. I could drive over..." Greta collapsed onto her knees and attempted to uncurl her fingers from around her mug but she had been gripping it so tensely and for so long that both arms had gone numb from the elbows down. She felt as if she was trying to wake up from a nightmare, everything in slow motion. "...gets to its peak at four a.m. – it's half ten now, so if you'd like to come with me, there's plenty of time to drive into the middle of nowhere..." Still on her knees she left the mug of cold coffee on the floor and crawled towards the phone."...you can't see anything in the city ..." Her hand groped at the receiver. "...you might be asleep of course..."

"Liam..." Her inert fingers slithered across the plastic bumps of the phone with no sensation of touch at all.

"... If you get this message before midnight give me a ring and I'll come and pick you up."

"Liam, wait..." She gripped the receiver; hauled it off its cradle and was speaking to him. "I'm here," she said. Pins and needles crowded into her hands.

"Hello? Did I wake you?"

"My Mum is in hospital."

"Oh no. I'm sorry... Is it bad?"

"Yes. I'm stuck here Liam, I'm physically stuck." Her voice shredded itself to a whisper.

"I'll come over. Just stay put. Will you be able to let me in?"

Swallowing helped to steady her voice. "I'll put the catch on the street door."

"Tell me your address. Hang on, I'm writing it down. OK, I'll be there as fast as I can." He hung up. She lay on the floor until the pins and needles stopped fizzing through her hands. Eventually, craving warmth, she rose and switched on her table lamp, lit the two candles on the mantelpiece and turned on the gas fire; shivering.

When Liam knocked she was waiting, her bag hugged against her chest. There was a stinging smell of blown-out candles. Only the gas fire lit the room. Liam had to duck his head to avoid her wind chimes. She looked away because the sight of him was so beautiful. "Thanks for coming," she said.

"I'll drive you to Leicester as soon as you feel ready. That's where she's in the hospital... Leicester right?"

"Yes. But we'll see the meteor shower on the way, won't we?"

"We will if we take a detour into Warwickshire or Northamptonshire but don't you want to go straight to the hospital?"

"No, I want to see the meteors. Your message... it was... I have to see the meteors."

He gave her a sharp look. She could see that he thought it was peculiar that she was more interested in meteors than in her mother.

"Press the button," she said, "listen to the message from Matthew."

They both listened. "Social Services?" Liam's voice was full of incredulous urgency, "no wonder you're so... winded," he said. "Shall I make you a drink? Christ. This is a shock, Greta. Take your time." He touched her shoulder briefly as he spoke.

"I'd really like to see the meteors," she said. He looked at her as if gauging something.

"OK," he said. The gas fire hissed. "So shall we go?"

"I'm still... stuck." She stood shivering, unable to set off. Maybe any action would do, so she bent and switched the fire off. "Will I be alright... in this... do you think?" She pulled at the collar of her denim jacket. "I'm... ...stuck." Her teeth were chattering.

"I could carry you out," he said.

"Yes. Do that." She shut her eyes, clamping her jaws together to silence her teeth. Their noise was bizarre, she felt her face convulsing. Weakness was affecting the backs of her legs as if her calf and thigh muscles were dissolving.

He picked her up and bumped her gently through the doorway, dragging the door shut with his foot. He carried her down the stairs and held her pressed against the wall to steady himself as he undid the catch of the front door. Then he carried her down the steps to the pavement and put her next to his car as if she was a rose growing in a pot. Greta was thinking that she was retracing her steps, going back in time. It was like the car journey from the abortion clinic but in reverse. She was being brought, paralysed, from the house into the car and then being driven to the hospital. Soon she would arrive at the table and there, a man would put back in the pieces of her daughter and set her speck of a heart beating again. One way or another, a daughter was going back to a mother.

They drove up the M1, branching off westwards into Warwickshire at Newport Pagnell. The movement of the car and the sense of travelling soothed her and she kept falling asleep then jerking awake out of fleeting dreams. As they skirted Stratford-on-Avon the skies became clearer. Liam was making for Meon Hill. "My uncle lives in a village near here called Pemberton," he said, "me and my sister used to come down and stay with him in the school holidays." The roads were narrow but then Greta gasped as they turned into a lane only just wide enough for the car to scrape through. Grass grew down the centre of it. In the darkness between high hedges, branches clattered and swished against the bodywork. It was like heading into a midsummer night's dream and maybe it focused everything that was bothering Liam because he turned towards her with determination. "Look, are you sure about this?" His gaze returned to the lane and he wound his window down. A gust of air swept the scent of mown hay into the car. "You don't think we should just head straight for the hospital?"

"I'm sure." She stared into the night at the mesh of branches that brushed at the sides of the car, "we'll get to the hospital anyway in the end."

"OK, you know best."

Greta looked at him suspiciously.

"I wasn't being sarcastic," he said, "it's right for you to trust your instincts." The car bucked slowly over the uneven surface of the lane. They were heading uphill. Liam pulled into a gateway and switched off the engine. Around them Warwickshire lay hushed under a sky patched with cirrus clouds. The moon shone through, outlined in blue haze. Liam hauled a bundle off the back seat, got out and opened the boot. He hefted a cylindrical case with a wide strap over his shoulder. Another, boxier one he handed to Greta. Opening a five-barred gate he ushered her through. "Your eyes will get used to the dark," he said, latching the gate behind them.

"Are we allowed in here?" Her voice was low, as if they were in church. "I can feel the silence," she said, "it's like skin."

"You're a complete townie aren't you," said Liam. The quiet humour in his voice was one of the things she liked so much about him. There was friendliness in his speech; humane concern. He walked with confidence along the line of the hedge. The ground sloped up more steeply. A stile led them into an even steeper field. Liam struck off into the centre of it. Out of breath, her heart thudding with exertion, she followed over the rough ground. They were nearing the summit. Thistles pricked her ankles like knifepoints. At the top Liam spread out the sleeping bag and travelling rug he carried. "Lie down and look up," he advised. He took the case off her, unlooping the strap from over her head.

She liked the care he took; his calmness; getting the strap off as if every hair on her head mattered and might feel pain if it got touched too hard. Kneeling on the rug she felt the resilience of tussocky grass under the two layers of fabric and as she patted at the lumps and bumps, she could feel bent and flattened shapes of more substantial plants. But the thistles couldn't get through the layers so she lay down, feeling the wool of the blanket slither over the nylon of the sleeping bag. Above, clouds blew across the sky. Canopies of stars hung between them.

"Look through these," said Liam, handing her the binoculars she had been carrying. She focused them as he instructed and was astounded and began crying out in excitement at what she could see. The sky was criss-crossing with arrowing lines of shooting stars. Against the velvet of the deep universe, billions of clusters, of spirals, formed a galactic backdrop where swarms of stars had her panning in great arcs. Again and again she tried to follow the incandescence of star after star, from flash point to extinction, as they fell. She imagined she could hear the magnesium plosives as each one ignited; the faraway rush, like air through wings.

Liam was setting up a telescope. "You're watching things that happened before you were born," he said.

Carmel Aurora

In the ochre light of dawn, she and Liam entered the hospital. A nurse with dark shadows under her eyes looked up as Liam told her who the silent Greta was. There was a pause. Then: "I'll take you in to her." The nurse seemed about to say something else. She looked at Greta with a little smile. Her hands closed the lid on a box of implements and with her knee she shoved her desk drawer shut. "Take a seat," she advised Liam and walked away with Greta trailing behind.

Greta was chilly. She looked at the figure ahead. Fatigue emanated from the nurse's rounded shoulders. "Will she be asleep?" Greta asked, trying to draw level. *What's the matter with my mother?*

"She may be. You're welcome to sit by her." The soles of their shoes squeaked on the polished floor. "She's there, third bed on the left." The nurse withdrew.

Greta walked towards the bed with her mother in it. This was it, the mother-shaped portion of space; the mother-shaped arrangement of matter. *If I'm silent she won't wake up and I'll come back tomorrow.* Her mother's head on the pillow became recognisable in the low light. She appeared shrunken; child-size. Her scalp gleamed through tufts of hair. The chart at the end of the bed said: *Carmel Aurora Buchanan.*

Greta stepped closer. At that moment her mother's eyes opened. Nightlight shone in the gloss of her pupils and as Greta arrived at the bedside her mother smiled at her. "Greta," she said. The smile lit her face. Her voice had a far-away sound. It was the wispy chime of a tarnished glass bell. Her mother had no teeth.

"Hello Mum," Greta whispered. Her mouth mirrored her mother's smile. "Where are your teeth?"

"In the glass," her mother's glance flicked sideways to the bedside cabinet.

"Why did you have your teeth out?"

"To save any more fillings. My teeth were finished. I knew you'd come, Greta. What time is it?"

"About quarter to six."

"Will you stop for a cup of tea? They'll draw the curtains in a minute and we'll see the dawn. They bring tea at six."

"What's wrong with you?"

"I had an accident." She started to cough.

A different nurse appeared. "Hello," she said giving Greta a quick smile. Her smooth black hair was pinned into a bun. With her narrow face she was like a painting by Modigliani.

"Nurse, this is my youngest. Isn't she beautiful?" said the whispery, tinfoil voice.

"Yes, she is, Mrs Buchanan," said the nurse, raising the pillows, angling the backrest, helping her patient sit up.

"She brightens my day," said Carmel Aurora, looking up at the nurse."

The nurse smiled at Greta, then gently put her hand on the forehead of her patient. "She's a beautiful girl," she said, "she's a credit to you Mrs Buchanan." Slowly she smoothed the covers, lifting the delicate hands one at a time to straighten the counterpane and fold its edge beneath them. Greta felt humble. The nurse was showing her how to be calm. In here, she was the giantess, Gargantina, with carthorse limbs to knock the jugs and sputum dishes flying.

"You can have morning tea with your daughter," said the nurse. She whisked the curtains around the bed before moving on to wake the next patient.

"How did you get here, love?" Greta told her mother about the message on her answering machine; about Liam giving her a lift. "They didn't know where you lived," said her mother. "The address I gave them was wrong."

A tea trolley was approaching. Greta could hear cups and saucers in descant on a trembling metal surface. She listened to the growing number of teaspoons that joined in, as one patient after another stirred sugar. Voices murmured. Someone at the far end of the ward opened the blinds. Daylight filled the long room. The trolley arrived at their curtains and a nurse with stiff wheat-coloured hair came through nodding at Greta pleasantly. Her cheeks were bright with beetroot capillaries. "Do you want your teeth in, Mrs Buchanan?" she asked. The nurse put the teeth into her mother's mouth. "So this is your other daughter..." she said. Greta's heart lurched as if she had almost tripped over. *Your other daughter...*

The nurse angled the adjustable table expertly over the bed and put a cup of tea on it. "Now you can stop worrying at last."

"Yes," said Carmel Aurora, her smile gleaming with glamorously level teeth. The nurse pushed the tea trolley to the next bed.

"That one has a beige uniform," Greta whispered, her throat contracting... *Your other daughter...*

"She's an auxiliary." Her mother's eyes, behind the rising steam from her cup, were blue and bright. "They're so kind in here," her mother sipped tea. To Greta, whose heart was now beating twice as hard as usual, it looked as if at any moment, she might drop the cup and saucer so shaky were her wrists.

When Greta came out, Liam was talking to a nurse. The look on his face was angry and he held a newspaper that they were referring to. "Of course he shouldn't but that isn't her fault," she heard him say.

"Pleased to meet you Greta," said the nurse, giving Greta's hand a brisk shake, "I'm Sister Wakefield." Her smile was the wrong way up giving her the air of a comedian telling a rueful joke. "Your friend will explain how it happened and then later you can talk to the doctor." and she strode off, back into the ward.

"God it's hot," Liam pushed open the swing doors to the corridor. "Sister Wakefield says to eat some breakfast."

"I don't want any."

"Your mother had an accident."

"Yes." *Why was Liam angry?*

He stopped in a dead end that led off the main corridor. A trolley piled with folded green cloth stood in the alcove. Liam took two plastic chairs off a stack and sat her down. He sat by her. "Did your mother tell you about her accident?"

"No." Greta listened to him saying that her mother had been hit by a pick-up truck; that the accident had happened a year ago. She heard *coma.* "In a coma?"

"Yes," he said.

"Are you angry?" Greta asked.

"No. Well… kind of. I'm shocked. And I don't know how to do this; it feels barbaric." He unfolded the newspaper; it was the *Mercury*. "It's this morning's," he said, giving it to her. "It's too hot in here," he stood up and wrestled his way out of the sweater he wore. His tee shirt underneath came half off, exposing his long ribcage and lean stomach. Roughly he pulled it straight and dropped the sweater on the floor as he sat back down. He raked his hair with his fingers, ending up bent forward, elbows on knees, head in hands as if in despair. When he had stopped moving she looked at the article in front of her.

Coma Victim's dream comes true… she read …by *Danny Scott.*

*As our headlines of fifteen months ago reported; on April 24th 1978, Carmel Buchanan had a narrow escape from death when a delivery driver tragically died at the wheel of his van…*Greta tried to think. What had she been doing fifteen months ago? …*Mrs Buchanan was thrown through a shop window by the impact and impaled on the broken glass…* She drew in a sharp breath. … *the facade of the building collapsed… during the rescue and she sustained a massive blow to the head… coma…* Greta's eyes blurred. A strange lassitude began to spread through her. 1978. Last year; when she met Rhonda; when she felt that things were getting better; when she went to visit her Dad's niche. She tried to read further and her left eyelid began to throb and quiver in a tic. … *Dubbed 'The Glass Lady' by staff at the hospital* …Greta struggled to focus, her eyes trembling and blinking more and more… *police contacted Deborah Buchanan, one of her two daughters,* … The words on the page were merging with one another. … *remained in a coma as the months went by… miraculously woke up a week ago asking for her second daughter Greta, a playwright. Greta Buchanan has now been contacted…* "I've finished it," Greta looked at Liam.

He didn't move. "The police got your name from the Edinburgh Fringe office and linked you to your mother to identify her. Social Services went into the house for next of kin addresses. They found your sister's…"

"They found her," Greta broke in, "she comes here. Is she here?" Greta's words were incoherent as realisations penetrated her brain.

"I don't think so, I don't know. I don't know why you haven't been in touch with your mother," he said, "all that time..." There was a pause. He began again, "I realise that you have problems of some kind with your mother... I don't feel qualified to be the one who..." Again he stopped speaking and this time twisted his head sideways to look at her. "I'm sorry," he sat back, "I feel," he raised a hand, let it fall onto his thigh, "...inadequate."

"She looks so tiny," blurted Greta, "she had..." Her voice was dissolving.

"What?" He leaned forward and touched her elbow. "What?" he said, more gently.

It was a struggle to speak. "She's had her teeth... out," she managed.

"The journalist who wrote that article is the guy who covered the story originally, the nurse told me," said Liam. "He says he knows you. Sister Wakefield is fed up with him because he keeps trying to get an interview with your mother."

"Oh God," burst out Greta, "what have I done?" and she wrapped both arms around her ribcage and rocked, tears running down her face. "I put..." she couldn't go on.

"You haven't done anything." Liam's mouth was solemn; eyes in shade. "Greta," he said, "nothing you put anywhere caused the accident." And he stood up.

"I'm sorry," she said, "you haven't slept all night," and she wiped her eyes with the heels of both hands and with her sleeve.

"I slept after work yesterday. I was planning the meteor watch. It's you who's running on adrenaline. Where are you going to stay?"

"My Mum's."

"But she's been in this hospital for over a year Greta; what state would the house be in?"

Greta stood up in agitation, knocking her chair over. The newspaper fell. They both reached out. He caught her hands. The crush of his grip steadied her before he let go and picked up the paper. "The *glass* lady," he said, "it's a grim article." Greta lifted the edge of her jacket to wipe her eyes. She felt his hand on her shoulder. "Look," he said, "let's be sensible. Sister Wakefield; obey Sister Wakefield. She knows what she's talking about for certain and anyway I'm starving. Breakfast. Come on." He bent to retrieve his sweater and then he put one arm round her. And she put her arm round his waist, and held onto him as they walked and she could feel warmth from his skin through the cotton of his T-shirt.

They walked like that. And then, reaching to open a door, he let her go. The door opened. A draught of air blew. And Liam looked at his watch. "I'm leaving once we've eaten," he said. "I've got a meeting." She walked on; benumbed. He had restored himself to her and brought her all this way. And then he had let go of her. The draught of air had gusted through the open door. Her feet woodenly placed themselves one in front of the other. Her hands had only the bag and the edges of her jacket to hold on to. They breakfasted in silence: him, egg and bacon, her, coffee and two bites of toast. He couldn't leave her there on her own after bringing her all this way.

But he did. "Thanks for driving me up here," she said, raising a hand at his departing back as he set off down the steps at the entrance, "and thank you for showing me the meteor shower."

"I remember thinking it meant something to you; that time you said you'd seen the stars at your friend's place near Torrington," he said.

It links us – don't leave…. she wanted to implore.

But he carried on down the steps.

"There's a chapel here Greta," said her mother, "go and light a candle for me please." Her voice was air. Her eyes were closing.

"Of course she will, Mrs Buchanan. In a couple more days you'll be able to go yourself." The Modigliani nurse laid her mother down. Greta watched, like a child. "She tires easily," said the nurse, "don't be alarmed, it's always like that with head injuries." Greta found it hard to concentrate. She had spent the afternoon talking to a social worker. "See you in the morning then?" The nurse held the curtain.

"Yes." Greta came away from the bedside; "um…"

"You've spoken to the social worker about the rehab arrangements; she gave you the key?" the nurse glanced at the clock.

"Yes… but…um… is my sister coming, do you know?" Greta's tongue stiffened around these words and she felt herself blushing.

"I don't know. I think your sister comes whenever work allows. She hasn't been since your mother woke up though." Greta didn't move. "We'll see you tomorrow then?" The nurse clearly longed to get on to her next task. *Please have time to tell me what my sister looks like and what she says to you and where she lives...* But the nurse was gone; leaving Greta to tiptoe away from her mother's bed alone.

Go and light a candle.

In the basement the floor turned from cream tiles to a smooth ramp of granular concrete glittering uphill. Double doors led into a huge and gothic building; the old part of the hospital. Greta had a paradoxical sensation of going back in time to put things right while simultaneously running forward as hard as she could, to catch up with a window where she could burst through into the rest of reality; a place where nurses saw Deborah as if it was the most normal thing in the world.

An arrow, pointing at a curtain of heavy-duty vinyl hanging across the corridor in overlapping strips said: *Chapel*. Pushing through the mauve-tinted weight of them she walked on. A humming sounded on all sides. Pipes, lagged in silver, ran overhead. The corridor turned sharp right. It was lined with stacks of old desks, swivel chairs, filing-cabinets and typewriters. There were hat stands and dented paper-towel dispensers like unused props from old scenes; a dead-end in the gloom. But right at the far end, paradoxically, was an oaken arched door.

Inside the chapel Greta clicked a light on. The Nativity, depicted in a modern stained glass window, dominated the back of the chapel. Greta stared, repelled by the star, an explosion of bayonets. One pierced the Virgin's halo and touched her head, one pricked the blue of her shawl. In her lap a thin baby flung both arms wide as if performing the reaction test, as if Mary had just been demonstrating it to the shepherds and wise men. Greta lit a candle.

The wind blustered as she walked out of the hospital and crossed the road towards the turreted prison. Barbed wire snaked along the top the high wall. An unpleasant sensation came over her. It felt like disintegration. It flowed from her centre, outwards along each arm and leg, travelling right into the tips of her toes and fingers like sparks along a fuse wire and as it exited from her body she felt as if the glue holding her molecules together had evaporated entirely. Her numb obedient feet kept walking.

The paint on the faded front door of the house which used to be her home was a spectral version of its former rich maroon. The street was so quiet it was like deafness. She unlocked the door and stepped over the threshold. There was a smell of damp. It was strange to be walking where she and Deborah had so often walked, to be passing the stairs and entering the kitchen. The soles of her feet no longer recognised the floor. The drawer in the end of the kitchen table looked absurdly small. The sink, which she remembered as white, was a sepia colour. With no-one in it the house had shrunk. *"Your sister has been keeping an eye on things – she sorted out the junk mail and utilities"* the social worker had said. Greta looked out of the window. The garden was featureless and overgrown.

The sideboard drawer in the front room; just as her mother had said it would; contained an imitation-leather writing case; and inside, birth certificates. She took this upstairs, to her parents' room. The late sun had been pouring into the room since teatime. *Under the bed*, her mother had instructed. Greta lifted the candlewick bedspread and there was a polished wooden box. The lid opened to reveal a baize writing surface, coming adrift. The narrow compartment under the baize was crammed with papers. There were photographs. Greta recognised her sepia mother as a girl in a drop-waisted dress, her hair in a fringed bob that hid her eyebrows. To face the camera she was raising her eyes rather than her head producing the effect of a glower. On the back it said, *Carmel Aurora O'Brien, 1939*, aged 13. Greta checked her mother's birth certificate – July 21st 1926. It added up. In 1939 she had been thirteen. *"Find my marriage certificate*,*"* her mother had said, *"there are things you need to know."*

Greta glanced through more photos and was just going to put them on one side when all of a sudden there it was; the wedding photo, unmistakable, her mother and father. He smiled; black hair curling back from his handsome face. She, in high heels, stood one foot angled before the other like a model. Her white hat had a veil of spotted net dipping seductively over her eyes. Carmel Aurora was a pretty bride. Instead of a wedding gown she wore a flowery summer frock and her left hand held a pair of white gloves. Under this absorbing image was another photo of the wedding – this time of a small wedding group; Carmel and Walter Buchanan, three strangers and a girl of maybe eight or nine, frowning at the camera.

Find my marriage certificate.

Greta laid the photos aside and sifted the documents. After some letters of promotion to her father came the marriage certificate dated May 9th 1949.

1949.

Then Greta got it. Goose pimples tightened in a circle on her scalp. If her mother had been thirteen in 1939 she had to have been fifteen when she had Deborah because Deborah was born in 1941. The calculations clicked madly into place in her brain… and if the wedding was in 1949, and Deborah was therefore eight years old… Greta stared at the wedding photo; at the bride and groom, the strangers and the frowning little girl. There was no doubt at all. The frowning little girl in the photo was her sister, Deborah. She scrabbled in the writing case for Deborah's birth certificate. There it was. Mother's name: Carmel Aurora O'Brien. Father's name. It was difficult to make out the spidery copperplate. Greta stared. It said: *Ladislaw Kazmierski.*

There's one letter among the others… her mother had told her, *find that one. You'll see, then.* Greta's quivering fingers turned over document after document. She found several letters. How small the envelopes were back then, how dainty the notepaper and slanting scripts. Here was an envelope post-marked Norwich, addressed: *Miss Carmel O'Brien, The Blue Boar, Elvedon,* a single sheet inside. *Dear Carmel, Don't come to the base any more, the CO won't put up with it. There will be no news of Kazmierski. You have to accept he is gone. I wish I could pass on a keepsake but there is nothing. We have lost other planes since then. We are losing men every day. You will get into trouble if you keep coming here. He would not have wanted that. I know how sad you feel. We had some fun that day swimming in the river and all the evenings at The Blue Boar. Kazmierski carried your photo in his pocket, the one of you and him on the riverbank. That is all I can tell you. Good luck, Carmel. Yours sincerely, Alec Noone, RAF Mildenhall.*

Something that was there all along had become visible; like a landscape when the fog lifts; unbelievable in its hugeness, colour and complexity and ringing with sounds and echoes. There stood her mother, the bride, smiling in a landscape she had no reason to fear.

There stood Deborah, in a different landscape entirely. And there stood her father.

Greta's knees ached from kneeling and the goose pimples had flooded down over her making her fingers cold and limp. She put everything back in the box, got up and hobbled along the landing to the tiny room above the scullery that had been hers at the beginning. There on the windowsill was her globe with its old-fashioned colours, Tanganyika; pink. Siberia, faint green; had it been that small? The memory of being unable to fit it into her suitcase came to her. Everything was faded. She knelt on the bed and looked out of the window. Impossible that there had ever been seedbeds and bean sticks. The collapsing shed was hidden by buddleia and brambles: the pear trees next door had been cut down. Turning away, she went into the other room – Deborah's room. In the wardrobe hung three empty coathangers and below on the floor were her comics and her Hans Andersen fairy tales. Taking the Hans Andersen she hurried to retrieve the writing case then went downstairs to put it away.

She couldn't stay the night here. Leaving the house she hurried up the avenue making for the Belmont hotel in De Montfort Street. Out loud, as she swiftly walked, she said, "it was Mum's birthday last week."

In the hotel she had a bath and got into bed.

If.

If.

It wasn't her mother's fault. But so many secrets. The secret of the wedding photo, the secret of where Deborah went. Now more secrets she could never have guessed; of a Polish airman, of her mother's illegitimate baby who was also Deborah, her sister. Her mother had been an enigma. Greta went blank. The room darkened. Sleep took over.

In the morning, Greta woke up hungry and unexpectedly calm. For breakfast she enjoyed bacon and mushrooms with a sweet pigeon-shaped girl serving her tea and toast. Then she went shopping. Back at the hospital she explained to Sister Wakefield what she wanted to do. Sister Wakefield agreed and took charge of the balloons, cards and cake Greta had bought. Greta hurried off to her mother's bed with the rest of the shopping where she helped her mother open the various packages. Carmel gasped, touching the things and staring: a pink nightgown trimmed with lace, a matching fluffy dressing gown and a pair of pink sheepskin slippers. "Feel the softness of that lambskin Greta." Carmel fitted a slipper over her hand and held it out.

"Well Mrs Buchanan, what's this?" The nurse with the gentle Modigliani features put in the thermometer and took Carmel's white wrist, checking her pulse. "Your birthday?"

"Last week. I'm fifty-one."

"Fifty two remember Mrs Buchanan – you've been asleep in your coma."

"She thinks I need a bath, look at these bath salts: from Marks and Spencer."

"So will we give you one?" said the nurse. "French Fern," she read out, picking up the bottle, "ooh la la – let's get the wheelchair."

"Miss Buchanan." Sister Wakefield's crepe-soled shoes squeaked up to where Greta sat reading on her mother's empty bed. "We've got the cards signed so we're ready when you are."

"Thank you so much," Greta lowered her newspaper.

"There is a favour you could do for me," Sister Wakefield said.

"OK."

"Could you talk to this journalist? He's been plaguing us ever since your Mother woke up. We could get rid of him if you would give him what he wants." Sister Wakefield's soulful eyes quivered in their sockets.

"What does he want?" Greta stared at her.

"At the time of the accident there was a newspaper clipping in your mother's apron pocket which helped the police identify her. The journalist didn't find out about it until a few weeks ago and since she woke up he's called every day asking for an interview. He says he knows you. Your mother refuses to see him but maybe if you spoke to him he'd be satisfied and leave us in peace."

"What was the newspaper clipping?" asked Greta.

"It's in your mother's locker," Sister Wakefield's brisk hand clicked open the little door and she crouched to peer inside. "It got bloodstained I'm afraid," she held out a cutting and Greta carefully prised it open. *Gargantina and Pantagruelle at Old St Pauls.* It was her review.

238

"If they had this, why didn't they send for me when she had her accident?" asked Greta, "why leave it until now?"

"The police linked her to you through the Edinburgh Festival Fringe office," Sister Wakefield glanced at the tiny watch pinned to her apron. "Once they had the name Buchanan they traced your mother's address and when Social Services were let into the house they found addresses for you and Deborah. You weren't at your address so they went to your sister. They didn't need more than one next of kin. It was up to your sister to contact you after that."

But she didn't. "So who traced me now?" Greta asked, "why trace me now even?"

Sister Wakefield smiled. "Your mother," she said, "as soon as she woke up it was all she talked about. – Where's my Greta? I want Greta… poor thing, she cried and cried… Why can't I see Greta? " Sister Wakefield clapped her hands together as if waking Greta from a hypnotic trance. "Social Services went back to the Fringe office and said you were no longer at the address they had and the office gave them someone's number in London – a Mr Tarry?" Her head nodded at the recognition that appeared on Greta's face. Silence. Then; "The journalist's in the day room," she prompted, and swished away.

Greta went down the corridor in confusion. She felt as insubstantial as a seed in the wind; not floating but tumbling along. There was the day room and a ginger-haired man sitting on an orange chair. He sprang to his feet and she recognised him immediately. "Danny," she exclaimed. It was Danny Scott who looked the same as he had at Four Pools Secondary Modern, pale and small and the faint golden eyebrows of a baby. He stared at her, his hair bright as marigolds. Greta had an urge to blurt out an apology for having half strangled him. "I'm Greta," she said, "Greta Buchanan… we went to the same school, I'm Carmel Buchanan's daughter."

"I know." There was a pause. "I'm sorry about your mother. It was an awful accident. She's lucky to be alive."

"So, you became a journalist," she said, her mouth going dry.

"Yes," said Danny, producing a notebook and biro. "Will you answer a few questions Greta?" The first one struck her like a cosh. "Did you deliberately conceal your whereabouts from your mother?" He stared at her unblinking. "Let's sit down," he added.

"You can if you like," said Greta, "I'm fine here. And no, I didn't. I thought I told her. I usually did. Maybe I forgot that time. I move a lot."

"Yeah," acknowledged Danny, "but why did your mother lie here for so long without you knowing about it?"

And the deaf sensation flooded her ears. "Because I'm a bad daughter," she said. A sharp pain came into the hinges of her jaws and she burst into silent tears and couldn't speak.

"Jesus," said Danny Scott, in alarm, "don't be so hard on yourself. I meant what were the *circumstances*. The police found an address for you in the West End of London but you weren't there and the tenants at the address had never heard of you. You're not the only person in the world who never writes to their parents I'm sure," and he held out an institutional tissue from a packet on the formica table.

"What do you want?" Greta asked.

"A picture of you and your mother," he said, "and the headline can say…" his hands placed each word, "… *Miraculous Carmel Buchanan re-united with her daughter.*"

Greta managed a weak smile. "OK," she said, "that's fair. But promise me you'll send me a copy of the paper when it goes in."

"Attagirl," said Danny Scott.

The birthday surprise went ahead too. The palsied man in the bed next to her mother was smiling. The patient opposite, a man who looked like the figure in Münch's *The Scream*, raised his white face. The woman on the other side of her mother remained unconscious but the one attached to the drip trundled her trolley up to join them. A nurse carried in the cake with a dozen lit candles. Everyone sang Happy Birthday. Greta helped her mother blow out the candles and the assembly clapped their hands and gave a thready cheer.

"That's a mouth-watering cake, Mrs Buchanan," said the nurse; "your daughter got it from Beamish and Lane's."

"It's too pretty to eat but we'll eat it anyway." Carmel touched one of the sugar rosebuds round the edge. "What happened to your friend, Greta?" She looked up at Greta, "Would he like some cake?"

"He went back to London," said Greta. She cut through the pale yellow icing. *What if Deborah comes in now?* Her heart thudded as she went over to the opposite bed with a piece of cake for *The Scream*. Close up, his lemon-shaped face and grey lines resolved into a smile. "Thank you," rustled his cellophane voice. The tea trolley came round. It had a bunch of helium balloons tied to it: blue, silver and pink.

"It's not just the tea trolley today, it's the postman, Mrs Buchanan," said the nurse. She fixed the balloons to the frame of Carmel's bed and gave her the cards. Carmel opened them. The staff had written such sweet messages that Carmel kept crying and crying.

On The Bank Of The Thames

Riverside Studios held a welcome party for the Polish dance company. But Greta felt bedevilled, tripping on the stairs, colliding with people, dropping things. "Light the candles for me, Greta," called Rhonda. Greta's lighter somehow fell from her hand. It skidded off the table. A swipe to save it toppled a tray of glasses. "Jesus Greta, what's up?" demanded Rhonda. "No – leave it. I'll get the broom. In this state you'll cut yourself to pieces. Light the candles."

Greta's lips were stiff, "sorry," she mumbled cranking the lighter. Earlier she had knocked a tray of pizzas out of a customer's hands and her kids had cried. The café was beautified with rubber plants, geraniums and posters. The candle flames twinkled... *Before she met my Dad, Mum had a boyfriend in the air force...* The music had been turned right up... *She was only fourteen or fifteen for Christ's sake...* Everyone was dressed in party clothes and more and more guests kept arriving... *The boyfriend was killed in the war but she'd got pregnant and she had a baby...* Greta was asked to dance; called over to talk and many people tried to persuade her to stop going round like a waitress re-filling glasses. Greta evaded them all and still couldn't keep her mind on what she was trying to get straight.

An hour later Rhonda danced into the kitchen on the throbbing beat of *Boogie Wonderland*, and found Greta washing glasses. "*I find romance when I start to dance in...* that's not necessary, Greta, you can mingle now. What's wrong?"

"I feel ill," she said.

"Go home, cherub," said Rhonda, "this isn't like you at all." Rhonda took an armful of cold white wines from the fridge and boogied the door shut with her hip. It was hard not to smile. Rhonda loved disco.

"Here," said Greta," lending a hand with the bottles.

They went through the loud throng and Rhonda began pulling corks. "Greta," she said, "those candles need replacing... could you just..." Dancers surrounded her, eager for the cold wine and Greta became absorbed in setting candles; each one lit from a failing flame, extinguished as the new one was pressed into the hot gumminess of molten wax remaining.

"So you are here," said the voice she had been both wanting to hear and dreading. "Are you lighting a candle for your mother?"

"That's what she asked me to do."

"Am I allowed to light one?" He copied her actions. "I hope she's well." Liam was tall. Greta's fingers had to reach up to touch his face. His jaw was warm. The backs of her fingers rested against his cheek. Before she lowered her hand she felt the movement in the muscles that made him smile.

"She's OK."

"Did you see your sister?" he asked.

She shook her head. "To you," she said slowly, "it's as if Deborah has always been there. You can say what you just said and it doesn't feel strange. And in fact," she paused, struggling to find the right words, "that is the case. Her address was at our house, the police found her... she went to see my Mum who was in a coma." There was a silence. She stared into the flame of the candle she had lit. "But to me she was lost. She is, still. Lost," she said. Then, "are you socialising?"

His eyelids lowered then opened up again; his eyes steady, a look that was amused; kind. "I'm sure they can spare me." An unexpected surge of words threatened to burst from Greta's throat and she abruptly walked away. In seconds she had dashed into the kitchen, snatched her bag from its hook and was weaving between the uproarious people and out through the door. The hoot of a riverboat and the slop-slop of wash against the wall amplified the peace outside. Background traffic murmured and there was an unseen newsvendor's distant call. Greta walked away from the throb of music and laughter behind her. "Greta!" When she didn't stop he ran after her. "Don't just walk out."

She faced him. "Liam," she said, "when I was little my Father used to have sex with me. It lasted from when I was nine until when I was fourteen." There she stood on the bank of the Thames. Against her face the steady breeze maintained its force. And she had just said something so loathsome that she longed for retribution; an assassin with a machete to hack her skull and thorax in half so she could fall, like split kindling. Her whole body went deaf. But she heard Liam clearly.

"Your mother didn't know?"

"No." Her voice at one remove, echoed in her head.

"Do you think your sister knew?" His brows were drawn into a frown.

"How could she know? She'd … gone." It burst viciously forth.

"God, you're swaying." He sat her on a bench holding her arm with one hand while with the other he pressed her head down so she was folded forward over her knees.

It was a moment before she could straighten up. "Once I got older I kept away from him." Her voice was low. He was crouching in front of her and she faced him, feeling as if the words were sliding back into her gizzard no matter how hard she tried to force them out. "I never went home unless I knew my Mum was back." Her heart was thudding. "I used to go to my friend's house, I used to go to church and read. I used to stay behind at school and do masses of homework."

Liam inclined his head at her. He rubbed his forehead, stood upright. "This is; hard. For you, I mean."

"Why did you come after me?"

"You looked … distraught."

"I'm alright. I'm finding it hard to sleep. I'll be better in the morning." She got up and began to walk away, backwards. "Goodnight," she said, "thanks for coming out after me," then turned and hurried off.

Liam spent the whole of the next day in the studio with the company. Just as she was leaving for the day he emerged from the office corridor. "Very casual," she said, staring at his faded jeans and desert boots.

He held the door open as she reached it. "Are you off home?" he asked. He strode along the pavement next to her.

"Yes. And you look like a student," she said. He wore a black tee shirt and an unbuttoned shirt over it, the sleeves unevenly rolled back, one cuff splayed on his forearm. "Where are you going?"

"I'm walking you home," came the reply.

At the kerb she stopped. "I can manage, you know," she said furiously, keeping her eyes on the street, "I'm not some lame dog that you have to look after all the time," and she stalked across the road, leaving him standing. Once across the busy street she plunged into the park, walking quickly. She skirted the lake where the wind parted the willow fronds like hair and the ducks were discordantly quacking and raising their wings at each other. Several boys rode by on chopper bikes; Reggae blared from a ghetto blaster. Regaining the street she strode along, unsettled and self-conscious.

A motorbike roared up to the kerb next to her and stopped. "Greta, come for a drink."

"Christ," she said, too surprised to be haughty.

"Come for a drink."

"I thought you had a car."

"And a bike."

"Oh."

"Come on."

"On that?"

"It's only down to the end of the road." The unfamiliarity of hoisting herself onto a pillion using his shoulder to grip was a new feeling and then more feelings complicated the moment: the precarious sensation of being unsecured as she perched on the seat; the awareness that she was relying on another person's balance to keep her safe. But all this made it impossible to be angry. "Hold onto the edges of the seat," he said over his shoulder and she was glad because she was afraid to hold onto him although she was longing to and this close she could smell his shirt. The bike jerked and they pulled away; the surge in speed like a punch; like a scream that remained un-screamed. It left her stomach behind. It got her to the pub with her hair in her eyes and incoherent legs that trembled as if she had been running.

They sat on stools at a small high table sipping lager. "How did you get on at your mother's house?" he asked after a silence. She told him about her parents' wedding photos and explained, in words that kept tripping over themselves, what she had discovered.

"So Deborah is your half sister," he said.

"Yes."

She told him about the glass animals.

"So *that's* what you left at your father's grave," he said.

"Yes," and his instant comprehension brought a strange realization. "I feel happy," she said. "I just felt it then, just for an instant. My mother's at death's door, it's all my fault and yet I felt happy."

"The way you said that is so cautious that I don't think you're planning to let yourself enjoy the feeling much are you?" Liam smiled at her as he spoke. "And anyway it's not all your fault."

"Do you know what Matthew said?" she looked sideways, watching him swallow beer.

"No."

"*There speaks a Catholic*: my sense of guilt, he meant." Her happiness transmuted into a sorrow on the edge of tears.

Liam turned his glass round and round as if it had to be unscrewed from the wet circle of condensation it made on the table. "Well," he said, "It's not your fault." Bells and cherries twinkled on the fruit machine. She and Liam were the only customers in the bar. Everyone was at the wooden picnic tables outside in the evening sunshine. Greta stared out of the window. "What about your play," he said, "the one you're having so much difficulty with. Is the writer's block perhaps something to do with all this?"

She said, "I'm trying to make up a narrative that tells the truth but doesn't horrify people." She changed tack. "You'd be surprised how often you have to account for yourself. I've always had to keep quiet. It's a double bind. You refuse to tell your own story because it would be like having a crap on the floor in front of everyone; but you can't explain why you won't. So everyone sees you as the opposite of trusting and confiding." Liam nodded. Greta gulped lager.

"Don't you ever think of others who might be like you?" said Liam, cautiously.

"No. Never. I wouldn't wish it on anyone even to the extent of imagining myself not the only one."

"But you know, literally, that there are others like you," he said, "don't you?" He was angling his head trying to intercept her averted gaze.

"I suppose so." She thought of Clare's warm kitchen: of asking her if she'd had cases of children who'd been subjected to incest and she remembered Clare's calm affirmative. A stiff little dog with homely, ash-coloured fur went past outside, bowlegged and low slung like a small grate, throwing all its weight sideways against the taut line of its leash so that its legs were at an oblique angle to the ground. Greta pointed; "look; the dog is abseiling along the pavement!"

Liam smiled. "Everything can be sorted out if you keep trying," he gave her that steady look. "You haven't told your Mum about what your Dad did. Have you?"

"No," said Greta, "it wasn't the right time. But there's a lot you haven't told me about you."

Liam gave a small amused exhalation.

"Go on;" she insisted politely, "tell me some stuff about you. I feel sick of the subject of me." She badly wanted to make him get away from this pretence that she was content to be just his friend. Drinking lager was not enough to quell how fidgety it made her feel. She offered him a cigarette, lighting it, lighting hers, flicking her hair back, focusing on him as he spoke.

"I did a degree at Dartington, I had some acting jobs," he said, "I was an assistant director at Theatre Passe Muraille in Toronto for a year."

"Impressive."

"Then I went into administration."

"Don't you miss acting?"

"No, I like negotiating funding and so on – maybe I'm political at heart. I like the struggle and strategy of it all. Plus I do some directing anyway. I prefer directing. My Dad would have been pleased."

"Did he die of an illness?" she asked, less truculently.

"No. An accident at work."

"They do dance at Dartington don't they?"

"Yes," he said, "Martha Graham Technique. I loved it. I like watching the way people move. People betray themselves in their movements." He glanced sideways at her.

"Do I?"

He smiled. Took a metaphorical step back. "I think everyone should dance. The ancient Greeks agreed. They even had a word for people who couldn't dance."

"Really?

"Plebeian."

"So the plebs were the people who couldn't dance?" He nodded. "I'm learning to dance," she said.

"Thank goodness for that," his expression was droll.

"I wasn't looking for Deborah," she said. "I've never once really looked for her."

"Your parents said you had to shut up about her," Liam reminded, "I think you've been trying really hard. If you think back there's... oh I don't know, probably something you did that could be said to have been an effort to sort things out. Isn't there?"

"I left home to go to university; but I was running away from home really, I just didn't want anyone to know," said Greta.

"But that's it. You were doing something. Clearly it started much earlier – because at some point you must have reached the decision to even do that."

"Did you mean just now that I have to tell my mother what my father did?" she said.

"Yes."

"And ask my mother where Deborah went," she said.

"Yes."

"Even ask why she didn't tell me before?"

"Yes."

"Even though she's lying there half destroyed by an accident?"

"She's not half destroyed," said Liam, "she's miraculously survived. You could even see that as a sign. You can say anything, Greta, that's the point."

"At least your leather jacket was the real thing," she said.

"Well, thanks, how could you doubt it?" Liam glanced at his watch, "It's almost seven. I've got to go. The writer's arriving tonight and I'm having dinner with him. Will you be alright?"

"Stop treating me like a lame dog," she burst out.

Her annoyance stopped him in his tracks. They walked out to his bike. He swung his leg over and eased it back off the stand and quietly said, "I really like you Greta, just so you know. But I'm afraid of messing you up. You're a bit, well, a bit... vulnerable at the moment. You need to be left to sort things out." There was a pause and Greta was conscious of her left hand gripping the strap of her bag, of his forearms, his folded back shirtsleeves. He kicked down on the starter and the engine blasted out a fume of two-stroke. "I just want you to know, that's all. I didn't want you to be wondering," he yelled, over the engine's racket. He leaned over and gave her a brotherly kiss on the hair.

"Well," she said, "thanks again for the way you drove me up to the hospital like that," her words drowning in the roar of his revving.

"Ring me any time," he called as he pulled away from the kerb. Is that what he said? The bike swooped off and she watched his knees sticking out and his shirt flapping behind him. *Shit bugger and damn him to hell!* It was all very well for him. Greta began walking. Was she supposed to tell her mother the truth after all the trouble she'd taken to hide it? It was like being told she had made a devastating mistake. Homeward bound from their walk, the man and his abseiling dog came out of the park and Greta fell in behind them. So wandering the world in search of her sister wasn't enough. Only telling her mother would bring her back to Deborah. Maybe Liam was right and it was like *Alice Through the Looking Glass.* You had to head in the very direction you were trying to avoid to arrive where you wanted to be. Ahead of her the sturdy grey haunches of the little dog propelled it forwards. Greta imagined holding its leash and feeling the tug of progress. How dare Liam say that. He might be nothing more than a demanding idiot who didn't know what he was talking about. Did she trust him? Could she trust men at all?

For several days there was no sign of him.

He appeared again a week later after a cast meeting. Greta served him a slice of pizza. "So have you been back to see your Mum?" he said, looking up at her.

"Not yet," she smiled, uncertainly. "That was a loaded question."

"Well, yes it was," he said. "You can sit down you know." She sat sideways on the opposite bench, one leg bent beneath her. "But it's a loaded subject," he went on, "don't you feel that?" She couldn't answer; chivvied crumbs into a small cluster with one finger. "The fact is Greta, am I right in saying that I'm the only person you've told about what your father did to you?" She nodded. "Well, for me that's like being given a time bomb to hold." She had a hollow feeling. "I don't mind holding it," he went on: "only…what about you?"

"It's OK. I see what you mean." The side of her hand edged the crumbs off the table into her palm.

"Nice pizza by the way."

She glanced at him. "You don't like pizza," she said, "you told me that in Cheltenham."

"True, but this is artistic pizza."

Greta rose and went back to the kitchen unable to think of anything to say. After he'd gone she wiped the table he'd been sitting at. Then sat in his place. *So have you been back to see your Mum?* Images of her mother circled in her mind; the familiar one in pinafore and beret, the one who made a noise like a fried egg, the one who went white and screamed at her, the girl in a sack-like dress glowering beneath her fringe, a naughty teenage vamp in wartime who swam in the river with men from the RAF. What right did Liam have? Yes, she'd been putting it off but anger at his timebomb remark surged through her. As if she might be more dangerous to him than he might be to her!

"What's up?" It was Rhonda. "That was the guy directing the new play wasn't it?" Rhonda's face changed. "That was *him*! Wasn't it?" Comprehension lit her up and she slid into the bench opposite, "Liam Kennedy! He's the one isn't he?" Her hands pressed Greta's forearm against the table, shook it, demanding the truth. "Is he being a bastard Greta? Why aren't you happy? He'll be here all the time for rehearsals for at least three weeks."

"I don't think he's able to like me any more than he does already and it isn't enough. I think he feels sorry for me."

"No, no. He didn't have to order food did he? He never has in the past."

"You think so?"

"Absolutely. If I felt sorry for you I'd just shout Hi! And hurry out with a cheery wave. He's good looking – in a bony kind of way, isn't he?" Rhonda added with a sly smile. Greta groaned and let her head fall onto her folded arms. Rhonda laughed, reaching across the table to seize her, ruffling her hair, patting her shoulder.

But in bed that night Greta thought she would never be able to do what Liam said she had to do. Never.

The Mouse

This is the eleven forty-eight St Pancras to Nottingham service calling at Luton, Wellingborough, Kettering, Market Harborough, Leicester… Dread tightened her stomach. The train glided between cuttings lined with bluish brick. It plunged into a series of tunnels and emerged again to pass through Cricklewood. Bam! a train hurtled by in the opposite direction. They picked up speed through Mill Hill, racing the motorway out into the countryside. *I can't do it.* Ivy and brambles shrouded the embankment: bindweed, dying drifts of rosebay willow herb; she was still in the world of the dark wood. Humid air came through the open vents.

"St Pancras to Leicester…" The guard punched her ticket, speaking with a rising intonation like a priest. "St Pancras to Nottingham…" he chanted, moving on.

Nottingham. *What if I went there instead?* Drowsiness overcame her. Chin propped on hand Greta leaned on the glass. *To fall… asleep and… not wake up… until the train… reached… Nottingham …*

With a jerk, she woke. Her mouth had slackened and she felt dribble cooling as she wiped her cheek with her hand and forced herself awake. One ear popped as the train plunged into a tunnel. The cackle of wheels on rails changed key as it rushed out again. Her skull juddered on the window. *Liam rang me up to ask if I'd like to see a meteor storm.* Beyond the glass the landscape was devoid of life. Further down the carriage, out of sight, a child started crying. They passed a lonesome broad pit with water in it. Nearby were thin brick chimneys like pencils on end. Smoke rose; the only movement in the stillness. They crossed a river and rumbled through Bedford before gliding back out into countryside again. Ponds dotted a flat expanse; she glimpsed swans, horses, caravans. *Does Liam like me or is he just being kind?* At the dinner in Edinburgh he had been kind. He had only just met her. *You're clearly very brave.* An unexpected assessment. Blue mist hung in a valley. It had been raining. There were puddles in the shale at the trackside. *We shall soon be arriving into Market Harborough.* The train stopped at a dramatic tilt. And now Leicester was the next stop and Greta was nearing her mother.

Mum I need to tell you something… No.

Hello Mum, are you feeling better? OK then, I'll tell you what Dad used to do. Preposterous; every version. A man carrying two lagers and a dangling paper bag came by. A smell of onion wafted from the sandwich in the bag.

Mum! You look great! Dad used to have sex with me and Liam said I ought to tell you. The train shimmied hard to the left and then to the right. Its wheels howled; metal to metal.

Soft drizzle misted the fields. Clouds had settled on the horizon. A train going the other way whumped by. The landscape slowed. What's that? In the corner of a field stood a flamingo with a turquoise body. Its curved neck was orange. The train drew level and Greta twisted her head to see the bird. It wasn't a flamingo. A tuft of neon rope and a blue plastic bag were caught on a metal marker pole driven into the ground. And Greta thought: I'm not pretending any more. And once again she felt the lurch of dread, the gulp of her interrupted breathing. With a wrenching jolt the train hobbled over points on the approach into Leicester. It stole into the tunnel, pitching Greta from side to side. Gazing into the window, a black mirror, she saw herself and half herself again, gazing anxiously back. The half-self was wavery at the edges, as if drained by the completion of arduous tasks. She had been in exile, she had been mute, she had stitched theoretical shirts from woven nettles and not complained. *Liam thinks I need to sort myself out.*

Walking towards the hospital, Greta turned right at the footbridge over the ring road and the hot August sun parted the clouds. A little rain still fell and people beneath trees looked up at the sky. Outside the museum, children climbed on the cannons, their tee shirts bright against the white walls of the building. Greta stared down the avenue towards the church and in between, the air was full of torn sheets of silver rainlight.

Pray for me
Please things have
Gone so wrong now…

She carried on towards the hospital.

In the ward, a nurse was feeding banana custard to *The Scream*. Opposite them, Carmel Aurora lay against her pillows, eyes closed. "She's not asleep love. Carmel! Your daughter's here to see you."

"Mum?"

Carmel's eyes opened, she smiled. "Greta," she lifted up her hand. Instead of the drooping frond it had been two weeks ago, the hand had strength. It gripped and drew Greta close. Carmel put her arm around Greta. "My girl," she said. Greta heard tears break and dissolve the two words and her own eyes stung with emotion. "I must ask you something," said her mother, "I've asked myself – it must be something I did. It couldn't be your father; he's dead and anyway he adored you. Why did you never come home? Will you tell me what I did wrong? Should I have got a telephone put in?"

Greta sat up straight. She took her mother's hand and placed it flat on the coverlet and began giving each of its knuckles a soft press downwards with the pad of her own forefinger. "It was Dad."

"No." Her mother had spoken to thin air. Her eyes looked vacant. Had she understood?

Now Greta began fanning her mother's fingers out on the coverlet by taking each of the fingertips between her own thumb and forefinger and placing them a little further apart. Neither of them spoke. Greta glanced at her mother, who in turn looked at the hand that Greta was still arranging, one finger at a time, over and over. "Pass me the tissues Greta." Carmel pressed one to her face and against her mouth. Greta saw her trying to control her lips; stop them peeling back to let a gush of weeping come out. "Oh dear God." The words wobbled from her mother's collapsing face.

Greta saw the tea trolley pushed into the ward. Her mother took a deep breath and sighed, making a thin lamenting sound. "I don't suppose you remember the day I smashed her glass animals with a hammer." And there, at last, was Deborah.

"Yes," said Greta. And found she was filled with a kind of painful gratitude and could hardly speak.

"I found her and your Dad together." Tears spilled over and Carmel pulled more tissues free. The pink dressing gown was too big. The sleeves fell away from her brittle arms as she raised the tissues to her face.

Greta wanted desperately to help her mother. "It's OK Mum. I put the animals in the dustbin." The tea trolley was two beds away.

"Deborah and your Dad," whispered her mother. "You were only eight; so little. I said you must never find out. Never." Again her voice tailed off into that thin lament.

"So she ran away from home?" said Greta.

"She didn't run. I…" Her mother's face was clamped into silence. A terrible alarm grew inside Greta. She saw again her mother raising the bolster hammer over and over. "… I banished her." Greta felt speechless, just as she had the day her mother told her Deborah was gone. Carmel Aurora was rigid, gasping for breath so as to speak and not cry. "I couldn't bear to see her any more. And I had to protect you. You were so little. … there's more to it… oh God…" she laid her head back on the pillows. The trolley reached them; the tea was being poured.

"Mum?" Greta passed a cup and saucer to her mother. Her mother took the tea nodding mute thanks.

"Do you want your curtains round?" The sympathetic nurse already had her hand on the fabric.

"No thanks, nurse." Carmel uttered these unexpected words with her eyes closed. The trolley moved on. Greta looked at her mother. At last; run over and crushed as she was, hit by a toppling building and stabbed by glass as she was, light had come in and the truth was revealed. There sat her mother, defying fear. "I thought she was somehow bad," she said, "you know now that she was illegitimate. I lied about my age, I lied and said I was a widow so I was bad and she was like me. It was my fault. All the trouble she brought would contaminate you. So I banished her."

Greta sipped her tea. Then couldn't cope with it and had to put it down. "What trouble did she bring?" she stared at the crisp, fawn coverlet, the white starched pillowcase. A pigeon was cooing outside in the clock tower.

"When you were really little, Deborah had a baby." Whispered words.

"The Special Hospital," Greta said.

"We had it adopted. I went with her to a place in Liverpool so she could have it there. You don't remember do you?"

"Kind of," said Greta slowly, "I remember wanting to know where the Special Hospital was – wanting to go there." A breeze from the open window stirred the curtains around the adjacent bed. Time stood still at a warm, rainy summer's afternoon moment. It was quiet and safe here. Carmel Aurora had recovered from subdural haematoma here and a terrible wound had healed in her back.

"If Deborah had a baby, who was the father?" Greta said, guardedly.

"We never found out. Deborah wouldn't say." Tears began flowing down her mother's face again. A fit of coughing racked her. "After I found her and your dad together I thought it over for a week or so and then I told her I never wanted to see her again," she sobbed.

Greta rescued the tea and put it on the cabinet then dabbed her mother's eyes with more tissues. "Don't cry Mum, don't cough."

"But I never found animals in your room."

"I only had a few. They were hidden in an old sock at the bottom of my wardrobe under a pile of stuff," said Greta. Her mother gazed at her. "And I went to visit Dad's niche and left them there."

"Why didn't I see them?" her mother's agitation was pitiful.

Greta couldn't think. "It was last year," she said, "you were… in a coma by then." Her mother's face was harrowed and tears rolled down her face. "Didn't you ever suspect?" Asked Greta.

"No. No. Never. Not his own child. His own child." Her voice faded and then her lips moved but no sound emerged although Greta could clearly tell that she said: "he loved you the best," before her mother's hands jerked in front of her face as she fought to claw air into her lungs.

"But I'm perfectly all right Mum," cried Greta, shocked at the agony of the spasm her mother endured, "don't cry. I shouldn't have told you. It was Liam's idea and he was wrong."

Hot fingers grasped her hand and shook her. "No, he was right," said her mother, choking the words out. "I'm sorry. I was useless to both of you. No wonder you left me."

"I'm back now." Greta moved closer and stroked her mother's arm. They sat in silence for a moment, then: "the nurse said, *your other daughter*," Greta spoke cautiously, "does that mean Deborah comes here?"

"She came while I was in the coma but not since I woke up."

"Ask her to come," said Greta, "write to her and say we want her to come," her breath used itself all up such was the force of her excitement.

"It's too late now," was the reply. Despair struck Greta as if a lance had pierced her body skewering her completely. As a swimmer might fight to reach the surface she rose to her feet unable to breathe and her mother prevented her instant flight only by seizing Greta's wrist and hanging on like a terrier.

"Greta," she gasped, "sit down again. You haven't changed a bit. It's just like the time you left Twig out on the lawn."

"It can't be too late," said Greta passionately, trying to wrench free.

"Alright, alright – it isn't. I'm wrong. I'm wrong. Sit down." Carmel's voice was piteous and tears fell from her chin onto her pink ruffles. "Please. Sit back down." Greta sat. Passed her mother a tissue. Her mother cried. Greta tried to breathe more calmly. After a while: "Give me that tea. I can manage that tea now. Let's drink the tea, Greta." They sipped like dazed boxers. "Deborah lives in Stroud," said her mother. "She's got one of those kennels where people leave their dogs when they go on holiday."

"Stroud?" Greta's voice went up high and cracked so that she had to cough to ease a sensation that her trachea was sticking itself together. Her eyes watered as if she was choking. "Stroud in Gloucestershire?" she managed to splutter. Her mother was nodding. "Didn't she ever ask about me?" Greta felt scarlet.

"She never got in touch. I only ever had one letter and that was in 1970; just a piece of paper with her address on it. They say she came here twice when I was in a coma." Greta had a glimpse of her mother as an ancestral figure; the high draped bed like a marble monument that Deborah had come to mourn; this woman; once a fearless fourteen-year-old who had fallen in love with a Polish airman and conceived a dark-eyed daughter on a riverbank. Her mother drank the tea down. Then she leaned over and put the empty cup on her locker. "I'd gone on the bus to visit your Dad's ashes," she said, head down and arm stretched out, her hand groping at the bevelled edge of the locker door. "I was going to buy yellow gladioli…" her hand scrabbled and prised, "I don't remember that truck coming…" her pale neck turned scarlet, the flush mounting into her tufty hair and Greta couldn't bear to watch the struggle and opened the little door for her. "God, what's the matter with me," cried her mother in mortification, "I just want my handbag. Thanks, Love." Her hands flustered in the bag among the old receipts and folded lists written on blue Basildon Bond; "Where's my pen?" On a scrap of paper, beneath the tremulous nib of her biro, words appeared, one letter at a time. "There," she said, "Deborah's address. I'm good for something at least. There's no reason why you can't go and see her yourself now." Her eyes looked straight into Greta's. "Will you tell her about...?"

"We can tell each other anything," Greta said, "nothing bad can happen because of anything we say." She seized her mother's hand. "Come with me!" she urged, "we can catch the bus to Stroud."

Her mother made an ironic face. "More like about three buses," she said. The simplicity of this vision wrung Greta's heart. Buses; winding their way out of town, among the lanes into villages, back to the main road and, much juddering and gear-changing later, arriving in the next town; like the ones that used to take her and Deborah to Mrs Griffin's kennels. And there would be Deborah, in Stroud.

"She won't want me. You go," her mother sighed.

"Look," said Greta, and she took her glass twig out of her pocket and held it out to show her mother.

Her mother touched the glass and smiled. "Tell me how the visit goes," she said.

Greta caught the train back to London in a mood of pure elation. She was right at the front of a huge intercity. The carriage was almost empty. She felt as if she was on the back of a motorbike, leaning into the curves as they flew along. She was flying! She was flying to London. Leicester was a launching pad and she had taken off again and the engine hissed with power. Now she saw life in the landscape: birds, sheep, pubs, cars, farmyards and villages. She did it! She did it! As they flew into Kettering the aprons of concrete, the Honda showroom, the spire, portacabins and rows of cars were all gilded with beauty. They curved out of town, flying under a bridge; a water-tower on the horizon. The driver was hurling them southwards and the carriage juddered and bucked under her. Swans on the lakes raised their wings. They crossed river after river, raced alongside a motorway, passed a cats cradle of pylons then hurtled through Bedford. She started to believe that England was tilted, that they were racing down a slope. What else could explain such headlong speed?

"You must get out more," said Rhonda the next day and gave Greta a little push through the lifted hatchway, "out from behind this counter. Your problem is you're thinking like a waitress instead of like a writer. Go on; check the inside of the auditorium for me. There's loads of coffee mugs missing."

"But the company are rehearsing," Greta dawdled, irresolute.

"Speaking of which – one of them fancies you. His name's Vavchek. He was asking me about you yesterday. Go in; put the mugs on a tray then sit and watch. Here, take this as well." Rhonda thrust Greta's notebook into her hand and then took the biro from behind her own ear and gave that to Greta as well. "You're a writer, Greta. It'll be inspiring. Vavchek's the one with the spiky blond hair. Go!"

Inside the dark auditorium Greta sat on the floor at the top of the raked seating and allowed the transforming power of the space to calm her. If her mother had been a queen in ancient Greece, she would have been tragic. On stage someone thumped the boards with a stick and the actors knelt as if they were a single organism, reacting. Greta hugged her drawn up knees. She had imagined finding Deborah many times. Surely, it would be simple. Gears grinding, the bus would ascend a Cotswold hill. The rattle of the empty seat in front of her would thrum in her fingers like a manifest vibration of her final effort. In her imagination she saw herself come to the top of the hill and there below, sparkling in the evening light, was the place where Deborah would be; the sound of barking an added clue. In her imagination she ran down the hill, past the crossroads and up a lane. And there it was; the place where Deborah lived; joyful with dogs.

When she carried the tray of mugs out, Greta found Rhonda sitting with a man in a wheelchair. He was about forty-five, heavily built, black hair receding from a high dome of forehead. His eyes were prominent and mild. "Greta," said Rhonda, "this is my friend, Vic Amey. We're catching up. Vic is from Maesteg like my Mum. I've told him all about you."

"Hi Greta. She tries to pretend she's a London girl but she was born in Maesteg, got it written right through her like a stick of rock." Vic teased Rhonda as he shook Greta's hand. Like Rhonda he had a captivating Welsh accent.

"Did you write anything?" Rhonda asked. Greta shook her head. "Vic started writing after his accident – I must get on. See you later, Vic," she took Greta's tray with her. Greta felt awed, alone with the author of *Coal!*, the play whose rehearsal she had just been watching.

"Sit down," Vic, genially slapped the table, "tell me about writing your Rabelais play, I'm doing a one-man show for my next piece."

"What is it about?" Greta perched on the bench, clutching her notebook self-consciously.

"It's about a man who gets injured at work and then finds he's become invisible; can't get his wheelchair up the step into the pub," said Vic laconically.

"Were you an actual miner?"

"I was the last miner in our pit to be disabled before they shut it down."

"Oh God; when?"

"Nineteen seventy-four," he said.

Liam came in and waved as he went into the auditorium.

"Liam's father was killed in an accident at work," Greta said. She noticed that her heart rate had gone up.

I'm a playwright, she said to herself as she wiped the tables at the end of the day. And not only that; I wrote and told my sister I'm going to see her this Saturday.

Next day, unprompted, Greta slipped into the back of the auditorium with her sandwich at lunchtime. The Polish dancers were enacting the work of miners. *My sister is half Polish.* Sudden shouts punctuated their moving tapestry like gunshots raising dust. Whatever they were using to make the dust swirled up from the dancers' feet. Beams of light from their helmets intersected. Greta was mesmerised and couldn't chew her baguette.

When her shift finished at five, she took her notebook and crept back into rehearsals. She found a different world this time. Blue light was released in bursts from a lantern as an actor covered and uncovered it with a blanket. Others carried away a still figure at shoulder height. A voice reading a bulletin came from one side and a spotlight shone on a pristine newsreader. The stamping of the dancers' feet now raised flecks of white into the air, like moths fluttering. Hunched in the darkness, Greta tried to transcribe it into words.

"You are the mouse, yes?" the Polish dancer, challenging her next morning as she served him coffee, sounded as if he had laryngitis. His face was aquiline and unsmiling, the hazel eyes fixed on her. His chin receded a little and was spiked by blond stubble.

"I didn't think you'd notice," said Greta. Several of the other dancers were drinking coffee at one of the tables. Greta could see Sue among them. "I won't come in if it disturbs you."

"No. You are a mouse. Black coffee please. I don't think we can be disturbed by a mouse. It was a mouse with a pen, yes?"

"Yes."

He turned towards the others. "I found the mouse!" he called. "Tom and Jerry," he said to her, "I like mice. Your name is Greta."

"Yes." She served his coffee.

"Tell me what you wrote. Come over this side of your – what is this thing?" He slapped her counter.

"The counter." She was amused; his unsmiling style had stopped disconcerting her. "I can't come that side, I have to work."

"You can come," he shrugged his shoulders, "this place is empty except for…" he waved an arm at the others. "And I am Vavchek." She went with him. He introduced her to Malgorzata and Tomas. Vic Amey joined them.

"You already met Greta, Vic?" Malgorzata's exquisite black eyebrows arched even higher, "that is good. Two writers together." She threaded her pipe cleaner legs into woolly legwarmers, adjusting the purple folds over the heels of her ballet shoes.

At lunchtime, shouting her name, Vavchek came to fetch Greta. Rhonda pushed her away from the till, taking her place. "Go on," she said, "…and the hot chocolate? Thank you. You're on your break in ten minutes anyway – That'll be four pound sixty please…Thank you. Go on Greta…"

"This is Katya," said Vavchek, while introducing her to a golden haired girl with the whitest teeth Greta had ever seen. He was hugging Greta possessively with one arm. His body was hot and writhy as he twisted and waved, calling to others, beckoning them over.

"I'm so pleased I meet you," Katya seized her hand in a warm grasp, "I wanted to tell you I saw your play *Gargantina and Pantagruelle* in Toronto two years back. It was wonderful." There was an upsurge of Polish-speaking as Katya shared something of this with her friends. Vavchek released Greta to wrestle abruptly with one of the others and amid the racket Liam appeared.

Greta said: "Liam, I've been to see my mother."

"Good." He was smiling at her. The racket got even louder; roars of laughter as the wrestlers surged among the tables. "And your sister?"

"I've written to her. I'm going to see her on Saturday."

"Greta!" Katya claimed their attention, " – Gargantina! She is a giantess, a giantess is it not?"

In the Flash

Deborah's house was on a hillside just outside Stroud. Stone cottages clung in slanting terraces which intersected in a quixotic fashion mapped by cobbled paths. Like overflowing trays, their gardens displayed a profusion of flowers and vegetables, creepers and trees. Set back from the lane with a magnificent view over the steep valley, two cottages knocked into one made Deborah's house. At the back were pens for the dogs in one garden and an orchard in the other. The grass beneath the trees was red and yellow with fallen apples. Chickens roamed among them. The annexed gardens were separated by a stone wall upon which stood a hen, pecking at the ivy, her stately feet like a dowager's gloved hands. Greta marvelled at her smooth metallic plumage; the inca gold of her breast feathers.

"Her name's Amber," said Deborah, whose hair, just touching her shoulders was a defiantly glossy chestnut threaded with crimson where henna betrayed grey hairs. Her fringe was defiant also as was the sparkly green hairslide that caught back most of her hair but left tendrils around her face.

"She's gorgeous."

"She's just a brown hen," laughed Deborah.

"Brown is an understatement," protested Greta. Topaz gave way to shades of cedarwood and cinnamon. In the sun, like a hologram, the wing feathers evoked other contexts of colour: river water running over tawny stones; polished onyx like the beads of Brother Isidore's long-ago rosary. "I didn't realise hens were so exotic," she remarked, "Look at her eyes." The hen's eyelid rolled upwards when she blinked, not down.

"Pick her up," invited Deborah, "they're all tame."

Greta put her hands on the hen but in a seething mash of feathers the bird flapped to the ground evading her with an exasperated cluck and Greta jumped back with a scream of laughter.

"Do this to her. Look!" commanded Deborah and held her hand flat out, palm down. "Over her back, like this." Deborah put her stretched hand above the hen and the hen crouched down and became still.

"Oh," Greta exclaimed, "will it work for me?"

"Do it," encouraged Deborah, "And then you can pick her up. Hold her wings shut and just lift her. Go on."

Greta hovered her hand over the hen and down it crouched. For a second, her palm rested on the feathered back and then the hen limbo-ed out from under her touch. It felt like stroking soft metal rolled out to a foil; sunwarm, smooth as water. Again she subdued the hen, and this time clasped her hands either side of its body to keep the wings shut. Under her hands she felt the wing muscles pulsing but she held on firmly. She lifted. The bird was light; delicately boned in its armoured gloss of feathers, bewitching and tame. It settled in Greta's arms.

"That's how you used to feel when I lifted you up," said Deborah. The hen uttered a small thoughtful syllable. Deborah leaned close and stroked the bird and the wind blew strands of Greta's hair across their faces.

Deborah had set the table with a white cloth and a bone china teaset. There was ham and salad, scones and jam. "I thought I'd feel too worried to eat," said Greta, "but I'm starving."

"Yes, reunions always make me hungry," observed Deborah, dryly. Neither commented on how little they had actually eaten. They smiled at one another. Greta felt shy. She knew all about the tea-set and the cottage and the kennel business and the neighbours and the Stroud winters. There was no more small talk. Surging up were questions. Realising she had been cramming food down to swallow the questions Greta put down her scone. "I thought you ran out on me," she said. A carriage clock on the tiled mantelpiece chimed five.

Deborah took a deep breath. "I wouldn't have," she said, "I wouldn't have..." she fell silent. Her pointer bitch, Sukie, uncoiled from the rug and placed her muzzle on Deborah's thigh. It was as if the dog heard the unuttered part of the sentence.

"Mum kicked you out."

"Yeah." Deborah nodded. There was a pause. Then: "I'm surprised you came," she said. "I thought you'd hate me too much." After more silence, her chair scraped on the stone floor and she got up and came round to Greta's side. A plaid shirt tucked into jeans gave her a trim, cowgirl look and her knitted waistcoat was jaunty but lines fanned at the corners of her eyes and the skin of her once plum-smooth eyelids was creased and soft. She sat by Greta on the old bench. The dog followed, crowding under the table, unsure which lap to lay her head in. "They assumed I'd get in touch with you," said Deborah. She patted Greta's knee. "There," she coaxed the dog, "good dog. Make a fuss of Greta." There was a pause.

"But you didn't."

"No."

"You didn't do it even when she woke up."

"No." Deborah's voice had gone quieter and gruffer. "Bugger," she said, "I need a bloody tissue." She fetched a box of them off the dresser, flapping her hand in front of her face, blowing her nose forcefully as she sat back down; settling Sukie again. "There," she said, "that's better." She cleared her throat. "I…" Silence again.

It was dawning on Greta that Deborah had been afraid. "You were scared to phone me," she said, "and I was scared to go and see Mum. So I didn't."

"Yes," agreed Deborah, "that's us." The dog licked her hand.

"Mum said …" began Greta, "…She told me about your baby." Silence. "I can understand… I know what he did." Greta felt desolate. The dog broke out panting, her yeasty breath smelting Greta's knee. "Mum said you didn't want me to be contaminated." Silence. "I can understand… I know why you went; why you couldn't come back. I know what he did. But why didn't you come and find me once I'd left too? You could have found where I was, why didn't you come?"

"I did," said Deborah.

"You did?" Incredulous relief replaced the tight painful feeling in Greta's chest. Words came scattering out: "When? Why didn't I… I didn't see you…" *Deborah had come.* "Did you come to Nottingham? To the university? Did you see me?" Images danced in her head; Deborah under the archway of the Trent Building, Deborah beside the fountain in Slab Square, Deborah at the bus stop by the boating lake. She seized Deborah's hand ecstatically and held it tight. "When was it? What was I doing? Did you see me?"

"I was walking towards your Hall of residence and you came the other way on the opposite pavement. There were girls milling about all over the road. I don't think any cars used the campus did they? You were laughing and talking to some others… it was a cold day; enough to turn your breath into steam. They had university scarves on but you didn't; you little rebel," she smiled at Greta. "Your friends were kicking up the fallen leaves."

"I didn't see you," Greta was filled with anguish.

Deborah squeezed Greta's hand. "You were happy," she said, "that's all I ever wanted. You looked happy and I saw you were doing well. Nothing else mattered."

"I wish I'd seen you."

"Well I saw you."

"How did you know I was there?"

"I always get the *Leicester Mercury*," said Deborah, "my one link with home. The school results are in every year. I saw it when you got A levels and I saw your name in the list of who went to what university. I rang the girls' halls at Nottingham and I said: *can I speak to Greta Buchanan please?* until I hit on the right hall and then I went there and lurked." She smiled at Greta's face. "You had a lurking sister," she said. Greta laughed. "That's better. This isn't meant to be a story that makes you cry."

"I wish you'd come over," said Greta, "or shouted to me." There was silence. Greta stroked the dog's head.

Deborah pressed a tissue to her eyes, very precisely, each eye in turn. "When I was young," she began, "when it first…" Her hand pulled more tissues free and she made a sighing sound as if impatient with herself. "To begin with I didn't even know I was doing anything wrong." There was a long pause. "After the baby…" they exchanged a glance. "… yes, his," she confirmed.

"Does Mum know?"

"No. She thought it was some lad."

"Oh Deborah…" The dog shifted her head onto Deborah's knee, upraised eyes going from one sister's face to the other's.

"It was a little boy," said Deborah. "After that I knew how bad it was." She stroked the dog's velvety ear forward like a soft lapel. "When I came home I didn't think he would ever do it again. But he did. Then she caught us that day. I think I wanted her to. For a couple of weeks he stopped her from chucking me out. But she told me she couldn't look at me. She used to turn her head away." The clock ticked. Deborah blotted a sudden rain of tears. "I knew he was dead. The one time she wrote it was to tell me that. I never answered of course." The dog made a groaning sound and subsided into a heavy curled shape lying half off and half on their feet. "When they first told me about her accident," Deborah continued, "it felt like she'd been punished. But I couldn't bear to think she might die. I missed her all that time and to think she might die and I'd never see her again... So I went to the hospital." Anyway," she said, "for some reason," she paused...

"What?" Greta urged.

"...The second time I visited I went to the Garden of Remembrance."

"Oh," said Greta, her scalp prickling.

"And I found... " she stopped speaking.

"...You found my glass animals," finished Greta.

Deborah leaned forward, elbows on the table, her forehead resting on the heels of her tissue-filled hands. "Up to that moment," she said, "I'd thought you'd always been safe. I sometimes even hated you because you had my mother and I didn't: you were good and I was bad. But I never thought he would ever do anything to his own child. When I saw those animals ..." Deborah straightened up and looked at Greta. "I feel as if my insides have been torn out. I didn't get in touch. I couldn't face you."

Greta put both arms round her sister. "I don't care," she said. "You'd have stayed if Mum hadn't made you go away. You'd have protected me." Fresh tears rolled down her sister's gaunt face. "What did you do with the animals?" said Greta.

Deborah gave a sob that could have been a laugh. "I dropped them one at a time onto the paving slabs and stamped them into dust," she said.

Clare, Ray and the kids went to the Isle of Wight for a week. Greta dog-sat. *Think of all the writing you can do, Greta.* Sweet Clare. On the first morning, she woke up and went to the top of the stairs. At the bottom there was a thud as Jazzy's dog elbow levered her upright and she switched in an instant from dog-shaped rug to alert collie. Her ears were cocked and her tail swished once, then again, like a radar scanner. Her eyes were fixed on Greta. "Hello, Jazzy," said Greta. Jazzy's body expressed a serpentine shudder of joy, a sneeze, a quick box-step of encouragement. Her tongue panted and every hair on her black and white body said: *come down now*! Greta came downstairs and the dog cast herself into a curve against Greta's legs and then swivelled over to lie on her back. Greta crouched, crooning endearments, to rub her chest. Relaxed paws bobbed against Greta's arms, the pink tongue reached to lick her hands. Greta tested the sprung shape of the doggy ribcage under the fur and her fingers felt how soft Jazzy's ears were, how gentle her lips and how warm her breath.

By day three Greta was feeling almost drugged with relaxation. Sitting drinking her morning coffee, her notebook open on the table in front of her, she wrote: *The dog is my shadow. What more could I want? She sits by me as I lie still, writing. She walks with me along the track by the water: she licks my hand. She leads me through the fields and into the village to buy the milk. Even when we walk through the valley and the tractors roar past I don't have to worry. She stays right by me. With her ears pricked up, she watches me. I prepare the table for tea and put bread and cheese on it. I make salad dressing, spill olive oil, the dog rushes over. She lies down behind me when I chop garlic, the tips of her fur touching my naked heels. How have I done without her? I'll be blessed for the rest of my life. I'll be calm now forever.*

Early next day, Greta woke from a dream. As she sat up in bed, she could hear words from the dream. She reached over to the bedside table for her notebook and wrote them down. *The best stories are about a man. I can see him, his red child's lips. He walks down a hill carrying a small suitcase. He is fourteen. The sleeves of his jacket come down over his hands.* That's all there was. The morning outside was full of birdsong. Greta padded to the window and opened it wide, breathing in the scent of earth and grass. Autumn had come. Towards the river, an elemental envelope of air and vapour contained the fields. Cows dipped their heads in the wreathing scrim to graze. *What I want to say isn't a tide of filth.* This was the thought in her head. She stared at the river, which was marked only by an extra density in the winding trail of mist. Taboo was the word. Exile. Where she had been all her life. Deborah, too. Both of them; silenced.

Two jackdaws flew in a chasing arc down to the lawn where they hopped and squabbled. "I know how to do *Why Some Women Don't Like Sex*," she murmured. It wasn't one play; there were too

267

many women and all had different reasons. Bit by bit you could do it. One play at a time. One of the racketing jackdaws took off into the trees. It was an apple they were competing for, fallen from the gnarled tree by the wall. The remaining bird bent its stubby head to peck the fruit. Feathers, closely scaled, stood in a ruff at the back of its neck. How would she write the play that would have her father in it? Or Gordon? Maybe she didn't have to write about it at all. Maybe just having to go through it was enough. It was enough that she had rescued herself. To recover would be the best thing of all – if she could achieve that. Greta closed the window.

To her surprise a letter arrived. It was from Liam: and hoped she was enjoying the peace. And then she had to go out and sit on the stone doorstep in the October sun to savour what he began to say to her. The woollen polo neck of her sweater comforted her chin and the wiry softness of the dog's fur was warm under her hand as she read his words. *I need to explain something. My Dad had an affair with another woman and left my Mum. I didn't speak to him for a year. Then he had the accident and died. I feel as if I criticized you for not speaking to your Mum all that time but who knows how long I'd have gone on not speaking to my father? And then he died. I said you had to do it – because I wish I'd done it. But I didn't. So I'm sorry. I'm a hypocrite. I'm almost afraid now of what you think of me. So I know I said this before, but I mean it – I really like you. More than just a friend. I like the air of rawness about you. I've always noticed that you're very warm, as if you're made of electrical current. Your hands are electrically warm. You hold on too loosely. I want to shout 'Hold tight!' as if we're standing up and the bus is about to go round a really sharp corner and you haven't noticed. It's like a film – you're the one balancing on the roof of the train and you don't see the bridge over the track. It's going to knock you off or leave you imprinted like a spreadeagled cartoon animal while all the bad characters win prizes, get promoted, cash in their investments and fulfil their lifelong ambitions....* Greta smiled. *Just so I get something else out of the way; this is what's been going through my mind based on what you told me about the colleague of yours who raped you. You were kept prisoner for one whole night and most of the following day. You were frightened but you blamed yourself and yet you knew that you had been deceived. But you expected a friend to be honest and a man of principal to be consistent. That man devised a trap for you. He refused to respect your wishes. He forced you to have sex with him repeatedly. He refused to use contraception. He didn't listen to you when you said he was hurting you. He detained you against your wishes. He continued to harass you on subsequent occasions. He forced his way into your flat causing you to run outside for safety. Your decision to have an abortion was a direct consequence of his actions. I find him guilty of rape and assault Greta. I want to beat him to a pulp.*

On the bus to Torrington Greta thought about holding tight whenever they went round one of the sharp bends in the lane. It made her smile. She was going to visit the glassworks.

"My father was a glassblower," she told the man.

He was a big man with a curved stomach that stretched his grey shirt out like a pregnancy. His eyes were as round as a tuna's. He wore a shiny white surgical collar around his neck, which angled his face upwards and gave him the appearance of a brawny fish coming out of a bottle. He had a line of patter like a comedian and now he looked at Greta and smiled. "Your father was a glassblower was he? Is this the third time you've been round today?"

"Yes."

"We can't keep meeting like this," He quipped, "it's time we were introduced." He tapped his name badge. "I'm Glen Hobbs."

"Greta Buchanan." They shook hands as other visitors filed past. Overhead the viewing balcony was full.

"You stand there, Greta," he said, and she stood on the metal staircase. The volcano mouth of the furnace glowed with a scarlet, pulsating light like a canned planet. The glassblowers, in leather aprons, became silhouettes as they approached it to take their gathers. It looked as if their movements were causing the lambent air to quiver. The church-like space was quiet. Glass is a quiet thing. But heat, as it smelts the air in the furnace, makes a noise like a hive of bees. "Who wants to have a turn?" asked Glen Hobbs. "You do," he said, beckoning Greta. "This young lady will be able to do it," he pointed at her dramatically, "even if she is a bit on the small side…" ushering her within the embrace of the barrier, "… because it's in her genes," he declaimed. Her leather apron engulfed her making her giggle and there was amusement all round. She stepped onto the platform with the glassblowers. "We'll take what we call 'the gather' for her – safety considerations prevent us from cooking her." Glen Hobbs had them all laughing; Greta too.

They gave her a Perspex facemask. The oversized equipment made her feel like a child. A glassblower helped her, passing the long metal gather with its blob of molten glass attached and she began to blow, listening as he spoke instructions into her ear. The commentary faded into the background and she swivelled the gather as she blew, watching the sheen on the bubble her breath was making. The glass integument ballooned. It was so fragile that she could see it quivering as her hand turned the tube. She stopped to breathe in. "More?" She asked.

"Yes, go on; I can't guarantee what shape it'll be," he said with a smile. She put her lips to the tube again. The bubble became a teardrop then a pear. It was a massive glittering pear, so thin that it was almost invisible.

"Look at that; a huge lopsided pear." boomed Hobbs. "You'll need a big fruit bowl for that." The spectators laughed.

Greta stared at it, holding it clear of the ground. "What now?" she asked.

"Knock it into the cullet." Her glassblower fetched a copper bucket from down by his bench. In the bucket already were blobs of glass: triangles of glass: wafers and splinters of glass. And she saw a perfect wineglass in there.

"What's wrong with that one?" she said, amazed.

"Pass it here," said Glen Hobbs, and Greta's glassblower tossed it over. "Air bubble, see?" Hobbs held it aloft. "If it isn't perfect it goes in the bucket. But we're nice to our rejects. We put them back in the furnace and they have another chance: which is lucky really because only about one in three is perfect."

Greta knocked her undulating pear gently against the edge of the bucket and watched its flaky crumple. Against the blunt metal it made the sound she imagined snowflakes might make if you amplified them falling onto fresh snow. Yet it was a hot sound, it had the crispness of something glazed by an inferno.

"See that? It's like cellophane." Hobbs reached down to pick up a piece of her delicate wreckage, crumpling it into flakes with his fingers.

270

"My Dad used to call it the flash," the term came into Greta's mouth from nowhere.

"She's an expert. Yes, I've heard it called the flash," he rolled his tuna eyes, "but none of it is wasted; it all goes back in the pot. Anyone got a bit of broken glass? Anyone got a milk bottle they forgot to leave behind on the doorstep?" The audience laughed.

"I've got this."

Glen Hobbs angled his body round and stared at the glass fragment Greta had dug out of her jeans pocket. He leaned over and took it, holding it up to the audience. "It's a glass twig ladies and gentlemen." His eyes twinkled, comical above the surgical collar. "Is that what it is – a twig?"

"Sort of. That was my sister's nickname for me."

"Right." He reached it back to her. "In she goes then."

Greta dropped it into the bucket with a plink.

"There you are," beamed Hobbs, "it all goes back in the pot. And then," he declaimed, "it comes back out like that." He swept his arm towards the tall glassblower working on the far left of the stage. The gesture rushed the heated air. The people turned their gaze as one. Greta felt as if she heard the sound of wings. The tall glassblower had just finished blowing a perfect, flute-shaped glass. Another glassblower snapped it off the end of the gather with forceps. Before their eyes he bore it off-stage and away: perfect and intact.

*****

271

Other fiction by Frances Clarke:

Unusual Salami
and other stories

With humour (*Imaginary Col*) or strange lyrical horror (*Unusual Salami*, the visceral title story) the characters in this collection struggle to make sense of life with sometimes dreadful consequences. Greg is weirdly empowered by reading a book, Anna escapes an enchantment (or does she?) God creates the world and Arkle is... well, Arkle.
And what IS that raggy brown stuff under the tree in *Pneumonia*?

Unusual Salami and other stories is available on Amazon

Lightning Source UK Ltd.
Milton Keynes UK
UKOW052011170113

205055UK00001B/162/P